the **BOATMAKER**

the BOATMAKER

A NOVEL BY JOHN BENDITT

 TIN HOUSE BOOKS / Portland, Oregon & Brooklyn, New York

Published by Tin House Books, Portland, Oregon, and Brooklyn,
New York

Distributed to the trade by Publishers Group West,
1700 Fourth St.,
Berkeley, CA 94710,
www.pgw.com

Library of Congress Cataloging-in-Publication Data

Benditt, John, author.
The boatmaker / John Benditt.
    pages cm
ISBN 978-1-935639-98-5 (paperback)
1. Dreams—Fiction. 2. Self-disclosure—Fiction.
3. Boatbuilders—Fiction. I. Title.
PS3602.E66145B63 2015
813'.6—dc23
                2014037936

First US edition 2015
Printed in the USA
Interior design by Jakob Vala
www.tinhouse.com

In memory
Earl Philip Benditt
(1916–1996)

But if the self does not become itself, it is in despair, whether it knows that or not.

—Søren Kierkegaard

CHAPTER 1

The man of Small Island is dreaming of a wolf. The wolf has blue fur and green eyes, eyes unlike any the man has ever seen in waking life. The boy, really, because in the dream he is a boy again: eight years old, with skinny legs and short pants. Just the age he was when his brother went into the sea and never came back.

In his dream, the boy walks toward a big tree standing by itself in a clearing not far from the sea. On Small Island nothing is very far from the sea. The tree is an oak, one of the tallest on the island. The wind blows hard on Small Island most of the year, and not many trees grow to be tall. Above the boy's head, oak leaves rustle in a light breeze. Everything else is quiet; no insects or birds are singing. It's high summer, the time of afternoon when the sun stands still and everything hushes. Even the sea.

The boy walks to the spot where his brother is buried. Awake, he has never come to this place. He refused to come to the funeral, a tiny gathering that included only his mother, a few of her relatives and the pastor. His father stayed away, drunk for three days. His mother insisted on his brother being put into the earth here and not in the little cemetery, overgrown with stones, where all the other dead of Small Island are buried. He doesn't know why she wanted this. Many things are mysterious to him—and nothing is more mysterious than whatever was between his mother and his brother.

His brother went into the sea and did not come back for three days. On the third day, the sea decided it had had his brother long enough and returned his body gently to a rocky beach not far from this oak. The boy is not sure he wants to see where his brother is buried, and he moves slowly but is unable to stop. He is small and thin, and with each step his boots weigh more. As he approaches the tree, he feels as if he is lifting the entire island with every step.

His brother's stone is a small rectangle facing the sky between gnarled, polished roots. He moves toward it, helpless. In daylight he doesn't feel this way. In daylight he is a man of Small Island, with a man's tools, a man's drink. But in the dream the flat stone seems magnetized, and he moves toward it step by step, with no will of his own. Extending from the stone is a patch of grass as long as a fourteen-year-old boy and darker than the grass around it.

He puts his left foot on the darker grass, and the wolf comes into view, long forelegs appearing first from behind the tree. The wolf's coat is the blue of the sky. On his belly, legs and muzzle, the blue shades into white. His eyes are green: glowing and human, full of sorrow and knowledge. They look straight into the boy. At first he thinks the wolf means to eat him, and it takes every bit of his courage not to look away. He knows the wolf has something to tell him and that if he looks away, wolf and message will vanish forever.

In the daylight world, there are no wolves on Small Island: They were hunted away long ago. There are still wolves in some parts of the Mainland, and every child has seen them in picture books. While the boy stares, the wolf's eyes soften, as if the beast has decided to spare this child. The wolf says nothing that ears can hear, but his eyes speak clearly, telling the boy what he must do.

The man wakes slowly under sheets heavy with sweat. He can't tell whether he is hot or cold. He knows he is still sick, sicker than he has ever been before. People on Small Island don't get sick often. When they do, it is usually just before they die. But mostly they die in other ways than from sickness. They drink themselves to death, fall through the ice into the sea, cut each other with knives on Saturday night in Harbortown. All of this they understand and take for granted. But they don't know much about being sick.

The man doesn't know how to do it or what it requires of him. He looks to the woman sitting on the edge of the bed, which is her bed, for a sign. She is small and dark, barely denting the mattress. Her palm takes some of the heat from his forehead.

"Have I been sleeping long?"

"A little while." To tell him the truth about how long he has been in and out of waking would frighten her. She reaches a towel into a basin of water, twists the water out, folds the towel and presses it to his forehead. He lies back and closes his eyes.

He has been in her house above Harbortown for two weeks with a bad fever. She has been changing the sheets, bathing his forehead with the towel dipped in water, wringing a few drops into his mouth, trying to see that he doesn't burn up.

"How did I get here?"

It is the first time he has slept in her house. In the time they have been together, he has met her at her door, walked away with her through the snow in winter, over the wet earth in spring, the grass in summer, but until now he has never been in her house more than a few minutes at a time. The sheets are scratchy. He has a fever. He knows what fever is, as the children of Small Island know what a wolf is without ever having seen one except in books. But he doesn't know what to do about it. In his world, there is a tool for every job. For sickness, he has no tools.

"Don't worry about how you got here." She wrings the towel out into the basin and presses it to his forehead. His face is narrow, his eyes a brown so dark it is almost black. His mustache droops over his mouth, gold sprinkled through the brown. There is dark stubble on his cheeks. Usually he is cleanshaven, except for the mustache. By Small Island standards he is a tidy man, though frequently drunk, sometimes for weeks at a time. On Small Island, this is not worthy of notice or comment.

She brought him to her house in a wheelbarrow, the one that usually stands outside his shed. He was in no shape to walk. When he hadn't come to see her for three weeks, she was frightened. She knew he had been drinking. When he is drinking, he doesn't come to see her for days, and she knows he will be in one of the bars in Harbortown. But they've been growing closer recently—at least she feels they have—and three weeks is too long for him to give no sign. Ignoring her shame, she asked after him in town, but no one had seen him.

She walked up to his shed, standing in a grove of maples away from other houses. He was sweating and delirious, lying on the floor. He didn't recognize her, pushed her away when she reached for him. His wheelbarrow was outside the shed under a tarp, his hoe, axe and shovel piled in it. She took the tools out, went inside and took him under the arms. She has no idea how she got him into the wheelbarrow.

She wheeled him out under the leafless maples and over the packed snow to her house, his arms and legs dangling. The snow squeaked under her boots and the barrow's wooden wheel. It took hours to get him to her house and walk and carry him up the narrow stairs to her bed. For the two weeks since, she has slept in the next room with her daughter, sleeping lightly, waking at every sound.

"Was I drinking?"

"Yes. But that's not it. It's fever. I brought you here to get better."

What she does not say is: *I was afraid you would die.*

He looks at her, not knowing what to think. His dark eyes glow above purple half-moons. With his head against the pillow, the bald spot at the back of his head isn't visible.

Under the stubble he is paler and thinner than when he's healthy, and there's a red spot on each cheek. The way he looks tears at something inside her.

Waking this way, helpless in her bed, he feels suspicious. Suspicious of her and also grateful to her—not an easy combination. She reaches to touch his shoulder above the bedclothes. His body is hot. She knows the fever is not finished with him. And she is reaching the limit of her powers. She is tired, all the way to the bone. She thinks of calling the doctor, then puts that thought away.

He hears a soft noise and turns his head, his neck painful. The girl is in the doorway. In her build she resembles the woman: small, tightly knit, strong. But where the woman has dark hair and eyes, the girl has thick blond hair and blue eyes. The girl watches him in bed, making him feel weak, exposed. He has spent little time with the girl, and not all of it has been easy.

"Is he going to die?"

"Of course not." The woman is off the bed, sweeping the girl up, moving her into the other room, tucking her back in bed. Hushed words pass between them, protests, then murmured agreement.

When she comes back, he is asleep. She pulls the covers around him, goes downstairs, refills the basin and balances it up the stairs. Sits on the edge of the bed wiping his forehead, trying to keep him cool. If the fever doesn't break soon, she will have to call the doctor. Like asking for the man in the town, fetching the doctor will require her to overcome her embarrassment.

In his sleep he turns and almost upsets the basin. He begins to speak, a word at a time. She can tell it is a conversation, that others are present. She hears his mother's name, his father's, another name she doesn't recognize. She leans forward, holding the basin, trying to bring her ear close enough so that she can hear everything.

Then she hears the knock on the front door: two soft, one loud, the tone demanding. *Valter.* It's been a while since he's come, and she knows a visit from her husband is due. Since she moved to this little house from the big house Valter's family owns in Harbortown, he has come to see her from time to time, usually at night after he's been drinking. He says he comes to see his daughter, but that's not it. He comes to see her and have his way with her, short and sharp, with no preliminaries. To show he can. To show that, even if she's left his house, some things don't change on Small Island. She has never even thought about divorce.

Usually when he comes to her door, she lets him in. It's easier that way. And if she is honest with herself, it is also because Valter's brutal way occasionally still excites her the way it did in the beginning. Valter comes from one of

Small Island's rich families, although on Small Island the distance between rich and poor is not as large as it is elsewhere. The people of the island are close to one another and close to the sea. Everything they do goes into the sea or comes out of the sea. And they all share the experience of the sea and the unceasing wind and cold in winter.

She wraps herself in an old blanket, plaid on a red ground, and goes down the stairs slowly, thinking her way through it all: Valter at the door, the man in her bed in his fever, her child awake in the dark watching the moonlight on the ceiling. She stops in the kitchen and picks up a long boning knife, folds the blanket over it. The man upstairs has sharpened her knives to a fine edge. She runs a finger over the blade, cuts and licks, enjoying the salty flavor of her own blood.

She opens the door and stands, not inviting Valter in or moving aside so that he can pass. Her husband is large and red-faced, two heads taller than she is and much heavier, smelling of whiskey. The moon over his shoulder is almost full. Covered in moonlight, Valter is dark and bulky, his coat of black fur, his hat the same stuff, fine and broad-brimmed. He is prosperous and hard. Life submits to a man like Valter. Three fat salmon, strung through their silver gills, dangle from a gloved hand.

"Not now, Valter."

"And why not, Kipfchen? You have a visitor?" He laughs, a brutal laugh that echoes like a voice in an empty barrel. Among the things Valter's family owns is a prosperous fish business. Much of what they sell is herring, pickled, packed in barrels and sold all the way to the Mainland.

She runs her thumb along the blade under the blanket, makes another small cut. "It's not a good time."

"I brought fish for her."

"Thank you. She's already asleep. You can't come up."

As if he hadn't heard, he takes a step toward her, his boots squeaking on the hard-packed snow. She pulls the blanket tighter, holding the handle of the knife. Since they were children, the woman has always felt a current of fear when she faces Valter. It ebbs and flows, but it has never gone away completely—until this moment.

Like a bear, Valter can smell danger. It is an unfamiliar sensation. He is used to ownership, to wearing a heavy fur coat and hat, the weight of it keeping the cold away. Used to well-made boots that come all the way from the Mainland on the Big Island steamer. He is not used to being even a little bit afraid. But he won't force things. Valter is patient. He can afford to be. He is rich.

Before what's happening has even registered in her mind, Valter has turned and is moving away. From the big dark form comes a song. Valter is famous on Small

Island for the number of drinking songs he knows. The fish, string quivering through their gills, lie in the snow where he dropped them, filling the prints of his expensive Mainland boots. She closes the door of her house, leaving the fish lying outside like visitors waiting for permission to enter.

In the kitchen she puts the knife down, washes the blood off her cuts, bandages her fingers and goes upstairs. The girl is asleep, golden curls covering her arm, thumb in her mouth. She tucks the blanket around the girl, turns down the lamp, goes across the hall and stands in the doorway. The man is asleep, quilt falling from his shoulders.

She stands looking at his lean form, thinking that he drinks too much. She never drinks. On Small Island, some drink all the time, others never. And it affects everyone differently. Valter drinks just as much as this man. But it never alters his bearlike nature, only expands it. This man, it undoes. As she watches, he begins to move, turning from side to side. His jaw clenches and unclenches. She leans in, but she can make out only fragments.

His dream is beginning again where he left it when he woke. The eyes of the wolf told him what he needed to do. Now he is doing it, and taking his task very seriously—more seriously than he has ever taken anything. He has never been able to take himself or what he does seriously. It is one of the reasons he drinks so much. He is a wonderful worker in wood. Every piece he works on comes out right, with nothing wasted. But this skill came to him without effort. And because it came with no effort he has never respected it—or himself for it.

In the dream, it's different: Every step matters. He is following the wolf's instructions carefully, taking the path through the woods. His parents' house is the same as always, with the sloping roof, wooden walls, joist-and-beam construction of every house on Small Island, except for those of one or two wealthy families, such as Valter's. A few pines overhang the house, making it seem dark even though it stands by itself on a bluff overlooking the sea.

As he approaches, he hears his father and mother, their voices loud and getting louder, clanging as they collide. The conversation is unhurried, as if they have spoken the same harsh words many times before, and each knows exactly what the other is about to say. As usual, they have both been drinking. His mother's voice is like a knife on a whetstone. Underneath it is grief. His father's voice is louder and more violent, but he is pleading.

He climbs the three steps to the front door, trying to avoid making the wood creak so he can hear what his parents are saying. His dream has a silvery quality that enters it from the room where he is sleeping. The curtains have been pushed back and moonlight pours across the bed. She watches him silently, then goes down the narrow stairs to check the stove.

The door to his parents' house is open. He eases across the threshold into the darkness, making himself small as he listens to the voices from the bedroom where his parents sleep, fuck and tear into each other in their drunkenness.

You killed him.

I never would.

You took him into the sea and he never came back.

I couldn't stop him. You know what he wanted. And he was good at it. The sea was in his nature. You can't change that. Any more than you can change your nature—or I mine.

He could have been anything. He didn't have to be that. He could have left this godforsaken little island and gone anywhere.

You're dreaming. Nobody leaves Small Island.

He could have. He was different. Better than you. Better than you can imagine.

You know I didn't do this. It's no one's fault. Why can't you stop hating me? It won't bring him back.

Stop hating you? You're asking me to forgive? Forgive you? You half-man. Quarter-man. Less than that. You—nothing.

Everyone on Small Island has lost someone to the sea. Many families have lost more than one. You're lucky. You have another son.

That sniveler? He's a little too much like you for my taste.

He's a good boy. Or he would be—if he had a mother who said a kind word to him now and then.

He's a weakling. Weaker than you—if such a thing is possible. He'll grow up to be a sack of whiskey just like you. The other one was beautiful. He could have been anything in this world, if he hadn't gone in your filthy boat, stinking of seaweed, and never come back. You killed him. And you know it. I hear it in your voice every time you speak. You're guilty. You're weak. You're hollowed out with dry rot. And nothing you do can ever change that.

The boy hears silence and then an explosion. His mother has thrown her bottle, and it's missed, smashing and making another mark on a wall that already has many marks. He knows what will happen now. They will fall on each other, hitting each other with anything within reach, couple like beasts, then pass out in a heap of clothes smelling of sweat, salt water, fish and alcohol.

The door of his parents' bedroom is partly open. He makes his way across the boards of the living room floor, laid down by his father and his father's father when his parents were newlyweds, before they lost his brother and wound up sodden on the floor, clawing each other in rage.

Against the far wall is a huge sideboard: dark, solid and heavy, with glass doors under an arching top. Inside are the few pieces of his mother's china that have survived the years of throwing. When he was little, nothing in this sideboard was ever used. Like everyone else on Small Island his family ate off simple plates and wiped their hands on rags.

The sideboard was made from hardwoods by a famous company on the Mainland. No metal was used in making it, aside from the hinges, lock and key. Every piece is attached by its own shape or by pegs of the same wood. It could be taken apart, piece by piece, and put back together without a single tool. Even on Small Island, where many are good with tools and wood, this piece has always seemed exceptional.

The sideboard has been in the boy's life from the beginning. And it was often talked about. People made fun of his mother for it. To her face, they were not eager to make her angry. Even before his brother's death, her anger was nothing to trifle with. But behind her back they mocked her for the airs she gave herself for owning the finest piece of furniture on Small Island.

The boy knows the drawers by heart; he began opening them when he was small. At first he pulled himself up by the handles. When he could stand up on his own, he opened the lowest of the three drawers. The stages of his childhood were marked by when he was able to reach the second drawer and look inside, then the third, always careful to slide them back with everything just as it was before the drawer was opened.

He slides the second drawer open with care. There is little light in the house, but he knows everything in the drawer by touch. There are three stacks. In the center, he feels the thing he has been asked to bring. Its texture brings the creamy white linen into his mind's eye.

He pushes the drawer back slowly, even though he's sure his parents have passed out on the floor. He backs away from the sideboard and passes the open door to their bedroom without looking in.

The man wakes clutching the covers, drenched in sweat, the sheet twisted in his hand where the napkin was in the dream. For a moment dream and waking life are wrestling, neither one strong enough to pin the other to the ground. Then he hears footsteps coming up the stairs: heavy, definitive and male. He leans his head back against the pillow, not knowing who is coming, too weak to fight.

CHAPTER 2

Downstairs the woman is waiting, having left her child and gone out into the winter night to fetch the doctor.

When she fell in love with the man upstairs in her bed, she didn't intend to change her world. But her world has changed. When she lived with Valter, the outer world was orderly. The people of Small Island were welcoming and respectful: She was the wife of a big man. But inside her, everything was like a dammed river. Now the river has broken the dam and over-flowed, foaming and surging downstream. Inside she has been freed, but the outer world does not give her the respect it once did. Going to fetch the doctor was not easy. Now she waits in her overcoat, snow melting on the green lodencloth and soaking her dark hair, for the doctor to come down the stairs and say words she is afraid to hear.

He descends a segment at a time, like a roundworm emerging from the damp earth in spring. First come black boots. Then trousers, the part below the knees tucked into the boots. Then the bottom of a fur coat, like Valter's, though not as grand. A gloved hand holding a black bag. A belly snug in dark fur. Chest, shoulders. Finally, a round face with pale blue eyes and white hair. The doctor is vain about his full head of hair. He comes out to see people, even late at night in winter, without a hat. He has seen everything—from birth to death and everything in between—many times. None of it has changed him very much. He is the only doctor on Small Island.

The doctor stops at the bottom of the stairs. His look is controlled, but the woman feels his condescension. She is Valter's wife—and yet she is not. Another man is up-stairs in her bed, sick with fever.

"Nothing can be done."

"Nothing?"

"It's in God's hands now."

"Nothing?"

"Good night."

He walks past her without a word. She feels her anger rising. Small as she is, she isn't afraid to hit the doctor. If Valter was up there sweating in the bed, she thinks, he wouldn't say that. It would not be *in God's hands*. At this moment, he would be scurrying to do *something. Anything.* Not *nothing.*

He hesitates at the door. She realizes that in her anger she has forgotten the money. She takes folded bills out of the pocket of her coat, slides them into the pocket of the doctor's, between warm fur and fat.

"My best to you and your daughter."

"And to you."

She closes the door and leans her forehead against the wood. The anger recedes, and she feels as if she might cry. Although the door is closed, she knows exactly how the doctor looks as he walks away in the moonlight. Despite his roundness and his white hair, he looks as if he might rise, click his heels and waltz away on the snow, which is as hard and smooth as a dance floor.

She takes her forehead from the door. Ribbons of light drip down her cheeks. After a few minutes, she takes off her overcoat, hangs it on a peg on the back of the door, leaves her boots in a corner, pads up the steps in stocking feet. She falls into bed beside her daughter, still wearing her clothes.

In the morning he is singing. She hears him and thinks she is dreaming, then realizes she is awake. Her daughter is curled into her mother's body, still asleep. She untangles herself from the sleeping child, gets up, crosses the landing and stands in the open door. He is sitting up, his brown eyes open, purple half-moons under his eyes. She knows he is not seeing her—or anything in the waking world.

> *Oh, on land the duck is a clumsy thing*
> *A clumsy thing like a pregnant woman*
> *Waddling from side to side when it walks*
> *Not made for land, not made for land*

He sings as if he were in a choir, head up and shoulders squared. There is only one church on Small Island, a little wooden building in Harbortown with a small congregation, mostly old women. In the days leading up to Easter, the women congregate to hear the broken-down pastor preach the eternal guilt of the Jews for crucifying Our Lord.

Small Island is a far-flung possession of the Mainland. The Mainland has been a Christian kingdom for almost a thousand years, since a peasant boy named Vashad converted the king from his pagan gods to faith in Jesus Christ. Vashad had been urged to journey to the capital and convert the king by a flock of shrieking blackbirds whose message only he could understand.

Every child in the kingdom—from the capital all the way to Small Island—knows the story of Vashad. But the woman can't imagine this man has ever been inside the church in Harbortown. And yet here he is, just as though he were in the choir, singing at the top of his lungs. She can't imagine how the girl can sleep through it.

He has a finer voice than she would have thought, rough from smoking and drinking, but clear and tuneful.

> *In the water, when the duck is swimming*
> *He's a little less clumsy than on the land*
> *But not much better, really, not much better*
> *Bobbing on the water like a child's toy*

It's a folk song from the part of the Mainland where his father's people come from. She knows the song, though her people come from a completely different part of the Mainland.

> *But, oh, when he takes to the sky*
> *Then the duck is filled with grace, filled with grace*
> *Because the duck was made for the sky*
> *And when he flies, there's none more graceful*

The verse about the duck taking to the sky, being a thing of grace, comes back again and again. There are many other verses that tell how the duck learns his nature, who he learns it from and many other things. It is the kind of song that can be made to last for a whole evening— accompanied by fiddle, guitar and bottles. The man sings several verses, his voice growing louder and firmer. She watches, as surprised as if her little girl had suddenly been changed into a beautiful golden dog, barking and licking her leg, asking to be taken out for a run.

Then his voice begins to slide down and away from good clear singing. It blurs until he is mumbling. His eyes close, and he topples over into fever sleep, his head missing the pillow. She lifts him and slides the pillow under his head. Her hand comes away wet. She tucks the covers under his chin, hoping they aren't drenched, that he won't freeze in bed. She doesn't have the strength to get him up and change the sheets one more time.

After this strange burst of singing, she begins to feel that despite her anger the doctor was probably right. Nothing can be done. All of this is beyond her: his fever, sweats, talking in his sleep and now his singing. Nature must find its course and take it, whether it is the will of God or not. It is time for her to go back to her life. She works at the general store in Harbortown. Her boss has given her time off. He has been understanding—because Valter's family owns the store—but it is time to go back to work.

She dresses herself, gets the child up and dressed. They walk out over the frozen snow, the girl rubbing blond hair out of her eyes. As they walk, warmth flows through their mittens, reconnecting them, and it feels the way it did before the man with the mustache and the bald spot entered their life.

By the time they leave the house, he is back in his dream. He has accomplished the first task the wolf gave him. Now he must go back to the oak, where he knows the wolf will be waiting. He holds the linen napkin with care. As he approaches the tree and puts his foot on the patch of grass darker than the rest, the wolf comes out from behind the oak, stepping so lightly the grass does not bend. The green eyes take in the napkin, and the boy thinks he sees approval in them.

The wolf steps closer on its long white forelegs. The boy knows the wolf will ask much of him, and he wonders whether he will be strong enough to do what is asked. He knows that if he shows fear, the wolf will leave in a blink of its green eyes and never return. The boy takes a step forward, holding the napkin. He knows that he must fasten the napkin around the wolf's neck and then hold on. He twines and knots the ends. Like all males of Small Island, the boy has spent his life near the water and on the water, tying and untying lines. The knot is firm.

He stands shoulder to shoulder with the wolf, holding the napkin, which circles the wolf's neck like a priest's white collar. Their shoulders are the same height. The boy's head is higher than the wolf's, which extends forward, with its white stripe down the muzzle. They stand for a moment, linked by the napkin. Then the wolf pads forward, slowly at first, then faster and faster, with a power unlike anything the boy has ever felt. All he can do is hold on and try to keep up. Amazingly, he can.

They trot across the familiar surface of Small Island: grass, trees and rocks spilling down, gray on broken gray, to the ocean. They pass Harbortown, go down the bluff overlooking the harbor, the wolf picking up speed with every step, the boy holding the napkin as tightly as he can. As they descend the bluff toward the water, the boy closes his eyes. He isn't afraid. He doesn't want to know the way back.

Then, the boy's eyes still closed, they're on the water. In the coldest part of winter, Small Island is held in a ring of ice that reaches out toward Big Island. They move across the water as if it were midwinter ice: solid as a church floor. Holding the napkin, the boy keeps pace with the wolf. When he needs more speed, he has it. He's there, stride for stride, even though they are moving faster and faster, loping over an ocean that is strangely solid under their six flying feet.

They run for what seems like hours, the boy holding the linen napkin, afraid to let go. After a time, he feels a message come through the napkin into his hand and travel up his arm like a shock: He must open his eyes. There, coming up before them as they move across the ocean, is a body of land bigger than anything he has ever seen. They approach a rocky beach, move swiftly over it and up a bluff to the headland beyond. The land is covered in long grass, bent low in the steady wind off the ocean.

If the ocean they crossed seemed frozen solid, on this land it is summer: hot and still. Wolf and boy run, legs in rhythm, over grass, through meadows, across streams, up and down hills, into a forest so dense the boy can't see the sky. Then out onto a plain with farms bigger than any the boy has seen. Cows, goats, sheep and hogs, fat and peaceful, are settled in the pastures. Smoke curls from farmhouse chimneys.

They keep running, across another plain, this one drier, not farmed, covered in a stubble of grass. The fields are parched, the trees stunted. The wolf slows to a trot, then to a walk. They stop in the arid landscape, with its sandy hills descending to streams shriveling from lack of water.

The boy looks around. He releases his grip on the napkin. His left arm feels so heavy that it might drop to the ground. Instead, it falls to his side, his hand holding a linen ring. The wolf is gone. The boy lifts the napkin and examines his mother's careful green stitching and the emptiness at the center, where the wolf was. He is alone among stunted trees in a landscape dying of thirst.

This must be the Mainland, he thinks. It is the only place that could possibly be as big as this, the only place that has as many landscapes as this place does, the only place he's ever heard of where the sea is not always close by. He's seen pictures of the Mainland in books. All the people of Small Island came from there centuries ago. Their ancestors were sailors, pagan warriors.

The man's eyes open slowly, crusted with sleep and fever. He feels as if he's been unconscious forever, as if he's not just waking up, but being born again. He has to think hard to know where he is, who he is, what his name is, how he came to be in this bed. Then it comes back—his waking life and his dream. He can feel the place where he held the napkin that was looped around the wolf's neck. It feels as if there should be a place rubbed raw on his palm, as there is after you work a rope without gloves. But he feels his palm and finds nothing but smooth skin.

When the woman gets home he's sitting up in bed. He is thin and pale, but the red spots on his cheeks are gone. He still has dark half-moons under his eyes, but the sheets are dry. So is his undershirt, which he hasn't taken off the entire time he's been in her house. She tried once or twice to get it off him, but he wouldn't give it up, wrestling with her even in sleep.

"You're awake," she says. What she means is: *You're alive.* After the doctor's visit, she had tried to let him go. She hadn't known what else to do. She feels guilty that she tried to do that. Guilty and overjoyed, overflowing with gratitude. *He is alive and on the mend.*

"Awake," he mumbles, his voice raspy. Even when he is healthy, he is not a man of many words. He seems to believe words are precious, to be doled out a little at a time. Perhaps he believes each man is given only a certain number for a lifetime and, when he speaks the allotted number, must die.

She goes downstairs, still wearing her coat, makes a fire in the stove, heats soup. Comes back up the stairs, sits on the edge of the bed and spoons broth into his mouth. The broth is made from the salmon Valter left behind in his bootprints. They were beautiful fish, and they made a rich broth to which she added carrots and turnips. She and the girl have been living on this broth, and the fish in it, for days. He accepts the soup gratefully and cautiously.

Awake now, his head clearing, his first thought is concern that he has been a burden to her. He feels clumsy and unused to his body. Soup drips from the corner of his mouth. She lifts the napkin she has fastened around his neck and pats the clear drops. He doesn't enjoy being touched, except at certain moments, but he wills himself to allow her touch.

"How long have I been here?"

"Not long."

"Have you been working?"

"Yes, I went back to the store."

"That's good."

"The doctor wasn't sure you would get better."

"The doctor?"

"You don't remember?"

"I think I don't remember much until today."

"You're cooler. It looks like the fever is gone."

"I'll take myself off your hands."

"That isn't what I mean. You're not a burden. And you don't have to leave right away. You're still weak. Wait until you've got your strength back. Then you can go."

Still wearing her coat, she spoons more soup into him, asking him without speaking to stay and take care of himself until he is fully recovered. She knows better than to try to make him stay. If she is careful, and doesn't say anything, perhaps he will do what's best for him. She will bring him back, gently, from where he was when he was dreaming, talking in his sleep, singing about the duck.

After all, she thinks, she had him when he was unconscious and burning with fever. Shouldn't she have him in her house when he is awake and mending? Why does he need to go right back to his cold shed?

As she holds the spoon up, he nods over, eyes closing. But she's gotten some broth into him, and even a few pieces of fish. He lists like a ship capsizing until he's down again and sleeping. She covers him and leaves. His sleep is less broken. He's not talking, or singing, or turning. Just rising and falling under the covers. She realizes how tired she is from caring for him. How, even though she tried to let go and let everything take its course, as the doctor had advised, her body was still hoping and fighting.

Now she feels how much the fight has cost. She goes down to the kitchen, feeds herself soup, goes back up to her daughter's bed. The child is asleep, thumb in her mouth, golden curls across her face. She undresses, feeling as if her clothes weigh a hundred pounds. She folds them over a chair and climbs in bed next to the child. Then all three of them set sail together in the dark from Small Island out onto the waves, cold, gray and numberless, that have beaten on that tiny speck of land since time began.

The next morning she and the girl leave early and go walking over the snow to Harbortown. When they have been gone an hour or so, the man wakes and gets up from the bed where he has been lying for two weeks. When he stands, he is shaky. He goes down the stairs in his underwear, long bottoms and long-sleeved top not particularly clean. He sees her house as if for the first time. He looks around the kitchen. There's little enough in it. He is ashamed of himself for taking her time, making her miss work. He owes her a lot—and he is a man who cannot bear to owe anything.

He goes upstairs, finds his clothes balled behind the bed and gets dressed. His denim overalls and brown corduroy jacket are loose. Once dressed, he starts coughing, feels the pull of the soft bed. It would be easy to get back in and wait for her return. He knows she would like him to be there when she comes home. Coughing interrupts his thoughts, cutting his chest and throat. He sits on the bed, pulls on his boots and laces them. They are tall boots like the woodcutters wear, with thick gripping soles.

He goes down, his boots loud on the stairs. He stands in front of her door, his breath pluming into the cold air, feeling thin and chilled.

It's not spring yet, but there have already been days of thaw. The crust on the snow has melted and refrozen. His tall boots break the crust, push down into soft white.

Around the side of her house he finds his wheelbarrow, filled with snow, ice packed between the spokes of the wooden wheel, like slices of an icy pie. Now he sees how he got to her house. He admires her, pushing him over the frozen snow in the wheelbarrow. She is small, and it would have been a heavy load for her, alone in the dark.

He looks at the snow and ice on his barrow, reaches with the toe of a boot and kicks a wedge of ice out from between the spokes of the wheel for the pleasure of seeing the shards skid away over the frozen ground.

He looks around the clearing that stretches away from her house. On the far side smoke floats from one chimney. He can smell cooking. He's hungry for the first time in his new-born life.

He scoops snow out of the wheelbarrow, regretting that he has no gloves, wipes his hands on pants and jacket and starts pushing his barrow across the clearing, over the hill and into the woods.

In the evening when she comes home from work, she knows even before entering her house that he's gone. She goes upstairs and pulls the covers down, sees where his body has compressed the mattress in night after night of sweating half-sleep. She wants to lean over and breathe in his smell, but she is aware of the girl beside her, who already asks enough questions.

Before the events of this past year, the woman always knew what she wanted. When she was seventeen, she knew she wanted to marry Valter, even though she didn't particularly like him. Two years ago, she knew she wanted to leave Valter's house, because she was ready to be on her own. Those things were clear. Like Small Island, they had definite outlines. Now, nothing is clear. Her life is like the sea: huge and formless, always in motion. Sometimes she even misses Valter. That frightens her. She strips the bed and lets the mattress air, then carries the sheets downstairs and leaves them with the other laundry that is waiting to be redeemed.

CHAPTER 3

After he leaves her house, she doesn't hear from him for many weeks. It's the longest she's gone without hearing from him since they began spending time together a year ago. She wonders whether he's angry with her for following the doctor's advice and leaving things in the hands of God. The doctor's a fat, smug fool, she thinks. And she was weak. But that can't be it. He can't know what the doctor said. He didn't even remember that the doctor had been in to see him. He was unconscious, tossing on her bed, singing about the wild duck. Men and their drinking songs. Idiots. No one is worse in that way than Valter, who knows hundreds of songs. She thought this man was different: quieter, less a fool, in spite of his drinking. Perhaps she was wrong.

But if he isn't angry at her, what is it? What keeps him away after she has lowered herself to run after the doctor, made the fish Valter left at her door into soup, nursed him until he was well? The man's silence makes the woman sharp and cranky; the girl keeps her distance.

As she goes about her business, winter is finally coming to an end. The snow loosens and slides down from the roofs to the ground, where it lies in piles under windows, next to doors. Water drips from the eaves. The earth re-appears between her house and the others. Small dark patches spread and link with their comrades until the snow is surrounded: a defeated army, retreating to lick its wounds, regroup and counterattack at the beginning of November. She leaves her door open, looks out to see her neighbors doing the same.

On a day when the snow is almost gone, she comes home from work to find a table sitting inside her house next to the front door. The table is simple but well made. The four legs mark a square on the floor, lean in, braced halfway, ending in a smaller square under the top. The table comes to her waist, which is small and she knows he likes.

Her coat still on, the girl beside her, she lets her hand fall to the surface. Cherry, she thinks. Her favorite. On the table is a pale blue envelope. It's been in and out of pockets, folded and marked in pencil and ink. Figures march from top to bottom like twin columns of ants. She doesn't want to touch the envelope. But the girl reaches for it. In a swift gesture, the woman picks the envelope up and lifts it out of reach.

"What is it?"

"Something someone left us. Look at the table. Beautiful, isn't it?"

"What's in the envelope?"

The girl is at an age where she has to know everything: what something is, where it belongs, why it belongs there, how it got there, what it's made of, who made it, why they made it. Sometimes the woman feels as if the questions, many of which can't be answered by anyone who has learned to think like an adult, will drive her mad. She wishes the man were here. Even though his relations with the girl aren't always easy, he sometimes has a way of answering her questions that makes her laugh and then silences her.

She stuffs the blue envelope with its double file of ant tracks into her coat pocket. Mother and daughter stand in the doorway, faces bearing the same expression, one dark, one light. The sun, slanting in, is higher than it has been all year at this time in the late afternoon.

"Is the table from Papa?"

"I don't think so, sweetheart."

"Did the man who was sick make it?"

That's what she has taken to calling him: *the man who was sick*. The girl can't imagine her father sick that way, sitting up unconscious with his eyes open, howling stupid songs. Her father is dignified. His house is large. His family is rich. She knows her mother doesn't want her to feel this way, but she waits for her father's visits with excitement, loving the fish he brings, along with his smell, his dark clothes, his voice and his power.

"That's enough. I'll tell you more when I know."

Of course she knows who made it. The man's hand is in this table. There's no mistaking it. And no doubt whose ant-track calculations are marching down the envelope. If there's one thing she can't stand thinking about, it's money. That's one of the things she grew to loathe about Valter: Everything was money. *Money, money, money.* She wishes she had never seen the envelope. The table is different. It has his hand in it, the hand that touches her secretly. She sees it in the glow of the surface, the way everything fits together neatly. He is not good with words, it often seems difficult for him to let them go. But sometimes the things he does without words—like making this table—are so deft that they take her breath away. She steps into the house, bringing the girl with her. After dinner she will take a walk.

She makes dinner, tucks the girl into bed, goes downstairs and pulls her boots on. She takes the envelope out of her coat and opens it. It is just as she thought. There are no words, just banknotes of the Mainland, folded to fit.

She pulls the bills out. Some are pale blue, others yellow or buff. Each note has the face of the king looking out from an oval frame. The king's face is narrow, thoughtful, with a fringe of beard, oval glasses and alert, intelligent eyes. He's not old, the reigning king, but he's been on the throne since he was a boy. He's already had a long reign, but he's never seen fit to visit Small Island. But then, why should he? The island is just a dot on the sea, a world away from the capital and the wonders of the palace. The woman knows why the man has left her this money. It makes her sad and angry in equal measure.

When she's sure the girl is asleep, she leaves her house, pulling the door closed quietly behind her. As she walks, the earth under her feet is dark, moist and yielding. Next to the path, shoots are nosing up: crocuses tightly wrapped in green. She's still angry with the man, but also excited and uncertain. She doesn't know what to expect when she gets to his shed. He may be angry, drawn into some place where she can't follow. Or deep in drink, passed out on the floor, tools scattered around. When he's sober—which can be for days, weeks, months at a time—he's a hard worker. But when he starts to drink, there is no stopping him. It might be weeks before he emerges, torn and dirty, pockets empty, like something that's been dragged through the woods by an animal.

She hates his drinking, but she feels a tenderness for the part of him that is unable to resist. She believes her love could change him if he would accept it as fully as she wishes to give it. She is mostly a sensible woman, but this feeling has remained with her for a year. As she walks, the almost-spring wind picks up. The path leaves the open field and dives into stands of fir, pine and spruce. Most of Small Island has been logged at least once, and there isn't much of the original forest left. A quarter moon stands out from the sky like pitted silver. She pulls her coat tighter against the cold.

Coming out of the woods, the path leads her first along the side of his shed, then around the front, a rectangle of unpainted boards with a door and window. It was built as a shed for storing tools, open in front to the woods. When he moved his tools in, it hadn't been used in so long no one could quite remember who had built it. He began by storing his tools in the shed. Then, when he wasn't working on other jobs, he started to rebuild it, closing the open front, hanging a door and a window, replacing rotten boards. His hands started the work on their own, without his having to think much about it. Then he went on a big drunk, ran out of money and lost his room in the Harbortown flophouse. He moved into the shed. In the year they've known each other, she's been in his blankets on the floor of this shed many times.

Standing in front of the shed, she can see that something is different. He's taken down sections of the walls at one corner; a white shape extends from the corner out into the woods. It looks as if the shed has given birth to a smaller version of itself in canvas. Lantern light shines through the canvas and meets the light of the quarter moon.

She walks to the door and knocks. He opens it, holding the lantern up to see who is at his door at this hour. A cigarette glows in the corner of his mouth. He seems unsurprised at her presence.

"Are you going to make me stand here?"

He moves aside to let her pass. Inside the shed, the flooring is gone, revealing hard-packed dirt. The little furniture he had is also gone, except for a toolbench. On the floor sit the spine and ribs of a boat, bow nosing out into the woods under the canvas. To the woman, the thing on the floor looks like the skeleton of a sea monster, something huge and dark sliding through the sea, far below the surface.

"What are you doing?"

"Building a boat."

He stands looking at her, holding a hammer in one hand and a chisel in the other. He is wearing the same longjohns he had on at her house when he slept and sang in his fever. It doesn't look as though they've been washed. Over the long underwear is a pair of dark blue overalls marked with paint, pencil and wood dust. She is relieved not to smell alcohol.

He puts the lamp down on his bench. His cigarette has burned to a glowing dot. He drops it to the floor and grinds it out.

"I can see you're building a boat. What I want to know is: *Why?*"

"To sail to Big Island."

"Big Island? Why in the world would you do that?"

She feels light, but not in a good way: She is empty and panicky, like a cloud floating on the spring wind above the trees outside. She wills herself back down into the shed and onto the dirt floor, wills herself to stay there.

"Because I'm going to do it."

She knows from his tone that he won't say anything more about his reasons. He's drawn a line, like the ones he draws with his carpenter's pencil. On the other side of the line there is nothing to say.

"You don't know how to build a boat."

He smiles, looking at the thing on the floor of the extended shed. The skeleton is well on its way to being a classic Small Island double-ender. The keel is oak. Also the upcurving ribs that remind her of a sea monster. The bow and stern are almost symmetrical, the bow a little higher and longer. It is a boat that can easily be sailed by one, though it would usually carry two, or even three. It looks frail, but Small Islanders have sailed and rowed boats like this into the northern sea for generations— and usually returned.

"The boatbuilder families will be angry. You know they don't allow anyone else to build boats."

At this he does not smile. He crosses behind her and closes the door, puts the hammer and chisel down. Stands close to her, leaning down, his face close to hers. He still looks thin, after his illness, but then he always looks thin.

She feels like a field mouse on the snow, hearing the whir of owl wings in the cold air above. He reaches down and unbuttons her coat, one button at a time, with a carpenter's roughened fingers, until her coat hangs open. Then he slides his fingers under the coat, feeling for her, finding her.

He is rough and gentle at the same time. It feels as if he is reaching right into the center of her. After a time, he begins opening and closing her again, many times, on the dirt floor, next to the skeleton of his boat.

When she comes back to herself, several things are in her mind. She lies there running over those things while she feels the two of them cooling apart where they were connected. She feels him shrink out of her and slip away.

He gets up, finds the threadbare blanket he sleeps under, lies down and pulls it around them. On the roof and walls of canvas extending from the shed, shadows of new maple leaves move back and forth. The small leaves move away in the wind and then return to their original places, as if they know where their homes are.

She rolls on her side, looking him square in the face and says, "If you want to go to Big Island, why don't you just take the steamer?" As soon as the words leave her mouth, she is embarrassed and wishes she could reel them back in.

He looks into her eyes, as dark as his own. He pushes the blanket off, gets up and stands with his narrow back to her, the bones of the spine showing clearly, the skin pale where the sun doesn't reach. He walks around the unfinished boat, touching it here and there, bending over to pick up her clothes and bring them to her. He finds his own clothes, slips into his longjohns, overalls and boots. Strikes a match, relights the lantern. From the lantern lights a cigarette. Stands, lantern in hand, cigarette in the corner of his mouth, smoke rolling up around his face, looking at his unfinished work without speaking.

She came to this shed with a purpose in mind: to give him back the money he left in the blue envelope. Now that she's here, she knows she can't return it. He won't accept it. She's angry, not sure exactly who she's angry with. Angry or not, she knows that the envelope in her coat pocket must go back down through the woods with her. As she walks home, she will think about what to do with his money, which she cannot keep but cannot return. She gets up from under the blanket and dresses herself.

She looks at him where he stands examining his work as if he has forgotten she is there with him. Suddenly she is sure he will drown, like his brother. Everyone on the island knows that story. For her, there is no death worse than drowning. It's bad enough when men fight in Harbortown, slashing each other across the throat and bleeding to death in the sawdust on the floor. But drowning is worse: There is nothing to say goodbye to. Even if the sea generously chooses to return his body, as it did his brother's, it will likely be on some other shore.

She pulls on the rest of her clothes, walks to the door and lets herself out into the night without disturbing him. She takes the path through the woods, being careful not to crush the green crocus shoots before they have their chance to bloom. The blue envelope in her pocket is a riddle, but she is good at riddles. She has liked them ever since she was a girl.

By the time she reaches the clearing where her house stands, the moon is setting on the horizon, out past Harbortown. The sky is pale. She walks faster in order to be home before her daughter wakes.

Inside, she takes off her coat, hangs it behind the door, puts the envelope in the drawer of the table the man made for her. She has to press it flat to get the drawer closed. Why, she wonders, would a carpenter who has never been out on the ocean decide to build a boat and sail away from Small Island? Especially one who has been frightened of the sea since his only brother drowned.

The answer must lie somewhere in the story of his family, she thinks. But where? It's such a tangle. After the man's brother died, their mother, the best seamstress on Small Island, raged, drank and beat her husband and anyone who tried to pull them apart. One night in Harbortown it took three men to get her off him and drag her back to her house, where she passed out. The husband followed, yelling the whole time, then passed out next to her with his arms around her. No one could understand why he stayed. Finally she threw him out, and he built a house on a bleak finger of land called Gallagher's Point, where the wind is so steady and strong that there are very few houses among the pines, stunted and twisted, that cling to the cliff. People say he has a woman up there, but no one goes to visit.

When the mother isn't drunk, she is still a seamstress who can sew anything. She makes embroidery more elegant than anything else on Small Island, a tradition passed down to her from her mother and her mother's mother. Even when she drinks, her hand is steady, but ultimately she reaches a point where the work blurs and she blacks out. After his brother died, she shunned the boy. People on the island felt pity, but they didn't want to have much to do with him. He was bad luck. Despite her shunning him, he is much like his mother in one way: He has hands that can make anything.

When the package arrives, the woman is working in the general store. The bell over the door rings, and the postman steps in. They get a lot of mail in the store addressed to *General Delivery, Harbortown, Small Island.* Only the well-to-do, like Valter, have their own postal address. Mail comes on the steamer from Big Island once a week, except in the dead of winter, when the ice is too thick to cut through. The steamer anchors in the harbor and a lighter is rowed to the stony beach carrying mail for the shop and orders for customers, things not found on Small Island. Many on the island cannot read or write, and she helps them with their letters. It has always surprised her how well the man who was sick can read. It was something his mother taught him.

"Here's one for you," says Finnarson. The postman has the Small Island look: narrow and wiry, drooping mustache. He holds out a package along with a pile of letters. The package is small and square, tied with twine. It has come all the way from another world: the Mainland, near the capital. For a moment, the sight of the package freezes her.

"One for you, I said."

"I hear you, Finnarson. There's no reason to shout."

"I wasn't shouting."

Finnarson is sweet on her. She is even-tempered, accepting Finnarson's timid advances in good humor. When she and Valter were living together, she was invisible to men. Now they seem alert to the slightest change in her, as if they can smell it, the way dogs do. It tires her.

Normally she would stop and chat for a while with Finnarson. Not today. She takes the letters and package without a word, sets them down and turns back to what she was doing before the postman entered.

Finnarson stands still, startled by her rudeness, then turns and clumps out and down the wooden sidewalk, the bell ringing behind him as he wonders: *What in the hell is wrong with her?*

She takes the package home in her coat. It stretches the pocket, but she doesn't want it in her hands as she walks through Harbortown, doesn't want anyone asking slyly: "A package from the Mainland, eh?"

She leaves her coat unbuttoned, almost doesn't need it. The spring air smells of mud. His boots will be wet. He is working again. She hears of him from time to time but pretends not to notice. He's stopped drinking. But he's stopped before; she doesn't expect it to last. This boat is nothing more than foolishness. He won't finish it. He'll give up and go back to what he always did before: drink and work, drink and work. And even if he does, by some miracle, finish his ridiculous boat, he'll never actually leave. Sailing to Big Island. What nonsense. She is afraid. But part of her cannot help but admire.

CHAPTER 4

In his shed the man of Small Island works on his boat without thinking. When he is sober, he can always find work. After he got well, he took the jobs he found until he had enough money to repay her, with something left over for his journey. Now that the debt is paid, he can work far into the night, as quickly or as slowly as he wishes. No one expects this boat; no one is paying for it. No one even knows about it, except the woman. As spring deepens, the boat grows and takes shape under the maples, whose leaves, now fully open, make shadows like hands on the white canvas extending out into the woods.

After laying the keel and joining the ribs to it, he fills in the hull, steaming and bending cedar planks into shape. Although he is afraid of the ocean, he has been fascinated by boats since his brother was taken by the sea. He has watched how the boatbuilder families assemble the parts in time-tested ways. But as he works in the shed, he is not exactly imitating: He is making something that is his own. And the boat is teaching him how to build it, showing him at each step what needs doing next.

He squats on the dirt floor, smoking a cigarette and examining the hull. Cedar planking is now three-quarters of the way up to the gunwales. Spring is almost full. The beginning of summer will be a good time to put the boat in the water. As he looks over his work, he considers how he will get his boat over the bluff and down through the woods to the beach below Harbortown. But before that can happen, there are things to be fashioned, including the sail. And a visit he needs to make.

At the woman's house, things are moving easily. She hasn't seen the man in a while, and when she doesn't see him, her life takes its own pace, like the pansies coming up in her window box, the crocuses blooming in the woods, the mud drying on the plank sidewalk in Harbortown, sending up showers of dust as heavy boots come down. She goes to work, leaves the store, collects the girl, comes home, makes dinner. She hears Valter has a new woman in Harbortown, which doesn't surprise—or even particularly interest—her.

Occasionally her husband comes to her door and knocks his familiar knock: two soft and one loud.

Sometimes she lets him come in and take her upstairs. Valter has a violent temper and it wouldn't be good for things to get any worse than they are now. But it isn't just to keep the peace that she lets Valter have his way with her. She isn't strong enough to say no every time. If the other man would claim her—really claim her—perhaps she could. But he doesn't. He stays in his shed in the woods, working on the sea monster growing up from the dirt floor.

The package from the Mainland, addressed to her at the general store in a blue clerical hand, sits on the table he left her. The girl asks what is in the package, hoping it's for her, a birthday present, even though her birthday isn't until October. The woman doesn't answer. The days are warmer, and they don't race toward sunset; they dawdle. Spring has come forward and possessed Small Island. Now in its turn it is beginning to give way to a new invader: summer. The maple leaves in the grove above his shed will be large and green. She knows that the thing she has ordered for him, all the way from the Mainland, must be delivered.

In the woods, he works into the night, leaving the door open and letting smoke from his cigarette drift out. Almost every day the boat teaches him something new, and he pauses to think: *I didn't know that.* This doesn't happen when he builds houses or does carpentry jobs. When he's doing those things, he knows exactly what will happen, even before the job starts. Not with this.

He has wrapped cedar planking around the oak ribs. The hull is now formed all the way to the gunwales, and he has begun putting in decking made of seasoned maple from trees nearby. The centerboard well has risen from the keel. The place where the mast will be stepped is visible. Less and less imagination is needed to see what this boat will be when it is finished: a classic Small Island double-ender, gaff-rigged, the mast stepped well forward. Made for fishing and transport. Sturdy, and capable of surviving the storms off Small Island. He stands in the doorway of his shed, smoking and waiting for the boat to show him what to do next.

He flicks his cigarette through the doorway into the dark, orange sparks pinwheeling as they fall. He follows the pinwheel out into the darkness, crushes the end of the cigarette under his boot, buttons his jacket and sets off for his mother's house. As he walks, he begins to envision how he will get the boat down the bluff and into the water. He will make a set of rollers, made of pine logs stripped of their bark. He will tie the boat to trees at each stage to prevent it from overpowering him and shooting down the slope. As he lets the boat slide down the bluff, he'll take each roller out from under the stern and move it to the bow. Done alone, it will be a long, hard piece of work.

The door of his mother's house hangs open. Around the house is the smell of wet earth. He walks up the path to the front door and climbs three wooden steps.

Inside, a kerosene lamp hangs from a beam. His mother sits in a circle of yellow light under the lamp, round embroidery frame in one hand, needle in the other. The smell of whiskey greets him like an old friend. She looks up, her face and nose broad, gray hair pulled back. Her round metal spectacles are tilted on her nose; one of the earpieces is missing. In spite of the fact that he hasn't been here for more than a year, she doesn't look surprised to see him. On the floor, outside the circle of yellow light, he can make out flat empty bottles lying on their sides.

"You're still sewing."

"*Of course I'm still sewing.* How do you think I live? You think I get money from your father? Or from you?"

She lists to her left, spits and pushes the needle into the fabric. Holding the hoop carefully in her right hand, she reaches down with her left, brings a bottle up into the light and takes a pull without offering a drink to her son. He has been staying away from alcohol while he builds his boat, and it's hard for him to smell it without wanting some. He isn't usually a man who can have one drink and easily stop. If he takes one, he's likely to be drunk for weeks, never finishing his boat and missing the summer winds favorable for Big Island.

"Where is he?"

"Who?" She sets the bottle down in the same place on the floor so she can reach it without looking, pulls the needle out and resumes her work.

"You know who I mean."

"Where do you think? *Up to Gallagher's Point with his whore.*" She spits again on the same spot. The needle, poised above the embroidery, dives down and in. For all the anger, her hands are sure.

He stands foolish and awkward, feeling shamed by her brutal lack of interest in him. Her face is fleshy, cracked and reddened. After all that has happened, after every blow she has delivered, psychic or physical, he needs her love exactly as he did when he was a boy. When his brother died, he wanted to save her. He knew he could never take his brother's place, but he thought he could save her from darkness and drink. He couldn't. When he reached out to hold and comfort her, she pushed him away, more roughly each time. His boat will make her see him differently. He is sure that in her eyes he will never be as good as his brother, but perhaps he can be better than his father—better than he feels at this moment, shamed in yellow light. His mother works methodically, her jaw clenching and unclenching as the needle passes through and out of cream-colored fabric.

"Why don't you ever talk about how he died?"

"*Who?*" She looks up, her face flushing a deeper red. His guts turn to water, and he wants to run, but he makes himself hold his ground.

"My brother." His breath is tight. He can't believe his audacity in mentioning his brother. He is sure she will explode. But she doesn't. Her tone is low and even. It feels worse than an explosion, if that is possible.

"You know what happened. Everyone on this nasty spittle of an island knows it. You can hear them whispering in the dark."

"I want to hear it from you."

For a moment, she just looks at him, then says, in a deep, raspy voice: "Your father killed him. *You know that.*"

"I don't know it. You never talk about it. All I know is what people say."

Her face darkens until the red seems black. "There's no mystery. *Your father took him into the sea and drowned him.* He knew how much I loved that boy. He did it because he hates me. And because he's a weakling." She leans over for her bottle, brings it up and drinks.

He is getting what he came for, and that is important. But it is harder to bear than if she had exploded and beaten him.

She looks straight ahead, away from him, in her own thoughts. "*He was the one,*" she says quietly, as if to herself. "He was so beautiful. What a man he would have been. He could have been anything he wanted. He could have left this spitfleck of an island and gone anywhere. Big Island. The Mainland. Europe, even. He could have been anything. Not like his father—that half-man. Or the other one—another weakling. Crying and wanting what I don't have."

Tears run down her face. She wipes her nose on her sleeve, takes another pull on the bottle. As she swallows, she looks up at him as if she is surprised to see someone standing in her house. He knows that when he leaves this house, he will want a drink—badly.

"I'm leaving."

"You left before."

"I'm leaving Small Island."

"And how would the likes of you leave Small Island? You have money for passage on the steamer? *I doubt it.*" She spits.

"I'm building a boat."

"A boat? How do you know how to build one? On this island, only the boatbuilder families do that."

"I know."

"When are you doing this?"

"Soon."

She looks at him long and hard, sets the bottle down and gets up, leaving her embroidery on the chair. The floorboards creak under her bare feet, which look as large and tough as tree roots. She leans over, opens the top drawer of her sideboard and takes something out. She closes the drawer, turns and comes toward him holding what she removed from the drawer. When she is close to him, her head is level with his shoulder. He wants to touch her, but he's sure that if he does, she will slap his hand away.

She takes his hand, lifts it up and puts something made of linen into it. "Take this. It's all I have. *Now leave me.*"

He turns and walks down the wooden steps, leaving the door open. The boards are loose. He should come back and fix them. He doesn't want her to fall. His boots find their way along the path, which is invisible in the dark. The grass catches at his feet and tries to trip him, but he pushes through into the woods. When he gets home, he falls to the floor next to his boat and sleeps.

He wakes up in his clothes, cold and sore. It comes back to him slowly: going to his mother's house, her not seeming to know he was there some of the time, telling her about the boat, being given the handkerchief. He rolls out from under the hull, stands up, goes to the pitcher in the corner, drinks some of the water and pours the rest over his head. Takes off his corduroy jacket, hangs it on a peg near the door. Reaches into the jacket pocket and pulls out the handkerchief. It's creamy yellow-white linen, decorated with his mother's needlework in green. He would know her work anywhere.

The embroidery shows the harbor of Small Island. On the bluffs above are a few tiny houses; below is the curving shoreline. In the foreground are three harbor seals, their heads sleek and pointed, nosing above the surface. One is nearby, on the right, the other two farther away, toward the land, facing each other. He folds the handkerchief carefully and replaces it in his jacket pocket. No matter how far from Small Island he goes, he must never lose the thing his mother has given him.

He turns to look at his work. The boat is almost finished. He has filled in maple decking between the gunwales and completed the centerboard well. In the town, he has purchased the few pieces of hardware he needs, avoiding the woman while he was there.

Now that the boat is almost done, he can indulge himself. He goes outside and sits, smoking and thinking, enjoying the warmth. Sitting with his back against the shed, he sees her come up the path carrying a parcel. She stops in front of him, the toes of her boots almost touching his.

She sits down beside him without saying anything. The silence excites him. He feels the excitement rising in his chest, arms, legs. He waits until his cigarette burns to a glowing nub, then crushes it into the earth. He takes hold of her, rough and tender at the same time, feeling the thing that always joins them, regardless of how long it has been.

He gets up, leans over, puts one arm around her back, the other under her legs. He lifts and carries her into the shed, then lays her down in the shadow of the boat. He pulls at her clothes, then at his, and enters her, quick and sharp. Her legs are raised, his overalls falling around him, his buttocks white in the darkness of the shed. She feels herself flow around and into him. As always, she loses her sense of where she is.

When he is done, the first thing she's aware of is the coolness of the air on her body. She straightens her clothing, gets up, brushes herself off and walks out the door. He watches her without moving from the floor.

The package is where she left it. She picks it up, brushes off a few pine needles and some crumbs of dirt. She goes back into the shed, holding the parcel out, her hands trembling. He stands and gets a folding knife, cuts the twine, which falls twirling to the dirt. He slices the paper, removes it and sees a light blue box with dark blue lettering raised from its surface. The name of the famous maker of nautical equipment means nothing to him.

He squats next to her on the dirt floor. What's inside the box is heavy, wrapped in tissue paper. He unwraps the tissue and lets it fall. What's left is a marine compass, designed for big ships but scaled down to the proportions of a small boat. It has a solidity and precision beyond anything he is familiar with. The black dial is lettered in red and gold. The needle moves slightly, as if eager to show him his course away from Small Island. He knows this compass must have cost every one of the bills he left her with the table—and perhaps more. He sets the compass back in the box, puts the box on the dirt floor and lies down, curling into her.

Two weeks later he and his boat are on the rocky beach below the town. Everything he needs is in the hull, packed in nets fastened under the deck. He's rigged a canvas cover over part of the cockpit to keep the spray out. The steamer makes the trip in two days. He might need four or five, depending on the wind.

One of the last things he did was to sew himself a sealskin bag with two straps to go around his shoulders.

In the bag he put the handkerchief from his mother, along with what is left of the money he earned from carpentry jobs. The bag is strapped to his chest under his clothes; the compass is mounted on the foredeck just behind the mast. He'll have to leave the tiller and step forward to read it, but when the wind is fair, the boat should sail itself.

Before leaving, he swept the shed, leaving the door open for the next man who wants to use it. He took the important tools with him, in case he needs to find work on Big Island. Any honest man of Small Island is welcome to the rest.

His final job was to step the mast, which he did when he got his boat down the steep slope to the beach. Now he pushes the boat out into the water, leaving the stern on a rock. He waits a moment, going over a few last things. Then he takes off his boots, ties them together and throws them into the cockpit. They land, one on each side of the centerboard well, dangling from their laces.

He steps into the water in his bare feet and frees the stern from its rock. The boat floats in the green water, waiting. He steps in, feels the boat take his weight and settle. He sits on the stern thwart, lifts the rudder and sets it in place on its two brass pins. He raises the gaff-rigged sail he sewed in his shed from heavy canvas. The breeze picks up—a summer breeze, no more than a puff, but enough to move his boat. He trims his sail, and the boat springs forward, leaving a hissing wake. He reaches forward and slides the centerboard down. When the centerboard is up, the boat will draw only a few inches. A little water comes through the seams onto his feet. This doesn't matter. As he sails, the hull will swell, seal itself and become watertight. Sitting on the thwart, he holds himself still, looking straight ahead, not turning around to see Small Island shrink out of sight behind him.

CHAPTER 5

When the boatmaker reaches Big Island, it is hot and dusty: high summer. The boat sailed beautifully for four days and three nights, letting him know he had done the right thing in building it and sailing out onto the open sea. He steered by the sun and the compass the woman ordered all the way from the Mainland, his wake bubbling behind him. The summer winds were fair and steady, and he ran downwind almost from the moment he put his boat in the water. It took a few minutes to work out of the wind shadow of Small Island and catch the prevailing winds. From there it was like sailing in a dream.

The best times were at night. The moon gained fullness on his journey until it lay whole and round on the water, his boat gliding over the wide white disk. The sea was calm, a big lake, the waves little more than ripples as he ran downwind, the gaff-rigged sail far out over the gunwale, held by a pole he had cut and stowed before setting out.

On the water, he wasn't hungry. He ate a little of the pemmican he had brought, along with water from a stone jug. When he needed to, he relieved himself over the side, feeling that the ocean belonged to him and his boat, a Small Island double-ender made from nothing but the tools at hand and an understanding of how wood fits with wood.

After leaving his mother's house, he kept himself from drinking. And knowing himself, he didn't bring anything other than water to drink while he was at sea. But when he was on the water he didn't even think about drinking. While he was working on the boat, the work kept his mind off alcohol. He thought perhaps on the water, work on the boat done, he would want it again. But he didn't. The moon on the green water was enough: full and still, the bright field undulating as the keel of his boat cut through it and left the waves, their crests painted with moonlight, behind.

He finds a pier and ties up without asking for per-mission. There doesn't seem to be anyone around to ask. Farther down the bay big ocean-going ships, sailing and steam, are tied up at long piers. Among them he can see the steamer that goes to Small Island once a week. He knows he could walk down there now and board the steamer. When he woke from the dream of the blue wolf, all he knew was that he would build a boat and sail to Big Island. Now he's done that—a remarkable thing for any Small Island man, especially one who is not of the boatbuilder clan. Perhaps what he's done is enough. He has enough money for passage back to Small Island. He could walk down the bay, buy a ticket, find the woman a present and go on board, leaving his boat to rot against this pier. He would have done everything he set out to do. And he knows that, even if she was angry with him for leaving, or for trying to give her banknotes to make up for having taken her away from work, she would take him back.

As he ties up his boat, he can see himself returning—and the future they would have after that. They will live together, in her house or a house he builds for them. They will have a child of their own, a brother for the girl. He will drink, but not as much or as often. He will work more regularly. Her love will change him a little. Occasionally, when he's drunk, he will hit her—but not as hard as Valter does. She will be happy he belongs to her. She will love the new child as much as she loves the girl. Sometimes in the winter, when everything is frozen and the four of them are sitting around the fire in their little house, she will laugh and tell the story of how her man had the crazy idea of building a boat. And not only had the idea, but did it, sailing all the way to Big Island and coming back on the steamer like a rich man. She will laugh and the children will take their cue from her and laugh also, tentatively at first, then harder, the girl almost grown, the boy sitting on her lap, firelight on their faces in the winter night.

He climbs up onto the pier, looks up and sees stairs—wood below, stone above—climbing the bluff. Three boys are playing at the foot of the pier near the pilings, which are rough with mussels, limpets, seaweed. The boys are brown and nearly naked, throwing stones at crabs that scurry out of sight behind the pilings or race into the water. They look to be seven or eight. On Small Island no boy of eight would be playing this way. He would be working alongside his father, on land or sea. He would not be working only if his father was too drunk to work, or in the still of winter when everyone is inside and people live on what they have put by before everything froze. In any case, on Small Island there are no piers to play under, and no sandy beaches. The shoreline is rocky all the way to the water's edge.

The boatmaker passes the boys and climbs the steps. Once he's over the top of the bluff, the sea disappears and he's in the middle of a dusty road. It's bigger than any road on Small Island, even though it is far from town and must be a small road for this place. The dust is deep and soft. He walks through it, following the road as it leads inland, joining and leaving other roads just as soft and sunbleached.

He walks slowly, finding his land legs. It reminds him of being drunk. As he walks what he thinks is a straight line, the island sways to the left, then to the right, then back to center. He hasn't had anything on his feet since he pushed off from Small Island, and his boots feel unfamiliar, heavy and confining. In this awkward fashion he walks away from Small Island and everything he knows.

In the noon heat the road is mostly empty. Occasionally he passes a man or two, dusty as the road, wearing wide-brimmed hats, wide pants and loose-fitting shirts. The boatmaker has never seen such clothes and doesn't know how to place their wearers. Are they rich? Poor? In between? Some of them are carrying tools—adzes, scythes or buckets; they must be workingmen.

The men he passes seem friendly enough, but they look at the boatmaker sideways as he moves by. His corduroy jacket is over his arm, the sealskin bag strapped to his chest under his clothes. He begins to feel he's worn his clothes too long without washing them, a feeling he never had on the water and rarely on Small Island. The spinning feeling slows and finally stops. As he walks inland, the trees thicken. His shadow peeps out from under his boots as if it is afraid of Big Island.

The road widens, the trees open and the boatmaker sees a big old building that has been patched and added onto many times. It is framed by a grove of tall oaks. Hanging from the peak of the roof is a sign with faded cream letters on a purple background. The sign, which reads *Mandrake Inn*, hangs motionless in the heat. Underneath the name a mandrake root is painted in the same faded cream color. The big oaks, their leaves dusty and still, shade the building even in the middle of the day. In their shadow, the roof shingles look purple.

In front of the inn on a little patch of dying grass is an unfinished pine table. At the table a woman sits smoking a cigarette, the smoke drifting up over her head. The smoke is almost invisible in the summer heat. In front of her is a glass filled with a clear brown liquid the boatmaker knows well. Her head is bare, her hair a dark-blond mane shot with lighter strands. A clip at the back of her head is attempting to hold her hair back—and half succeeding. She is wearing a dress of dark red, the bodice tightly fitted. The opening of the bodice is cut square and her breasts fill it as if they were in a picture frame. The boatmaker has no idea what to make of this scene. No woman on Small Island has ever sat exposed this way in public.

As the boatmaker comes down the dusty road toward her, the woman of the town looks without expression at what the sea has thrown up on Big Island. He is mute as a stone. The woman at the pine table seems elegant beyond imagining—and available in a disturbing way. He walks up and takes a seat on the bench across the table from her, one seat down so that he is not facing her directly.

Sitting this way, it is hard for the boatmaker to know what to look at: her breasts, framed in the square open-ing, or the drink in front of her. He resolves his dilemma by not looking at either the woman or the drink, which she now lifts to her mouth, showing sharp white teeth. She pauses before drinking, her lips the same red as her dress, her tongue clearly visible, before letting the liquid slide in. The boatmaker sits stiffly, strangled by thirst. He feels that if he doesn't get a drink and then another imme-diately after, his body will turn itself inside out. But he has no idea how things happen on Big Island. They sit there in silence. She is coolly appraising; he is trying not to look.

Behind the woman of the town, the open door of the Mandrake is a rectangle, cool and dark. The boatmaker stares into it as if he could make someone appear with a drink by willing them to.

The woman of the town exhales smoke and fingers a box of matches. On the box a pink swan swims serenely in profile on a green diamond, which floats in turn on a yellow rectangle. She holds the box so the swan faces the boatmaker, then spins it in her fingers, hiding the swan, her face giving no sign she is doing anything at all.

A man emerges from the doorway holding a round tray with a drink. He is wearing a nightshirt, not very clean, that reaches below his knees. He sets the drink in front of the woman of the town and blinks, examining the boatmaker as if he is surprised to see a customer.

"You too?" he says, letting the tray fall to his side, where it makes a wet spot on the nightshirt. The boatmaker nods.

The man retreats into the door of the inn. A little while later he comes back with another drink. He sets the drink in front of the boatmaker and then stands motionless, waiting.

The boatmaker looks at him, not immediately understanding. On Small Island, there is no need to pay for anything when it arrives. Everything that is delivered has its place in a specific account. These running accounts stretch back over generations, connecting everyone on the island, laid over ties of blood, marriage, death and history. Occasionally someone will come into money through gambling or an inheritance and make a debt smaller. It is not considered right to eliminate the debt altogether: that would break a bond.

Understanding that on Big Island things are done differently, the boatmaker rises and goes around the corner of the inn, watched closely by two pairs of eyes. Out of sight, he reaches under his shirt into the sealskin bag and pulls a bill out by touch. He brings it back, sits down and puts the banknote on the table. It is pale blue, enough for many drinks, even if two people are drinking.

The woman of the town sits watching, spinning her matchbox round and round. She looks up at the innkeeper, nods with her eyes. The innkeeper picks up the blue banknote, leaves the drink and vanishes into the inn.

The woman takes in the strange little man's discomfort, her eyes alive, her mouth a red smile on the glass. She lowers her glass, puts a forefinger into it, stirs the liquid slowly. Its motion amuses her. She decides that on her husband's next trip she will have him bring her a glass of water cooled by some ice from the precious store in the cellar.

"You're not from around here," she says, crushing the red end of her cigarette out in a saucer while thinking about the next one.

The boatmaker can't say anything. The noon heat, the woman of the town, his arrival on Big Island after four days at sea, have rendered him dumb. He dips into the drink, his first in many months, knowing what's coming, feeling the burn in his nose and throat as fumes rise up to his brain. As always, the drink seems to know him by name.

"No."

"And where are you from, my friend of not too many words?"

"Small Island."

"Small Island. Now isn't that *something?*" A smile pulls at the red corners of her mouth. "You don't see many here from Small Island. More from the Mainland. Rich folks from the Mainland think Big Island is a *picturesque* sort of place these days."

The woman of the town has seen men from Small Island before; they haven't impressed her. This silent one seems as though he might be different in some way she hasn't figured out yet. But she will, with a little effort. Men aren't difficult to figure out. There are only two things to keep in mind when you're trying to understand a man. Those two items cover ninety percent of all situations. The other ten percent you figure out as you go along.

This one, she thinks, does look the same as all the others from Small Island, which is a tiny rock at the end of the world, a very shithole. He has the grime, the overalls, the drooping mustache, the long underwear worn even in summer. They must have a depot over there that issues every man a pair of longjohns when he's born. After that, they grow with him, never needing to be washed—until the funeral maybe. He's got a little stash of money on him that he doesn't want anyone to see. Funny the way he went around the corner to get into it.

He doesn't seem too bright, possibly even stupid. But there is something alive about him, like a healthy animal. The image of a seal comes to her mind, its fur smooth, wet and flashing. There aren't many seals left in the waters off Big Island, because their fur is fashionable on the Mainland, and being fashionable is a death sentence. Mysterious how they live down there in the dark and cold. Yet they're like us, breathing air, warm, not like fish, which are cold and alien, barely alive. In spite of her contempt for the boatmaker, at the thought of the seal, the woman of the town feels a motion in her chest.

"You came on the steamer?"

"No."

"So how did you get here? Fishing boat? Whaler? Sealer?" He doesn't look like he would be working on any of those, but there aren't many ways to get from Small Island to Big Island. She has named them all, as quick and efficient as a businessman.

The boatmaker doesn't feel like telling her about building his boat or the nights he spent on the water. Once he starts talking, he might tell her about the woman on Small Island, about being sick, the wheelbarrow, the money he tried to give the woman, the compass she ordered for him. He might not even stop there, going on to babble about his mother, his brother—even the blue wolf. Better to stop before he says anything.

His silence begins to unnerve the woman of the town just a little. Perhaps that is how he is different, she thinks: by being able to remain silent. In her presence, most men start talking right away and then don't stop, boasting about this or that, thinking they can impress her. This one is uncomfortable, she sees, but he can hold his peace. And that bothers her. She has worked so hard to keep the layer of ice around her heart intact. Any feelings she might have had for a man she pushed into the ring of ice and let them freeze solid. Here and there one touched her in a way that might have begun to melt something inside her. When that happened, she pushed him away and froze him right up again. It has always worked. She uses them, pulls the money out of them in a steady stream while she dreams about the capital and the beautiful things they have there.

But it is hard work to keep things frozen inside. She has always known that some man might find a way to begin to melt that ice. And then it could all be over very quickly. This thought often flickers at the edge of her mind. But the grimy silent little man from the shithole at the end of the world won't be the one to do that. There's not a chance of it, regardless of his unnerving silence. It won't even be much of a challenge.

The innkeeper comes out of the inn. The boatmaker orders two drinks for himself and one for her. While the man in the nightshirt goes to fill the order, the boatmaker slides one seat down until he's directly across from the woman in the dark red dress with the square-cut neckline and the mesmerizing cleft between the two roundnesses.

He reaches into her bag without asking and takes out two cigarettes. Removes the matchbox from her hands, puts both cigarettes in his mouth and lights them, holds one out to her. She is not sure she wants to accept anything from this man. While her mind debates, her hand reaches out, apparently of its own accord, takes the cigarette and brings it to her mouth. She begins to smoke in rhythm with him, taking the smoke in and letting it go when he does.

The innkeeper returns and sets the drinks down: two on his side, one on hers. The blue banknote has plenty of room for these drinks and many more, stored invisibly in the long face of the king, his royal eyes sad and knowing behind his glittering lenses in their oval frames.

CHAPTER 6

The first thing he notices in her room under the eaves are two dresses hanging in an open cupboard, both identical to the one she is wearing. They have the same fitted bodice, square opening and three-quarter-length sleeves, all made of the dark red silk that makes her hair and skin seem tawny. He wants to ask her why she has three of these and why they are the only dresses in her tiny room. But he doesn't ask. These are the mysteries of the woman of the town. And yet if he doesn't speak, he is no longer frozen in her presence. He holds her down and takes her like an animal.

The boatmaker stays in her room for three days with the curtain drawn over the window. From time to time the innkeeper comes up the stairs with a new bottle. They have moved from glasses and ice to a place where glasses are unnecessary. Neither of them feels at home, yet neither has any doubt that they belong in this room together. They drink from the bottle, fire flaring between them, burning their bodies with the sting of a jellyfish and sealing them in one continuous spasm. Occasionally they ask the innkeeper to bring them a little food.

After a while he moves on from paying with one bill at a time to turning his money over in clumps. When he left Small Island, the money he had seemed to him like a lot. He had worked many jobs to earn it, not drinking and saving. It wasn't the most money he had ever had. And he knew that even on Small Island there are people to whom his cache would have seemed a small thing. Valter, for instance. Or the doctor, who has been stuffing the bills his patients give him under his mattress for so many years he has trouble getting into bed. Or so the people of Small Island like to say. To the boatmaker it seemed like a lot. Now it's going fast, like the ice in spring around Small Island, melting first slowly, then fast. One day it's gone, and the sea opens.

Up in her room he is sometimes her child, other times her father. Sometimes both of them are animals howling in red heat. Regardless of the madness in the little room, the innkeeper always seems to appear with a new bottle at the right moment. The boatmaker slowly understands that the two of them are working together, the woman of the town and the innkeeper. But his understanding remains distant, and the knowledge unimportant. All that matters is what's happening in this room with its narrow bed and the desk built into the wall under the window.

Sometimes he is rough with her. The boatmaker hasn't been with many women, and he has never been rough with any them. The woman of Small Island didn't arouse this feeling in him, which holds desire and anger, affection and loathing, mixed until they are inseparable. Sometimes he wanted the woman on Small Island more, sometimes he wanted her less, but he never wanted to hurt her. This one, he wants to hurt. He wants to break into her, tear her into pieces. Then suddenly he feels tender. The two feelings seem to intensify each other—the desire to hurt and the tenderness. They are poles; an electrical force runs between them as he raises himself above her. His body fills and empties. She is willing to be whatever he wants. It makes him feel powerful, a feeling he is not used to having in the presence of another person. Usually the boatmaker feels his power only when he is alone.

But if she will be whatever he wants, she remains just out of reach, and she wants to keep it that way. She is frightened. She can feel something inside beginning to give way. The winter ice is beginning to chip, break up. When she feels it, she tells herself: *Be hard. Be as hard as you can. Don't let that start. Do whatever it takes to make him pay. That's the only thing you need to think about: making him pay.* She aims to keep the stream of the boatmaker's banknotes—yellow, blue and buff—flowing to the cashbox in the office under the stairs where the innkeeper sleeps. She will drain his cache and throw him into the road, like a rag she has used to wipe herself with.

That is what she tells herself. But inside where there are no words, she feels things warming, melting. It enrages her. And so she prods him, does things she knows will make him angry. She wants him to be a beast, to be crude, to hurt her, rip her so that she can despise him. More than anything, she wants the confidence she felt when she first saw the boatmaker walk up the road to the inn looking grimy, confused and out of place. But in the red heat of her room, among the crumpled sheets and the sweat, her confidence is harder and harder to find. And so she puts every ounce of her will into draining his cache.

Days later—he's not sure how many—the boatmaker finds himself at a wooden table sitting across from a large man wearing a broad-brimmed black hat, black coat and trousers stretched tight across his flesh. His face is ruddy and yellowish, the glow of a man who has fed well, drunk well, smoked well. His black clothing is summer weight, elegant despite his bulk. His thick graying sideburns drop down his cheeks and rise to meet on his upper lip. He waits, fingers knitted on his black vest, in no hurry, as he watches the boatmaker try to drink coffee from a white mug.

They are sitting in a large room with two lines of tables, their surfaces darkened by years of spilled food and drink. The sides of the room are open above waist level; awnings outside offer shade. The smell of the sea fills the room.

The boatmaker looks at the light from overhead reflected on the surface of his coffee. It reminds him of the moon on the nights he sailed. He wants to pick up the coffee and drink, but he knows that when he does, his hands, which he is holding together under the table, will shake like an otter's tail. He curls over his stomach, waiting for the spinning to stop and the burning to subside.

"Sick, eh?" asks the man in the black coat, sipping his coffee: a normal, healthy man after a hearty breakfast. The idea of food makes the boatmaker wish to die. Like a thoughtful walrus, the large man whistles breath through large teeth to cool his coffee. "We've all been there. Though perhaps not so far in as you." He appraises the man across the table while he lets the coffee run down his walrus gullet.

The boatmaker knows he can't lift the mug with one hand, but he wants coffee so much he doesn't care. He reaches one hand toward the handle, the other steadying his arm. He begins to raise the cup, all his vital force concentrated on not spilling. The mug shakes and some of the hot liquid dribbles onto the stained table anyway. But he manages to get the mug to his mouth and slurp a little.

More coffee spills as he uses both hands to set the cup down. He feels he's going to be sick, but he fights that. He may tremble like a maple leaf, he may have to reach for his coffee with both hands, but he will never allow himself to be sick in front of this fat man who looks like a bull walrus sunning itself on a flat rock.

"We've all been there. And it's not a problem. But the thing is, *we can't have fighting on Big Island*. The drinking, what you do up to the Mandrake with Elise and Enrik—that's your business. No one cares about that."

"Enrik?"

"The innkeeper. Her husband. Don't tell me you don't see him up there, scurrying around in his nightshirt. Elise and Enrik seem to go their separate ways. But somehow it turns out they're always together—and more than it would appear." The walrus whistles through his teeth onto his steaming coffee.

The boatmaker wants to throw up whatever is in him, which can't be much. But it's not what the walrus is telling him that is making him sick. So they are married and working together. It doesn't matter. Not at all. The boat-maker felt what he felt. She felt it too. He knows that. He reaches with both hands for his mug and manages to get it to his mouth without spilling more than a little pool.

"We don't care about that. Elise is Elise. She does what she does. Or perhaps I should say: She is what she is." He sets his coffee down, gives a fat walrus smile, show-ing tusks. "That's as may be. No one's going to change that. But the thing we don't take to on Big Island is *fighting*."

The boatmaker's face hurts. A purple moon circles one eye, and there is a scythe of dried blood on his cheek. His body is sore, as if he'd been punched and kicked when he was down. What he doesn't want to admit, even to himself, is that he doesn't remember much of how he got the marks. The last thing he remembers is being in her room at the Mandrake, thinking his money would soon be gone.

That is all his memory holds before he woke up in a big room above the one where they are sitting: a bare open space with iron-framed beds extending from the walls. On most of the beds, the mattresses were rolled up on metal springs. One or two had the mattresses down flat, their sheets crumpled. When he woke, there was no one else in the room. At first, he thought he was still on Small Island, dreaming. Then he knew he was awake.

Slowly the story came back, up to the moment when he knew he had to leave the Mandrake. After that: nothing.

A woman with an apron around her middle approaches their table, supporting the bottom of a coffee pot with a dish towel. "I'll have some more, thanks. I think our friend still has most of his," the walrus says. The woman pours coffee into his mug, looks at the boatmaker, turns and walks away.

The few others who were sitting at the tables when the two of them sat down have left. They are alone in the big room open on one side to the bluff and the harbor below, its blue surface etched by the long commercial piers.

The boatmaker lifts the white mug and manages to get some coffee down without spilling. The feeling of being sick is subsiding. He knows that soon he will need to find an outhouse and sit for a long time while everything leaves his body. He sets the mug down with only a slight tremor.

"As I was saying, the one thing we can't have on Big Island is fighting. And you seem to find a lot of that. Or it finds you. Maybe you should think about leaving and going back to where you're from—to your people."

His people, the boatmaker thinks. Who are they? His mother, with her drunken breath and beautiful needlework? His father, in the shack on Gallagher's Point? His brother, under the rectangle of dark turf? The boatmaker doesn't know who his people are—or if he has any people at all.

He also doesn't understand what the walrus is upset about. On Small Island fighting is just fighting. From time to time, every man on Small Island, even Valter and the doctor, gets drunk and gets in a fight or two. It's nothing special, and no one tells you to leave the island—or mentions any punishment whatsoever. Unless you've killed someone.

"I'm not going back," he says. The two men regard each other, one round and flushed, the other drawn, a sickle of dried blood on his cheek. They lift their mugs. The boatmaker can now pick his up with one hand and convey it to his mouth almost like a normal person.

"That may be," says the walrus. "I'm not going to lock you up—yet. But I'm warning you: Big Island is a civilized place. We don't tolerate people behaving like animals here."

The boatmaker looks in his mug. At the bottom he can barely see the moon on the sea. He picks it up and drains it, pushes himself off the wooden bench and stands. He is not steady on his feet, but he manages to turn and walk away, placing his boots with care. There is no doubt in his mind about where he is going after he stops at the outhouse and sits a good long while.

The woman of the town is where she was when he first saw her. Her drink, translucent and brown, sits in front of her. The smoke from her cigarette is almost invisible. He wonders which of the three dresses she's wearing. The one she took off the night they went upstairs? Likely not. That one will need mending.

Through the open door, his carpenter's eyes can make out the stairs in the hall. They were cut from the edge of a walnut tree and were never perfectly square. Their edges ripple and curve, scalloped, no two alike. With time and wear, the grain is showing. The Mandrake is older than almost any building on Small Island.

"You're back," she says, smoke streaming from her nostrils. He stands, sweating a cold sweat in spite of the heat. He's thirsty but everything in him turns away from water and alcohol. He stands with his boots planted as if he were a tree that had sprouted in the road outside the Mandrake and grown there for centuries.

"*You're back, I said.*" She speaks loudly, as if to a half-wit.

"Yes."

"Is that all you have to say?"

"I came back."

"I can see that for myself." She takes whiskey and cigarette, sips and smokes to conceal her smile.

"*I want to be with you.*" He feels as if the words are ripped from him the way seed was ripped from him again and again in the little room up the stairs. It went on that

way until each act was done in a realm far beyond pleasure
or pain.

"I hear you met Stig," she says calmly, giving no sign
she has heard what he said.

"Stig?"

"The Warden."

"The Warden?"

She inhales smoke and drink, looks him up and
down with contempt. The innkeeper emerges from the
doorway in his nightshirt, carrying a tumbler of whiskey.
He sets it down in front of his wife, takes the empty and
goes away, paying no attention to the boatmaker standing
in the road.

The boatmaker notices how the clip holds her hair,
which is the color of the drink in her glass. The hair is
too thick to be caught completely. Strands push their way
out and fall over her ears. From time to time she notices
one and pushes it back, where it stays a moment before
escaping again.

"I came back to be with you."

She sips, appraising the boatmaker's unshaven cheeks,
the purple around his eye, the dried blood on his cheek.
She wants to feel nothing but contempt. But his condi-
tion and directness begin to soften her. She thought she
had driven him away for good when his money ran out.

But now he is back, standing there bloodied, without pretense. There are no men like this on Big Island. Even the dumbest are smoother than this, better at presenting the face they think she wants to see. This man, who apparently lacks the shrewdness to put on any face at all, is beginning to melt the ice around her heart.

"The Warden takes care of things. Like a sheriff. Or a parson." She waves her cigarette. She isn't slurring, but her gestures are bigger than usual. He knows that she never seems drunk, even when she's been drinking for days.

The need to hold her, pull her to him, is overwhelming. He feels like a man trapped in a burning house, walls and ceiling flaming down and every door and window blocked.

"Did you hear what I said?"

"A sheriff. Or a parson."

"Yes, he's the Warden—of this end of the island. There's another on the other end. Stig may seem like a fool, but believe me, he's not. And he's not keen on having you around. I hear there was a lot of fighting. That wasn't smart. Doesn't do *me* a lot of good, now does it? Stig seems to think you should be on your way back to Small Island."

"No."

"Stig can be persuasive. And not just with words. He can have you locked up. There are worse things than the Hostel."

"The Hostel?"

"The place where you slept last night. And the night before." She snorts to show that he is as low as the dust on her many-buttoned shoes.

The boatmaker feels electricity flow through him, completing the circuit between the desire to protect her and keep her from harm and the need to choke her until her face turns blue, slap her until there's blood at the corner of her mouth. He stands stock-still, clenching and unclenching his fists.

The woman of the town sees his reaction and is pleased. If she is hard enough, this will turn out fine. She must simply ignore the warming she feels around her heart.

"Stig doesn't take kindly to residents of Big Island being beaten bloody. It seems you did that to several of our citizens before you were subdued. Of course, you look a little the worse for wear yourself. But Stig isn't concerned about that. It's *outside his jurisdiction,*" she says, drawling the fancy words as she exhales rivers of gray-brown smoke. She sees his face redden under the brown that comes from sailing on open water.

"*I came back to be with you,*" he says again with as much emphasis as he can manage. On Small Island, when a woman has been with a man, it usually means she wants him to build her a house. Sometimes she wants to get married, though not always. He knows this woman is married. The woman of Small Island was married, too, and it didn't matter. He's pushed that knowledge aside and returned to claim her, to find out whether she wants him to build her a house.

He is deadly serious; she can feel that. *Don't soften*, she tells herself. One more hard blow should finish him.

"Do you have any more money?" She looks at him from under her thick unplucked eyebrows.

"Money? It's money you want?"

"Is that a surprise?" When he says nothing, she adds: "Well, do you have any?"

She lifts her glass and lets the warming, cooling whiskey run into her. She knows she's done it. The silent little man is crushed. She begins to enjoy herself the way she usually does when she's with a man. This one gave her a scare, but in the end he was no different from the rest—just less talkative.

The boatmaker knows how much he has left from their nights together: almost nothing. When he was in her room, it didn't feel as if he was paying for anything. He just let go and his money flowed out of him in a trickle, a stream and then a mighty river. Now the flood is spent. He turns away and heads toward the harbor, back the way he came when he landed and climbed the stairs, first wood and then stone.

The woman of the town watches him walk away. The bald spot on the back of his head is round, the hair around it thick and brown. Monks have their hair cut that way. There is a word for it, but she can't remember it. They would know on the Mainland. Everything is different there. She remembers, as she often does, the beautiful restaurant she saw on her single visit to the capital. It was so elegant: the champagne flutes reflecting candlelight, the waiters buttoned into their starched shirtfronts, music pouring out over the snow-covered sidewalk. That is where I belong, the woman of the town thinks. Among violins, beautiful dresses, refined manners, heavy silver and leaded crystal. I will find my way there in the end. No clod of earth from Small Island will hold me back. He is gone—and good riddance. If he has the nerve to return after the way I have just humiliated him, I will handle him with ease. She lights a cigarette with a match taken from the box with the pink swan floating on the green diamond and inhales, feeling powerful and well protected.

CHAPTER 7

The boatmaker retraces the route he took to the Mandrake. On the crest of the bluff above the stone staircase he pauses, looking out over the sea, broad and green in the heat. He is in no hurry. No one is expecting him. On Small Island there are times when no one knows exactly where you are. But they know you are on the island or on the water nearby. Now he is in a place where no one knows him or his family, where no one will know if he walks out into the bay. He could find some heavy stones, put them in his pockets and keep walking, far enough so that the water comes up over his head. After a time the woman of Small Island would realize something had happened. She might think he had simply decided not to return. Or she might decide he had made it to Big Island, stayed there and drunk himself to death.

On this island, he thinks, life is not as it is on Small Island. Things have odd names. The Warden. The Hostel.

And some of those things seem to belong to no one—or to everyone. On Small Island each thing is owned by a particular person. Every house, boat, board, saw, adze, nail, bottle and glass, every table. Things are easily borrowed, often without much need for asking. But each thing belongs to someone. Nothing belongs to everyone. Except the sea.

The boatmaker thinks of the woman of the town, her half-smile as she looked at him standing in the dusty road and asked if he had any money. A tremor runs through his body from top to bottom. It is the rage he felt in her room. But now it is without the tenderness that mixed with it and made it something else. He begins to shake with so much anger he can barely stand. He makes his way slowly and carefully down the stone stairs.

His boat is as he left it, tied fore and aft. The tide is low and the double-ender seems to hang from its bow and stern lines. Two fishing boats, larger than his boat and painted dark blue, are tied farther out along the pier.

He goes down the last wooden steps, crosses the sand and climbs the pier. Two of the boys who were there when he arrived are playing with a crab, standing on either side of the cornered creature with a stick, pushing it back and forth between them. As he crosses the sand, the boys lean together and whisper. He knows he doesn't look right. And not just because of the purple eye and the crescent of blood on his cheek. Behind their hands, the boys are laughing at him in a way they would be afraid to laugh at their fathers, the fishermen whose boats are moored to this pier.

In a few hours the tide will be higher. His boat will come up closer to the pier, and he will be able to step aboard easily. But the prickling sensation of rage under his skin won't allow him to wait.

Holding the stern line, he reaches until he feels the deck with his boots. He drops down, eases himself into the cockpit and releases the stern line. Everything is in place: tiller and rudder under the gunwales, centerboard stowed, sail lashed around the boom. Standing in his boat, he is aware of his body in a simple healthy way for the first time since he started drinking with the woman of the town.

In the bottom of the boat is a little water: an inch or two of brackish green that moves as he steps aboard. Although the boat has been tied to the pier for only a week, it already needs to be bailed out and hauled up onto the beach. Each of its seams needs to be worked over and caulked. He thinks about taking off his jacket and starting to work; it's a calming thought. He squats in the boat, feeling the healthy part of him return. He sees that while he has been on Big Island he has been changing into something else—something that was in him but unknown. The woman of the town did that. At the thought of her, anger surges through him again.

He straightens up, moves toward the bow, the boat sliding under him. The compass is behind the mast, wrapped in canvas held down by a rope. He unties the rope and pulls the canvas off. Under its glass dome, the compass is almost as pristine as the day it was made in a factory on the Mainland, before it was mailed to the woman on Small Island, before his fever, before the dream of the blue wolf—before everything. He has polished it and kept a light film of oil on it. He feels the difference between the woman who gave it to him and the woman of the town; rage goes through him again. He reaches underneath the compass and pulls. Nothing. The compass is bolted with all his craft at the four corners of its base. He pulls again. Nothing moves. Red rage surges through him, blinding him. He pulls one last time. The compass comes up, tearing, splintering and leaving jagged holes in the deck. One of the mounting bolts is bent; the base and glass dome are unharmed.

He sets the compass down, takes off his jacket, reaches into the sealskin bag strapped to his chest. Inside is the handkerchief from his mother with the image of Harbortown and the three seals in green. He wraps the compass in the handkerchief and puts on his jacket.

With the compass cradled in his arms, it's not easy to climb up onto the pier. But he manages and goes along the pier and down to the beach. The boys are gone, leaving behind their prey, a translucent crab stepping into and out of a thin line of foam. The crab moves with a delicate, high-stepping motion, as if it wanted to avoid contact with the water.

At the top of the bluff the boatmaker hesitates. He knows he is going to a place he saw while walking the roads of the island. He doesn't remember exactly where it is, but there's a homing instinct in him, like a salmon's knowledge of the place where it was born. The salmon-instinct takes over, and he sets out on the dusty road to the main harbor and the town on the bluff. He has a feeling that the place he's looking for is on the outskirts of the town.

On Big Island people often stop to say hello to a stranger and offer him a ride to town in a farm wagon. But they don't stop to ask the small man carrying a bundle wrapped in an embroidered handkerchief. In fact, as they pass some people make a mental note to ask the Warden who the stranger is and whether he is dangerous. Paying no attention to their looks, the boatmaker keeps walking until the dusty trees at the side of the road are replaced by buildings, first old one-story houses, then larger houses with stores nestled in between. Ahead is a wider road, the dusty wagons and buggies on it headed for the center of town.

He comes out of his salmon-trance in front of the place he's looking for. He must have passed it while he was deep in drink, at some point after he left the Mandrake and before he woke up at the Hostel.

His destination is a simple storefront with a big window in front that reaches almost to the ground. Behind the window is a space that looks as though it should hold a display of goods. But there's nothing on display—just a field of green, flat across the bottom and covering a wall in back that comes up to the height of the boatmaker's shoulders. On the window three disks are painted in gold, one above and two below. Under the three golden balls is the name *Cohen*.

The boatmaker knows almost nothing about Jews. On Small Island there are no Jews in the flesh. They are present only in the pastor's Good Friday sermons drawn from the Gospel of John. But there have always been whispers on the island about people from certain parts of the Mainland who came and settled, blending in and concealing their origins. Along with everyone else, the boatmaker heard the whispers, but they never concerned him one way or the other. If he knows anything about

Jews it's only because he read about them. Reading is an odd faculty for a house carpenter from Small Island. But his mother always had books in her house: the Bible and a few others, including a picture book with plates showing Vashad surrounded by his cloud of blackbirds.

He pushes the door open and enters a large room with counters on two sides. Behind one counter is an arched opening filled by a beaded curtain. The room is bare, with nothing on the countertops, nothing on the shelves behind.

The boatmaker knows he's in the right place. He feels he should be ashamed to be here, but he isn't. He is focused only on what he came to do—and what will happen afterward. He pulls the door closed behind him, walks to the counter and sets down his compass.

A man comes through the arched opening, pushing aside the beads. He is tall and thin, dressed in black and wearing a skullcap. Light brown curls dangle in front of his ears like corkscrew shavings left behind by a plane. The boatmaker is startled: He has never seen such curls on a man. What surprises him even more is how closely the man resembles the face on the banknotes. The king doesn't have curls dangling in front of his ears, but apart from that the men could be brothers, with their long faces and dark eyes behind oval lenses.

The man in the skullcap moves to the counter, appraising the boatmaker and his shrouded parcel with the eyes of someone who has seen everything that is for sale in the world and knows how to evaluate each item to the penny. He reaches out with long white fingers to remove the handkerchief. The boatmaker's hand shoots out, takes the man's wrist and stops him before he can touch the linen. The shopkeeper pulls his hand back, curling his lips at the unclean touch. The boatmaker unwraps the handkerchief and stows it in his jacket.

"You don't have to do business here," the shopkeeper says. When the boatmaker stares at him without saying anything, he adds: "We don't need your compass."

"I came here to sell it."

The Jew looks at the boatmaker as if he were a wild animal in a zoo: dangerous but safely behind iron bars. He picks up the compass, examines it and sets it down on the counter. He pulls a loupe out of his pocket, pushes his glasses onto his forehead and uses the loupe to peer into the glass dome. His eyes come alive and the look of having seen everything the world offers for sale disappears.

He puts the loupe away, lifts the compass above his head to examine the underside, the hanging bolts. "One of these is bent. Did you rip it off your boat?"

The man pulls his glasses back down onto his long nose. Behind the oval lenses, he looks at the boatmaker as if he can see every drink that has poured into him since he put in at Big Island, every beating he has taken, the talk with the Warden, even the way he had to reach for his mug with both hands.

"This *is* yours, isn't it? It didn't by chance come from someone else's boat? We don't accept stolen goods here. We follow the law to the letter."

The boatmaker says nothing. His mother's handkerchief is a lump inside his jacket. He stares. The man in the skullcap stares back.

"Not talkative, I see. Not from Big Island either. Well, that's as it may be. And this compass may be yours, and it may not. I would guess it is. A Stenysson. Lovely piece of work. A miniature version of the ones they make for the big ships. Don't see many of these hereabouts. Not much call for them."

The shopkeeper goes quiet, calculating what he knows about the compass and the boatmaker, fitting each figure into the right account. Then he names an amount.

The boatmaker says nothing, but his small erect figure gives assent. The shopkeeper turns and pushes through the beaded curtain. The boatmaker flicks at an itch near the crust of blood on his cheek. He doesn't want to scratch it and make blood flow. But he can't help touching his face. Crumbs of dried blood fall to the floor.

The storekeeper comes back and places some bills on the smooth wood of the counter, along with a few coins. The boatmaker picks up the bills without counting them, turns and walks out of the shop, leaving the coins.

The shopkeeper looks at the retreating back, the round bald spot, the worn corduroy jacket. What a savage, he thinks, almost without human language, not so different from an animal, a beast of the field, lowing to its fellows, with no soul and no knowledge of Ha-Shem. Then again, he thinks, I live in a land of savages.

In the mind of the shopkeeper, the people of Big Island are no better and no worse than Gentiles anywhere, among whom the Jews have always been condemned to live. From Abraham in Mesopotamia to Joseph in Egypt, from the destruction of the Second Temple to the harlots of Paris or Berlin. They are all savages. This one is a little stranger than most, that's all. He did have a fine compass, though, a beautiful instrument. Which is odd. Assuming it isn't stolen. If it is stolen, that will be found out soon enough. And the way he wouldn't let me touch the handkerchief, which was embroidered after some strange Gentile fashion. Perhaps the handkerchief is a fetish of some kind, a thing sacred to the savage.

Without thinking, the shopkeeper lifts the strings that extend from under his dark jacket and brushes them to his lips. He picks up the compass and carries it through the curtained archway into the room behind. After sliding a ladder along the cases, he puts the compass on a high shelf, among other valuable items that have parted company with their owners.

As he puts the compass on the shelf, the shopkeeper stops thinking about the boatmaker. Long experience and deep study have taught him not to waste time trying to understand the ways of those who live beyond the Word and apart from Ha-Shem. They may seem close to beasts, like this strange little man with his round bald spot, or dignified and cultured like the men he does business with on the Mainland: experienced and tolerant, some of them as world-weary as Jews themselves. But deep down, he knows that, whether they are wearing overalls smelling of cow dung or bespoke suits scented with expensive cologne, they are nothing but animals: hot breath without mind, unsanctified clay. He comes down the ladder feeling the need to wash his hands, read a midrash and pray to Ha-Shem from the depths of exile.

CHAPTER 8

After pawning his compass, the boatmaker wanders until he finds a place to sleep in the brush by the side of a dusty road. He has enough money to stay anywhere on Big Island, eat wherever they serve food. But he isn't willing to spend any of it on anything but what he pawned the compass for.

He wakes up under the bushes to the sound of wagon wheels. The sun is up and it's hot, hotter than it ever gets on Small Island. He rises, stretches, feels the sealskin bag strapped to his chest, money and handkerchief inside. The purple moon around his eye has faded. The scab on his cheek has shrunk to a scratch.

He undoes his overalls. Yawning and stretching, he lets a hot stream run against the folded bark of a tree and then shakes out the last drops. Even though he's had nothing to eat since the day before, he's not hungry or thirsty. He stretches again and walks out onto the road that leads to the Mandrake.

When the boatmaker reaches the inn, the pine table sitting out in front is empty. He realizes it must be very early. He walks up to the inn and opens the door. Inside it's dark, cool and quiet.

Leaving the front door open, he walks toward the stairs, their scalloped edges showing walnut grain. He goes up slowly, a step at a time, trying to make his feet quiet. But a door under the stairs opens, and the innkeeper comes out of the office where he sleeps in the same nightshirt he wears during the day. The only difference is that at night he adds a nightcap, equally unclean, with a long tail. The innkeeper doesn't care about his appearance. But he does care deeply about the cashbox under his bed. On the floor next to the metal box is a large, well-oiled shotgun. Box and gun are rarely parted.

The innkeeper steps out and comes close enough to the foot of the stairs to recognize the boatmaker in his corduroy jacket and overalls. He goes back into the office, pulls the door closed behind him and touches box and gun with a big toe before climbing back in bed for a few more hours of half-sleep in the endless daylight.

On the top floor there are only a couple of doors and no noise coming from behind any of them. The boatmaker walks up to hers and pulls it open. She's asleep, wearing a cream-colored shift under sheets that look the same as when he left.

He enters and walks across the room to the desk built into the far wall. Like the stairs, the desk is made of walnut. A lot of walnut was used in building the Mandrake, which means it was originally a respectable establishment: a summer hotel with striped awnings, men in linen suits drinking and playing croquet in the garden behind the main building, watched by women under parasols. The boatmaker leans back on the desk, waiting for his presence in the room to penetrate her sleep.

She turns over once or twice, mumbling things he can't catch, then opens her eyes and looks straight at him. At first, she's frightened. There's something strange and different about the boatmaker, the way he's looking at her, his unannounced presence in her room while she slept. Then she relaxes, pleased that her power has brought him back. He must have found money somewhere, she thinks. He wouldn't have the nerve to return without it. Unlike her husband, the woman of the town has little regard for money in itself. But she does like the elegant things it buys. And most of all she enjoys receiving it as a tribute to her power over men. They draw near her offering it, eager to be enslaved. Their submission pleases her. The money itself is nothing.

She reaches back, plumps the pillow, arranges it under her. Locks her fingers behind her head and looks at him as if she had no doubt that when she woke on this day, just past Midsummer's Eve, she would find him in her room, leaning on the edge of her desk.

At the sight of her, luxuriating and complacent, the boatmaker's anger rises up. She is playing with him, he thinks, happy to see her prey. She seems to be licking her lips. He feels the redness swell until it reaches his eyes, and he can barely see. His body feels clumsy, immensely strong. He feels as if he's not wearing his clothes but is caged within them. He tears at his brown corduroy jacket and opens the sealskin bag.

Reaching into his bag, he pushes the handkerchief aside and takes out his money: all the bills from the pawnbroker, along with the coins that were left when he stumbled away from the Mandrake. He raises the money over his head, turns, and brings his hand down on the desk. The coins leap and fly into the room. The bills flutter like summer rain, falling on the floor and on the worn sheets molded to the body of the woman of the town. She is no longer smiling; she is frightened. He pulls the rest of his clothes off and stands naked, the core of his body white, his arms and face sunburned.

"Here's the money you wanted!" he shouts.

"Hush. You'll wake everyone."

He crosses the room in two steps and rips the sheet from her. She lies back, giving in to his anger. He takes the scalloped neck of her nightgown in his right hand and pulls. A strip of fabric comes away from neck to hem, uncovering her. He drops the fabric and slaps her hard across the face with his right hand. She says nothing, but looks at him, flushed and out of breath like a boxer.

For four days they stay in her room, eating nothing, drinking only from the bottles the innkeeper leaves outside the door. It is as if they are demons living on nothing but each other's flesh. When they were together before, their lovemaking was often rough, but not all the time. Sometimes he felt tender, even admired her as a woman who knows things no woman on Small Island knows. Whose relationship with the keeper of the inn is different from any relationship between man and woman on Small Island. Whose beauty has awed him from the moment he saw her.

Now all that has been left behind, and they are demons in a death struggle, caged, tearing each other to pieces, each piece with its own pulse, the way the pulse remains in every fragment of a heart that has been cut in pieces. Even when he is inside her, it is a death match. He is much harsher than before. And she is just as harsh, digging her nails into him as soon as he stops holding her wrists together, biting whatever is within reach until his blood flows.

They don't stop, day or night. In this room, the clock has only one hour. It is always the same time, whether they are on the floor or on the bed or he is bending her over the desk. Money mixes with clothes, bodies, blood, seed, streamers of nightgown, sheets. They stop briefly, then begin again as if they had never stopped. She sleeps from time to time, while he leans over, watching. He does not allow himself sleep. He is sure that if he falls asleep, she will kill him.

The whole time they are together he is in a rage, convinced that she is laughing at him, peasant of Small Island. And she is fighting to keep him away from her heart. To keep the coating of ice intact, deep and thick as in the deadest time of winter.

On the fourth day, when he stands naked and looks down at the tangle of clothes on the floor, her body at the center like a bird in its nest, she knows she has lost. She knows what he will say before he opens his mouth, then feels it rip her open just as he ripped her nightgown from neckline to hem.

"I'm going," he says, looking straight at her, his face and arms red-brown, the rest of him white, framing a bush of brown, red and gold. "The money's gone. That's what you wanted, isn't it? *Money*. It's yours. All of it." He gestures to the tangle on the floor.

She wants to open her mouth and tell him it's not about money. It never was about the money. He can stay as long as he wants. She won't ask him to leave. She will take care of her customers elsewhere and then come to him in this little room, and they will be together in their disorder, where they have everything they need. She wants to tell him this. But her mouth will not open.

She sees the welts on his sides from her nails. She has written on his body. She didn't know she had it in her to write anything, but she has written a story on him, a story that will fade slowly from view. She wonders whether another woman will read it before it fades away completely. She sees purple marks from her teeth on his neck, shoulders and arms. His body rivets her. The words he has just spoken have made him even more vivid, powerful. There is a light around him: the aura of farewell. She knows this time he won't be back. And now, having lost, she wants him, deeply.

He bends over and paws the layers. He moves carefully, not touching her, as he finds the pieces he needs to reassemble a version of himself.

When everything is on, he stands dressed, his clothes askew. The drooping mustache. The dark eyes. The stubble.

She isn't sure whether she is laughing or crying but her eyes are doing something, something is flowing from her into the world.

He doesn't seem to notice. He walks across the wreckage as if walking on waves, his Small Island boots lifted over flying foam. Then he is out of the room and gone, not bothering to close the door behind him. She hears the sound of his boots, fading on the stairs.

She throws things this way and that until she finds a robe, wraps it around her and hurries down the stairs, pulling the belt and taking a pin from her mouth to keep tawny hair from her face. She reaches the bottom of the stairs in time to see him from the back, receding in the dust: a slight figure in a corduroy jacket, with a round bald spot. He walks stiffly, like a man getting out of bed and walking for the first time after a bad accident. She feels the ice pack around her heart give a huge crack and give way. In its place is a rush of warmth. She is surprised to find her eyes are not wet.

Behind her, the door to the office opens, and the innkeeper stands in the doorway, watching his wife at the foot of the stairs. Beyond her, the figure of the boatmaker is growing smaller. The innkeeper knows the boatmaker's money is gone. Counting the days on his fingers, he can guess very accurately how much the boatmaker had when he came in the front door and walked up the stairs trying not to be heard. Within a few hours every bill and coin will be in the box under his bed, next to the well-oiled shotgun whose twin triggers have a very light action.

The boatmaker walks away feeling the soreness right through his body. On Big Island he has been to places he did not know existed when he put his boat in the water. He doesn't know whether he has found what he came here for. He does know he will need to get himself some work and a place to sleep. He thinks he will return to the Hostel. This stay will be different. For the first time since he saw the woman of the town in front of the Mandrake, sending her barely visible plumes of smoke into the summer air, the need for drink is gone.

A few weeks later he is sitting in the big room of the Hostel, where food is served on rough wooden tables. The hall is filled with the crews of the two ships that are in port, a whaler and a trader. Both are big sailing vessels, the whaler with three masts, the trader with four. All around the boatmaker comes the buzz of three languages: the language of the Mainland and the islands, including Small Island, English and the whistling, clicking speech of the natives.

It is said that no white man has ever mastered the native language, never been able to use its clicks and pops properly to tell a story, which is all the natives seem to do in their own culture: sit and tell stories. Stories of the origin of the world, the wrestling of the mighty twins whose struggle created the world, stories of the spirits of the ancestors, of whale, seal, walrus, bear and salmon, stories of the endless expanse of winter ice, the way the world was before the white men arrived with their mechanical movements, their stilted language, their gunpowder and alcohol. Drink has changed many of the natives. The Mainland mostly holds them in contempt, though the king has established missions to bring them the Good News about Jesus Christ. They often sail on the big ships and are good sailors: strong and willing, unafraid in storms, though very drunk in port.

The crews of the two ships have been in port a few days and the worst of the drunkenness is over. In his sobriety the boatmaker is quiet, almost invisible. He wonders how many of these sailors, whose voices, rough as saws, fill the dining hall, have been up to the Mandrake to visit the woman of the town. Many, no doubt. She isn't hard to find. It's still more than warm enough to sit outside the Mandrake with her box of matches, a drink in hand, advertising more vividly than the faded sign with its mandrake root ever could.

As always, it has been easy for the boatmaker to find work. As soon as one person hires him, the word spreads that he has a gift for wood. And there are always things that need building or repairing: houses, furniture, barns. People are used to work being done half-right, a quarter-right—or even mostly wrong. They are pleased to find the boatmaker does his work so that everything fits and everything lasts. He does this with the tools at hand and the wood that is available. He never haggles: He does the work and accepts the offered pay. Sometimes his employers think he is slow, since only children and half-wits are indifferent to money. Yet he is rarely cheated.

Because he is working and not drinking, money silts up in his sealskin bag. He sleeps at the Hostel, in the big room upstairs, for almost nothing. The mattresses are rolled down and filled with sailors who stink and dream in their three languages. Although it was not easy, he has learned to sleep through the commotion. It is the first time he has lived, eaten and slept among many men. He has learned to manage the smells, the dreams, the arguments, the talk, the songs, the scrimshaw, the cribbage. He slides through it all and remains alone. By the time the Warden settles heavily into the chair across from him, his scratches have healed. His color is better and his breath is good. His mustache is bushy. His animal spirit has returned.

The boatmaker has no trouble picking up the heavy white mug in one hand and lifting it to his mouth. The

Warden signals for a mug, and a waitress brings one. She leans and whispers into the Warden's large red ear, looking at the boatmaker as she speaks. Actually, she may not be whispering. She may simply be speaking in an ordinary Big Island voice. But the wash of sound makes it impossible for the boatmaker to hear.

"She says you look better," booms the Warden. They drink. There is no moon in the boatmaker's cup. Nothing but coffee, dark and oily. "She's right. You do look better. You've been working. I hear you're good with wood. *Better this way, isn't it?*"

The boatmaker drinks his coffee, waiting for the Warden to come to the point or leave.

"Still not saying much, eh? Well, believe me, it *is* better this way. We're happy to have you here while you're like this—working and not fighting."

The waitress comes back and fills both mugs. She goes away, looking at the boatmaker out of the corner of her eye.

They sit there for a while in silence while the room empties and quiets down. Now the Warden doesn't need to bellow. "Haven't been up to see Elise either, have you?"

The boatmaker begins to think about getting up and leaving. He doesn't know anywhere else on Big Island to stay. But the price of staying at the Hostel may be getting to be more than he can afford. He reaches into his clothes and pulls out a banknote. It's yellow: five crowns.

He holds the bill in front of him, his hands resting on the table as he stares at the king of the Mainland and all its farflung islands. He looks into the engraved image, feeling that it is about to speak. He has no idea how long he remains sitting there holding the edges of the bill. When he returns to himself, the room is empty and the Warden is gone.

After his conversation with the Warden, the boatmaker knows he will keep working a while, then move on. There is nothing more for him here. When he woke up from dreaming about the blue wolf, all he knew was that he was going to build a boat and sail it to Big Island, something no one he knew had ever done. At that time Big Island seemed like a different world, enormous and complicated. Now he knows it isn't all that much bigger than the place he comes from. He has found everything there is for him here; he must move on. He will work, retrieve his compass from the pawnbroker, make his boat seaworthy again and put to sea.

As he makes his preparations to leave Big Island, the boatmaker finds he is beginning to be interested in money in a way he never was before. He has already learned some important things. From the woman of Small Island he learned that money can be used to repay certain debts but not others. From the woman of the town he has learned that money can be used to deceive and hurt. But these experiences feel as if they are only the first steps toward a deeper understanding of what money is. There must be more to learn, in places where history stretches back farther. On the northern islands, the history of settlement is shallow. The people of the Mainland have lived permanently on these islands for only a few hundred years. Before that, they were the province of the natives in their skin boats.

His plan is no clearer than the notion he had while he was building his boat of what he would do after landing on Big Island. All he knows is that he must move on, go deeper. And in the world the boatmaker comes from, the realm of green islands scattered on a cold northern sea, going deeper means only one thing: the Mainland.

CHAPTER 9

Two months after leaving Big Island the boatmaker has sailed to the Mainland and made his way inland all the way to the capital. Mostly he has walked, sometimes hitching a ride in a farm wagon. As he travels, he learns about the country, mostly by listening. He doesn't ask many questions, but he finds that people are happy to talk about what they know and offer their opinions of what is happening in the kingdom. While he listens, he notices what people wear, what they eat, how the houses are built. It is a different world from Big Island—much larger and stranger.

One of the things he hears people talking about is the modernization program undertaken by the king. Running in the blood of the reigning king is the urge for victory inherited from his pagan sea-warrior ancestors, along with the visionary ecstasy of Vashad. The spirit of the peasant boy who converted the king hovers over the country. The main cathedral and the river flowing through the capital are named for Vashad. In the cathedral are displayed six huge carved wooden panels depicting his life. The workmanship of the panels is famous. But the current king is a man of reason, and his passion is neither for conquest nor for the Resurrection. Instead, he dreams of bringing his small, backward kingdom into the century of progress.

As he moves inland, the boatmaker sees signs of the huge modernization program all around. New telegraph lines are rising on stout poles carved from the forests of the Mainland. Half-finished roads and bridges are everywhere. In even the smallest villages there are new schoolhouses, waiting for teachers trained in the latest pedagogical methods, whom the king hopes to lure from the wealthy and advanced nations of Europe, to the south.

It is still warm enough to sleep on the ground. The boatmaker has no need to find lodgings, and he spends little of the money he brought from Big Island. But by the time he reaches the capital, his money has begun to run out.

The boatmaker has never had difficulty finding work. But when he arrives in the capital, it is particularly easy due to the construction boom that has accompanied the modernization program. The city is expanding rapidly, bringing blue-and-yellow tramcars out from the old center to places that had been farms only a year or two before, running along newly paved streets that had been country roads. The fields are full of buildings going up. When work on one site is finished, it is easy to get a job on the next. The boatmaker works from first light until dark and often beyond. Work is almost as good as drink was on Big Island before he stopped drinking.

As the boatmaker moves from one building site to the next, he makes the first friends he has had as an adult. On Small Island there is only family, then everyone else. His own family is tiny and broken. But as he works in the midst of the construction boom that surrounds the capital he becomes friends with an oddly matched pair called Crow and White. And these two men become something new for him: neither family nor everyone else.

White is huge, with tangled white-blond hair and stubble the same color on a broad chin. His surname, which no one ever uses, is Weiss. White is helpless with tools, which splinter in his paws, but he can lift and carry timbers that two ordinary men couldn't budge, as well as sacks of gravel that would usually be hauled in a wagon. He is entranced by what the boatmaker can do with a hammer or a chisel and must be prodded by the crew boss to move on when he is caught staring like a child as the boatmaker fits two pieces of wood into a complicated joint.

Crow is a small man with dark hair slicked back from the widow's peak that curves down his forehead like the beak of the bird he is nicknamed for; his surname is Kravenik. His eyes are dark and his features sharp. Although Crow's hands look clever, they are soft and pale, and the boatmaker never sees him do anything that could be interpreted, even charitably, as work. Everyone who knows the two of them refers to them together as if they were a business, perhaps a dry-goods store: Crow-and-White.

In the morning, Crow arrives with White at the construction site where they are working. The two of them come out from the city on the tram or in a wagon. Sometimes Crow stays all day, drinking coffee or pulling from the curved flask he keeps inside his jacket. On other days he stays only briefly, returning at the end of the day to pick up White.

The crew boss and the men who own the building sites, who don't usually welcome anyone who isn't working for them, seem perfectly comfortable with the small dark man. They take him away from the workmen and talk quietly, sometimes sharing a drink from his silver flask. Sometimes the boatmaker hears them laughing and pointing at one or another of the men. Once he even thinks he sees them pointing at him. But he dismisses the idea. What reason could they have to talk about him? He is a stranger here, with no family, just another worker. He shrugs it off, as he does Crow's habit of writing in the small black notebook he keeps in his inside pocket with the curved flask.

As the boatmaker and his friends move from site to site, the tie among the three of them deepens. The boatmaker tries to teach White the things that can be done with tools, beginning with some of the simplest. The huge man is slow and tentative from having been laughed at all his life. But he is not stupid. Just clumsy, untutored and so immensely strong that other men have naturally turned him into a beast of burden.

The boatmaker has never taught anyone to use tools, as he himself was never taught. He learned by watching his father and taught himself, the tools fitting easily into his hands, moving the way they were intended to move. Tools don't move that way in White's paws, and helping him learn is a long struggle. The boatmaker doesn't mind. When he is teaching White, he finds in himself a patience that is rare with people—though common enough when he is working with wood.

The relationship between Crow and White is unlike any relationship the boatmaker has seen before. White's wages vanish into Crow's purse, re-emerging at Crow's discretion. White seems to accept this arrangement as a law of nature, gazing at Crow with the same wonder that comes over his face when he watches the boatmaker's hands. Crow doesn't appear to mind that White is growing attached to the boatmaker. In fact, he seems to enjoy it, nodding and winking from behind White's back when only the boatmaker can see him.

After their work for the day is done, the boatmaker follows Crow and White into the city. The three of them go to cheap restaurants in the Old Quarter, where they tear into lingonberry pancakes or share big bowls of steaming goulash. As the weather turns cold, they invite the boatmaker to sleep on the floor of their room, which is on the second floor of a boardinghouse that was once an elegant townhouse; their landlady is the last member of the family that built the house centuries before. The upper floors, once richly appointed living rooms, drawing rooms and smoking rooms, have been carved up into rooms for boarders.

As snow falls and construction stops, a room opens up at the boardinghouse, and the boatmaker moves in. His room is up the stairs on the left, across the landing from the room where Crow and White sleep in one large bed. It is an easy move, since the boatmaker wears all his possessions.

The room is small and spare, the floor painted dark green by a previous tenant, perhaps an absinthe drinker. The walls are covered in antique paper splotched with roses, the pattern cut off arbitrarily where new walls were built. On the wall above the bed is a single window looking down onto a narrow alley paved with cobblestones. On moonlit nights, the rounded stones break the moonlight into islands of brightness.

Outside the boardinghouse, the streets are packed with crowds far larger than any the boatmaker imagined before landing on the Mainland. During the day there is a steady drumming of hooves. But even that noise is swamped by the sound of thousands of people shouting to make themselves heard, doors slamming, hammers smashing paving stones, police whistles, buggy whips cracking, crates of produce landing with a crash on sidewalks, coal rattling down tin chutes. The noise of the streets is a whirlwind, always howling, except very late at night.

As it turns bitterly cold, the air fills with the smell of coal dust. Snow sifts along the streets. Amid the snow and noise, portraits of the king are everywhere: on kiosks set up for them, on telegraph poles, looking down from tall buildings. The image on the posters is always the one on the banknotes: the narrow face, dark eyes behind oval lenses, mustache shaved to a thin line, military tunic with high collar, diagonal sash, medals.

Slowly the boatmaker gets used to the constant movement, the noise, the smells, and he sleeps soundly. Having no work, living on what he's saved, he wanders the streets with his new friends, accompanying them to dark taverns and houses filled with women of the town. But he doesn't join in, just watches.

One thing the boatmaker does on his own is visit the main cathedral to see the famous carved panels that tell the story of Vashad. Leaving the boardinghouse around mid-day, he makes his way to the cathedral. Inside it is cold and dim, the light filtering from clerestory windows high above. There is no one visible and the huge interior of the church is quiet.

The boatmaker takes his time moving from panel to panel, examining the wood and the craft. Each panel is twice as tall as he is and six feet across. They were carved over decades, centuries after the death of Vashad, in workshops established by the king specially for that purpose. The panels are oak, polished and darkened by age. The carving is detailed, adoring, the carved figures raised above the surface, glowing and lifelike.

In the first panel Vashad is a peasant boy among farm animals, listening to the blackbirds, who have just arrived to change his life. In the second he has left his father's farm and is living in a tiny Christian community—at a time when Christians were persecuted and such communities were illegal. In the next he is shown on the road to the capital. In the climactic panel Vashad is in the palace, the blackbirds a mighty halo around him. The king is lying face down in surrender. Behind him three of his knights stand astonished, mouths open.

After the king was converted, the blackbirds flew away, never to return. Vashad moved to a tiny hut near the river, living on alms left at his door by grateful Christians. The fifth panel shows him there. In the sixth and final panel Vashad, now a saint, smiles down from Heaven on a rich, peaceful Mainland. Smoke drifts up from cottage chimneys; cattle are well-tended and fat.

The boatmaker doesn't have any particular feelings about Vashad. But he does admire the workmanship of the panels. As he puts a few coins in a box and leaves the cathedral, he is thinking about the workshops where the panels were made, the men working in silence, each knowing his task, the work unfolding with meticulous care over decades. Outside it is late afternoon and almost dark. But the days are already slightly longer.

As the snow recedes and the ground unfreezes, construction begins again at an even faster pace than the year before. The modernization program is accelerating, bringing with it increased speculation in land. The currency is inflating, the price of land soaring. Speculators are snapping up the best parcels and building ever more houses for the workers of the city, especially the government employees, whose wages are rising faster than anyone else's.

Sadly, the royal treasury, depleted after centuries of rule by weak kings and cliques of barons and earls, cannot bear the weight of the modernization program. His funds exhausted, the king has been forced to turn to the only source of capital on the Mainland capable of supporting his ambitions for progress: the House of Lippsted.

The House of Lippsted is a merchant bank owned by an ancient, aristocratic Jewish family. Its roots are in Vienna; it has interlocking relationships with fraternal banks in Paris, Berlin and London. The Lippsted holdings on the Mainland include thousands of hectares of the country's richest farmland, plants for making cheese, a railroad and provincial banks, as well as fisheries, mines and rich stands of timber.

None of these enterprises is visibly connected to the House of Lippsted. The only businesses that bear the family name are the merchant bank itself and a furniture workshop in the capital, which produces furniture known throughout Europe for the unchanging simplicity of its designs, the remarkable quality of the wood used in its manufacture and the fact that not a single nail or screw is used in making any of the pieces.

Hesitantly at first, then with growing confidence, the king has turned to the House of Lippsted to finance his modernization program. As the boatmaker is finding his footing on the Mainland, the relationship between the Crown and the House of Lippsted continues to deepen. A bond has grown between the king and Jacob Lippsted, who is the head of the family on the Mainland. The two are the same age, both educated in Europe, the king in Berlin, Jacob Lippsted in Paris.

The rates of interest Lippsted charges the royal treasury are always reasonable; Jacob Lippsted sees to that. But repaying the loans depends on the modernization project coming to fruition, increasing the kingdom's productivity and the revenues flowing into the treasury. As long as the project lies everywhere unfinished, the principal and interest the Crown owes the House of Lippsted will grow even faster than the project itself. By now the debt is so large that both sides are fearful of the consequences if it were to be revealed.

Although the relationship between the House of Lippsted and the Crown has not been made public, there have been whispers about it in the capital. With these rumors in the background, the modernization program and the construction boom are moving forward rapidly. The boatmaker is finding more—and better paid—work than he has ever known. He has accumulated so many banknotes he no longer keeps them all in his sealskin pouch. Some are hidden in a cache that he built by pulling up a section of green floorboard in his room and refitting it so the hiding place is invisible to a casual examination.

In spite of having piled up what seems to him like a lot of money, the boatmaker has not made much progress in understanding more about what money is and where it comes from. But he has not given up trying to answer those questions, along with all the questions he still has about what he is seeking in the capital. Late at night the city quiets, and in his little room over the alley he takes his mother's handkerchief out of the sealskin bag yet again. He has folded and unfolded the cloth so many times he must be careful to prevent it from falling to pieces like a map read once too often. He smooths the linen across his knee and looks at the scene, trying to read the message embroidered there for him.

CHAPTER 10

Just before Midsummer's Eve the boatmaker hears of an opportunity to learn more about money. Every year on the king's birthday, the Royal Mint is opened to the people. In the old days on his birthday the king gave each of his subjects a gold coin; the kingdom was smaller and richer then. Now in place of a coin, the king offers his people knowledge. Volunteers, mostly women from aristocratic families, educated in Europe, give free public lectures on the history of money. After the lectures, citizens are taken on tours and shown the huge presses, imported from England, that print the kingdom's banknotes. At the end of the tour, they are allowed upstairs to a special room where they may exchange a few old bills, soiled from being passed through many hands, for fresh new ones.

The birthday of the current king is on the fourth day of July, in the middle of the brief, brilliant Mainland summer. The weather is always beautiful on that day, the sky still light at midnight. After the endless darkness of winter, the people of the capital are in a frenzy of eating, drinking, talking and dancing, feeling no need for sleep. The boatmaker decides he will go to the Mint for the lecture and tour, hoping to learn at least some of the secrets of money.

On the morning of the fourth, the boatmaker rises early to a sky already bright and rushes out to join the queue around the Mint. The oldest portions of the building are the remains of an ancient armory. Around that ancient core, the Mint has been expanded many times; it now presents to the world an imposing façade of dark brown stone. The queue circles the building before snaking up broad stone steps, passing under a round arch and entering massive double doors. In front of the doors stand two large policemen with brush mustaches wearing dark-blue dress uniforms. At parade rest, rocking on the balls of their feet, they look like twins.

The line inches forward, starting and stopping. The people on the pavement stand and talk, feeling the July sunshine on their faces. They are in no hurry. There are not many holidays on the Mainland, and most of them are religious, requiring the pious to spend long hours kneeling on stone church floors, cold in winter and hard always. The king's birthday requires little of anyone. Families picnic and drink on the grounds of the Winter Palace, which on this day are open to the public under the eyes of the police and the King's Own Guard in their scarlet tunics and round bearskin helmets. Some people choose to visit the Mint, drawn by the opportunity to enter another place that is off limits three hundred and sixty-four days of the year—and to be in the presence of vast amounts of money.

Most of the people in the queue are workingmen in their Sunday clothes. Here and there a man has brought his wife, or a woman not his wife who makes a living in the taverns, but mostly it is a long file of workers: stevedores, hoopers, teamsters, carpenters, ironworkers, roofers, butchers, delivery boys, clerks, fishmongers who squeeze lemon on cracked hands to hold down the smell before coming out to join the crowd, boilermakers, laborers from farms on the edge of the capital, printers, tram drivers, conductors. They stand laughing and talking, shuffling forward, sweating under wool suits worn a few times a year, wiping creased necks with big handkerchiefs. Many eat bread and sausage from paper parcels and drink from flasks or bottles stowed inside their jackets. It is a day of celebration; the men of the capital are at their ease.

After two hours the boatmaker is two-thirds of the way to the doors flanked by the burly policemen. He moves forward haltingly with the line, speaking to no one, wearing the only clothes he owns: blue overalls over longjohns, brown corduroy jacket, heavy boots. The same clothes he wore when he pushed off from Small Island, though by now somewhat the worse for wear. His landlady has offered to have her maid wash his clothes, a service she performs for Crow and White. The boatmaker always refuses.

Standing in the sun, he notices a man four places ahead of him in line. The man isn't drawing attention to himself, and yet he commands respect. It isn't his clothing that is noticeable: an ordinary brown tweed suit, like those worn by hundreds of others in the queue. Nor is it his body, lean and hard under his clothes, or his face, which shows the red of someone who has spent much time outdoors. What draws notice is the eyes. They are cold, clear and blue, like the water in a mountain stream running over spring ice. The boatmaker notes the man, the newspaper folded in the pocket of his jacket, the sausage he is finishing and washing down with a pull from a flask. His curiosity satisfied, the boatmaker turns his face up to the sun of the capital, which feels different from the sun of the northern islands.

The city, twenty miles inland on the brown flux named for Vashad, does not smell of the sea. Instead, rising into the air is the smell of horses, their droppings bursting green on the pavement, day after day and week after week. The droppings pile up and are ground into a dust that floats up in every season of the year and can be sensed even on a holiday, when the workshops and factories are closed and tramcars run infrequently. Beyond the dust and the smell, the sky is an infinite blue.

The man four places ahead takes the newspaper out of his pocket and spreads it open like the wings of a seabird. At the top of the page *The Brotherhood* is printed in the old-fashioned spiky lettering that not all residents of the Mainland can read, even those who can read the modern letters. The narrow columns below are set in round modern type. The newspaper gives the impression of seriousness, anger—and a message not meant for everyone. The lean man with the ruddy face is absorbed. When they reach the steps leading up to the Mint, he folds the newspaper and puts it back in the outside pocket of his jacket.

The line climbs the steps and eases between the twin policemen. Inside, the boatmaker is out of the heat in a hallway with a stone floor and ceilings so high they seem like another sky. Light comes down over a balustrade from windows on the floor above. In the hall everything is shaded and cool; everyone keeps their voices down without needing to be told. As they enter, the boatmaker sees that the man reading *The Brotherhood*, the three who were in between them and the two who were behind the boatmaker, along with the boatmaker himself, make up a group of seven that is being guided to the right.

The seven of them go down the hall toward a lighted doorway on the left and turn into a room resembling a classroom, lit by bare electric bulbs. At the front is a heavy desk with wooden folding chairs set facing it in a semicircle. Behind the battered old desk is a chalkboard and two glass-fronted cases. In one case the boatmaker sees three shells he knows: whelks prized by the natives who long ago made their summer homes on Small Island.

As the men enter, a woman stands writing on the dusty chalkboard, her back to them. She is slight. Her hair, drawn up at the nape of her neck, escapes in unruly black curls. Her purple dress is high at the throat, long in the sleeve and skirt. In a clear, unfussy hand she is writing: *The Three Epochs of Money*. She finishes writing, sets the chalk in the tray at the bottom of the board and turns to face the seven men of the capital in a semicircle before her on folding chairs.

"Good morning," she says, brushing her hands together to remove chalk dust. Although this woman carries the scent of wealth about her, the only jewelry she wears is a cameo with a woman's profile, ivory on a black background. The profile on the cameo bears a striking resemblance to her own. She smooths the front of her close-fitting purple skirt.

"My name is Rachel Lippsted. I welcome all of you to the Royal Mint on this occasion of the king's birthday." The boatmaker feels a subtle tremor go through the men at the name Lippsted spoken in this place. "We'll talk here awhile and then go for a tour of the Mint, on the one day of the year we're allowed here, a place that is normally closed and under the highest level of security in the kingdom—second only to the palace when the king is in residence, and of course the person of the king himself.

"Let's begin at the beginning," she says, "or near the beginning." She smiles, trying to put her audience at ease. She's small and trim, but there must be a boldness in her, the boatmaker thinks, to be here, giving a lecture to seven workingmen of the capital. Not many women could do that. He wonders how the others feel about being lectured by a woman. The boatmaker himself is both pleased and irritated.

Rachel Lippsted walks to one of the glass-fronted cases, the toes of her black boots showing beneath the skirt. She takes a key from a pocket in the front of her dress and opens the door, reaching in to remove two of the three whelks, which are conical and delicately flecked in black and white. The boatmaker knows that these whelks need just the right conditions in order to thrive. They must be covered by the sea most, but not all, the time, living in water that is cold but not too cold, with the right amount of salt. If any of these conditions are not met, the whelks will disappear. On Small Island they grow in several places, holding tight to the rocks in clusters of three or four, always covered at high tide. To the natives these whelks and the places where they grow are sacred.

Rachel Lippsted holds up the pointed shells and asks: "Does anyone recognize these?"

The boatmaker does. But there is no reason for him—an anonymous carpenter from Small Island—to draw attention to himself in the Royal Mint on the king's birthday. He says nothing. None of the others speaks.

"It's not so surprising that no one knows these," she says, brushing the curls from her eyes. As she holds the shells up for inspection the boatmaker notices that the first two fingers of her right hand are stained yellow-brown, like his.

"These shells are rare and precious, almost gone today, though still found on some of the remote islands of the kingdom. They have a fancy scientific name in Latin and a lovely one in the tongue of the native islanders. But we needn't be concerned with all that. Our own Main-land speech will do just fine—and in our language they are called tidal whelks."

There is a shifting in the room, a shuffling and creak-ing on the wooden chairs. It is not a comfortable sound. The boatmaker senses the discomfort but doesn't know where it comes from.

"Why do I bring them up?" the woman asks, putting the shells down on the desk and turning to face her audi-ence. Unlike the dress of the woman of the town, Rachel Lippsted's dress is made to conceal rather than reveal; it cloaks her from wrist to neck. Nevertheless, the boatmaker can see that within the dark silk is a small, firm body.

"I show you these shells because for the natives who lived on our own northern islands and beyond, all the way to the Arctic, these shells *were* money. They were the carriers of value as well as a medium of exchange. To be sure, the natives had other forms of money: polar-bear pelts and teeth, and the wing bones of certain seabirds. But these shells were their most valuable form of mon-ey, real currency—every bit as much as our banknotes, printed on the remarkable presses you will shortly see.

"Now, can any of you gentlemen tell me why these shells should have become the medium of exchange for the natives of those remote islands?"

There is no answer. The boatmaker feels a resistance building in the little crowd, a resentment at being addressed in a lecture tone by this small woman, with her exotic name and deep confidence in her own intellect. This truculence comes to him along with the men's smell, mixing tweed, underwear changed once a month, heavy shoes, tobacco, drink, sausages and machine oil. There's something else in the smell, too, something like fear and anger, shared among them. It is a smell the boatmaker doesn't recognize; it doesn't exist on Small Island.

Receiving no answer, Rachel Lippsted leads the men through a history of money in three stages, pausing from time to time to make notes on the board in her clear, educated handwriting.

The first stage, she explains, exemplified by the tidal whelks with their mathematical markings, is the use of rare and beautiful natural objects as the medium of exchange among small groups over short distances. This is followed by the growing use of rare and precious metals—copper, silver and gold at first, later mostly gold—by great nations reaching across oceans to take, absorb and exchange. Then she comes to the final phase, their own: the era of banknotes, which stand for gold but have no value in themselves. In spite of their lack of intrinsic value, the ghostly abstractions bearing the long face of the king can measure the value of any other thing: animal, vegetable or mineral, including the labor power of men. This is a remarkable capacity.

"After all," she asks, holding up a Mainland banknote, a pale-green-and-pink rectangle only one of the men in the room has ever seen, in a denomination large enough to purchase a house, "what is the *value* of this note? Beautifully printed as it is, is it not simply a piece of paper?"

The smell in the room, of shared resentment, deepens. Rachel Lippsted pauses, hands clasped on the front of her purple skirt, then tries another tack.

"Can anyone tell me what is the same in all three phases of the history we have just covered? As different as they are?"

Her questions are met with more moving of feet and creaking of chairs.

"Let me tell you, then. The thing that provides continuity, the thing that is the same in all three periods is faith."

"*What do you mean by that?*" demands the man in the tweed suit who was standing ahead of the boatmaker in the queue, reading his newspaper. His face is redder, his brown hair curly, electrified. He twists in his chair, obviously having difficulty remaining seated.

"This is what I mean," the small woman says. Her voice is steady, but the boatmaker sees in her eyes and clasped hands that she is, if not frightened, then alert to possible danger. "What I mean is that unless the people have faith in their money, it is worthless."

"*Gold isn't worthless!*" the man in the tweed suit bellows, the folding chair trembling under his lean legs.

"Gold has value because we *believe* it does," Rachel Lippsted says; keeping her voice steady clearly requires an effort. "Gold is beautiful, yes, and easily worked. It makes wonderful jewelry. But as currency it has nothing but the value we endow it with. And this has always been true: Money has the power we bestow upon it by putting our collective faith in it."

The man in the tweed suit stares, his face raw.

Rachel Lippsted continues. Her voice wavers, but her logic is clear. "Faith is present in all three stages of money. In our stage, the final one, the true nature of money becomes clear. Banknotes have no value in themselves. Yet they are immensely valued. Men will do many things— both good and bad—for just one of these colored notes."

She holds the pink-and-green bill up to the room. The man in the tweed suit can no longer hold himself back. He stands, the folding chair flattening and falling behind him with a bang.

"*The currency is worthless because the Jews have made it worthless!*" he yells. "The king is in debt to the bloodsuckers up to his eyes. And you know that don't you, Miss Rachel Lippsted? *Because you're one of them."*

His lips arch from his teeth in disgust. He takes a long stride toward the woman at the front of the room. The boatmaker wonders whether the ruddy-faced man will assault her. He wonders what the other men in the room would do if that happened. Surely they would not sit by while a woman was being beaten? Would they? He is far out of his depth.

Rather than raising her arms over her head to shield herself, as the boatmaker expects, Rachel Lippsted steps back and leans against the heavy desk. The boatmaker sees her feel behind her, finding something set in the wood. She must be signaling, he thinks.

Sure enough, a moment later, while the man in the tweed suit is still shouting about the Jews and the inflation that is sucking the life out of the kingdom's money, the door swings open. The twin policemen muscle in and grab the shouting man by his shoulders.

"You Jews will get what's coming to you!" he shouts over his shoulder as they flank him and march him out. He seems surprisingly unafraid. In fact, as he leaves, he looks as though he might break into laughter.

Outside the Mint, the stone steps are empty. The tours are at an end until the king's birthday next year. The man who had been shouting stands chatting in a familiar way with the policemen who marched him out. A man in elegant civilian clothes approaches, chats briefly with the other three. Then he turns and walks off, arm in arm with the man in brown tweed. They are not in a hurry, but not wasting time either, one a little taller, a little leaner, than the other, both carrying themselves in a manner that suggests marches, parade rest, attention and conversation in the field over cigarettes cupped against the wind.

CHAPTER 11

In the classroom the semicircle of folding chairs shows a gap
where one chair lies flat on the floor. The two whelks glit-
ter on the desk, their checked surfaces reflecting light from
bare bulbs. Rachel Lippsted resumes her lecture, slightly
unsteady but determined, proceeds to the end, locks the
pink-and-green bill in the desk and puts the whelks back in
their case. Turning the lights off and closing the door, she
escorts her six remaining pupils out of the classroom and
down broad worn stone stairs. At the bottom is a heavy
door guarded by a soldier who nods them past.

They enter a huge space in which they must stop to
let their eyes adjust to the dimness. Light trickles from
small windows high on the walls, at the level of the street
outside. The floor is bedrock. Cut into it are four bays. In
each bay sits a huge piece of machinery, as tall as two men
and much longer. A serpentine of rollers of different sizes
leads the eye from one end of the machine to the other.

Over everything is the smell of oil and ink and the melancholy of machinery stopped in the middle of its task.

Rachel Lippsted, neatly buttoned into her purple dress, toes of black boots peeping out from under her skirt, explains that the presses are as modern and powerful as any in Europe. Made in England and brought by specially reinforced ships upriver to the capital, they can print thousands of banknotes an hour. The Mainland has moved out of the second phase of the history of money, she says. The country's wealth is no longer tied to gold or to conquest: It increases with the skill and productivity of its workers.

At the end of the tour the group assembles in the high-ceilinged entrance hall, and the five other men leave without a word. In spite of the strange events of this day, the boatmaker still wants to exercise his privilege of exchanging worn bills for new ones. The woman in the purple dress shakes his hand goodbye. The boatmaker has never shaken hands with a woman. Her palm is cool and dry, smaller and smoother than his.

After leaving her, he climbs stone stairs and walks through offices, asking for directions, until he finds himself in a small room with frosted glass rising from a wooden divider. There are two arched openings in the frosted glass. Etched in the glass between them is an oval enclosing the king's initial surrounded by an intricate floral design. Against the far wall, under the familiar portrait of the king, are benches. The benches and the arched openings in the frosted glass are empty.

Although no one can see him, the boatmaker turns away, screening his sealskin bag. Reaching under his overalls and long underwear, he opens the bag and draws out three notes: one each in blue, buff and yellow. Money in hand, he turns back.

A woman appears in one of the openings in the glass, next to the oval bearing the king's initial. She is middle-aged and small, her hair pulled back in a neat silver bun. At the throat of her blue blouse is a gold pin shaped like a beetle. Her blouse is dotted with yellow butterflies, their wings spreading until they almost touch.

"May I help you?" she asks in a tone that is correct, even chilly.

"I've come to change," the boatmaker says.

"Change?"

"Exchange, I mean," he says, blushing under the color of a man who works outdoors. "I was told I could exchange old bills."

"Let me see."

The boatmaker moves forward, stiff and apprehensive, as if one cross look from this teller, a small woman behind frosted glass, could vaporize him. He places his bills on the counter, its oak worn smooth by thousands of banknotes moving back and forth—the silent, invisible pressure of money.

The woman picks his bills up by the edges and sets them aside. The forefinger of her right hand is covered by a rubber tip. She reaches for a ledger bound in red leather and pushes it through the arched opening, indicating with the rubber tip where the boatmaker should sign. He signs his name and hands the book back. She reads the name, looks at it again, picks the book up and carries it down the counter to another woman about the same age. They peer into the book, gray heads poised over the fine blue lines bearing the names of the people of the capital. Without leaning forward, the boatmaker tries to hear their whispers, but he can't make out the words.

The woman with butterflies on her blouse returns and puts the red ledger down. She reaches into a drawer and removes three crisp notes. She counts them once, twice, then a third time with her rubber finger and pushes the bills through the opening. Although it is not hot in the room, the boatmaker is sweating under his overalls. He takes the bills and turns, slowing his legs so that he can depart at a dignified pace.

He retraces his steps through the warren of walls, stone stairs and wooden doors to find his way out into the July evening, still noon-bright though it is past six. The broad stairs leading to the Mint are deserted. It is the evening of a holiday; the festive energy has been spent. Everyone is home with family or in a tavern settling down to a nice quiet drunk to avoid thinking about what awaits the next morning. The boatmaker has no family and tries to avoid taverns, especially when he is alone. This evening he is tempted, but he knows it isn't just one drink he is avoiding: It is a whole world, with many places he would rather not revisit.

He returns to the boardinghouse. The landlady's room is on the first floor. She is in her fifties, straggles of iron-gray hair pulled into a disorderly bun. She is rarely without a cigarette and a volume of Kierkegaard; she often smells of drink. Sometimes she darts out at the slightest sound on the stairs, cigarette burning, wiry hair flying. Other times, nothing rouses her for days, and then she reappears wearing a look the boatmaker knows all too well from the inside. This time, as the boatmaker passes the door stays closed. No sound comes from within.

Lining the walls of the narrow stairway to the second floor are portraits of the landlady's ancestors, the oldest at the bottom and the newest at the top. Most of the portraits are paired: man and wife. At the foot of the stairs knights with rude faces under bowl haircuts stare out of severely carved gothic frames. A little higher up, burghers in urban black with ruffs that curve and recurve like mathematical functions gaze from frames heavy with gilt. Higher still, elegant patrons of the arts, slightly bohemian, lounge in simple frames with classical lines. At the top is a portrait of the landlady herself as a young woman, painted in a daring style, then new, with patches of bright color that make her face resemble the flag of an unknown country; the frame is a simple line of black.

As the boatmaker climbs, the landlady's ancestors regard him with their varying degrees of piety and pride. Although her home has become a shabby boardinghouse in a questionable neighborhood bordering on the Jewish quarter, the landlady's family is one of the oldest and noblest in the land. The boatmaker, who has no lineage to consult, cannot imagine what it must be like for her to live among pictures of her stock going far back into the history of the Mainland, almost as far back as the time of the sainted Vashad. At the top of the stairs he turns left and goes down the hall to his room. He lies on his narrow bed without taking off his corduroy jacket or boots.

Since he arrived on the Mainland, understanding money has become something like a mission for the boatmaker. Now, after what happened at the Mint, he knows the Jews are somehow bound up in his questions.

Lying on his back, he reaches into his sealskin pouch and pulls out the three banknotes the woman in the butterflies gave him. He holds them above his head to look at them. Pulls them down and smells them. Rubs them against one another, feeling the very slight roughness, like that of unimaginably fine sandpaper. If you worked with new bills a long time, they would probably sand your fingers to the bone, he thinks. No wonder the woman at the Mint wears a rubber tip.

He holds the bills up toward the ceiling, squinting at the image of the king. It brings back the image of the Jew on Big Island, silently estimating the value of his compass, the whispered words of the woman at the Mint over her red ledger, the violent outburst in the classroom, the shaky determination of Rachel Lippsted to continue her interrupted lecture, the enormous power of the machines that print the banknotes. The boatmaker knows that all these things fit together, but he does not see how. When he came to the Mainland, he wanted to understand more about money, which seemed to him like just another part of everyday life. But the desire to answer some apparently simple questions has led him into a dark confusion. Lying on his bed, he feels as if a swarm of bees, trapped and angry, is buzzing in his head.

He lets the bills drop and fumbles a cigarette and matches out of his pockets, lights the cigarette and watches smoke rise to the ceiling, flattening like the cap of a mushroom as it meets ancient plaster. He wonders how many thousands of cigarettes it would take for the ceiling to be as stained as his fingers, Rachel Lippsted's and his landlady's are. He wonders whether he should simply lie on his bed and smoke until answers appear on the ceiling.

He hears a knock on his door, and Crow enters without waiting for a reply. Behind him, White is an enormous shadow.

"Why are you lying there?" asks Crow. "Are you ill?"

"I'm thinking."

"*Thinking?*" The little man gives a laugh that shows his opinion of the boatmaker's capacity for thinking deep thoughts. "Better leave the thinking to me. Or better yet—to our friend White here." He gestures with his thumb at the man behind him, who fills the room like a polar bear. White chuckles at Crow's cleverness.

The boatmaker says nothing while he lets smoke drift to the ceiling. He knows that Crow understands all the curves and angles of the world, all the places where things are fastened—and what holds them in place. The boatmaker is often amused by Crow and impressed by his worldliness. But today the little man's words seem to be coming from far away. Outside the window the July day is ending slowly, the sky covering itself up like a boxer seeking respite from the unrelenting assault of daylight.

"I went to the Mint. For the king's birthday."

"Wanting to find out about money, eh? Well, aren't we all, my friend from Small Island? You're not going to get any closer to it at the Mint, though, I can tell you that. They don't leave it lying around loose over there." White laughs a white bear's rumble. To Crow and White, the boatmaker is the king of the rubes. They like him partly because in his presence they feel tougher and smarter than usual. Even White feels superior in worldly knowledge to the man from Small Island.

To Crow, the boatmaker, with his remarkable skill at working wood and his Small Island origins, is something of a novelty. As always when confronted by novelty, Crow has been trying to figure out how to turn it to profit. When it comes to calculating how to get his cut, Crow has nothing but patience. And he knows a drunk when he sees one. The boatmaker's dryness is a ruse Crow will sooner or later penetrate. He's not worried. He's been getting past deeper ruses, from much trickier customers than the boatmaker, all his life.

"At the Mint," the boatmaker says, looking at the ceiling, "there was an argument with the woman giving the lecture. Rachel Lippsted. A man was yelling that the Jews are parasites. The police came and took him."

"What did he look like?" asks Crow, senses alerted.

"Tall. Curly hair. Tweed suit. Like someone you don't want to mess about. The girl was cool. Frightened. But tough. I think she pushed a button in her desk to call the coppers. They came and hustled him out. But they weren't rough. More like acting." The boatmaker feels as if the two men, one small and dark, one large and white, are making an effort not to exchange glances.

"Well, not everyone likes the Jews," says Crow. "Even all the way out on Small Island, where they dress in animal skins, you must have learned that."

Another time the boatmaker would have laughed. Not now. "Never knew any. Oh, and another thing, the man who yelled about the Jews had a copy of a newspaper called *The Brotherhood*. What's that?" He raises himself on an elbow, cigarette burning down, so that he can look directly at Crow and White. They stand still, expressionless.

"Forget all of that," says Crow. "It's not important. Come on out and have a drink with your friends for a change."

The boatmaker knows he shouldn't go with them. But his head is buzzing like a beehive, and so he agrees. He won't drink, he thinks. He'll sit in the Grey Goose with them and watch while the men of the Mainland drink themselves into oblivion to mark the end of the king's birthday and the imminent return of the working week.

After that night the boatmaker is drunk without stopping for three months: from the first week in July through the blinding Mainland summer, when night is no more than a single inheld breath in an endless day, through August and into September. He continues to work, not drinking quite as much when he is actually on the job. When he's on the building site, he removes his corduroy jacket and works in long underwear and overalls, letting alcohol steam out of him in the sun. He doesn't say much, and people keep away. He accepts beer from White and the occasional pull on Crow's flask while he's working, enough to keep his hands from shaking.

As soon as the crew stops for the day, the sun still high in a white sky, the boatmaker starts in again. He drinks on the tram back to the city and in his room. He goes to the Grey Goose with Crow and White and spends his wages on alcohol, letting it burn its way into him. He's never cared for beer, hates the feeling of it sloshing inside him when he's drunk. He likes grain-spirits: ethereal and burning, whispering demon-thoughts in his brain. He gets in fights, beating or being beaten, waking up in his bed or on his green floor with no memory of what happened the night before, his mind no more substantial than a fresh shaving of wood from a chisel.

While the boatmaker sinks into drink, tension over the modernization program grows all around him. In spite of the precautions taken by the king and Jacob Lippsted, rumors are spreading about how much the Crown owes the House of Lippsted. Many are outraged by what they hear. There is a widespread feeling that an illness has struck the crown—and the Jews are to blame. Though Jacob Lippsted and the king enjoy each other's company, these days they take care not to be seen together in public.

The hatred of Jews on the Mainland is not as virulent as it is across the narrow neck of land that connects the Mainland to the continent of Europe. There hasn't been a pogrom in the capital for more than half a century, a length of time that would be unheard of in certain countries to the south and east. But there is a disgruntlement in the kingdom that cannot be wiped away, a hatred that seems to rise from the earth itself, bubbling up like a volcanic hot spring, expelling poisonous gas across the fertile land.

Crow and White understand far more of what is happening on the Mainland than the boatmaker does. But they don't bother to enlighten him. Crow knows he is getting closer to being able to profit from the boatmaker; the boatmaker's drunkenness may be good for his plan. Crow and White watch as the boatmaker engages the world with his fists and his rage.

The man from Small Island has changed from a skilled carpenter who worked hard and said little into a man who is continuously drunk, yelling in his muddle about money, the Jews, the king, Big Island, a woman of the town, a compass, a wolf with blue fur, his mother, his brother, and other things equally unintelligible to normal, healthy people.

The boatmaker's yelling fits usually begin at the height of his drunk, just before he gets into a fight with someone bigger than he is or passes out, listing, sinking and needing to be carried to his room in the boardinghouse, a task Crow and White perform with good humor. That is, White carries while Crow supervises, pulling on his flask and pointing out holes in the pavement that White should avoid while he shoulders the boatmaker's dead weight.

Within his spirit-haze, the boatmaker begins to feel that Crow and White are regarding him differently. Now that he is drinking, he would think they would make even more fun of him than they did before. But the mismatched pair don't make fun of him. Instead, he feels them watching him, as if they are trying to decide what to do with him. He assumes it's because of the drink. He's seen others eye him this way when he was drunk for long periods: as if they couldn't decide whether to try to help or walk away. But they do neither. They simply watch him with interest as they drink their own drink. Crow and White are professional drinkers: slow and steady, rarely drunk or out of control.

The boatmaker quickly gives up trying to figure out what Crow and White are thinking. In any case, there is little room to spare inside his head, which is filled by the only two things that matter: the way wood speaks to him, which never goes away no matter how much he drinks, and the buzzing that sounds like a swarm of angry bees. The angry buzzing, the intensity of his confusion about money, the Mainland and the Jews, makes him fear he will lose his mind, something the boatmaker, for all his strangeness, has never been afraid of before.

Not even the deepest drunk or the worst beating can silence the buzzing for long. When he's working it recedes a little, but it comes back as soon as he wraps up his tools and leaves the building site for the city. And then he can't get to the Grey Goose fast enough. Or someplace rougher: a cabin on the roadside where they serve spirits, distilled in the cellar from wheat or potatoes, that are guaranteed to produce blackness in a hurry.

One night in September, under a moon about half full, Crow and White are walking him back to the boardinghouse. The boatmaker is drunk, but for a change he hasn't started spouting the usual gibberish about the Jews, the king, the Lippsted girl, and so on and so forth. On this particularly lovely fall evening, Crow and White have not had to shut him up or carry him home. But they are still leading him, and he notices that they do not seem to have drunk as much as usual—perhaps nothing at all.

Rather than going to the front door, they guide him by nudges and shoves into the alley behind the boardinghouse. There are only a few clouds in the sky, and the moon is reflected on the cobbles, still warm from the sun. Moonlight rolls down the stones and collects in rivulets.

For a moment the buzzing in the boatmaker's head quiets. In the familiar alley near their boardinghouse, he is pleased to be supported by his friends. What does it matter if they do not go inside directly? For a breath or two he is almost at home, feeling much as he would under a Small Island moon. He pauses to wonder what the woman and her child are doing.

Then White's massive arm shifts and the boatmaker finds himself held up from behind by two huge paws that he has tried to educate in the use of hammer and chisel, bit and brace. Crow moves in front of him, moonlight picking out the sharp features under his widow's peak, and reaches inside his coat. He takes out his curved flask and holds it out to the boatmaker, dangling in White's arms, toes above the cobbles.

"Drink?" He knows Crow is acting drunk. He has no idea why.

"No."

"That's alright. You've had plenty."

"I guess so. What's this, then?" He tilts his head to indicate White, holding him from behind.

"We think you know."

"You think a lot of things," the boatmaker says, laughing. He is finding himself funny, a rare occurrence. He feels as if he should shut up, but in this moment he can't; it feels too good to laugh.

"You think a lot of things, Herr Kravenik," he says. "And know a lot of things. And you do a lot of things. Only none of them seems to involve work. And why is that?"

The small man is silent. He caps the flask and starts to put it away, then suddenly uses the bottom of it to smash the boatmaker's face. His mouth fills with blood, as if fed by a warm underground spring.

"Where is it?" Crow asks.

"Where is what?" He knows that later his face will ache. Now he feels nothing except the blood in his mouth.

"The money. *Where is the money?*" Crow nods over the boatmaker to the white giant, who spins the boatmaker around like a ragdoll and begins punching him—face, shoulders and gut—with a huge balled fist, bracing him with the other hand. It all seems to happen slowly. It doesn't even hurt much.

The boatmaker, who usually fights like a demon when he's drunk, takes blow after blow until he is lying on the cobbles, peering down into the rivers of moonlight that flow between the stones. The two men, big and little, lean in like shadows speaking strange tongues. "The money," says Crow. "Where is it? This is your last chance."

The boatmaker tries to move his arm. It doesn't move. He wants to ask: *What money?* And add: *I thought we were friends.* But nothing comes out. He lies spreadeagled as White kicks and punches him into blackness.

CHAPTER 12

The boatmaker wakes slowly, not knowing where he is. His body is a lump of pain. He sends thoughts into his trunk and legs, but they don't respond. He stops trying to move. Light rakes in from windows on the far wall, leaps the empty bed next to his own and paints a stripe on the ceiling. The stripe seems motionless, but if the boatmaker is patient, he can see that it changes position. First the light is on one side of a thin crack in the plaster of the ceiling; then it is on the other. He feels as if he has seen this stripe of light before.

He knows he is in a hospital, though there is no such thing on Small Island. He focuses on the ceiling, trying not to feel the throbbing in his head and his body. He waits to see when the stripe of light will move and leave the fine, meandering crack behind. It seems important for him to remain awake: He is afraid that if he goes to sleep he will never return to this room.

When he wakes again, it is dark. The door opens, admitting light from the hall. A woman enters, dressed in white. Starched straps hold up a long skirt. A white band crosses her forehead under a headdress falling to her shoulders. A nun, the boatmaker thinks. Like *hospital*, it is a word he knows from books.

The nun circles his bed, wrings the cloth she carries into a bowl on the stand beside his bed, places the cooling compress on his forehead.

"You're awake. That's good. Can you hear me?" He can feel something warm seep through the bandages around his right ear.

"Yes." His voice is rough and faint.

"Even better." She pours water into a glass, supports his neck and bandaged head while she helps him drink. Pain, white and unforgiving, shoots through his head as the cool water flows into him like water flowing into a desert. Finishing the glass, he signs that he wants more; the sister gives him another. It is still a miracle, but more like water this time, less like the mercy of God. She eases his head back onto the pillow. White pain cuts through his body.

"That's all you can have. The doctors are worried about your insides. From the look of you, they have reason to be. Something big hit you. What was it?"

She smiles, a little self-conscious, making clear he doesn't have to answer. Her teeth are small, even, white. He wonders what color her hair is under the white headdress. Then thinks: blond, to go with the blue eyes and pale skin.

"How long have I been here?" The pain returns when he speaks, but a little less each time he opens his mouth.

"Three days and three nights."

Three days. That's why the stripe of light is familiar.

"You've been drifting in and out. And talking. We couldn't understand much of it. But you did keep saying *The Brotherhood*."

She takes the cloth from his forehead, wrings the water out into the basin and replaces the cloth on his forehead. "The Brotherhood. Why were you talking about that?"

The boatmaker looks at the ceiling. It seems to him that there are things everyone on the Mainland understands—everyone except him. Perhaps even this nurse, a nun who looks not yet twenty.

Though he could speak, he asks for water with his hands. She shakes her head. "And you have had visitors."

The boatmaker tenses under the plaster and bandages. The pain returns. He assumes Crow and White came back to finish him off. He has no idea why they would do that. Then again, he doesn't know why they assaulted him in the first place—the men he thought were his friends.

"Who?" he croaks.

"Father Robert, and the one they call Neck." She smiles at the memory.

"*Who?*"

"Father Robert. A wonderful man. He often visits the sick here. No matter how ill or poor they are, regardless of whether they have friends or family. Even the doctors admire him—and they are not easy to impress." She smiles. "Neck is one of those Father Robert has saved. You'll understand why he's called Neck when you meet him. His name is Brother George."

"Why?"

"Why what?"

"Why did they visit me?"

"To help you. And to save you." As she speaks, he sees how young she is. Younger even than he had thought: maybe only seventeen. Calm and competent even so.

"And I would say you could use a bit of saving, judging from the way you came here. Are you fond of drink, then?"

The boatmaker says nothing. He wonders whether a cloud of alcohol was sweating out of him as she dressed his wounds. Out of a man who had decided, firmly, that he wasn't going to drink on the Mainland. He groans.

"What?"

When he doesn't answer, she props pillows under him, goes into the hall, returns with a bowl and begins feeding him beef broth, a little at a time from a heavy, nicked hospital spoon.

Taking in the soup, the boatmaker puts his feet, tentatively, on the path that leads back to the world. Broth spills into dark stubble on his face, and she wipes it away with a clean cloth.

At first he is awake only an hour a day, then two, then a few hours, which he spends watching the stripe of light. Then he is awake for almost a whole day, waiting for the sound of her steps in the hall.

He is not listening for her because he wants to be saved. The boatmaker has no interest in being saved. For him, being saved can mean only one thing at this moment: not drinking. And he doesn't see how anyone can help him do that; it seems like something he must do for himself.

But he can tell the sister wants to see him saved, and he is willing to hear whatever she has to say, because he is grateful to her. And he is grateful for something else. Saved or not, he will be able to take care of himself. Though his jaw and several ribs are broken, his hands are unharmed.

When he has been sitting up for a full day, is nearly ready to get out of bed to try to walk, the nurse comes in to inform him that his visitors have returned. She asks whether he wants to see them. He tells her that he does. He would like to know who wants to save him.

The first man to enter is of medium height, taut and well-built, with a body like a wrestler's: strong arms and a chest larger than you would expect for his height. He is wearing the black robe of a priest, belted at the waist, a square of white showing through the collar. He is blond, with sharp blue eyes behind steel-rimmed glasses. His movements are graceful and purposeful. He is a man accustomed to being obeyed. The man behind him and to one side is shorter, almost squat, wearing a much-lived-in woolen robe and leather sandals. His head, tilted to one side, joins his shoulders directly. He has no neck.

The boatmaker feels himself staring at the neckless man, then pulls his gaze back to the priest. The priest is examining the boatmaker's discolored face with a look much like that of the doctors who visit patients in the afternoon: kind but distant, evaluating the patient's state against a large body of unshared knowledge.

"How are you feeling, brother?"

"Alright."

"I am glad to hear it. You must be on the mend. We came to visit you several times when the outcome was very much in the balance. I'm sure you don't remember."

Nothing in this requires an answer; the boatmaker offers none. The sheer novelty of having visitors is receding. Now he wants to know what has brought these men to his bedside. He is curious—and suspicious. The beating he took from Crow and White has changed something in the boatmaker.

"Pardon my rudeness," says the priest. "You must be wondering who we are. We feel we know you already, having been here with you when you were struggling for your life. But of course you do not know us. I am Father Robert. And this," he says, turning toward the neckless man, "is Brother George."

"I am," says the other, bowing slightly, hands clasped in a gesture that might express prayer or embarrassment. His hands are strong and rough, the hands of a man who works the soil, the brown nails cracked and broken.

"I am Brother George, but you may call me Neck. Everyone does, sooner or later." The man named for what he does not have laughs. His head is broad, his brown hair close-cropped, his nose dented as if he had been a boxer. It is a face difficult not to like: the face of a man who is not pretending to be anything other than what he is.

The neckless face makes the boatmaker want to weep. He holds himself still. I must be getting soft, he thinks, lying here in this bed. Soft like the bed itself, or the young nurse. Everything around him is soft. He knows he must harden himself, rise and walk, rejoin the world before he splits open like a milkweed pod at the end of summer, revealing soft seeds.

He struggles up and pushes the covers off. His visitors look at each other, wondering whether they should call the nursing sister to prevent the man in the bed from rising.

Instead, they decide without a word to move to him and steady him as he attempts to rise. The boatmaker comes up shakily, braced on one side by the priest, on the other by the monk. His legs feel weak. Pain shoots through his left foot. All the blood in his body pours into his head. He is sure he will black out, fall to the floor and smash into fragments of plaster and bandages. But the strangers support him.

Holding his breath, he extends a foot from under the long nightshirt and takes a step. Pain shoots from his foot up to his head. He stops to rest. He can feel each man, left and right, smell their different smells. He takes another step, the pain and dizziness lessening. Without a word, he makes a stiff-legged, halting journey to the window and back. Father Robert and Neck help him into bed and exchange a meaningful glance above his head. The boatmaker feels tears he knows he must not shed.

"What was done to you was dreadful," the priest says, when they have covered his bruised legs with bedclothes. "A sin. Do you know who did this?"

"Crow and White." It sounds to him like someone else's voice coming from within the bandages.

"Crow and White? Odd names."

"Their real names are Kravenik and Weiss. I thought they were my friends."

"Why would they do such a thing?"

"I don't know. They asked about money. I don't know what they meant. I would have *given* them money." He laughs. It feels as though someone is breaking his ribs a second time.

"*Money*," the priest says, thoughtful, his hand on his smoothly shaved chin. "I see you are tired. You must rest and heal. We will return when you are stronger. Where will you go after this?"

"I don't know."

"Perhaps we can offer you useful work. In a godly place, where the love of money does not enter. But we can discuss that later. Until then, we pray for your recovery. All of us will pray: Brother George, myself and the rest of our brothers."

After they leave, the boatmaker spends an hour watching the stripe of light on the ceiling as it embraces, then abandons, the wavering crack. He is moved by his visitors. Not because they offered to pray for him. Nor because they promised him work. It was simply their bodily presence as they supported him in his painful journey to the windows and back. The warmth. The feeling that they would not let him fall. After watching the light a long time, the boatmaker falls asleep, worn out.

Over the next few days he begins to walk on his own, first around his room, then in the corridor outside, finally out on the grounds behind the stone wall that separates the hospital from the city. It is the beginning of winter, gray and cold. The days are already short, though no snow has fallen.

The bandages and plaster come off little by little, leaving the boatmaker bruised and swollen, white and soft in places, but intact. He even has his teeth. He runs his hand over his face and jaw, covered by rough, dark beard.

The nurse comes every day, first feeding him and changing his dressings, later just being in the room, engaging in what passes for conversation with the boatmaker. It amuses her, when she's not busy with sicker patients, to see how many words she can get out of him in one visit. When she tires of that game, she counts silently to see how many minutes he will go without giving up a word.

The boatmaker enjoys her presence, though she seems less like an angel than she did when he first came back into the world and more like an ordinary, lovely Mainland farm girl. He is beginning to be healthy enough to think of leaving. He does not know where he will go. He would like Father Robert to return and talk more about the place built by brotherhood, where the love of money does not enter.

Bundled in a blanket against the gray cold, he goes out into the hospital grounds, picks up scraps of wood, brings them back to his room and puts them in a pile on a table against the wall. He pushes the beds apart and pulls the table into the middle of the room. Then he sets to work with a clasp knife borrowed from one of the hospital workmen.

The sister sees him working and is pleased. Though she is young, she has seen many patients: those who mend and those who do not. Instinctively she knows that for this man making things with his hands is part of the road back. She comes into the room and watches without speaking.

As the boatmaker works, the great purple bruises turn blue, then green and finally fade to yellow. The soft white places become firmer.

One day he stops his work and asks the nurse for various implements; she brings them. He uses scissors to cut through the dark beard and shaves with a straight razor. He trims the thick mustache, gold mixed with darker brown. The nursing sister sees the healthy animal emerge.

When the weather has turned dry and sharply colder, the young priest returns, alone. The boatmaker is sitting at his table working scraps of wood with the clasp knife. He sets the knife down and stands up in his robe and pajamas. They are about the same height, the priest more muscular, healthier and sleeker, his blond hair combed straight back.

The boatmaker wraps himself in a blanket and the two men walk in the hospital grounds. The priest tells the boatmaker of the community called The New Land that is growing in the countryside not far from the capital. The New Land will renew the kingdom's spiritual foundation, the priest says, in the voice of a man who enjoys speaking to crowds, carrying them along with him to action. The people of the Mainland have been corrupted, fallen away from God. Even the king, defender of the faith, has been degraded. A great cleansing is needed, a new beginning in Christ. The land itself, the very earth, must be purified.

As they walk in the cold, the boatmaker feels the priest's authority. In a simple black robe, no weapon in hand, he is a warrior, a spiritual chieftain. Men would do many things for this man—almost anything.

"The men who are making the New Land are humble. They are like Brother George: close to the earth, working with their hands. We don't need the wealthy or the powerful, the nobility. They are covered in the mire of their own corruption. When we raise the banner of the Lord, they will run after us so as not to be left behind, but they will never really be with us. And we don't need them. We need men like you. You could be one of us."

"I don't know."

"You don't have to know now. There is time for you to consider my offer. But I ask you, brother, where else is there for you to go? The capital? Small Island? What awaits you in those places?"

The boatmaker has no answers. He turns and walks back to the main building, pulling his blanket tight around him.

Inside, he takes off his blanket and goes to the table where the scraps of wood are becoming a house. It is his gift for the nun: a Small Island house in miniature. Snug and close to the ground, with small rooms on two floors. He has carved the ground floor and the corner posts, the beams to support the roof. For the moment, the house is open to the sky, but he knows how the roof will be. He wonders whether she will like it. He knows it is not fancy or polished. But it is what he has to give.

As he heals, he considers the priest's invitation to become a brother on the New Land. He is drawn by the feeling he had when he stood between the priest and the peasant monk. He can see himself as a brother among men working toward the same end, and not for money, wearing a robe like the one Neck wears. Putting his hands in the dirt. Not even working in wood but in the earth. Though he knows little enough about this monastery and the brothers there, he feels in himself a growing desire to shed what he has been and join them. As he carves the pieces of his little house, feeling these things without being able to name them, he realizes that the buzzing in his head—the confusion of king, money, Jews, hate—isn't there anymore. It hasn't been since the priest invited him to join the brothers on the New Land.

He works on the house and walks the grounds, wearing his blanket. Snow falls every day, covering the dead grass. The boatmaker knows he can't stay at the hospital much longer. No one has told him he must leave or mentioned any form of payment, which is a good thing, since he has not a bill or coin. He thinks of his cache under the floorboard. Was that the money Crow was yelling about while White kicked and beat him? He wonders whether the two of them found his hiding place. It was concealed. But the room isn't big, and they would have torn his things apart. He knows that, despite his skill, nothing stays hidden forever.

One day the nurse brings him the clothes he was wearing when he was brought to the hospital. Everything has been washed and folded, mended and darned. It must all have been covered in blood, he thinks. She leaves the room, and he dresses. Everything fits, though it is all loose.

At the bottom of the pile is his sealskin pouch. The top of the bag is torn where Crow and White forced it open. Unlike his other things, the bag has not been mended. The money is gone, including the new bills from the Mint. That doesn't matter. What matters is that at the bottom his fingers touch nothing but sealskin, the seam held tight by gut thread. The handkerchief embroidered with the picture of the harbor and the three seals, which he carried next to his chest all the way from Small Island, is gone.

He can imagine how it happened, White tearing at the bag with his bear paws, Crow grabbing it away as soon as it is ripped open, pulling out the contents, pocketing the money, dropping bag and handkerchief near the boatmaker's unconscious body. A passerby finding him and calling for help to rush the injured man to surgery. One of the Samaritans picking up the bag, thinking it must be valuable, and piling it on the stretcher with the boatmaker, in the urgency of the moment not noticing the handkerchief. The handkerchief lying in the rain under the wheels of pushcarts, under shoes and boots, until nothing is left but a few threads, green and white. Finally even the threads washed down between the cobbles to the sewer drain at the end of the alley and from there to the mighty flux named for Vashad. As he imagines this slow progression of decay, the boatmaker feels he is taking a beating ten times worse than the one White's giant fists delivered. After it is over, he is as empty as the sealskin bag.

When the nursing sister returns, she sees that he is dressed in his own clothes, sitting in the chair in front of the little house he's been making from scraps of wood. At his feet is the torn sealskin bag that was with him when he came in, the thing he clutched as he floated in and out of consciousness. He seems utterly without animation. The boatmaker is often quiet, but the nurse has never seen him quite like this. She has the urge to touch the shoulder of his corduroy jacket. But she refrains and leaves the room; the sound of her shoes, squeaking on the marble floors, and the swish of fabric under her white skirt trail behind her. When she comes back, hours later, the boatmaker has not moved. She decides to send for Father Robert.

When the priest arrives with Neck, the boatmaker is lying on his bed, fully dressed. He has not eaten or slept since he discovered the handkerchief was missing. He has gotten up only to drink a little water and use the chamberpot. The priest stands over the bed, looking down at the slight man in his corduroy jacket. It is the first time he has seen the boatmaker in his own clothes. Neck stands behind him.

The boatmaker has no idea why the priest has come at this moment—but he knows it is the right moment. When he sees the two men of God, the desire to be part of something larger than himself surges up in him like the sea surging and foaming around Small Island. Life has exhausted him. He cannot survive any longer living for himself alone. He has come to a place of terrible dryness. If he does not find his way out of it, he will die.

Father Robert, who has brought many to the light, knows more than to give a long sermon at this moment. All he says is: "Are you ready to join us, brother?"

The boatmaker looks up and sees a softness in the rounded face, a brotherly welcome in the blue eyes.

"There may be a special role for you there," says the priest. "An important calling. I can see it in you. Isn't that right, Brother George?"

The neckless man steps out from behind the priest. "Yes, Father. Very special. I see that too."

"Now, brother, will you join us?"

The boatmaker, feeling his tears beginning to flow at last, can only nod.

CHAPTER 13

After Father Robert and Neck leave, the boatmaker lifts himself up, sits on the edge of the hospital bed and cries silently. He has not cried since his brother drowned off Small Island. After that, he felt he had to care for his mother, even though she seemed more angry than sad and pushed him away when he came near. To protect her he stopped crying, has not cried since. Until now, when he feels a hot gratitude to Father Robert and Neck for finding him in his darkness.

The men from the New Land are to return the next day. That evening the boatmaker eats again and smiles at the nurse. After dinner he goes back to his work on the miniature house. He works through the night, feeling the pleasure of working in wood return, renewed. When the weak winter sun appears, the house is finished, the walls up, roof on and door hung amid a pile of wood scraps. He has left the front of the house open so the nurse can reach in and arrange the furniture he has carved for her: beds, chairs and tables.

The house is the one where he stayed with the woman of Small Island when he was ill. There are private jokes carved in the gift. A wheelbarrow sits by the side of the house. Three salmon hang from the knob on the front door by a thread through their gills. The nurse will not get these jokes, but she will feel his gratitude in the thing he has made.

The priest and Neck come for him and bring him out into the country in a farm wagon on roads covered with snow. The community is set by itself, surrounded by fields and close to a stream. The cold is harsh; the animals are already in the barns for the winter. The boatmaker is given a bed in a room with many other men and a robe like Neck's.

He has been looking forward to being among brothers working together. But he has come to the New Land at the time of year when life slows and much energy goes to staying warm. The men take their meals in silence in the refectory at heavy wooden tables while one of the brothers who can read sits on a stool at the front and reads from the Gospels. The boatmaker is surprised to find that Neck is a frequent reader; he had assumed

Neck was unlettered. The neckless man reads in a warm, clear voice from the witness of Matthew. Neck asks the boatmaker whether he would like to read. He declines.

The snow deepens. Time begins to stand still. The boatmaker finds quiet corners and reads the Gospels, swept up in their repetition, their strangeness, the unknowability of Jesus, the acts of magic that seemed designed to impress His audiences but in which the carpenter of Nazareth appears to have little interest. He goes for long walks through the snow with Neck, both bundled against the cold, the boatmaker wearing his tall woodcutter boots, Neck in his sandals.

Neck shows him the fields where the cattle will be pastured in the spring, the pens for goats and pigs. In the warm weather, the ducks will wander freely but will usually stay close to the pond that is now under two feet of snow and visible only in ghostly white outline. He shows the boatmaker where the bees, now inside, will be kept.

Their long walks often end in the square that lies in the center of the New Land. On one side is a small church made of boards painted white, on the other a handsome two-story building of local stone housing the office and living quarters of Father Robert and the few administrators who keep the community's books and manage its common funds. None of the brothers owns anything: A brother will give his robe and sandals freely to anyone in need of them.

On a cold winter day Neck and the boatmaker stop into the church. Inside it is empty and cold. There are no images, none of the stained glass that provides the beautiful colored illumination in most churches, the warmth and fire. Yet when Father Robert preaches, as he does every Sunday and sometimes during the week, the room blazes with light and color.

The pews are divided in thirds by two rows of thin white columns that support the roof. Neck and the boatmaker go to the front and sit in the first pew. Facing them is a simple lectern, behind that a large round window of clear glass. Strips of lead radiate from the window's center, crossed by other strips in widening circles around the central point. The window looks like a map of the world seen from the pole.

The two men sit in silence. Neck's eyes are closed. His lips move slightly. The boatmaker wishes he knew how to pray. He assumes he will learn in his new home. Outside, snow falls heavily, as it has for many days. The outside world is as white as the walls of the church, covered in quiet. The boatmaker closes his eyes and recites to himself the words of one of the prayers he is learning. It does not feel satisfying. He waits until Neck is finished, and the two of them go back out into the snow that is already covering the prints they made when they entered.

The snow accumulates in drifts as tall as the sheds. The animals go into the fields less and less, until they never leave the barns at all. The air in the barns is thick with animal breath, animal smells. The animals are never eaten on the New Land, but they are occasionally sold in a nearby town for cash. With the proceeds, Father Robert directs Neck to purchase salt, tea, nails and other essentials. Aside from these few purchases, the New Land survives on what it makes or grows.

As winter deepens, the meals in the refectory dwindle. Fresh fruits and vegetables are long gone. Then fruits and vegetables preserved from the golden summer begin to disappear. The stored grain goes slowly, but one day there is no more bread. Toward the end, only turnips, potatoes and carrots from the root cellars are left, along with dried lentils. The brothers eat stew made from these root vegetables day after day, a little less in their bowls each week.

The boatmaker is amazed at how little grumbling there is despite the lean rations. There is some. The brothers are human, after all. It is cold and their diet puts them not too far from starvation. But as he looks across the dark tables while Neck reads from the Gospel of Matthew, he sees that these unshaven men in their stained robes, many unable to read the words they are hearing over their vegetable stew, believe honestly and deeply in the New Land and Father Robert. And if following him means eating gruel made from potatoes and lentils for weeks in the deepest winter, that is what they will do. It is unlike any other group of men the boatmaker has ever seen or heard about.

As the brothers' meals shrink to nothing, the snow subsides. The days begin to be more than a brief interlude between acts of darkness. Tentatively at first, the animals leave the barns. The earth unfreezes. Snow comes again, but not as heavily, and it melts quickly. The brothers walk the fields, seeing where fences need repairing. They plan the first plantings and prepare to move the bees back out under the trees.

One evening, as they prepare for the evening meal, Father Robert joins them. The priest has not joined the brothers for a meal in weeks and has done so only occasionally over the winter. The boatmaker is far from the inner circle of the New Land, but even he has heard the murmured gossip from Neck and one or two others. Some say the priest has been fasting much of the winter—not every day, but many days in a row. Others say he is not fasting at all, that he is gone for long periods to the capital, where he meets in secret with supporters of the New Land: wealthy and powerful benefactors who believe in the priest and his mission of purging, renewal and purification.

When the priest enters the hall, he does look thinner to the boatmaker's eyes. He was never fat, but his face, which had been rounded, is more sharply defined, his eyes a heightened blue like the sky of a perfect summer day. He is pale, but it is a paleness underlain by fire.

"Brothers," he says, towering over them where they sit at their benches, "kneel and pray with me."

There is a shuffling of sandals and benches as thirty or more monks stand and then kneel as a herd.

"Father, hear our prayer from this New Land dedicated to You. The season for planting draws close. We ask You to make us ready, not only to sow but also to receive seed. We would be fertile in Your name, Father—this land and these men. Bless the beasts of the field whom You have entrusted into our care. Bless us, who have placed ourselves in Yours. Give us Your Grace so that this harvest is fruitful. Bring us a yield beyond what earthly hands can make, what earthly eyes can see. Grant our request that this season be the beginning of a special planting, cultivation and harvest. In Your name, amen."

"Amen" rumbles from the throats of the kneeling monks in an unmusical chorus. The boatmaker, who bows his head only sometimes during prayers, and rarely keeps his eyes closed, has the feeling Neck is watching him.

Not long after Father Robert's prayer, the rituals of plowing and sowing begin. The brothers work long hours, collapsing exhausted at night with little conversation, sometimes dispensing even with prayers and reading from the Gospels. When the planting is done, there is a lull, and the brothers sleep deeply in the fresh spring nights. The days lengthen and warm; female animals are heavily pregnant.

As the first shoots come out of the earth, the boatmaker finds in himself a love for what is growing from the earth that he has never known before. In particular, the lettuces draw him. There are six or seven varieties, from small mottled dark-green leaves that will form a head no bigger than a man's fist all the way to big pale floppy heads that will be capable of filling a child's arms when they are ripe. Each variety forms in its own way and at its own pace. The way each one knows exactly what it is fascinates the boatmaker.

He spends hours making sure that each plant has a good mound of dirt around it, that each pyramid is moistened at the right time, that caterpillars and slugs are picked off young plants, chopped to pieces and returned to the earth. He fights an ongoing war with insects and with hares. Some nights he sits under a big oak near the lettuce field, dozing, shotgun across his knees, waiting for the hares. But they rarely appear when he is there.

During the day, Neck comes to him carrying a heavy old wooden bucket with a ladle in it. The water is drawn from a small springhouse enclosing a spring that bubbles up at all seasons within a low circle of stone. Neck stops to offer the boatmaker cool, clear water and chat before moving on to his next task.

Though the misshapen man is not the brightest or shrewdest brother on the New Land, he seems to have more of the confidence of the young priest than anyone else. At Father Robert's order he goes all over the community, even into the capital. And everywhere he goes, Neck carries his belief in Father Robert. His faith in the priest and his cause is a light that connects all the brothers. To the eye, Neck seems like a creature from underground: neckless, snuffling and blind. Yet he is capable of bringing light up into the day where other men, less broken, dwell.

Aside from Neck, offering cool springwater from his bucket, the boatmaker talks to few of the brothers. Yet he is never alone. Around him the others are tending vegetables, orchards, goats, the chickens in their runs, the bees in their hives under a grove not far from where he walks slowly up and down the rows of lettuces with his hoe and watering can.

At their meals, which are growing steadily richer with the fruits of the season, the brothers listen to the Gospels. On Sundays they gather in the white church to hear Father Robert preach in front of the big round window with its polar map. The priest returns again and again to the virtues of silence and obedience, which go together like root and leaf. But as he listens, the boatmaker does not feel obedient. He knows he may never be, no matter how hard he tries. Silence, however, is in his nature. It is one of the reasons being at the New Land makes him feel he has come home.

As the year turns forward and the lettuces bloom, Father Robert shows special interest in the New Land's newest brother. From time to time he invites the boatmaker up to his office overlooking the central square. His office is on the second floor of the administration building, the only stone building on the grounds, quite old, made of the same dark brown stone used to build the Mint and many of the other royal buildings in the capital. When Neck calls him, the boatmaker tilts his hoe into his wheelbarrow, brushes his hands on his robe and walks slowly through fields now green and lush, past the springhouse, past the chapel, into the square.

He climbs stone stairs to the second floor and enters the office. The priest is sitting behind a heavy desk of dark mahogany. He looks up as the boatmaker comes in, puts some papers in a folder, closes it and gestures the boatmaker to sit. A carafe and tumblers stand on a side table of the same dark wood.

The priest gets up, fills a glass and hands it to the boatmaker. Moisture condenses in fat drops on the rounded glass ridges of the pitcher. The water from the spring is cold and delicious, with a metallic taste from deep in the earth. The priest goes back behind his desk and sits down. Father Robert never seems to hurry; his deliberate movements are part of his power. Often in the priest's presence the boatmaker feels he is being weighed and measured. That makes him suspicious. Yet he is grateful to Father Robert for bringing him to the New Land: for the calm, for the silence, the brotherhood—and because he feels no need to drink.

As he drinks his springwater, the boatmaker takes in the secretary against the wall behind the priest. It is a beautiful piece of work, probably a hundred years old and taller than a man. Most of the wood is walnut, inlaid with oak and woods the boatmaker has never seen, from trees that do not grow on the Mainland. Above are shelves behind glass-fronted doors, held by a lock with an old-fashioned key protruding. Below the shelves is a desk. The writing surface folds up to conceal drawers and pigeonholes.

"You like this secretary?" asks the priest, bringing the tips of his fingers together in front of his chest to form a globe.

The boatmaker says nothing.

"Of course you do. You are a man of wood—and it is a beautiful piece of work. From the famous House of Lippsted, no less." He looks intently at the man from Small Island.

The boatmaker is silent. He says nothing. The priest continues as if he has not expected an answer.

"Yes, a beautiful piece of work. Not a nail, not a screw in it. No metal but the key, lock and hinges for the doors. Made not just with wood—but with secrets. Clever. Clever as the devil. Ironic that it should be here." The priest smiles a knowing smile and swivels to face the secretary.

The two men, one blond, one dark, look into their own reflections in the glass-fronted doors, as if this piece of furniture, with its immaculate craftsmanship, made in a workshop thirty miles away, could tell them why they are sitting here.

"If only the Jews had stuck to making furniture," says the priest, swiveling to face the boatmaker, "we would all be so much better off. But they cannot stay away from money."

The boatmaker has no more interest in Jews and money. When he came to the New Land he left all those questions behind.

"But I didn't ask you here to talk about furniture. Or about the Jews. Or even about the House of Lippsted. I wanted to find out how you are doing on the New Land."

"I am grateful to you, Father, for bringing me here."

"So you have said. And that is a worthy sentiment. But before long you may have a chance to show your gratitude in a more concrete way."

"More concrete?"

"Yes."

"How?"

"That is a longer conversation. For another time," says the priest. He leans back in his chair, brings his fingertips together in the globe. The look he had in the hospital returns: an evaluation of the boatmaker against a great body of unshared knowledge.

The boatmaker has intense feelings for the young priest. Gratitude. Devotion. A willingness to do anything for the man who brought him here to the green shoots of lettuce, the springhouse and the silent companionship of his brothers. He feels embarrassed at how little of this he is able to express. He knows he has said before that he is grateful. Why can't he say more of what he feels? He knows he is stubborn. He is sure he is far from being saved.

"We will speak soon, my son," the priest says, his blue eyes sharp. "Until then, do me one favor."

"What is that, Father?"

"Please pay close attention to your dreams."

"My dreams?"

"You do dream, don't you? I think everyone does, from time to time."

"Yes, sometimes." From his life, the boatmaker remembers only a few dreams, the dream of the blue wolf by far the most important.

"As a favor to me, pay close attention to your dreams. When you have something to tell me, you may come here at any time."

As he stands to leave, the boatmaker notices something he hadn't seen when he entered. On a corner of the broad mahogany desk is a copy of *The Brotherhood*, the newspaper the tall man at the Mint was reading. He wants to ask the priest about the paper: who publishes it, who reads it, what connects the violent man at the Mint to this young man of peace. He stops himself. There is a barrier around Father Robert that does not invite questions. The boatmaker walks out and down the stairs, sweating under his robe.

It is a fine day. Hot and spacious, good for things that are growing. In the field, the lettuces are green and strong, anticipating summer. The boatmaker walks between the heads, some light, some mottled, some dark. He is still moved by the young leaves. His feelings for them are different from the feelings he has for wood. Wood calls him to shape, act, make: It calls forth his power. The lettuces he simply allows to have their way, providing as much of the right soil and moisture as he can, protecting them from insects and hares. The rest, they do on their own.

As he goes up and down the rows of leaves, thinking about the talk he has just had with the young priest, he sees the hare has been back. Some of the young heads are gone. Some show scalloped indentations. The boatmaker decides he will spend the night under the oak tree near the field, with a shotgun in the lap of his robe. There will be a large moon. And it should be clear, a good night to put an end to the hare once and for all.

He has come to believe there is only one hare: a big gray-brown animal, a cunning trespasser, a wily survivor who knows enough not to take everything at once, never to be seen in daylight. Although the brothers do not eat the animals they raise, a hare is different. It would go a long way in the kitchen. Even the fur would be useful as a collar for Father Robert's cloak in winter, soft brown and white against black wool almost as fine as silk.

The boatmaker feels rather than hears Neck come up behind him with the bucket. He turns around, and the neckless man offers him springwater. He takes one ladle, then another. When Neck turns to go toward the springhouse to refill his bucket, the boatmaker puts down his hoe and walks with him. They pass the beehives, which are under the trees and out of direct sunlight. A brother wearing heavy gloves and a veiled helmet moves slowly among the hives, holding a piece of honeycomb. The bees' low hum mixes with the wind in the trees.

Inside the springhouse it is dark and quiet, with the smell of wood that is always wet. The men take off their robes, get down on their knees, reach into the clear cold spring, splash themselves, then sit on the low stone wall surrounding the water, wearing only sandals. They sit awhile in silence, listening to the water gurgle. "What did the father say?" Neck asks.

"He asked me to attend to my dreams."

"He did?" Neck seems interested. The incline of his head is now just right, like a stopped clock at the moment it is correct.

"I don't dream much. I don't want to disappoint him."

"You won't disappoint him. Father Robert is rarely wrong. He sees more than others do in us—because he loves us."

The boatmaker considers this for a moment. Then he asks: "How did you come to be here?"

"Like you."

"What do you mean?"

"I was in hospital—the one you were in. Maybe even the same room. I'm not sure. This was quite a few years ago. I was still a boy. And already I wasn't a beauty. Never did have much of a neck." He laughs.

"I was kicked in the head by a horse on my father's farm. So now, not only do I not have a neck, but my head is permanently off to one side. And not only that, even if I recover and live, maybe I won't be right in the head. Not that I was so very swift before." He laughs a laugh without bitterness.

"While I was in the hospital, my parents decided they had had enough of me. God will forgive them. They had enough troubles already. Plenty of troubles."

The boatmaker is angry at the cowardice of Neck's parents, surprised that his friend is not. The two men get up and put on their robes. Neck fills his bucket and they step out of the springhouse and stand in the sun. The warmth feels good after the cold water.

"Father Robert found me in the hospital and brought me here when I was healed enough to come. The New Land was just starting. There were only a few brothers. All that was here was the main building. Father Robert made all of this happen," Neck says, gesturing to the fields with his ladle.

"He's powerful, you know. And I don't just mean spiritual power. He has that. But he has more. I know he seems like he's just a young priest, but he gets things done. In the real world. He has powerful friends. He is pure—but not unworldly. He knows a great deal that you and I can only guess at. And we don't need to know. He knows it for us. Don't worry about disappointing him. He sees who you are. I'm sure of it. Otherwise, he wouldn't have asked what he asked."

That night the boatmaker sits under the oak tree, shotgun on his knees, waiting for the cunning old hare to show itself. He doesn't care for guns: the noise, the way they jump. He prefers tools for working in wood, which make no sound and respond to the pressure of a hand. If you work with those tools long enough, they become part of you, like an arm or a finger. He can't imagine a shotgun ever becoming part of him. Still, every man on Small Island knows how to use one. And he's not unhappy to have the weight of it in his lap as he sits between the roots of the oak, promising himself he will stay awake until the hare appears. It's a warm clear night with a yellow moon, almost full, rising over the lip of the earth. The wind whispers the oak leaves. The bees are quiet.

He wakes with a start under the fat moon, now up over the horizon and turning silver. A big brown hare is making his way between the green heads, snuffling and chewing forward. In waking, the boatmaker must have made a sound, because the hare leaps away in a huge bound. The boatmaker raises the shotgun and fires at the place where the hare was, then discharges the other barrel out of sheer disgust at himself for having fallen asleep. Wisps of smoke curl toward the moon.

As he sits holding the cooling gun, he realizes he has woken out of a powerful dream. In his dream he was alone in the springhouse. The water was the same as in daylight: clear and gurgling. But a huge round wooden pole, like one of the posts of the telegraph the king is sending into every corner of the kingdom, rose out of the earth next to the spring. The post went up high into the darkness near the roof. The legs and feet of a man tied to the pole were hanging down.

The boatmaker cannot see the face or the upper body, hidden in darkness near the roof of the springhouse, but he knows that it is Jesus Christ, dressed in the robe of a brother on the New Land. The robe lifts slowly of its own accord to reveal calves, knees and feet. In each calf the flesh has opened like a wound. But there is no blood. Instead, salmon spill from the parted flesh, first one or two, nosing their way out, then more and more until an entire school is pouring, falling with a continuous splash into the spring. The far wall of the springhouse lifts, and the boatmaker can see that the spring now extends all the way to the sea. The salmon, thousands now, a gigantic school, roil the water, thrashing and swimming, breaking the surface in a spray that covers their flashing silver bodies, a churning mass on their way to an invisible home.

CHAPTER 14

Two days pass before the boatmaker is ready to go to Father Robert and speak of his dream. At dinner in the refectory he half-hears Neck reading from Matthew about the lilies that neither spin nor toil yet are arrayed more finely than Solomon. At night, the hare raids the lettuces, but the boatmaker is no longer at war.

On the third day, he climbs the steps to Father Robert's office. He has never been up the stairs before without having been called and he can feel his heart beating in his arms and legs. He stops outside the heavy oak door, which stands open a few inches. He pauses, feeling an itching discomfort spread through his body. He knocks and hears the young priest ask him to enter.

In the office all is as before: the heavy desk, the side table holding the pitcher and tumblers, the secretary, its shelves filled with books on the Gospels and the history of the Mainland dating back to the seafaring kings, files in neat piles on the desk.

Father Robert is calm, but also expectant. The silent man from Small Island can have come for only one reason: because he has had the dream the priest is waiting for. The circle will be joined, the priest thinks. The Brotherhood, sheathed in secrecy in the capital, has lodged its faith in him. That faith has been justified, as he knew it would be. Father Robert knows he is only the one who comes before, that standing before him is the thing itself: message and messenger in one. Still, pride swells him as lust would swell the body of an ordinary man. He wants urgently to ask. But he maintains his composure, gesturing the boatmaker to sit in the chair and then returning to his own. Beneath the fine black robe and the coarse white one, both men sweat.

"You said I should come and tell you if I had a dream."

"Yes." The priest's hands form the globe.

"I was afraid I would disappoint you."

"And have you?" The young priest is attentive, confident.

"I don't know. I did have a dream, though. The other night, in the field, when I went out to kill the hare that's been eating the lettuces." The boatmaker feels as if he is babbling. The priest flexes the globe of fingers and smiles to show that his patience is large, his spirit untroubled.

"And your dream?"

"I was in the springhouse."

"The springhouse." This is a new twist. But the priest knows the rest, at least in essence.

"There was a pole, like a telegraph pole, standing up next to the spring. A man was on it."

"A man?"

"Tied to the pole. It was dark. I could only see his legs."

"And what did you see?"

"There were cuts in his legs. Deep cuts. But no blood came out. Instead, fish were coming out of the cuts. Salmon. A whole school of them. The wall of the springhouse lifted up, and they swam out to the sea."

The priest is quiet, listening; the boatmaker feels that his dream is foolish, that he has wasted the priest's time.

"And how did you feel in all this?"

"I could hardly move."

"And after that?"

When the boatmaker is silent, the priest says gently: "Go on, my son."

"I wanted to leave my body behind. Take it off, the way you take off your clothes. I wanted to be there with the salmon, swimming away. And then I was grateful. Very grateful."

The priest leans back in his chair, closes his eyes, fingertips touching. All is well. He has found the needed fourth; the deep spiritual work can begin. He admonishes himself to avoid the sin of pride, reminds himself that he is merely a tool—and one of many, at that. It is little more than chance that he has been selected for this role, not a reward for any particular virtue. Unlikely as it might seem to the world, the priest thinks, the rough little man across the desk is far more important than the young and polished man of God.

In spite of these cooling and temperate thoughts, Father Robert cannot help the pride that warms and excites him. He is a fisher of men, a skilled fisherman. He has found them all, landed them, wriggling, at the end of his line in the name of Father, Son and Holy Spirit. They are all different, these little men, each with his own strange twist. This one with his springhouse and salmon. Fish springing from His wounds! It is almost blasphemous. It *is* blasphemy.

Still, he tells himself, he cannot judge. He has not been entrusted with the full plan. But he has been given a critical role. And he has fulfilled what has been asked of him: He found the fourth. The circle is closed. He has merited the trust of The Brotherhood, men who are powerful and wise in the ways of the world, who will help bring the young priest's vision out of this monastery and into every corner of the kingdom.

The priest opens his eyes and smiles at the small man from the tiny island at the end of the world and says: "My son, I am pleased with you."

After his visit to Father Robert, the boatmaker feels that the brothers are treating him differently. A zone of silence seems to surround him. And within that zone he also feels himself changing. Over a dinner rich with the fruits of summer, the words of Matthew now sound strange and ominous. The buzzing in his head returns. Only Neck remains the same, visiting the boatmaker in the field with his bucket to ask how he is faring.

The Sunday after the boatmaker recounts his dream, Father Robert preaches in the chapel. Bright summer light pours through the polar window behind him. Most of the thirty or more brothers are present, but even on Sundays there are chores that will not wait. As hymns are sung and the service proceeds, a few brothers make their way out and down the aisle; others enter from the fields to take their places. The boatmaker is sitting two-thirds of the way back, not wishing to draw attention to himself.

But as Father Robert begins his sermon, the boat-maker feels as if the priest is speaking directly to him. He even feels the priest looking at him, though the brilliance of the round window behind Father Robert means that all the boatmaker can see is a dark form within a glowing aura.

"Despair," Father Robert begins, in a voice so low the brothers must lean toward the round window to hear. "Despair is the greatest sin against Our Lord. Despair." He pauses to let the words sink in.

"There are many other sins. Sins we have all come to the New Land to rid ourselves of. The love of money, which, as Paul says, is the root of all evil. The sins of lust, which are as many and varied as the folds of a leper's skin, turning a man into a creature as low as one of the fat worms that burrow through our rich soil on the New Land. Think of these worms: You know them."

A rustle of recognition ripples through the congregation. Indeed, they all know the fat glistening worms, coated in translucent slime, that wriggle blind through the dark earth.

"You know these worms. They are wonderful—in their place. They aerate our soil, leave their waste behind and help us grow our crops. In a sense, they lie beneath everything we do in this community. And the Lord must love them, because He made them so well-suited to their task and made the efforts of us, his children, depend upon them. For in their absence, our crops would be poor shriveled things."

Father Robert bends down behind the lectern and comes up holding a glass jar of the kind the brothers use to preserve fruits and vegetables. The sun is higher, no longer coming straight in through the radial window, and the brothers can see that the bottom half of the jar is filled with fat earthworms crawling over one another. The priest unscrews the lid, reaches in, pulls out a long, fat worm and lets it dangle from his clean white fingers.

"Look, brothers. We know God must love these creatures. Without them the New Land would shrivel up like the Valley of Dry Bones. But look again! And ask yourself: Who among you would trade places with even the fattest earthworm?"

He shakes the long worm hanging at the end of his fingers. It curls and shakes, its slime glistening in the light from the round window.

"*Who among you would be one of these?*" He waits, but there is no response aside from a shuffling of sandals.

"Not one. Not one of you would be a worm in our soil." He lowers the worm slowly back into the jar, screws the lid on, replaces the jar in the lectern, reaches into a pocket at the front of his robe, pulls out a large, clean white handkerchief and wipes his hands.

"And yet that is what lust makes of you: a worm, wriggling and crawling in your own slime. Nor is lust the only sin that reduces you to something far down the ladder of His creation. *Anger.* Your rage against your fellow sinners. Many of you are familiar with that sin from your former lives. *Drink.* Some of you know that one too. Many a man who sits in this sanctified place have I picked up in my arms in the streets of the great city in drunken unconsciousness, covered in his own bodily wastes, and carried to the New Land to be bathed, cleansed and risen into a new life." The priest's voice has lowered and become that of a mother. Every man in this chapel can imagine being gathered in his arms, bathed and brought into the light.

"But none of these sins, bestial as they are, compare to the sin of *despair*," Father Robert says, his voice rising and gaining strength. Now it is the voice of a father, not a mother.

"All the other sins may reduce you to the level of a beast, brothers. Sometimes to the level of a warm-blooded beast, with a pumping heart and a backbone. Sometimes all the way down to the level of one of our flexible glistening friends here—with no backbone, wriggling in excrement. That low, brothers, *even that low*, sin can take you. And any of these sins may lead you to desecrate yourself, tear your family—your wife and loving children—to shreds.

"And yet, and yet . . ." He takes out his broad white handkerchief and wipes his hands. Then he grasps the lectern and looks squarely at his congregation, who are hushed and still, following every word.

"Yet despair is worse than any of these sins, brothers. Much worse. It may not seem so. After all, these other sins burn the sinner and his loved ones, scarring the landscape of his life like a forest fire raging out of control, leaving nothing but blackened, charred stumps. Despair, on the other hand, may seem small—quiet and innocent—meaning harm to no one. The man in despair may seem only passive and sad. Weak. Oppressed by himself. Worthy of our pity. Of the charity Our Savior offered even the weakest among us: not just a second chance, but a third chance, and a fourth chance, chance after chance until the end of time. Despair, the quiet man's disease, *would seem, then, to hurt no one.* And yet it is the gravest, wickedest sin of all."

Father Robert pauses, reaches down into the lectern, brings up a glass of water and drinks, letting his words sink in before putting the glass away. His sermons are always full of passion. But he seems to be pouring his full power into this one.

"And why, brothers, is despair such a great wickedness, when it seems so harmless? *Because the man who despairs seals himself away from God, away from Our Savior's healing mercy.* The man who despairs is arrogant—with an arrogance greater than most of us sitting here can imagine. We can imagine lust, sloth, drunkenness. All of them—easily. But this arrogance is beyond the comprehension of most of us. Enfolded in himself, the despairing man substitutes his pitiful human personality for the Creator and His Creation. The despairing man says: I know Salvation is not possible. I know that only darkness is real. I know the universe is empty and dead—nothing more than an elaborate mechanism, beautifully carved furniture: finite and inanimate. The despairing man offers up these falsehoods as common sense when they are *the most outrageous lies. And we know them to be lies! We know Salvation, brothers! And we know that the entire Creation is alive with the light of Salvation!*"

The priest pauses, holding the edges of the lectern in a wrestler's grip, color rising in his face. Although the chapel holds the cool of the night long into the summer day, he is sweating.

"Unlike other sinners, whose sins are merely the weakness of Adam and can be repaired, as the burned forest regrows from seeds dropped into blackened soil from unburned trees nearby, the one who despairs sets his vanity, his stubbornness and his spiritual pride, above the Mercy of the Lord, rejecting the priceless offer of Salvation. That is why despair is the greatest of the spiritual disasters that can possibly befall the human soul." Now he is shouting, the words flowing straight from his wrestler's chest.

"And if there is any man here who feels the ice of despair forming in his heart, he must ask for strength from the Savior to melt that ice, ask that he be bathed in the blood of the Lamb: the hot, cleansing blood whose heat will melt the coldest of hearts, the hearts of sinners who think they are lost forever from the sight of God and condemned to drift forever in a dead, mechanical universe."

The priest rests his forearms on the lectern, allowing his head to fall forward, showing lustrous blond hair. Then he lifts his head. He is spent, sweat running down his face. "Let us pray."

After the concluding hymns, the brothers file out into the mid-morning sunshine. They walk out two by two in silence, returning from Heaven to earth. Cows must be milked, eggs collected, vegetables nourished. When they have finished any tasks that cannot be postponed, they will retreat to the refectory to read the Gospels if they can, pray silently if they cannot.

The boatmaker is in no hurry. He wants to spend time with his lettuces. He needs to be alone to turn things over, as he would examine a piece of wood, the width and straightness of its grain, the knots where branches were born. He cannot shake off his sense that Father Robert's sermon was aimed directly at him. Almost all the lesser sins the priest described—lust, drunkenness, rage—are the boatmaker's own. And now that he is somewhat freer of those, at least while he lives on the New Land, he feels the weight of his stubborn despair.

Despite the dream of the springhouse, which seemed to promise salvation, the boatmaker feels he is a fraud on the New Land, not knowing how to pray, not knowing the meaning of being saved. He is a counterfeit banknote that looks like the real thing but comes from some hustle of Crow's rather than from the Royal Mint. He loves the lettuces, the humming of the bees, the rustling of the oak leaves. He is deeply grateful to the young priest and Neck for bringing him here. He knows it has saved his life. And yet, even wearing the robe of a monk, he cannot bring himself to believe in a larger way of being saved: a saving of his soul.

For a few days he keeps to himself, not speaking even to Neck. He avoids meals, taking a crust of bread and bringing it to the field in the pocket of his robe. He goes to and from the lettuces with his wheelbarrow, hoe and watering can, turning things over again and again, struggling with the renewed buzzing in his head and the questions that have returned: about the Jews, money, the king. When he is not working, he walks the fields by himself, unable to find stillness.

Walking by the chapel, in the square between the church and the main building, he sees four of the brothers digging two deep holes. Next to the holes two poles lie in the grass, like the one the boatmaker saw in his dream of the springhouse, like the telegraph poles the king is bringing to the remote corners of the kingdom.

Over the next few days, the holes deepen. Using chocks and block-and-tackle, the brothers raise the poles and slide them in. First one pole, then the other, is raised and earth filled in around it. When the work crews are finished, the poles stand side by side, each two feet across and twenty feet tall. By the time they are raised, the boatmaker, preoccupied with his own struggles, is paying little attention. He has decided he must go to Father Robert again, to confess his doubts and his questions.

When he is finally ready, he walks up the path to the stone building slowly, his sandals pressing down the dry summer grass. The New Land is well supplied with water from the spring and from the stream that runs near the pastures, but at the height of summer the grass turns brown and brittle; it crackles under his soles. He has no clear idea of what he should say to the priest beyond knowing that he needs to confess his doubts. He thinks Father Robert could answer his questions, some of which go far beyond salvation to touch on worldly matters. But his thoughts are confused, and he is hesitant to question the priest.

He walks into the shade of the entryway and up the stone stairs, worn in the center by decades of footfalls, most recently those of Father Robert in his elegant black boots and the monks in their sandals. At the top he sees the door is open a few inches. He stands at the door, feeling all force drain from his body. He raises his hand to knock, but the door opens farther before his knuckles reach wood. Father Robert is in the doorway seeming pleased, though not surprised, to find the boatmaker standing there.

"Father . . ."

"Come in, my son," says the priest, gesturing toward the now-familiar chair and moving to the side table to pour glasses of springwater. The boatmaker sits holding his glass with both hands, trying to find the place to begin. He looks at the secretary behind the priest, with its rhythm of dark and light wood, its hidden craft.

"Father . . ."

"I know, my son. You have come with questions."

The boatmaker is so startled he feels as if the priest can see right through him to the chair he is sitting on.

"And I am here to answer your questions. Now is the time. Many things have led to this moment. Many preparations have been made."

The boatmaker opens his mouth to speak, but the priest speaks first. "And you are ready for us. Ready to join in the birth of the New Christ."

"The New Christ?"

"Yes, the New Christ. I know you have been reading the Gospels, particularly Matthew. I hope you don't mind if Neck tells me these things. He has a great love for you, Brother George. The state of your soul is of consequence to him—as it is to me and to all of us."

"I don't mind," the boatmaker stammers, utterly perplexed.

"Good. Now let me explain the New Christ—and answer the questions you have come with. You know by now that Our Savior was foreordained in the Old Testament. He was not original: He was a reconsecration, a new Adam, who made good the sin of the Old Adam and paid the debt for all mankind."

"What I wanted to know . . ." says the boatmaker, struggling to bring the conversation back to his own questions.

"You know some of the Old Testament now, and the New. You read them from the outside, as most do. But there is a great secret, brother, that is not given to all, even to those who call themselves Christians—especially not now, in these dark, fallen times. There is another way of reading: from the inside. And if you read the Book from the inside, with eyes that can see, a great secret is revealed. And that secret is that the sacrifice of the Son of Man did not end in Palestine in the first century AD. It continues in our own times—*as a living matter*. Not in the pages of a book—even the greatest of books, the Holy Book—but as *flesh and blood, living and dying, here and now.*"

The priest's voice becomes a subdued version of the voice that gave the sermon on despair: quieter but very passionate.

"The sacrifice must be renewed to lift the darkness of a new age. And you, my son, are an essential part of the renewed sacrifice Our Father has offered us: the New Christ on the New Land."

The boatmaker is stunned into silence, deeply confused. These are mighty answers indeed—but they are not answers to the questions he carried with him into this office. And what the priest is saying is so momentous he cannot begin to comprehend it.

Suddenly he is ashamed of the questions he entered this room with. He must let go of them. He must put aside his doubts, his despair, and do whatever the priest asks of him. If he does, in the end he will find answers to everything he has asked—and much more.

At this realization, the boatmaker feels as if he will break down and weep for the second time in his adult life. But he is sure such a display would be letting Father Robert down. He composes himself and listens, obedient.

The priest feels the change, and his paternal heart softens. He wants to stand and embrace the rough little man, but he cannot possibly allow himself to do that. Instead, he proceeds to explain, as gently as he can, what lies ahead. He smooths his blond hair, takes out his handkerchief and blows his nose to hide his emotion. His heart is overflowing, swimming in proud, hot gratitude. He puts the handkerchief back and continues calmly.

"We have been waiting, and now the time of renewal is at hand. Your dream is one of the final missing pieces of the puzzle. Now that you have had this dream, your life will change. You will be preparing for the moment of rebirth, the sacrifice of the New Christ."

"Why has this happened?"

"I will tell you as much as you need to know—and no more," says the priest, the question returning him to his authoritative daily self.

"In every era there is a struggle between the forces of light and the forces of darkness. It happened in the beginning, between Satan and Adam. It happened again when the Jews freed Barabbas and chose the crucifixion of Our Lord. Now the forces of darkness are again rising and undermining our nation. And the Jews are again at the center of it. The House of Lippsted, who make this beautiful furniture"—the priest gestures with his thumb over his shoulder at the secretary—"have crept into the heart of the kingdom. Through his insatiable need for the money to support his schemes for *progress*, our weak and foolish king has delivered himself into their hands. Behind closed doors, the debt of the Crown to the House of Lippsted grows and grows. They take pains to conceal it, the king and his Jews. They have broken the debt up into many small pieces—each owed to a different subsidiary of the House of Lippsted. And they believe that that way the size of the debt will remain hidden.

"But nothing remains hidden from the eyes of God!" says Father Robert, bringing his palm down on the surface of the desk.

As he feels the heat in his palm, the priest fears for a moment that he has gone too far, even for a private conversation. The division of the Crown's debt into splinters to conceal its size has never been made public. That information comes from a network of spies loyal to The

Brotherhood that reaches all the way to the palace. It would be disastrous for the network to be exposed.

Father Robert pauses, breathes in, rubs his palms together. He feels himself calming. He is almost certain that the man from Small Island is not shrewd or worldly enough to understand the implications of what the priest has said.

The boatmaker is barely listening to what Father Robert is saying about the details of the king's debt to the House of Lippsted. The man from Small Island has crossed a threshold: He will join the priest's plan for the New Christ.

"How do I fit in?"

"You have come to us when the moment is ripe," the priest says, now feeling quite secure. "There have been signs—many signs—already. Our Father is merciful. When the forces of darkness are strongest, a new Redeemer comes. Now that you have been shown to us, we will show you the rest."

The priest watches to see the effect of his words. The boatmaker is silent. He has decided to give himself to this new purpose. All he wants now is to be taught how to serve.

"Now I will show you how powerful the love of your brothers is for you," the priest says, rising and moving to the window behind the side table. "Come and see."

The boatmaker gets up, sets down his glass and goes to stand next to the priest. Father Robert puts a wrestler's arm around the boatmaker's shoulder and points with his other hand down across the square. Suspended on the poles the brothers raised in front of the chapel are Crow and White. Their arms are wrapped behind the poles, and thick ropes are tied around their chests and legs. Their eyes are open as if they are surprised. There are no marks on them. Their faces are pale. It is not easy to tell how long they have been dead.

CHAPTER 15

The day after seeing Crow and White the boatmaker is moved out of the hall where the brothers sleep. Neck leads him to a small building tucked behind the chapel. He has never paid much attention to this building, which faces the woods stretching away to the border of the New Land. Neck shows him to a small single room.

"You have been chosen to give everything. What an honor. Beyond an honor." The neckless man would like to be in the boatmaker's place, would like to give even more than he already does to Father Robert and the New Land. But he knows envy is a sin; he pushes the thought away.

The walls of the boatmaker's new room are white-washed, the pine floorboards unfinished. On the wall above the narrow iron bedstead is a crucifix. He is given a new robe, finely woven, whiter than his old one and never worn before. There will be no more work in the fields for him. Taking off his old robe, stained and gray, putting on the new one, he feels himself enter a new life. It seems as if everything he has experienced—Small Island, the woman of the town, the Mainland, money, the Jews, the New Land, the lettuces, the hare, the dream of the salmon—was intended to bring him to this moment.

He sees that in each of his experiences he has been different: sometimes meek, sometimes hard, usually silent, occasionally talking too much, often gullible, sometimes suspicious, sometimes drunk for long periods, at other times achingly sober. All these versions of himself have played their part in bringing him here; he is grateful to each of them.

He no longer eats with the other brothers. Twice a day a silent monk comes to his door carrying a wooden tray that holds a glass and a bowl or two. While the brothers in the refectory continue to have vegetables every day and often eggs, along with their grains, in his narrow room facing the woods the boatmaker's diet diminishes day by day. At first there are summer vegetables: eggplant, tomatoes, squash and greens, served with barley. Then the vegetables thin out and disappear, first the tomatoes, then the eggplant and squash. Finally his beautiful lettuces stop appearing, and nothing remains but stewed barley, washed down with cold springwater.

The boatmaker knows he is being prepared for something, but he does not know what the task will be. His understanding of what the young priest told him just before he saw Crow and White staring from their telegraph poles is unsteady, transient. Sometimes he thinks he knows the sacrifice that will be required, at other times he is lost in confusion. He works to humble himself.

His only work is reading the Gospels and praying to the crucifix on the wall over the bed. When he can pray no more, he waits for the silent brother with his wooden tray to arrive. From time to time, between his two meals, Neck comes in. For the boatmaker, these are the best times, because Neck is willing to explain a little.

Neck tells the boatmaker he is one of four brothers, each of whom has a mystic and sacred seal set upon him. Now that the seals have appeared, a revelation is at hand that will change the Mainland, then spread out to transform the world, as the death of Jesus did, radiating from Jerusalem. Father Robert has not yet been given the full meaning of the seals: There is more to come before the revelation is complete. But the priest is busy, going frequently to the capital for meetings. Neck is vague about the people the priest meets with in the city and what they discuss. But it is clear that, young as he is, Father Robert has spent years laying the groundwork for this change—and the New Land is only part of the picture.

The boatmaker wants to know more about all of it: the bigger picture the New Land is part of, the men the priest meets with in the city, the other three brothers, the seal each one bears, the nature of their task. But he knows he must be satisfied with what he is given. If he asks directly, Neck goes silent.

Over time, his eagerness for answers fades. The diet of barley gruel, water and prayer has left him at a distance from the things of this world. He stays in his cell, reading the Gospels and waiting for his task to begin, praying for the strength to do whatever is asked of him. Despite all the steps he has taken on this road, he is not certain that he has completely vanquished his own stubbornness, the spiritual pride concealed within despair. And so he prays harder, eats less.

On a hot day toward the end of summer, Neck comes to his cell with a parcel wrapped in brown paper and tied with twine. While the boatmaker has changed during his time on the New Land, the neckless man has remained exactly the same since the boatmaker first saw him, entering the hospital room behind the priest. Neck has never offered more than he is able to give, never appeared when he was not welcome, never tried to explain more than he understands.

The boatmaker looks at the package under Neck's arm, but he asks nothing. In the last few days, the world has moved even farther away. The barley gruel shrank to a spoonful in the bottom of a bowl. Then the bowl itself disappeared, and all that was left was a glass of water from the spring. At first, the boatmaker gulped it greedily. Then he measured it out, drinking a little at a time. Now he barely notices the glass when it arrives. Sometimes when the brother comes to him with the second tray, the first glass is still full.

With the package under his arm, Neck leads the boatmaker to a covered walkway outside his cell. It is the first time he has been out of his room in many days. He steps out, head feeling light. Even in the shade of the overhanging roof, the sun is blinding. He closes his eyes.

Neck takes him by the arm and guides him around a corner. He feels Neck let go. He stands there, eyes closed, hearing Neck's steps retreat, a door opening and closing, steps returning. Neck undoes the boatmaker's belt, lifts his robe, guides him forward until he feels something cool against his thighs.

"Lift up and climb in."

The boatmaker lifts his left leg and puts his foot down into water that is between warm and hot. He lifts his right leg. Neck hands him in and down.

"Let me know if it's too hot."

The boatmaker opens his eyes to see Neck standing over the metal tub with a bucket. He gives a sign that the water is fine.

Within the metal tub, his body seems long and white. His hands and arms are dark from working in the fields. There are few marks left from the beating by Crow and White. He closes his eyes, welcomes the hot water. It is the first hot bath he has had since coming to the New Land.

As tenderly as a woman, Neck bathes every inch of him. When they are done, the boatmaker steps out. Neck towels him off and walks to pick up the package wrapped in twine, which is sitting on the seat of an old green kitchen chair pushed up against the wall of the building. He cuts the twine and breaks the brown paper, bringing forth a new robe, even finer than the one the boatmaker has been wearing.

He unfolds the robe, shaking it out and pulling it over the boatmaker's head. His dark hair is wet from the bath, his bald spot larger than when he left Small Island. The new robe is snowy, immaculate. Over the left breast a heart engulfed in flames has been stitched in red thread. Inside the heart the Roman numeral IV has been worked in the same bright red.

Neck takes him by the arm and leads him, dripping, back to his cell, where he kneels in the corner. The waiting is over. Knees on the pine floorboards, he looks up at the crucifix and prays.

Two days later, Neck returns. Leaning on him, the boatmaker walks in his flaming-heart robe, feet bare, eyes closed, under the roof of the covered walkway. They pass the spot where Neck bathed him in the metal tub and arrayed him in his new finery. They turn another corner, cross grass and climb steps. At the top of the steps the boatmaker feels the presence of an open door and other people.

He lets go of Neck and opens his eyes to find that he is looking through the door of a one-room building set right at the edge of the woods. The room is simple and whitewashed, the floor covered in deep, fluffy cotton wool. On the cotton wool, sitting cross-legged, are three brothers of the New Land in the same kind of robe the boatmaker is wearing. In a low chair, holding a worn Bible, is Father Robert.

The boatmaker takes a tentative step into the room, feeling the softness of cotton wool on his feet. On the far wall is a large round window like the one in the chapel, with concentric lead strips intersected by lines radiating from the center that form a polar map overlooking the woods.

Father Robert motions for him to sit. He sees that the other three also have Roman numerals stitched within their flaming hearts. The boatmaker sits down facing I, with II on his left and III on his right. He doesn't recognize the others from his days on the New Land. Number I is tall and sinewy, with a dark beard and piercing eyes, his hair close-cropped. II and III are doughier, II dark, III a redhead with flaming hair and freckles, a type seen from time to time in the capital, displaying the blood of a tribe conquered long ago by the sea-warriors in their longships.

Each day for the next week, after praying all morning, I, II, III and IV in their flaming-heart robes are brought to sit on the cotton wool and listen to Father Robert read from the Gospels. He reads from all four accounts in turn, not starting at the beginning, but going immediately to the description each of the Gospels offers of the dark hours before the Crucifixion, when Jesus, betrayed and abandoned, wrestled with His fear, revealing that He was both human and divine.

The priest says each word loud and clear, stopping occasionally to see whether his meaning has penetrated the four men before him in their pristine robes. Between passages the priest neither explicates nor preaches. He lapses into silence and waits.

After days of living on springwater, the boatmaker's mind is aflame, his senses acute as a hare's. Beyond the wind in the trees he hears the bees in their hives. He concentrates on that low hum as he struggles to make out what the priest is trying to convey through his readings. When his brain can no longer make this effort, he looks sidelong at the brothers beside him in their flaming-heart finery. Number I is clearly the leader: vigorous and powerful, in command of himself. II and III are just as clearly followers: nervous and sweating, willing to do anything to avoid disappointing their leaders.

After a week, the boatmaker is led to the open door by Neck, feeling light not only in head but also in body. Father Robert is not present. The sun is behind the building, away from the great radial window; the room with its cotton-wool floor is in shadow. The boatmaker enters and takes his place across from I.

"Welcome, brothers," says Number I, the boatmaker hearing the leader's voice for the first time. It is a reassuring voice but not one that invites discussion.

"We are all equal here," Number I says. "Each of us is essential. The number you wear indicates no precedence. We are four-in-one, one-in-four. We shall live and die together for the New Land. Let us pray."

Number I bows his head and leads them through the Lord's Prayer. The boatmaker no longer hears the bees even though the wind is now very soft.

When they finish their prayer, Number I raises his hand and looks at each of the others in turn. "By now, I think we all understand what is required of us. It will be a slow and painful end—like that of our brother Jesus, the First Christ—but when it is finished we will be on the right hand. And by the time we reach our appointed places, having sacrificed body and blood, the great transformation, with its unstoppable force, will have begun here below. Is anyone not ready? Speak now or forever be silent, brothers." The boatmaker feels Number I looking straight at him, trying to read his Small Island heart.

"Then we are ready." Number I reaches a strong arm behind him into the cotton wool, holding the other three in his gaze. He finds what he is looking for on the floor. His hand comes around in front of his chest holding a knife with a worn wooden handle and a long, highly polished blade. The boatmaker can see there is an inscription along the blade in the ancient spiky script of the Mainland.

"Our task will be long and slow, brothers, counted in days, not hours or minutes. Blood shall flow, and be taken up. In between, we will be in our cells, praying. Then we shall return here for the next round. Toward the end, we will be carried, but we shall return as long as we draw breath."

Outside the wind dies; the oak leaves hang in ripe green clusters.

"Finally, we shall leave our husks of bodies and be swept up in a great ascent, turning and turning until we join as one and are seated at the right hand of the Father."

Number I takes the knife, holds it up before him in strong tanned hands. "I will go first."

Their leader closes his eyes, lips moving. He opens his eyes and raises the knife. Holding his nose with his left hand, he uses his strong right arm to slice off the tip. The stub of pink flesh comes away in his left hand. He holds it up, showing it to the others, as blood washes down his face.

He wipes the blade and passes it to Number II, who takes it, his soft hand shaking. Number I buries the tip of his nose in the cotton wool. Red spreads around the spot. He pulls a tuft from the floor and holds it to his face. He pulls another tuft and applies it. His bleeding slows. Over the cotton held to the tip of his nose, he looks meaningfully at Number II.

Number II closes his eyes, reaches over and slices a small tip from his left earlobe, stifling a scream. Trembling, he holds the flesh out for the others to see. He hands the blade across the circle to Number III, puts the nub of flesh into the cotton wool and pulls a tuft for his ear.

The boatmaker cannot see the wound, but he assumes it must be bleeding less than I's. III does the same to his own left earlobe. As III puts the flesh down and stanches the flow with cotton wool, the boatmaker sees that although the wound is not deep, it is bleeding heavily.

Number III hands the knife to the boatmaker, who hefts the blade and wipes it across the knee of his robe. The blade is just as he thought: a beauty, remarkable for its strength, sharpness and balance. He would like to take time to puzzle out the inscription on the blade, but he feels the eyes of the others on him, staring in anticipation, while each man presses cotton wool to his bleeding flesh.

He tests the blade with his finger; the slightest pressure draws blood. No one has explained the rules to him. What part should he cut? An earlobe, like II and III? They are followers. Presumably he should do as they did.

The boatmaker had sensed that their task might be a deep sacrifice—possibly the ultimate sacrifice. And he prayed for the strength to see it through. But now that the moment has come, it is not fear that makes him hesitate: It is the absurdity of it. What strikes him most is not the wounding or the sacrifice. It is the tiny details.

Something about the blood seeping through the cotton wool makes the room seem like something from an asylum for the insane. The boatmaker feels giddy, crazed from hunger and the scene before him. He has to stop himself from laughing or shrieking.

The urge to howl becomes almost too strong to resist. As he struggles to hold it in, the urge changes into something else: a rage like the buzzing of the bees on the New Land, growing louder and louder until it fills the sky.

Without intending to move, he finds himself standing, already moving. In two steps he is across the room, leaping over the three stunned brothers in their flaming-heart robes, dotted with blood, cotton wool falling from their hands in astonishment.

Without knowing how, he is crashing through the radial window. Glass showers around him as he hits the ground. He lands on his shoulder and rolls to his feet. Running into the woods in the fine white robe, his feet bare, is clumsy work. Blood flows from a cut on his nose, which feels as if it might have glass in it, but he does not stop to check. He is surprised that his legs carry him so well after weeks of fasting. He finds a fierce pleasure in the animal act of running away to save himself.

His bare feet slip and he falls, bruising and cutting his body, but he does not stop to inspect his wounds.

He had no idea how deeply imprisoned he felt until he crashed through the window and began running. He thought all he felt was gratitude. Number IV, he thinks. I am no one's Number IV—Father Robert's or anyone else's. He wants to rip the beautiful robe to shreds and tear out the flaming heart.

He runs until he reaches a stream at the edge of the woods. On the bank he stops and holds still, listening over the thudding of his heart. He knows Father Robert, Neck and the other brothers, with dogs and guns, will soon be after him. To his surprise, he finds the knife still in his hand.

He touches his nose, finds an open wound, probes gently with the tip of the knife and removes a shard of glass. Undoes his belt, pulls off the robe, cuts it into pieces, binds his nose with a long strip, winding it round and round his head. Wraps the knife and strips of fine white wool into a bundle he holds over his head.

As he reaches the muddy bank that leads to the stream, the crazed exhilaration that has carried him this far ebbs, and he feels pain and hunger surging in. Blackness begins to cover him, but he knows he cannot allow himself to pass out here. He holds on to a sapling as he steps carefully down the muddy incline to the stream. At first the stream is so shallow that he must use his free hand and his feet to keep moving, but soon it deepens and widens.

In the deeper water the boatmaker turns on his back and floats, holding his bundle up to the sun with both hands while he allows the rippling water to carry him downstream toward the mighty brown tide named for the peasant boy who, led on by a flock of screeching blackbirds, converted the king of the Mainland to faith in Jesus Christ.

CHAPTER 16

A week later the boatmaker stands on one of the bridges that cross the Vashad and connect the two halves of the capital. On his way to the city he has stolen clothes from clotheslines outside farmhouses, and he looks something like his old self. The wound on his nose has closed. He is no longer wrapping it in strips of wool, but he will have a scar that looks like the letter *X*.

Standing on the bridge, he reaches into his pocket and pulls out the knife from the little house at the edge of the woods. He looks down at the blade, which still has a crust of blood on it. In the ancient spiky script one side reads: *Behold the lilies of the field, they spin not, nor do they toil.* He turns the blade over. On the other side it says: *Yet Solomon in all his glory was ne'er arrayed like one of these.*

He holds the knife up to the sun and then lets it fall. The knife spins and spins, circling its point, the blade fluttering in sunlight. It sails downstream above the river, still spinning, strikes the surface and disappears under the surging, rippling brown water.

When he reaches his room in the boardinghouse, he is surprised to find that his money is still under the green floorboard. As White was beating and kicking him down into the cobblestones Crow kept saying: "The money! Where is it?" Yet his cache is undisturbed. The room is mostly as he left it. The landlady has cleaned after her fashion. But the room hasn't been rented since he left it the morning of the beating.

There haven't been many looking for rooms to rent. Times have changed since the boatmaker left the capital. There is an unease in the streets, a feeling that hard times are coming. The roads, dams, schools and telegraph lines that have been started are still going up, but no new construction is being undertaken. Jobs aren't as easy to find as they were the year before at the height of the boom. Some of the workers who were drawn to the capital by the modernization program are returning to their villages.

The boatmaker sits on the edge of his narrow bed, holding his money, still wrapped in brown paper. Beside him on the blanket is the piece of green floorboard that covers his cache. He opens the paper and removes a few bills. He has no need to count: It would all be there or it would all be gone.

He wonders where on the New Land Crow and White are buried. Perhaps they are not buried there. It is consecrated ground, after all, and they were strung up as thieves. He slips the bills into the pocket of his stolen overalls, rewraps the rest, slides it back and replaces the floorboard. Then he sits on the bed with his head in his hands while it gets dark outside his window. The boat-maker has enough money so that he doesn't need to work for a while. But he knows he will begin looking the next day. If he does not, he will drink.

There is a soft knock on his door. The door, its inner face painted the same green as the floor, opens, and the landlady stands in the doorway, without Kierkegaard but with a cigarette burning between her knuckles.

"Is there anything you need?"

"No. The room seems the same."

"No one's been in it since you left. Except me, to clean. And your friends."

"They were here?"

"I let them in. They said you'd been hurt and they were helping you out. I thought perhaps they would take some of your things to you, so I let them in. But I don't think they took anything. There wasn't much here, to tell the truth. I watched them while they were here. For your sake. I don't know why I bothered. You never even came back to give notice."

"I'm sorry. I was away."

"I would say so," she says, looking hard at him to see if she can tell where he's been in the many months since he walked out of her house on an otherwise unremarkable day. The X across the boatmaker's nose is healing, but the crossed lines are still an angry red. A dark beard is attempting to join his mustache.

"I'll pay for the room—the time I was away."

"But that's nearly a year. It's too much."

"The room's been empty."

"Yes. But that's not your fault. No one came around wanting to rent it. Believe me, if anyone had wanted to rent it, I would have. I didn't keep it intact as a memorial to you." She laughs. A crackling, gurgling sound rises from her lungs.

"I'll pay."

Giving her the money for a year's rent will take a good bit of what he has under the floorboard and force him to find work sooner, which is all to the good. He is surprised by how deeply relieved he feels to be back in this room, with its green flooring, single window, washstand, candlestick and view of cobblestones and sky. He is moved by the landlady, too. He can tell that, whatever she may say, some part of her hoped he was safe and waited for his return.

"God bless you," says the landlady. No tenant has ever offered to pay for a room he hasn't occupied for a year. She feels guilty. But she tells herself that the man from Small Island won't change his mind once he's made it up—and so there's no reason to argue.

She offers the boatmaker the memory of a curtsey and pulls the door closed behind her. Before it has closed all the way, it swings open again. "And where *are* your friends? They never gave notice, either. There was just a tremendous commotion in their room one night and then—poof!—they were gone."

"Is that so?"

"Yes, that's what happened. Do you think they'll be returning?"

"I wouldn't hold their room for them."

"That's too bad. Tenants are scarce these days. Well, if they don't come back, and you do happen to hear from them, let them know a few things of theirs are down in the cellar. Good night." This time the door closes all the way.

After the landlady leaves, the boatmaker sits for a long time on the bed. His nose itches, but he wills himself not to scratch. If he scratches, the scar will be worse than it is already going to be. It is bad enough that his face will be marked permanently. He must work, and he knows he would never hire a man who looked the way he did a week ago. Since then he has eaten and been in the sun; he looks healthier, less strange. Still, he is afraid that people can see where he has been and what he is running from. He is sure the brothers from the New Land are still after him. Father Robert will never give up.

For a few days he walks the city, enjoying the end-of-summer heat, feeling the strangeness of being outside and free, an ordinary workingman, not a monk in a white robe. The boardinghouse is in the center of the old city, surrounded by many houses like it, built centuries ago by titled nobility and now divided into apartments or turned into rooming houses. Only a few streets away, the Jewish quarter begins. Under the current king, the Jews are no longer confined to a few crowded streets. Their neighborhood has begun to spread, its once-clear borders blurring.

The boatmaker walks through the Jewish neighborhood, looking in shop windows lettered in the unreadable alphabet of the Hebrews. Some windows display nothing but black garments and hats, some strange cuts of meat, others only books. There are no women on the street, only men in a variety of costumes. Some wear black knee breeches and white stockings from the previous century. Others are dressed in black suits suggesting no particular time or place. All wear hats of one kind or another, some of them large round fur hats that have the look of countries far down to the south and east. Most of the men, bearded or clean shaven, have sidelocks curling down their cheeks. They speak to one another in their Jewish language, moving quickly on urgent business. They do not seem to see the boatmaker, and he does not mind being invisible.

He turns into a shop with a striped pole outside next to a sign that says *Chirurg*. It's a narrow space, with a chair like a throne in the center. Leaning against the chair reading a newspaper is a man in a white apron, the sleeves of his striped shirt gathered in by garters.

"Welcome, friend. You have come to the right place," the man says, folding his newspaper and dropping it on a shelf next to the cash register, which sits on a shelf in front of a mirror covering much of one wall.

The boatmaker sits in the chair, tensing as the barber binds the white sheet around his neck. He relaxes as he realizes he is safe, free.

"Haircut and shave?"

"Yes."

The barber twirls the boatmaker toward the wall opposite the mirror. High on the wall in a thin black frame is an engraving of an elegant, muscular black horse, its coat shining, led by a dark-skinned man in pantaloons, slippers with the toes turned up, a short jacket and a turban with a jewel and a feather. Underneath the picture are the words *The Royal Champion.*

"Beautiful horse, yes?" says the barber, approaching from behind and stirring the contents of a white mug with a brush. "The king's," he says, covering the boatmaker's face in small white circles. "Never been beaten. Which is as it should be. Now, I'm not so sure we can say that about the king. There's something wrong there. Possibly *very* wrong. There are rumors about." He sets down the mug, picks up a razor and begins to strop it on a fat leather belt.

"But this is right, this horse. *The king's champion against all comers.* He may not be much of a man, let alone much of a king. *But by God his horse can run.* For some reason that makes me sleep just a little better at night when I lay meself down next to the missus." The barber tests the razor on his thumb and, having determined that it's plenty sharp, spins the boatmaker toward him.

"It's little enough, mind you—a racehorse—given everything that's going to hell in this kingdom. But at least it's *something.*" The barber whistles a broken melody as he shaves the boatmaker, saying nothing about his scar, though of course he is curious. It's not the kind of scar you see every day.

The boatmaker relaxes into the pleasure of the shave and the haircut that follows. When the barber is finished, he pulls the white cape away like a sculptor revealing his creation to the public: suitably modest but in the confident expectation of sustained applause.

"A new man!" He brushes the boatmaker's shoulders with a horsehair brush. The man from Small Island appraises himself in the mirror. Not a new man, he thinks. But at least he will be able to look for work without feeling he needs to hide his face. For that alone, it has been worth enduring the barber's nonsense.

"Quite a scar you have there, friend."

"If you say so."

"I most certainly do. Between the scar, the hair and the beard . . . Well, when you walked in here you were enough to frighten the demons of Hell, but now you're fit for polite company."

"Maybe."

"How'd you get that scar anyway, friend?"

"An accident. At work."

"I can imagine," says the barber, ringing the register. "And what trade do you follow, friend, to have such an accident?"

"Carpenter." The word hangs in the air behind the boatmaker, who is already on his way out of the shop into the streets of the Jewish quarter.

"Carpenter," mutters the barber. "Carpenter. Now, I wonder . . ."

The boatmaker doesn't seem like a fool. Too close-mouthed for that. In the barber's experience of men, which is vast and superficial, close-mouthed men are generally shrewd. But only a foolish carpenter would wind up with a scar like that across his face. Something about this carpenter doesn't add up, he thinks. But then, so few things do nowadays, with everything as disarrayed as it is in the kingdom—and a weak king reigning. The barber lifts his newspaper and opens it, looking for a place to pick up his reading about the shameful world he lives in.

In spite of the slowdown in the modernization project, it takes the boatmaker only a little longer than usual to find work. With the Jewish quarter overrunning its old strictly enforced legal limits, the neighborhoods around it are changing rapidly. The Jews do not seem to have been affected as much as others by the running down of the king's ambitious program. They are taking over many buildings. Townhouses like the one his landlady owns are being turned into apartments for six or eight families.

As always, the boatmaker quickly acquires a reputation for having a wonderful touch with wood, for working hard without complaining about the materials or tools supplied to him and for saying little, all of which endears him to his employers. He is hired by one landlord, then another, before being taken on as part of a crew that is steadily employed by a large property owner.

The carpenters, plasterers, roofers and brickworkers on the crew are all Gentiles. The Jews do not appear to work very much with their hands. They keep shops and run after each other in the street waving important slips of paper. The construction crews are made up of Mainland Christians who work with rough hands for their pay and mutter among themselves about the Jews taking over the Old Quarter like insects eating overripe fruit from the inside out. On the construction site, they whisper over their lunch buckets and then continue after lunch while pulling surreptitiously from bottles and flasks.

The boatmaker sits on his own and says little, refusing the offer of drink after lunch. Talk swirls around him, but he makes no effort to enter its stream. He is happy to have steady work and not to have to find a new employer after each job, but he is wary of the crew and their alcohol. The scar on his nose is becoming less noticeable, particularly among workingmen who bear many scars.

Although the boatmaker's employer has crews working on several sites, there is only one foreman for all these projects. When the foreman comes around, the mumbling about the Jews stops. He is a tall, lean man with curly reddish hair graying at the temples, a pipe smoker who wears a long tan canvas coat. The men respect the foreman, but they don't fear him. They are familiar, calling him by his Christian name, Sven, rather than the more respectful surname, Eriksson.

Sven Eriksson is one of them, a Gentile and a highly trained carpenter. He can lead, organize and get things done on a schedule. Those qualities have caused him to rise higher and higher until he oversees all the sites their employer is developing on the frontier where the Jewish quarter is pushing out into the historic center of the city.

When the boatmaker has worked for a month under Eriksson's guidance, the weather begins to turn colder, and the crew shifts to the interiors of buildings so they can keep working as long as possible. Most outdoor work on the Mainland halts from early December into March, and sometimes later, depending on how severe the winter is. This pause is deeper than custom: It is instinct.

The boatmaker has made no plans for the time when construction work halts. He knows he will continue to live at the boardinghouse, taking meals with his landlady or going out to eat in the dark taverns and restaurants of the Old Quarter. He has begun to eat in some of the Jewish restaurants, with their food from down to the south and east: strange grain dishes, pastes of chicken liver, purple soups dotted with sour cream. He eats this food with more pleasure than he would have imagined. And he could go on this way all winter; he has enough money not to work. But he has his own reasons for wanting to keep working, and when the foreman asks to meet him on a street corner a block or two from their latest site, the boatmaker is willing to go.

The next day he meets Eriksson, and they walk together through the no-man's-land where some stores are Jewish, some are not, and the peoples flow by each other without touching.

The foreman's strides are long, but he is in no hurry. The boatmaker keeps up without trouble, hearing the swish of the foreman's canvas coat, seeing the large pencils poking up out of his breast pocket. Everything about Eriksson looks well broken in, and it all fits easily together. It is a look the boatmaker, still wearing stolen clothes that make him feel patched together, can only envy.

After walking for a while, the man in the canvas coat stops, takes out his pipe and turns to face the boatmaker. His jaw is square, his nose long and straight. His eyes are a weathered blue-gray, not a clear, icy blue like Father Robert's.

The foreman tamps tobacco into the pipe, which has a short, curved stem. Clamping the stem between his teeth, he takes out a wooden match, lights the pipe and sucks to get the tobacco going.

"You are good with wood. You have the feeling for it."

The boatmaker feels as if he should say *thank you*, but something in him will not allow him to say the words. It is too soon since he was brought to a dangerous place by kindness, by gratitude.

"Very good with wood. But taught by yourself, yes?"

"I learned from watching others. Beginning with my father."

"Where are you from?"

"Small Island."

"As far away as that? Well, I knew you weren't from here. You don't talk enough to be from the capital."

"Maybe."

"You don't hate Jews enough, either, do you?"

"Hate Jews?"

"Yes. Do you?"

"No."

"Good. So you wouldn't be opposed to working for them?"

"I don't think so."

"That's good. Seeing as how you already are." The foreman takes out another match and relights his pipe, which has gone out while he was speaking.

"That's not the important thing, though. As I said, you have the feeling for wood—and that is something one cannot teach. But there is more for you to know. Much more. I don't think you've ever been in a shop where men make things using old methods, where every man has been trained by someone who was also trained by a master of his craft."

"No." The only thing remotely like that on Small Island is the clan of boatbuilders, and they never take in anyone who is not of their blood.

"Would you like to learn?"

The boatmaker hesitates. Learning a tradition rooted in working with wood sounds very tempting. And he does want to learn. But he is in no hurry. The last time he decided to be part of something larger than himself, he wound up leaping through a window and running for his life, his face covered with blood. Without thinking about it, he touches the bridge of his nose. The angry red has receded, but the crisscrossing pink ridges will be there a long time.

"I don't ask everyone," says Sven Eriksson, swinging to a stop at a crowded corner. The stream of people on the sidewalk parts to give the tall man room. "I leave most of them alone. And not just because of their mutterings about Jews."

The boatmaker looks surprised. The foreman fills his pipe, tamps it, lights it with a wooden match and smokes while looking at the boatmaker.

"You're surprised. But of course I know about their muttering. They shut up when they see me coming. But I know what they're saying. They forget that I was one of them, that I come from where they come from. But I had a conversation like this one long ago, with a man I can never hope to equal. And after that things were different for me. They could be different for you. You have the gift. It's waiting to be called forth and developed. But you'll never get there on your own. The knowledge you need is something built up generation after generation, not by one man alone."

Sven Eriksson inhales, then lets smoke run from his nose and mouth. He senses a hesitation in the smaller man, and he doesn't understand why it should be there. Usually the foreman is utterly dispassionate when he makes this offer, which happens once every year or so, but for some reason he wants this man to join them. He knows the value of the offer he is making; few refuse. This one could, he thinks.

The boatmaker waits, aware that the foreman is puzzled by his slowness. He turns the offer around in his mind, looking at it from different angles. The foreman does not seem to want him to join a family or give up everything to join his brothers. The offer seems to be about the wood, the secrets of tradition. He thinks of the workshops where the six great panels depicting the life of Vashad were made centuries ago. Of the men working in silence for decades, each knowing his part in the great enterprise.

"Yes."

"Good," says the foreman, relieved. "You've made a good choice. You won't regret it."

Sven Eriksson takes out his black notebook and holds it open while he draws on his pipe and writes something with a carpenter's pencil. Tearing the page out, he hands it to the boatmaker.

"Be at this address tomorrow. Seven sharp. Don't be late. We don't tolerate that. And know that when you arrive, you'll be no more than an apprentice—regardless of what you think you already know."

The foreman snaps his notebook shut and extends his hand. The two men shake hands. Then the boatmaker stands watching as the canvas-covered back recedes, smoke billowing over its shoulder, blooming and crumpling like the trail of a powerful long-distance locomotive. Around him stream the workingmen of the Mainland, Jewish men in their varied costumes, even a few native islanders, hollowed out by drink inside their fur parkas—all giving off the rich smells of life and decay. The stores are full of food and dry goods. The streets are filled with horses, wagons and blue-and-yellow tramcars. The spaces between the cobbles are packed with dung.

CHAPTER 17

After his conversation with the foreman the boatmaker stops in at the barbershop. The barber is sitting on his throne, holding a newspaper. On a bench under the engraving of The Royal Champion is an unusual sight: a native in his fur parka. On the small islands in the north, the natives still follow their traditional ways. On the Mainland, they are mostly single men, far from the sea, often drunk. They aren't hated the way the Jews are. Instead, they are despised and pitied, treated more like animals than human beings. Most of the capital's shopkeepers do not allow native islanders into their stores.

Seeing the boatmaker, the barber closes his paper and jumps out of the chair with surprising agility for a large man. He sets the paper down next to the cash register. Since returning to the capital, the boatmaker has had the opportunity to read copies of *The Brotherhood*. By now he is familiar with its black hatred of the Jews and the king.

Though he has no more interest in reading the paper, he is still wary of it, half-expecting to see it everywhere he goes. But the newspaper the barber sets down by his register is not *The Brotherhood*; it is *The Commercial Register*.

"Welcome, my friend," the barber says, rubbing his hands. "Haircut and a shave? Just the thing. Hope you don't mind our friend here," pointing with both hands, palms together, index fingers pointed like a pistol, to the native, who is slumped over, head covered by the parka. From under the fur comes the smell of whiskey.

"No."

"That's good. So many in this presumably Christian nation of ours forget that these men are our brothers."

From this remark the boatmaker concludes that the barber is trying to convert the native to the barber's own Christian church. He loses interest in the native's presence. He eases himself onto the throne, leans back and allows the barber to begin.

In the mirror behind the cash register the boatmaker examines himself. He knows he looks different from the way he looked when he put his boat in the water and sailed from Small Island. But he's not a man who has ever spent much time looking in mirrors, and it's difficult for him to see exactly where the difference lies. He is older, which shows around his eyes. He barely notices the scar across his nose. He knows his bald spot is expanding and his hairline receding. At some point the two will meet, and the dome of his head will be shiny and hairless. When that happens, he decides, he will wear his hair cropped short. His mustache is the same: full and drooping, gold shot through the brown. Perhaps as he loses his hair he will keep the mustache and grow out the whiskers on his chin underneath it, leaving his cheeks bare, as he has seen men of the capital do.

The barber finishes the haircut and spins him around for the shave. He looks up at the horse with the turbaned man holding its lead. Part of the engraving must be fanciful: There are no turbaned men on the Mainland. But the horse must be a good likeness. Below the colored image the fur parka moves up and down like a bellows, pushing the smell of alcohol out into the shop, where it mingles with the scent of shaving cream, the barber's aftershave and the odor of cut hair. No matter how lowly the apprenticeship the foreman is offering, the boatmaker thinks, it will be enough to keep him from drinking through another winter on the Mainland. That in itself would be enough. But perhaps it will also give him a taste of what the men felt in the workshops where the great panels showing the life of Vashad were carved.

The next day the boatmaker goes to the address the foreman has written in script that is as clear as a mathematical equation. Sven Eriksson is waiting outside an old stone wall of the kind that enclose the grandest townhouses in the Old Quarter. An arched gateway filled in by wooden doors painted brown was probably originally built to allow carriages to pass. A smaller door set into them stands partially open. Through it, the boatmaker sees men in canvas coats carrying tools and wood across a paved courtyard.

"So you've come."

"Yes."

"Are you ready to work?"

"Yes."

"Do you know where you are?"

"No."

"Can you guess?"

This teasing question reminds the boatmaker of the riddles of the New Land. The sensation makes him uncomfortable. For a moment he thinks perhaps he has made a mistake in coming here. But he stands his ground.

"My apologies," the foreman says. "There is no need to guess. It's just that a man from the capital would probably have guessed already. Or been told by the men on the building site."

"I don't gossip." The boatmaker's face flushes with irritation.

"No," says the foreman. "And that's a good thing." He pulls out his pipe, tamps, lights, inhales. "This is the House of Lippsted."

The foreman waits. When there is no response, he continues: "I've asked you to become an apprentice of his house because I have no doubt you'll learn to be a craftsman in the Lippsted style—over time. I won't mislead you: It's a slow process. Many don't have the patience to follow it all the way through. Others, even some very gifted ones, drink themselves out of a job in their impatience. I don't tolerate drink. We must be clear about that from the beginning."

Sven Eriksson inhales and exhales pipe smoke, looking over his newest apprentice. A strange one, he thinks, but a man with a definite gift. It is a gift that might go in any one of several directions. The foreman likes gifted apprentices—though not too many at any one time. He knows that in any enterprise there must be the right mixture of the brilliant and the steady. As in making concrete, sand and gravel must be balanced.

"You'll begin at the bottom. Maybe you think you're already a carpenter. And out there you are," he says, pointing with his short, curved pipestem at the world beyond the fine stone wall.

"Out there, you are a carpenter. And not a bad one. Plenty will take you on right now, no questions asked." The foreman lets smoke run out of his nose and mouth. The morning air is pleasantly cool.

"In here, you'll be less than that. Much less—a boy in the yard, doing anything anyone asks of you. Starting with stacking boards and carrying them where they're needed. By the time you're allowed to form an oak peg, you'll think you've been given a huge promotion. But you'll still be an apprentice. And for a long time. It takes years to absorb this: the way Lippsted makes furniture. Not a pin, not a screw, not a nail. And when you learn our way, you don't learn it with the mind only. No, you learn through your skin and get it into your bones."

The foreman laughs, puts the pipestem between his teeth and speaks around it. "The pay's not much, either. Barely enough to hold body and soul together."

"It will be enough."

"How do you know? I haven't named an amount."

"It's enough."

"Alright. It's enough. So are you ready? Now that I've made it sound so appealing?"

The foreman removes his pipe, knocks the bowl against his hand and lets the ashes float to the pavement. He takes a last look at the man of Small Island, more than a head shorter. Then he turns and goes through the open door, the boatmaker following him into the compound. At the center is a beautiful townhouse with a tapering Seventeenth Century façade. Clustered around the townhouse is a warren of workshops and storage spaces where men in canvas jackets, some short, some long, move quietly and purposefully as they practice the art of making furniture held together by nothing more than the affinity of wood for wood.

As the foreman warned, the boatmaker begins at the very bottom of the ladder that leads to mastery. Day after day he does no more than carry wood, aged and sawn, from the places where it is stored to the shops where the journeymen and masters shape it. He carries the woods of the Mainland—oak, pine, three kinds of walnut, spruce, maple, cherry—along with woods from far away, which he has never seen before: rosewood, ironwood, hornbeam, teak.

While he is becoming familiar with these woods, the boatmaker learns to find his way around the workshops, storage areas and outbuildings, all organized according to a plan centuries old. Through this tangle Sven Eriksson moves smoothly, smoking, cleaning his pipe, making notations in his notebook, overseeing everything without raising his voice or appearing to oversee anything. After the boatmaker is admitted to the compound, the foreman says nothing to him for weeks, seeming, in the buzz of the workshop, to have forgotten hiring him.

From time to time, the hum of work pauses as a finished piece of Lippsted furniture is loaded onto a wagon, wrapped in big quilted blankets, like a racehorse after a workout. At the moment of departure the men in the compound stand for a moment and bid Godspeed to wood they have lived with for years: as logs, sawn boards, then pieces planed and sanded, fitted together before receiving many coats of oil or varnish and standing to cure before shipping.

As a particularly beautiful piece is loaded onto a delivery wagon, the men watching in the yard can only imagine the richness of the city or country houses, on the Mainland or in Europe, where these pieces will be installed. Sometimes the drivers of the wagons, dark green with no identifying marks, return with stories of the places the furniture has gone. Over the decades, many have gone to the two royal palaces: the Winter Palace in the capital and the Summer Palace fifty miles to the north, in the fertile plains around the port of Christaborg.

But beyond the occasional tale, not much is said in the compound about where the furniture goes, about the people who buy it or, for that matter, about the outside world in general. The boatmaker is surprised at how little loose talk there is among the workmen of the House of Lippsted. There is none of the muttering about the Jews he heard when he worked on the construction crews, and which he has heard in the background since arriving in the capital. Perhaps that is not so surprising, given where he is. Still, he notes its absence as he is called from workshop to workshop, carrying boards, pausing to watch pieces being fitted, carrying away excess wood, sweeping up sawdust or the curled shavings that remind him of the sidecurls of the men on the streets of the Old Quarter.

As he moves through the compound, he wears the canvas jacket he was given on his arrival. It is not a long one like the masters wear but a short jacket without pockets, signifying that he is not yet authorized to carry pencils to mark the wood or tools to shape it. In fact, the boatmaker is not authorized to use any tools at all, except the big pushbroom and his two Small Island hands.

He is surprised to find that being at the bottom of the ladder, mostly invisible, quite insignificant, does not make him angry or make him want to drink and fight. After all, he is not a boy but a man—and a carpenter who has been told since he was small what a wonderful touch he has with wood. To compound his insignificance, the pay of an apprentice is, as the foreman warned, a laughable amount meant for a boy still living with his parents. Most of the other apprentices are younger, some the sons of Lippsted craftsmen. If the boatmaker didn't have money in the cache under the green floorboard, he would be eating potato soup for every meal and washing it down with water.

In spite of his low station, the boatmaker is, in his way, content. He eats well. He has a place to lay his head down at night. And six days of the week he is at the compound at seven o'clock, ready to work. He has never worked in a place where so much reverence is paid to wood, where each piece—from a board of precious African rosewood to a plain pine plank—is seen for what it holds within. This reverence makes it easier to bear being an apprentice in a short coat, easier to work without the obliterating fire of alcohol as the days shrink, darkness expands and winter conquers the sky. The first flakes are yet to fall, but the air already smells of snow. Those who have warm beds are grateful.

Soon the first snow dusts the city; it will not be long before the ground is covered. As he walks to work in the morning or home at night, the boatmaker can imagine what is happening on the New Land: the harvest in, livestock in the barns, the ground turning hard and cold, life narrowing down to reading and prayer as the winter solstice approaches.

When he thinks about the New Land, it is always with a small note of fear. He is sure Father Robert is still looking for him. He doesn't know whether the priest wants him to return and resume his role as Number IV in the New Christ or whether he would like to hang the boatmaker on a telegraph pole for all the New Land to see. In either case, he needs to avoid anyone from that community, especially Neck and the priest. He is surprised they haven't found him yet. He assumes one day there will be a knock on his door in the middle of the night and Father Robert and Neck will be there to march him away.

As he thinks it over, day after day, he concludes that Crow and White must not have told the priest where he lives. Perhaps, he thinks, the thieves never spoke directly to Father Robert. It is a reassuring thought. Still, he never feels completely safe. He has repaired his sealskin bag and it rides on his chest under his jacket at all times, much of his money inside. If he sees Father Robert or Neck—or anyone he recognizes from the New Land— he will turn and run without looking back.

As winter begins, the boatmaker moves up one short rung on the ladder that leads slowly to mastery of the Lippsted craft. In addition to carrying boards and sweeping, he is now allowed to make the pegs that hold much of the furniture together. Many of the joints require no fastenings: They are just one piece of wood fitted cannily into another. But some require wooden fasteners, pegs carved from the same wood as the furniture itself. To make these pegs, a journeyman first turns out dowels of a specified diameter. Then the dowels are sawn to the right length. Only after they have been sawn is the boatmaker allowed to take an old wicker basket filled with the raw pegs and use a knife and sandpaper to round them into the correct shape.

From time to time Eriksson looks in on him, but most of his contact is with the journeymen who make the dowels. These journeymen never praise. They tell him what needs improving. Anything done correctly is passed over in silence. It seems the road to being a master in the House of Lippsted is endless: Praise would be nothing more than time wasted on an infinite journey.

The boatmaker attends to their correction without protest. He does not need to be corrected often—and never for the same fault twice. As he works, he makes a discovery that pleases him: His gift is more than something that flows directly from the wood into his hands. When he entered the compound, he was drawn to being part of a tradition. But having learned everything about his craft on his own, he was afraid he could not begin at the bottom and learn from others without destroying his gift. Once inside the walls he finds this is not so. He is learning from the others—and his skills are improving.

Like the reverence for wood he sees around him, it makes his status as an apprentice easier to bear.

The days grow shorter. His apprentice tasks now begin and end in darkness. Each trip from one building to another requires the boatmaker to button up and make his way through drifts of snow, feeling with his toes for solid footing. He knows from experience that if he falls, there will be little sympathy for his bumps and bruises and much concern for the precious wood.

One day, as he carries a basket of his pegs through the falling snow to be inspected, the main gates swing in. A carriage clips and rattles through, drawn by a pair of glossy black horses with plumes of the same shade rising from their foreheads. The carriage, a two-wheeler, luggage strapped to its roof, pulls to a stop, and the heavily bundled driver steps down. He opens the door and extends a hand to a small, elegant woman with a fur over her shoulders, her hands in a muff of the same fur. Holding his basket of pegs, the boatmaker sees that it is the woman who lectured the workingmen of the Mainland about money.

Rachel Lippsted is concerned about her footing. She does not look up to see an apprentice in a canvas jacket holding a basket of pegs, snow melting on his thinning hair and thick mustache. A man with a dark beard edging his jaw steps out of the carriage behind her without a hand from the driver. He is compact and wiry. He and the boatmaker could be brothers, though this man's hair and skin are darker. He wears a black overcoat worth more than the boatmaker has ever been paid for any job. The man of Small Island carries his basket across the yard through a curtain of white flakes to a workshop where he finds the others buzzing with the news that Jacob Lipp-sted and his sister have returned to the townhouse after many months in Europe.

CHAPTER 18

After the boatmaker sees Jacob and Rachel Lippsted, they do not appear in the courtyard for many weeks. But the two of them are in his mind as he lies on his narrow bed, smoking and watching the moonlight move across ancient flowered wallpaper.

Even in the brief moment he saw them, something emanated from Jacob Lippsted and his sister that adds to the puzzles the boatmaker has been accumulating since he arrived on the Mainland. On the New Land, as he prepared for the task Father Robert offered him, he had let those questions go. But now that he is back in the capital—and working in the House of Lippsted—his questions have returned full force, with Jacob Lippsted and his sister at the center.

As they stepped out of the carriage into the falling snow, there was something powerful about them. They looked infinitely well cared for, as if they had never had a material need that could not be satisfied by lifting a hand, if not at once, then with little trouble, the outcome assured no matter where in the world the object of their need was to be found. And yet the boatmaker thought he also saw a tentative quality, as if the power on which their luxury rested, though generations deep, could not be fully relied upon. In these elegant, luxuried creatures the boatmaker thought he saw a wariness that he never saw in Father Robert. The priest never stopped to worry about the obstacles that lay before him: He strode into the world with complete assurance, always ready to deal the first blow.

Lying on his bed smoking, the boatmaker finds that his feelings for this pair, particularly the sister, are strong and complicated. Perhaps these feelings have been germinating ever since his visit to the Royal Mint. He feels a desire to protect the slender figure with the dark curls, along with a desire to overwhelm and take her. And now he works in the compound where she lives, glimpsing her in comfort and luxury, while he wears the short canvas coat of an apprentice, carrying baskets of pegs for the furniture her family's business makes. He pushes his feelings down and crushes out his cigarette. Then he concentrates on falling asleep, on what he must do the next day to continue learning the secrets of the Lippsted craft.

One evening as he sits on his bed he remembers what his landlady told him about Crow and White's belongings. It's a cold night, one of the longest of the year. The streets are quiet. A soft layer of new snow covers everything. Underneath it are the crusted layers that make up the history of the season. The boatmaker gets up and looks out his window down at the alley, at the cobblestones covered in white. The alley is empty, not even a cat or a rat scurrying through the snow.

Down there, he thinks, is where White bashed him with his huge fists. But why didn't they find his cache? He still doesn't understand that. Surely it was his money Crow was asking about while White beat him. And if they had searched, they would have found it. Yet apparently they didn't bother to look very hard. The question of why they didn't tear his room apart to find his money takes its place among the riddles, once left behind, that are returning with a new intensity.

Suddenly, he needs to see Crow and White's belongings—immediately. Somewhere in this house is everything that remains of the two men he thought were his friends. When he last saw them, their eyes were wide, staring. Perhaps they were held down and strangled in this house. That might account for the commotion the landlady said she heard in their room the night they disappeared. It would have taken more than one man to strangle White. The huge man would have fought desperately to prevent them from hurting Crow.

The boatmaker takes his candlestick and goes down the stairs past the landlady's ancestors, descending from the current century of progress to the darker centuries before. He stops for a moment at a portrait that reminds him of Father Robert. The painting, in a square frame, is of a young man, seated, wearing a white ruff over a steel breastplate, helmet in his lap. The man is young—fair and strongly built. He has the priest's blond hair, his stabbing eyes, rounded face, high cheekbones and snub nose.

The boatmaker examines the painting in the flickering light from his candle. Then he goes down to his landlady's door on the first floor in the rear. She comes to the door in her robe, wiry hair askew, book in hand, cigarette burning.

The landlady is never surprised when lodgers appear at her door. Her attitude is neither cold nor welcoming. Boarders have their rights; she has hers. She has her station; they have theirs. Her lodgers are simply part of what her life has become. With time and change, the landlady has shed many of the mental habits of her caste, but some of those habits go so deep they will be buried with her when she is placed between her mother and her father in the cemetery across the river reserved for Main-landers of ancient and noble blood.

Two black-and-white cats twine between her legs. The cats have the run of the house—and more privileges than the lodgers. Crow hated them. He insisted cats are unclean.

"You said my friends left some things here."

"Yes, I put them down in the cellar."

"I'd like to look at them."

"Can't it wait until tomorrow?"

"I need to see them now."

The landlady sighs. To any of her other lodgers she would have refused without a second thought and gone back to her cigarettes and the anxious Dane. But the boatmaker paid a year's rent without being obliged to.

She closes the door, then comes out, cigarette burn-ing, without Kierkegaard but with a candlestick of her own and a big iron keyring. The cats follow at her ankles, avoiding contact with the boatmaker.

She leads this little band to the back of the house, opens a door, and they go down rough stairs. The air is damp and musty between the stone walls. At the bottom of the stairs is a landing with old wooden doors left and right. The landlady pauses and draws on her cigarette be-fore dropping it and crushing it in the dirt.

"On the right, I think," she says, examining one iron key after the other while the boatmaker holds both candlesticks. The cats circle, thinking of juicy mice and rats in the storerooms, which they are rarely allowed to visit.

The landlady finds the key she wants. The lock groans and gives way. Inside, the room is filled with ancient dark furniture, huge crates. There are cobwebs over everything. Mice scurry in the darkness. The boatmaker thinks he sees some Lippsted pieces against the rear wall, but in the dark he can't be sure.

After inspecting the piled belongings, the landlady realizes she's in the wrong cellar. They back out, shooing the cats, before repeating the procedure and entering the opposite storeroom. Here there is also furniture, though it looks smaller and more recent. The boatmaker sees no Lippsted pieces. The cats squeeze between their legs and disappear into the center of the room, where lamps, boxes, old shoes, clothes, a chandelier, trunks and suitcases are piled.

"They must be in here somewhere. I'm not staying to look."

She takes the key off the big iron ring and hands it to him. The boatmaker hopes his friends' belongings are somewhere near the top.

"Make sure you don't lock Castor and Pollux in here. You're a good tenant—when you're not disappearing without giving notice. Better than those friends of yours. At least you came back. But if you lock my cats in here, there will be Hell to pay. Do you understand me, young man?"

"Yes, ma'am."

The boatmaker takes the key and steps into the room. In the light of his candle shadows dance up the walls then slide down behind the furniture, taunting him. The black-and-white cats slink through the piled goods as if they are hunting through underbrush, alone, then together.

The boatmaker advances slowly, moving boxes, shoes, lamps and suitcases. Everything is coated in layers of dust, deeper or thinner depending on how long ago the goods were stored. By the time he reaches the center of the room, the cats are in a frenzy near the walls, snapping at vanishing mice.

In the center, on top of the pile, is a cardboard valise, held together by twine, which the boatmaker recognizes as Crow's. The little man was secretive about its contents, as he was about his notebook, his money—and everything to do with his affairs.

The boatmaker picks up the valise. It is light. Inside, a few items rattle against cardboard.

The boatmaker puts the valise aside and looks for anything else that might have belonged to them. He finds a couple of old nightshirts that smell of Crow's cologne and a bundle of newspapers tied with string, which might have belonged to Crow; White could not read. On top is a copy of *The Brotherhood*. He finds nothing else in the storeroom that might be connected to two boarders of this house who wound up staring from telegraph poles on the New Land.

The boatmaker is ready to leave, but Castor and Pollux have gone silent, missing. He sets Crow's valise outside the door and calls the cats. It takes an hour of rooting through the remnants of lodgers' lives, and scratches on both hands, to get the cats outside with the door closed. One of them—the boatmaker can't tell the cats apart and doesn't care—has a fat mouse, nearly dead, in its mouth and is not sharing. He gets back to his room torn and bleeding, valise in hand.

By now there is little left of the night, but he feels no need for sleep. He lays the valise on the bed and unties the twine. Inside, neatly folded, are two of the white shirts with ruffled fronts Crow favored: shirts only a man who never worked at any honest trade would have chosen.

Lifting them up, the boatmaker sees the silver flask, recalling the hundreds of times the little man reached inside his jacket and pulled it out, offering it occasionally to the boatmaker, less often to White, who mostly drank beer. Perhaps Crow made White drink beer because it was cheaper than whiskey. The flask is thin and curved, its surface striped, matte finish alternating with shining polished stripes. Engraved on two of the matte stripes are the initials *A. K.*

Other than the shirts and flask, the only item in the valise is Crow's black notebook. It is much like the one Sven Eriksson carries, although in every other way the two men could hardly have been more different. Sitting on his narrow bed, the first hints of daylight at the window, the boatmaker holds the notebook, trying to decide whether to open it and read. He does not believe in spirits or an afterlife. But there is something about the way Crow died that makes the boatmaker hesitate before opening his book. He holds it on his lap for a while. Then he begins.

An hour later the candle flame makes flapping sounds as it dies. The boatmaker gets up to replace the candle, sits down on his bed and continues reading, looking for answers as he enters the secret life of the man who was his friend, then his assailant and finally a riddle stuck on a pole like a handbill. Daylight begins to open his room to the outside world for inspection. He does not have much time before the landlady will knock, offer him coffee and a soft roll with butter and he will have to leave for the compound.

Inside the front cover, in dark ink in Crow's best hand, as if he was trying to impress his final reader, is *Anton Kravenik*, with a flourish beneath it. Under the name, in smaller script, without a flourish, is the address of the boardinghouse. The boatmaker wonders how long Crow and White lived here before he met them. He could go to the landlady's room and ask. She will be up, perhaps never having gone to bed, ready to go down to the kitchen and direct the maid in preparing coffee and rolls. Instead, he keeps reading.

Crow's legal name inside the cover is the clearest entry in the entire notebook. The rest is a jumble, the writing large and crude, almost printing, in whatever implement came to Crow's small, clever hand. Much is written in pencil. The boatmaker remembers seeing Crow suck on a pencil stub, pursing his face and wetting the lead before writing.

The book is not a story, or even a string of sentences. It is a tangle of financial dealings: money coming in and going out, much of it from people indicated only by single letters. The record is not in chronological order, though the dates of transactions are noted, along with dates and places of meetings. Reading through these entries brings the boatmaker back to the beginning of his time with Crow and White, when he enjoyed their friendship. He had wanted the unfamiliar sensation to continue.

In Crow's notebook are three different kinds of entries for sums received or paid out. Though not large sums, they are more than adequate for the life Crow and White lived. In fact, based on the amounts flowing through his ledgers, Crow was a man of means, at least from the boatmaker's point of view. Or would have been, had it not been for the fact that one category of entries consists of what are obviously winnings—and much larger losses—at the racetrack.

Crow was an impulsive, careless gambler. Tips on horse and dog races, from Crow's friends in the shadow world, are decorated with doodles and exclamation points. Many are followed by angry, obscene entries, indicating that another sure thing had failed to materialize. Some are scored almost all the way through the tough paper. While he pages through the book, the boatmaker recalls Crow returning to the construction site from his mysterious comings and goings, occasionally ebullient, more frequently dark and withdrawn, lashing out at White and drinking by himself at the edge of the site, not inviting the boatmaker with them to the Grey Goose for dinner.

The second stream is a smaller, steadier flow into Crow's household economy. The amounts don't vary much, never huge, never too small, mostly weekly, disappearing in the winter. They are scattered through the pages but, unlike some of the other entries, these are not difficult to decipher: They represent White's pay, disappearing into Crow's pocketbook and reappearing as Crow saw fit. White never expressed any resentment at this arrangement. White was grateful to Crow, as if the smaller man were guiding him through a distracting world in which White would otherwise have been lost. The amount White was paid is larger than the boatmaker would have expected. He wonders whether that was because of White's unusual strength or Crow's connections to the shadow world, or both.

The third stream of amounts is impossible for the boatmaker to make sense of. Here there are no names— only dates, numbers and letters. P, Q and R appear repeatedly, appointments with each one scrawled in pencil, along with payments received from them. No payments seem to have been made to them, so they cannot have been bookmakers. In fact, in spite of his losses at the track, Crow does not seem to have had to resort to loans from bookmakers. The payments from P, Q and R are larger than any of the other sums, except a few of Crow's worst losses. They are irregular, beginning before the boatmaker met the mismatched pair and continuing to the end.

The boatmaker leafs through the notebook, trying to find patterns in the jumble. The only thing he can see is that payments from R increase in frequency and amount over time, while those from P and Q remain the same. The three largest payments from R, each larger than the last, are in the months before the boatmaker was beaten. He turns down the pages where payments from R are noted.

At a knock on his door he stuffs Crow's notebook under the rumpled sheets and rises, his body both light and heavy from lack of sleep. While he was absorbed in the book, morning has filled his room. He snuffs his candle.

At his door, the landlady holds a bowl of steaming coffee, heavily diluted with milk, as he likes it. The black-and-white cats are twining between her legs. There is no sign of a mouse.

CHAPTER 19

A few snowy nights later the boatmaker stands at the door of the Grey Goose, stamping snow from his boots. When he enters, he sees that the interior looks just as it did when Crow and White sat in the back at one of the rough, poorly lit tables. Around them, the tavern would be filled with workingmen and people from the shadow world, eating goulash, sopping it up with bread and washing it down with dark, yeasty beer.

But he's come early, and the Grey Goose is quiet. One or two men who are always there, alcohol their only company, stare into space, not registering the entrance of the man from Small Island. As always, Gosdon stands behind the bar, apron lashed around his substantial middle, polishing a glass. He turns when he hears the boatmaker enter, puts the glass down and lays his palms on the bar, arms spread wide in the classic pose of the bartender, ready to hear your confidences—or reach under the bar for his truncheon.

"Well, if it isn't my friend from Small Island. Haven't seen you for many a long day," says the owner of the Grey Goose in a tone of commercial bonhomie. "Nor your friends Crow and White. Left quite a tab, those two. Meaning Crow, of course. White never handled money. But *you* knew that. What's your pleasure, friend? Where have you been? In an accident, were you? Interesting scar that, on your nose. Been jumping through windows, have you?"

The boatmaker starts. The bartender sees the effect of his words and says: "Just joking, friend. Just joking. But seriously, where have you been?"

"Out of the city."

"Ah," says the bartender, picking up his glass and polishing. "A nice long vacation in the country. Like a man of means. A nobleman at his country estate. Seems to have done you good. All except your nose. Get that fighting, did you? I'm no fool. Even in the country they have fights."

"Yes."

"And how does the other one look? Tell me he looks worse than you. I always thought you were a man who could take care of himself. Even though you are not the largest fish in the sea." Gosdon laughs at his own wit and holds the glass up to the light to examine it for streaks.

"Even against that mountain of a man, your friend White, I think you might do alright. You didn't get that nose fighting with White by any chance?"

"No."

"Glad to hear it. Now, tell me, what became of that oddly mated couple? They haven't been here nearly as long as you—more than a year, I think. Until then, they were in here almost every day, running up their tab. Oh, I know Crow was drinking his own whiskey out of that silver flask even while he was in here: buying one from me and drinking one of his own and thinking I didn't see. *Too smart by half*, that one. Well, I keep my eyes shut and my mouth closed. That's my motto. Everyone knows that about Rickert Gosdon. As long as a man behaves himself in my tavern, I don't care what he does on the outside. And aside from running up a tab that maybe he intended to pay and maybe didn't ever intend to pay and sneaking some of his own whiskey out of his fancy flask, Crow never caused me any trouble. Too smart by half, though.

"By the way," Gosdon says, putting down glass and rag, leaning forward across the bar as far as his stomach will allow and lowering his voice: "*I hear those two came to no good in the end*. Which doesn't entirely surprise me.

But since they were friends of yours, I thought you might know something about it."

"No." The boatmaker's stare is steady.

"Alright. If that's how you want it." The proprietor, who had been hoping for gossip, is put off. He turns away and makes himself busy behind the bar before coming back and stopping in front of the boatmaker.

"Well then, what'll it be? I seem to recall that yours is whiskey. And if memory serves, not too particular about whether it's a fancy whiskey. I like that. A man who's not a snob about his drink." What the tavernkeeper means is: a man who drinks what Gosdon serves and doesn't complain.

"Nothing, thanks. But I've a got a question. Do you know anything about a man named *R*?"

"*R*? That's not a name. It's a letter." The bartender draws back. The question has an air he doesn't like in these troubled times. Perhaps the boatmaker, who always seemed to be a bit of a half-wit, a rustic foil for Crow and White, might actually be a dangerous half-wit.

"Maybe his name just starts with *R*. Could it be someone Crow knew? Someone he had business with?"

Under its fat the tavernkeeper's face goes pale. "I don't know anything about *R*, my friend. Or any other letter of the alphabet." He pauses, breathing a little harder. "And you would be well advised to forget the entire alphabet—up to and including *R*. Especially *R*. Our friend Crow may have been mixed up in things that are a little too deep for the likes of honest men like you and me. *Ordinary peaceful men.*" Gosdon reaches under the bar and wraps thick fingers around his truncheon.

The boatmaker can see that the owner of the Grey Goose knows more than he is letting on—and is frightened by his knowledge.

"One more thing. Do you know anything about something called The Brotherhood? An organization that publishes a newspaper, maybe does some other things."

"*I do not.* And now I *know* you're getting into things that the likes of us plain honest men should stay away from." The tavernkeeper is sweating.

"This kingdom's mad at the moment. I've heard about it being like this before—in the time of my grandfather. He started this bar, my grandfather. Built it himself. And based on what he told me when I was no more than a pup, when things get like this it means we're going straight into the mouth of Hell. Stay out of it, friend. Get yourself back to Small Island, and stay there. Forget your bloody questions. And for God's sake stop asking about The Brotherhood."

The tavernkeeper lets go of the truncheon and brings up an unlabeled jar of clear liquid like the ones the monks of the New Land use for preserving fruits and vegetables. He fills a shotglass and downs it without offering any to the boatmaker.

"Just one more question. How big was Crow's tab?"

"Big enough for a little chiseler," says Rickert Gosdon, pouring and draining another shot of clear stuff. He names a substantial sum.

"Drinking his own whiskey in here and making notes in that little black notebook. Did more of all that than paying up. Mind you, I wrote it off long ago. Learned that from my father. No use dwelling on the past." Talking about Crow's tab has brought them back onto safe ground; the fat man's breathing is more regular. The sweat on his face is drying. He sighs a long sigh.

The boatmaker turns away, reaches into the sealskin pouch and takes out a sheaf of bills. With his back to the bar, he counts. Then he turns and lays bills on the polished surface. "That should cover it."

The tavernkeeper looks from the money to the boatmaker and makes a calculation in which greed and fear are as delicately balanced as the mechanism of a fine old grandfather clock. Then he reaches for the sheaf of bills and shepherds it under his apron and deep into his trouser pocket.

Looking Gosdon straight in the face, the boatmaker reaches into his corduroy jacket, pulls out Crow's flask and lays it on the bar. The flask lies face up, the letters *A* and *K* glinting in their dull stripes. "Take this too. Let's call it the interest on Crow's tab. No doubt it's valuable. Might be solid silver."

Gosdon looks at the flask. His eyes widen. "Absolutely not! You're a good man, settling your friends' tab like that, but *take that thing out of here*. Take it off my bar. I don't mean to be rude. But pick that thing up off the bar, get out of here *and don't come back!*"

The tavernkeeper has raised his voice. He's sweating again, more heavily this time. He stares at the flask as if it were a poisonous snake coiled on the bar his beloved grandfather built with his own two hands. The boatmaker turns and walks out, leaving the flask glinting in the light above the bar.

The next morning he is back at work in the compound. Sven Eriksson is pleased with his progress; the boatmaker has taken a step up from shaping the pegs and carrying them through the snow in an old basket. Now he is allowed to watch as the boards are marked, then sawn, with the understanding that one day, perhaps in the spring, he will be allowed to mark the wood for cutting and sometime after that make a cut himself. He is still a long way from the rooms where the finely shaped pieces are fitted together and finished with many coats of oil, stain or lacquer without the benefit of any plans other than those stored in the heads of the master craftsmen.

Little by little, the journeymen, apprentices and masters have come to tolerate the boatmaker, even though he isn't really one of them. He comes from far away and has no father, uncle or cousin who worked at the House of Lippsted before him. He envies the workers in the compound, who fit in easily and seem to know their jobs without being told how to do them. In spite of his gift for wood, there are still many things he does not understand about how Lippsted furniture is made, how the pieces are so finely attuned that they fit together without fastenings.

Moving from workshop to workshop, the boatmaker feels both pride and shame as he compares himself to the others. Though he would never share his feelings, in secret he believes he has a talent greater than that of even the master craftsmen. And yet in the light of day he is a novice who is not even allowed to carry a pencil. He both envies and looks down on the others in the compound. In this awkward, divided fashion he goes where he is told to go, carrying sawn boards to where they are needed.

One day, as he carries boards across the yard through falling snow, he sees Rachel Lippsted step out of the townhouse and cross the courtyard to the waiting carriage. He stops, not wanting to stare but unable to prevent himself. The last time he saw her he was sure she had not seen him. This time, without her brother, undistracted, she can hardly miss him, standing in the yard in his short canvas jacket, shivering over sawn boards, his mustache rimed with snow, head bare, the scar on his nose faint in the cold.

She pauses, surprised to see a workman in the compound staring at her without reservation or concealment. She is wearing a long skirt of green silk. Her hands are hidden in a fur muff that matches the trim of a long wrap made from the same silk. Snow dots her dark curls.

She intends to turn and step into the carriage immediately to interrupt the unusual exposure, but she is caught, stopped, by a feeling of recognition. She cannot recall where she has seen this compact figure, the face with its drooping mustache. But there is something familiar about the small workman. The feeling stops her only for a moment. She resumes her movement, climbs into the carriage; the liveryman closes the door. Rachel Lippsted gives no sign, but she is musing as she is carried off within the comfort of black leather cushions.

After that, weeks go by without the boatmaker seeing her in her two-wheeled carriage with the matched blacks.

From time to time he does see Jacob Lippsted enter or leave, accompanied by important-looking men. Some are obviously elders of the Mainland's Jewish community. Others are Gentiles: clean shaven businessmen or government officials who move through the yard paying no attention to the workmen crossing between outbuildings.

Jacob Lippsted seems at ease with all of them, Gentiles and Jews, giving each man his due. Because he is a Jew, Lippsted can have no official position, cannot meet openly with the king. Still, he knows how to move the government, even move the king, if he must.

The boatmaker notices more than he lets on of these comings and goings, more, perhaps, than an apprentice should. None of the other workmen seem to take any interest in what the owners of the House do. The only one who speaks to Jacob Lippsted directly is the foreman, Sven Eriksson, who is always respectful and focused on the matter at hand.

Snow drifts into the courtyard and piles up against the walls. Across the river from the Old Quarter, in the ceremonial district, the ground is still frozen in the parks and gardens around the Winter Palace. But daylight has already begun to extend itself, a little at a time. In the early afternoon, when the boatmaker goes into the yard with a load of boards, he doesn't need to feel in the dark with the toe of his boot for each cobble, fearful of going down.

As spring approaches the boatmaker moves up once more in his craft. Now, not only is he allowed to mark boards for cutting under the supervision of a journeyman, he is allowed to make the cut and show his boards afterward for inspection, standing in a line with younger apprentices, some of whose fathers have worked in the House of Lippsted for most of their lives. Standing next to his peers in their short coats, the boatmaker feels his awkward, secret mixture of superiority and envy.

As he continues to work, these feelings grow stronger. His pride surprises him. There is something in the boatmaker that will not be satisfied even with being a master in this house, having at his command every tool and technique that goes into furniture famous throughout Europe. Even being the foreman, which would put him on a different level entirely, might not satisfy him. He realizes these feelings are mad, and he confides nothing to anyone as he stands in line to have his boards inspected. The masters linger over his work, perhaps unable to believe the man from Small Island can do what the other apprentices do. His feelings trouble him. But his boards pass.

Toward the end of winter the boatmaker makes a decision: He will begin a project on his own. He knows that what he intends to do goes against the grain of the House of Lippsted. In the compound, each man moves at the pace determined for him by his elders, and every step is examined and approved by men who have already climbed the ladder of their craft. No one undertakes anything on his own initiative. Indeed, the guiding and containing of individual initiative is one of the deepest secrets of the furniture. Each piece is formed by the accumulated wisdom of generations, not by the impulse of any one man.

The boatmaker knows all this, but there is something in him that will not be stopped. Having mulled his decision for days, he stops the foreman in the yard and explains, in his halting and awkward fashion, what he intends to do, using material left over from other projects. The foreman takes out his pipe, knocks it against his hip, fills the pipe and lights it to give himself time to think before he speaks.

Sven Eriksson's first impulse is to shout: "Of course not, that's not how we do things here! I didn't give you the honor of inviting you to this place so that you could do things your way. I invited you here to learn how to do it *our* way!"

But something about the small man's determination makes the foreman hesitate. Though Sven Eriksson is a man of tradition, he is not lacking in imagination. He can see how things might be done differently. After all, he has chosen the boatmaker to be an apprentice in this place, which to the foreman is as sacred as the massive cathedral consecrated to Vashad.

As he smokes, inhaling and letting the smoke flow out in a long stream like a flight of wild ducks, he finds himself, to his own surprise, acceding to the boatmaker's plan. He feels lightheaded, as if a heavy grip on his mind has been loosened.

That unfamiliar sensation lasts only a moment. The strictness of tradition returns immediately as he lays out the conditions of his permission, which can be revoked at any time. The work must be done on the boatmaker's own time, using nothing intended for any piece of Lippsted furniture. It is not to be a secret, but he should keep it covered when he is not working and avoid making a public display of his heresy. If even one of these conditions is violated, the project ceases on the spot.

The boatmaker thanks the foreman and tells him he will follow these rules. They are in any case the rules he wished for. He turns and walks away, leaving the foreman sucking on a pipe that has gone out, watching the small canvas-covered back diminish into a new season that is still merely a suggestion.

The boatmaker finds an empty place in the back of one of the storerooms where the wood is aged. There is little light in the storeroom, and it's always cold. But it's an excellent place for the boatmaker's project. He begins arriving before anyone else is working, even Sven Eriksson, usually first into the compound.

The boatmaker begins with a feeling, the way he did when he was building his boat. In his shed on Small Island, the boat taught him how to build it, showing him the next step at every stage, each piece appearing as it was needed. It is the same with this.

He continues with his other work, silent, efficient and pliable, but he is more comfortable: The disturbing mix of superiority and envy has disappeared into the thing he is making. When he leaves for the day, he covers his work with the heavy canvas used to cover planks being seasoned. As he goes about his other duties, he finds bits of wood left over from other work. Most are too small to be useful, but here and there he finds a piece big enough and sound enough; he carries it back to the storeroom and puts it under the canvas. He does not flaunt his project, and few come to the back of the storeroom. To those few who do have business there, the foreman has given orders to pay no attention to the shape growing under weathered canvas.

One night when he cannot sleep for thinking about his work in the storeroom, the boatmaker takes out Crow's notebook and turns the pages he has turned many times without understanding everything that is scrawled there. That Crow controlled White's wages was obvious long ago. That Crow wagered considerable sums on races and lost regularly in spite of tips from the shadow world is interesting but not surprising. What he can still make no sense of are the increasing payments from R. And in that respect this night is no different from all the other nights he has puzzled over Crow's untidy accounting.

He smokes until he needs to close the notebook and sleep. He will read this book until it falls to pieces, if that is what is necessary for him to penetrate its secrets. In the meantime, the thing he has imagined is growing in the back of a cold Lippsted storeroom. It is unlikely and out of place, but also inevitable: demanding entry to the world.

CHAPTER 20

Early in spring, on a day when crusts of snow are piled on the curb but the air is mild, Sven Eriksson walks along the wall surrounding the Lippsted compound, pipe clenched between his teeth. Beside him walks the boatmaker, not smoking, lengthening his stride to keep up with the taller man. Around them, the people of the capital no longer need to pull their coats tight or walk with shoulders hunched against the wind.

"It's not done!" says the foreman, pulling the pipe out of his mouth so abruptly his teeth rattle. "No one from the workshop has ever been invited upstairs to dine with Herr Lippsted and his sister. Never! Nothing like this has happened to any man in the three generations of men I have worked with here."

The boatmaker paces like a pony trotting a thorough-bred. He gleans from Eriksson's outburst that he has been invited to the beautiful old stone townhouse with its tapering Seventeenth Century façade. If he accepts, he will go up to the Lippsted family quarters, above the storeroom where finished pieces are packed for shipment, to places where the foreman himself, for all his years of service and his high station, has never entered. The boatmaker feels the foreman's confusion, anger, fear.

"There is the name, of course," says the foreman, putting the pipe back between his teeth and slowing down so that his walking, smoking and talking settle into a rhythm. "I suppose that's part of it. I don't know. One can't know everything."

He stops and turns to face the boatmaker, causing people on the sidewalk to step around the two men in their canvas coats, one short, one long, who are having what appears to be an intense and serious conversation.

"You are to appear one week from tonight. You own a suit? No? Well, then: Find one! God knows what you'll look like. I don't suppose it matters. I have no doubt you will never be back there. All I can ask of you is: Don't disgrace us! Even though you come from far away and haven't been here long, you are one of us. You work with your hands. You are learning your craft. They are different up there, believe me. In ways I am not able to express precisely."

Sven Eriksson goes silent, drawing on his pipe. Then he adds: "This must be some odd quirk of Herr Lippsted's. He is more than capable of it. Yes. It can be no more than that. But for this one time wear a suit and make a good impression for those of us who work down here."

And with that, agitation on features that are usually very orderly, the foreman walks away while the boatmaker stands on the sidewalk, continuing the conversation in his mind.

The boatmaker does not go back to work. He doesn't know whether he will accept the invitation to attend dinner with the heirs of the House of Lippsted. Like the foreman, he isn't sure he belongs at their table, even though his twisting path seems to have led him there by a series of coincidences.

If the boatmaker was a more mystical man, he might have taken those coincidences as signs. Many on the Mainland would have done so. In spite of the king's devotion to reason and science, many of his subjects remain deeply attached to portents and divinations. Some long for a time when things were clearer: when a cloud of shrieking blackbirds circling the head and shoulders of an earth-smeared peasant announced God's message to an entire kingdom. In this century of change it is not easy to tell where the voice of God is to be heard. Is it in the humming telegraph wire? In the ultra-modern chemical works overseen by scientists from Berlin? In the monstrous presses, imported from England, that print the Mainland banknotes? In the secret societies that belch their black hatred of the king and "his" Jews? The voice of God might be in any of these—or in none. In these confusing circumstances, a small minority of Mainlanders is passionate, certain they know where the truth is to be found. But most are deeply confused and longing to be instructed.

The boatmaker, who subscribes to none of these versions of the truth, has his own confusion to sort out. He disappears into his own thoughts. When he reappears in the world, he is standing in front of the Royal Mint, looking up at its imposing brown classical façade. It is a working day, and ordinary citizens are not allowed in. The stone steps are empty. At the entrance two of the King's Own Guard stand at attention. The tall guardsmen in their scarlet uniforms and round bearskin helmets look out, over and above the man in the short canvas jacket.

He decides to walk on. Surely on this day of all days the foreman won't complain. He walks into the Royal Gardens that surround the Winter Palace, down a long allée between plane trees to a round pool within an ornamental stone wall. In the summer there will be boys here, sailing their boats, using sticks to push them out into the center of the pond to catch the wind. In just a few weeks the bravest troublemakers will begin skipping school to come here. But today the pool is empty. Concrete shows at the bottom between crusts of snow.

The boatmaker walks through the gardens and out, past the Winter Palace, set inside a tall wrought-iron fence decorated with the gold-painted initial of the reigning king. Over the domes and spires of the palace flies the national flag, indicating that the king is in residence. The flag is divided into blue and yellow quarters, the golden crown in the center circled by golden versions of the blackbirds of Vashad. Flanking the gate are sentry boxes, a guardsman before each one.

As he passes the palace, the boatmaker wonders how much the king can know of what goes on in his kingdom, even with the network of spies and informers that he must have, along with the police and army. The king is only a man, after all, not a god: a small figure somewhere under all the domes and spires, walking from room to room, ringing for coal when the fire in his study goes out and the room turns cool, chilling his fingers as they turn the pages of the latest report on the modernization project, its pages filled with charts and tables, endless bureaucratic sentences.

The boatmaker passes the Winter Palace and walks on while the afternoon sky contracts to a deeper blue.

No plan in mind, he finds himself at the door of the barbershop. He goes in and asks for a shave and a haircut, realizing as he does that at some point on his path his decision fell into place. He will go to dinner at the House of Lippsted. Somewhere he will find the first suit he has ever worn. He will ascend to the living quarters in the townhouse that rises above the rough bustle of the compound. He will see what it is like to sit at a dinner table with Jacob Lippsted, scion of the House of Lippsted, and his sister, with her glowing eyes and small resilient body under the fur wrap. The boatmaker knows he is not the man the foreman is; he never will be. At the same time he is not restrained as the foreman is by tradition and years of service. He has been invited. He will climb the stairs and join them at their table.

The barber is sprawled in his chair, the *Afternoon Post* covering his face, his legs dangling toward the floor. Snores bubble up from under the paper, raising it, then letting it fall. As the boatmaker enters, the barber wakes and holds the paper out as if he had been reading. The native islander is on the bench, bent forward under the engraving of The Royal Champion.

The barber gets up and lays his paper on the counter. On the front page is an engraving of two horses facing each other in silhouette.

As he sits, the boatmaker tries to decide whether to keep his mustache or shave it off. Perhaps he should grow a beard. He wonders whether there will be other guests at the dinner. He loses patience with his thoughts, irritated with himself for deciding to accept the invitation. He imagines tearing off the sheet and running, half-shorn, out into the street, yelling. He can't stand the barber's chatter or the snoring of the native under the engraving of the glossy racehorse. Working to be presentable for others makes the boatmaker ill.

Something the barber says as he chatters on breaks into this circle of irritable thoughts. ". . . yes, they're going to race against the king. *Against The Royal Champion.* Can you imagine? These Jews! Daring to run their horse against the king's, who's never been beaten in twenty races. A single challenge at the royal track. In June. Says so—right there in the *Post.*"

The barber nods in the direction of the newspaper, on whose front page the two horses stand nose to nose like shadows cut from black paper.

He finishes with his scissors, lays them down and returns with his mug and brush. Spreading hot lather across the boatmaker's face, he bursts out: "Outrageous! That the Jews could raise themselves up out of their place and challenge the king! But it's not entirely their fault. If things had been right in this country, something like this would never have happened.

"Listen to this," he says, sticking the brush in his mug, picking up the paper and reading like a public speaker: "The king is said to have accepted the challenge in the spirit of sportsmanship and to show the openness and forward-thinking spirit of the Mainland under his rule. 'We are moving forward to join a wider world,' His Majesty said through the Lord Chamberlain in announcing that he was accepting the challenge from the House of Lippsted."

The barber snaps the paper shut. "*A wider world!* Isn't our world wide enough? He forgets what he is king *of*, this weak king, with his love of fancy foreign ideas. His father, God rest his soul, would never have thought like this. The old ways were always good enough for *him*. Under his father there would have been no Jews putting on airs and rising above their station to challenge The Royal Champion to a match race."

At the barber's raised voice, the native sits up, his face framed in fur. The smell of whiskey seeps out into the shop. "*No good*," the native says. Then he leans forward until only fur is visible, and his sleeping resumes.

When he reaches the boardinghouse, the boatmaker goes to his landlady's door. He hasn't seen much of her since they went down to the cellar to look for Crow and White's belongings. She never even asked whether he found what he was looking for. But now he needs her help. He has no idea how to find a suit for dinner at the House of Lippsted. The landlady opens the door after a silence somewhat longer than usual, alcohol on her breath. He explains what he needs. She looks at him carefully, up and down. She is concentrating, but she isn't thinking deep thoughts or judging: She is appraising the Small Island man with the eye of a seamstress.

She disappears, leaving him standing in the doorway. He hears doors opening and closing, drawers sliding in and out. He feels dizzy and begins to sweat a cold, uncomfortable sweat. He needs a drink.

The door, which has drifted shut, opens slowly. Castor and Pollux pad out, rub against his legs, ask him to take them down to the cellar. At this moment he would gladly go down there with them, replace Crow's notebook and suitcase on the jumble, watch the black-and-white cats in their frenzied hunting and never come out. But the door opens again as the landlady pulls it with her foot. Her arms are filled with a black dinner suit, a white shirt, a bow tie, studs and cufflinks, patent-leather pumps. The tie is in her mouth. The boatmaker gently removes the tie from between her teeth.

"My husband's," she says, breathing heavily. "He won't be wearing them. You can have them." The boatmaker had no idea his landlady had been a married woman with an elegant husband. Somehow he had assumed she was always as he knows her: midnight drinker, smoker, reader of Kierkegaard, person without family.

"You didn't know I had a husband, did you?" She laughs, and he hears the crackling of fluid in her lungs. "Take these to your room and try them on. I'll be up to see where they need to be altered. You're a little smaller than he was, but close enough—and the same in the shoulders, which is the most important part. I'll be up in a few minutes. You be decent!" She laughs again, crackling and gurgling.

In the days before the dinner the boatmaker works as if nothing has changed. He wears the short jacket of an apprentice, measuring, cutting and presenting his work for inspection in a line with other apprentices. He sees how seriously the others take the inspections, how relieved they are when their work passes and they are allowed to take the next step up the ladder that leads to mastering their craft. The boatmaker still envies them, but not as much. He knows now that he will not be staying in this compound long enough to become a master in this house. The thing he is building in the back of the storeroom has changed his path.

These days, the only time he is really comfortable is in the storeroom, working with wood he has picked up before it is discarded or given away. From time to time the foreman directs that the scraps be given to poor women outside the compound walls. The past winter was a long one, even for the Mainland; in most houses there is little firewood left. The Gentile women of the Old Quarter accept the alms, then turn their backs, cursing the Jews as they make their way to their homes, where their husbands have been drinking and not working since snow began falling in November.

In the storeroom the thing the boatmaker is building has begun to find its form. The outline is there, even if one or two pieces have not yet presented themselves. He knows they will. And they will fit, even if not in precisely the orthodox way. He does not allow himself to envision the finished piece. Instead, he focuses on the task at hand. And a feeling leads him on, a glow that surrounds each piece as it shows him how it should be shaped and where it will fit.

The boatmaker works early and late, keeping his promise to the foreman not to neglect his duties. From time to time Sven Eriksson enters the storeroom, walks to the back and stands, pipe clenched, towering over him as he kneels among the pieces on the floor. The foreman looks for a while without speaking before turning to leave. As he watches, the foreman has a different look than he did before the boatmaker was invited upstairs for dinner: a look very much like worry. Sometimes, when his work is up-to-date and he has no report to make to Jacob Lippsted, Eriksson paces the wall—once, twice, three times—puffing like a locomotive.

On a warm night, at an hour when he would usually be in the storeroom, deep in his unfinished work, the boatmaker walks through the Old Quarter wearing a black dinner suit in a style dating from three decades before. The landlady has taken in the waist and shortened the sleeves and trousers. She has done her work with skill and care, gratified that one of her lodgers will be dining at a great house in the Old Quarter. Gratified and—very surprised. She would never have expected it of the silent man from Small Island.

As she bends over the suit to take it in, memories rise in her, stirred by smells from the old fabric. There is the smell of her. From the time she was first presented at court as the daughter of an ancient and noble family she never changed her scent. And there is the smell of her husband, equally loyal to one scent throughout his too-short life. As she cuts and sews, her scent comes up from the fabric, mingling with his for the last time. She drops a few tears as she works, but the stitches are true.

The suit, like anything made to measure, is perfectly wearable, though almost comically out of date. The boatmaker, walking through a lovely spring evening in the capital, is unaware of changing fashions. To him, the suit simply feels confining. The vest, the stiff white shirt, the tie knotted by the landlady under his clean shaven chin, all of it holds him and shapes him in a way his own clothes never do. But if the suit is confining, wearing it is liberating, as if by putting it on, he has become someone else: a man who belongs at the dinner table in the House of Lippsted. Through the warm air he walks, smoking and carrying a parcel wrapped in paper.

On reaching the compound he lets himself in, nodding to the watchman, who has seen him many times at this hour leaving for the boardinghouse. He does not stop to see the look on the watchman's face as he takes in the man of Small Island wearing an elegant dinner suit in a fashion decades old.

The boatmaker goes to the storeroom, opens his parcel, takes the patent-leather pumps out, removes his boots and pulls the shoes on over the shockingly thin black socks the landlady gave him. Almost transparent, the socks are unlike anything he has ever imagined a man would wear. They remind him of the stockings worn by the woman of the town. The shoes fit in the length, pinch slightly in the width. He goes to the door of the town-house and knocks.

The man who opens the door wears a suit much like the boatmaker's. Without being told, he knows the man is a servant. The servant leads him up a flight of carpeted stairs into a drawing room with a big bay window that looks out over the compound where the boatmaker can be seen every day, wearing the short jacket of an apprentice.

Jacob Lippsted, dark and compact, wearing a suit of the same quality as the boatmaker's, but transported three decades into the future, stands in the middle of the room. He dismisses the servant and shakes the boatmaker's hand, drawing him into the light of a drawing room filled with priceless Lippsted pieces and paintings made up of splotches of color that seem to picture nothing but themselves.

The boatmaker finds himself moving toward the bay window. On a cushioned seat matching the curve of the bay sits Rachel Lippsted. Next to her is a man even smaller than she is, dressed in a rumpled dinner suit in a style somewhere between the boatmaker's and his host's.

"My sister, Rachel," says Jacob Lippsted. "And our dear friend, Rabbi Nachum Goldman."

The tiny man wears a skullcap, but he is clean shaven and without sidecurls. Around a large nose, his features are smudged with age. He looks weary, but his eyes are bright. The boatmaker shakes the rabbi's small, dry hand and turns to the woman next to him, who is wearing a closely fitted dress the color of the sky on a perfect October night. The cameo at her throat is the one she wore at the Mint, its profile echoing her own. Her hair is up and she looks more elegant and composed than she did at the Mint.

She does not extend her hand; the boatmaker has no idea what is expected. He feels as if the other men are watching him to see whether he understands the ritual of being introduced to a beautiful woman in a drawing room filled with daringly modern paintings and priceless Lippsted furniture.

He nods in the direction of her cameo, approximating a bow. Those who know Rachel Lippsted know she is on the point of laughing out loud—feeling both pleasure and a teasing superiority. But her face shows only gracious welcome.

"May I bring you a drink?" Jacob Lippsted asks, breaking in on the boatmaker's discomfort.

"Yes. Please."

"Any *particular* drink?" Jacob Lippsted has a bit of his sister's teasing humor, her combination of graciousness and superiority.

"Whiskey."

"Whiskey, we have," he says, moving to a sideboard where bottles the boatmaker has never seen before are arranged like soldiers next to their commanding officer: an elegant silver ice bucket.

The boatmaker is more interested in the sideboard than in the bottles. It is old, perhaps very old: Lippsted, in a style simpler and more austere than that of the present day. The front is light, inlaid with a geometric pattern of darker woods the boatmaker cannot identify, in spite of his months in the yard. Perhaps the wood is no longer used, possibly no longer available, even to the House of Lippsted.

As he accepts a tumbler filled with whiskey and ice, he worries about the drink. He has drunk nothing for many months, since waking up in the hospital, and does not know how he will react. In his life, he has rarely had just one drink. But he wants badly not to be drunk in front of these people, especially the woman on the window seat. He doesn't care as much about the men. But the thought of what he might do in front of her if he can't stop with one drink makes the sweat run under his old-fashioned dinner suit.

"Welcome to our home!" says Jacob Lippsted, raising a glass filled with the same whiskey he gave the boatmaker. They drink. It is smoother than any drink the boatmaker has ever tasted: perfumed fire.

"My foreman tells me you are a promising worker in wood. And Sven Eriksson, whatever his other virtues, is not a man to dispense compliments lightly. Though, come to think of it, that is one of his chief virtues to me, as a businessman."

Jacob Lippsted laughs, and it becomes clear that one of his ways of putting people at ease is laughing gently at all the participants in a situation, including himself. Like the whiskey, this kind of teasing humor is new to the boatmaker.

The host laughs and finishes off his drink in one swift motion. "Another?" he asks the boatmaker, rising. Neither Rachel nor the rabbi is drinking.

"No," says the boatmaker, who has drunk only enough to feel the perfumed fire in nose and throat.

"Don't tell me you are joining my sister and the rabbi in teetotalling?" Jacob Lippsted says, dramatically exaggerating his disappointment. "For them, one glass of wine is a celebration. Two is a debauch. Join me instead."

"Maybe later," says the boatmaker, relieved to find he can take a little of the surprising whiskey without being overwhelmed by his thirst. The sweat has stopped trickling down his back and sides under the antique jacket. He begins to feel as if an approximation of himself is present.

As he listens, he finds that Jacob Lippsted has a remarkable skill for drawing everyone into the conversation in rhythm. To be sure, the scion of the House of Lippsted has the assistance of beautiful surroundings, the warmth from aged whiskey and the frictionless, invisible attention of servants. But the boatmaker has the feeling that his host could do the same thing in a shed on Small Island, squatting on a dirt floor around a fireplace made of broken stones, surrounded by entirely different people drinking a much rougher whiskey.

CHAPTER 21

A servant whispers in Jacob Lippsted's ear, and doors slide back. They are escorted into a smaller room with wood-panelled walls in which a narrow dining table has been laid for four. The boatmaker and the rabbi face each other across the width. Jacob is seated at the head, Rachel at the foot. Tapers are lighted. Candlelight glows on silver and linen. A servant fills the boatmaker's glass with red wine.

The wine is as incomprehensible as the whiskey and the paintings. The same novel strangeness extends to the food. The roast and vegetables on his plate share names, shapes and colors with food he has eaten, but they don't have the same taste. As he assesses these novelties, he continues to be surprised that he can drink a little and not be devastated.

As he eats, drinks and speaks a few words under the persuasion of Jacob Lippsted, the boatmaker keeps circling back to the question he has been asking himself since the foreman conveyed the invitation to dine: *Why am I here?*

The boatmaker is not a man of many words. But he has never been afraid to speak up when it is necessary, to say what needs saying, ask what needs asking. For the first time in his life he is afraid to speak: afraid that if he does, he will wake up in the cold storeroom under an oil lamp, wearing a short jacket, pieces of his project scattered across the floor.

Rachel Lippsted spends the meal studying the odd man in the old-fashioned dinner suit. Again, she has a memory of seeing him but cannot put her memory-picture in its frame. Where was it? And when? Wherever and whenever it was, she knows he was not dressed as he is now. Beyond that, her memory is failing her in a way it seldom does.

She watches the boatmaker as the conversation flows in the channels her brother creates for it. She can follow, participate and remain watchful, thinking her own thoughts. Long experience has made her comfortable in drawing rooms and dining rooms where conversation and mood move on many levels. She sees that the boatmaker is uncomfortable in his ancient suit. He may never have worn a suit before. She sees that in his discomfort he naturally assumes a formality, a consideredness, a slowness that fits the suit as well as the suit fits him.

She is surprised to feel herself drawn to the odd man from Small Island. To his bald spot, the crisscrossing scar on his nose, the rough, knowing hands. She pulls herself back mentally, startled at how out of place her response is. Perhaps, she thinks, it is because the suit is the vintage of her father's, hanging in his dressing room upstairs, in the place it was the day he died. The suit is touched by no one other than his daughter, who takes it out occasionally to brush it, shake it out and bury her face in it when no one is there to see her.

"And are you a Jew?" asks the rabbi from across the narrow table.

The boatmaker is as startled by this question as if the room had changed into a different room, with different people in it. But he gives no sign.

"No."

"You are from Small Island?"

"Yes."

"And where on the Mainland are your people from?" The rabbi is fluent in the language of the Mainland, but he speaks with a slight accent, as if he came from the lands down to the south and east, in Europe.

The boatmaker names a region a long way from the capital, near the narrow neck of land that connects the Mainland to Europe. This narrow land bridge has been fought over repeatedly, belonging to three different nations over the course of its history. Now it is firmly in the possession of the Mainland, the border overseen by a toll collector in a booth guarded by one sleepy young conscript.

"What you say may be true," says the rabbi, removing the linen napkin he tucked into his collar when the soup was served. In spite of this precaution, there are dots of beige and brown on his lapel and shirtfront, corresponding to the soup and each of the three subsequent courses. "But there is the matter of the name."

The boatmaker feels himself tense. He has remained silent about the question of his name whenever it has come up on the Mainland. He has no wish to discuss it here. But he feels an obligation to be a respectful guest. While he is wrestling with his feelings, the rabbi stuns him again.

"Then again, you may be one of *the Secret Jews*," Goldman says, wiping his mouth with the big napkin, dark eyes sharp and bright. "Stranger things have happened. Baruch Ha-Shem."

"*Secret Jews?*" The boatmaker cannot believe what he is hearing. He wants to clean his ears out with his fingers. But he sits unmoving.

"Yes, the Secret Jews. There are twelve of them, hidden from the prying eyes of the world. Ha-Shem in his wisdom understood that mankind is weak, unable to keep the Covenant on its own, despite all its piety and good intentions. So he built a foundation."

"What?"

"A foundation. You are a carpenter, yes?"

The boatmaker's silence passes for assent.

"So you understand the importance of a good foundation. It is invisible—and yet essential. To last, a house must be built on a solid foundation. Even if the house burns down, it can be rebuilt on the same foundation. A single foundation can serve many houses, over generations. Not so?"

The boatmaker's relief that the conversation has veered away from his name has turned to disbelief. Many strange things have happened to him on the Mainland. What happened on the New Land was, in the end, shocking. But at the very least all of it happened within a Christian framework, the framework that holds the entire kingdom together, from the capital to the outer islands. The idea that someone thinks he is a Jew, secret or not, is incomprehensible.

The rabbi rumbles on, giving no sign that he is aware of the boatmaker's distress.

"In his foresight, Ha-Shem provided a foundation for mankind, who are as frail as the frailest wooden dwelling on our Mainland. This foundation consists of twelve men in each generation. These men are to all outward appearance ordinary men, simple, humble people. And yet they support the world. Who knows? Perhaps you are one of them. Baruch Ha-Shem."

The rabbi wipes his mouth, eyes twinkling.

The boatmaker has no idea whether the rabbi's speech is deadly serious or merely a fantastic joke played in this room every night on another unsuspecting guest. Perhaps he has been invited only to be the butt of this joke. The foreman told him Jacob Lippsted had an unusual sense of humor, that he was capable of anything. *A Secret Jew*. Nonsense! He is no Secret Jew. Any more than he was Father Robert's Number IV. He wants to get up and leave, but the eyes of Rachel Lippsted are on him, and he cannot rise.

The rabbi continues as if everything is fine.

"The final irony is that none of these twelve know who they are. And they cannot know. The virtue they need most to fulfill their task is humility. And what man, knowing he is one of the righteous twelve—pillars of Ha-Shem's creation—could possibly remain humble? No one! That is not human nature! They would tear off their rags and clothe themselves in jewels and furs. And the people, in their benighted state, would bow down and worship them."

The rabbi wets his throat with a little of the deep red wine in his glass, which is still more than half full. A servant enters, offering a carafe of the same wine. All except Jacob Lippsted reach out and cover their glasses.

"You see why this lack of self-knowledge is so important. Others may try to guess who they are. A foolish impostor may claim to be one of them. But in almost all cases they live out their lives unknown and unrecognized, to be discovered only later, after they have fulfilled their purpose and been replaced. Because there must be twelve in the world at all times. If one dies, a new one is born that very day, somewhere in the world. Only Ha-Shem knows where. It may be in the farthest, humblest corner of the world—even on your Small Island."

"There are no Jews on Small Island."

"Yes," the rabbi says, laughing and dabbing at his mouth with a corner of his napkin. "That is just what one of the twelve would say. And who is to know? None of us! All we know is that the humor of Ha-Shem is at work at all times and in all places. And He rarely makes our road straight."

The strange dinner concludes without further discussion of the Secret Jews, but the boatmaker is left wondering, new questions added to the ones he has been accumulating since he landed on the Mainland. No closer to answers, he resumes his routine, going back to long hours in the storeroom before and after his other tasks.

In the back of the storeroom, the thing he is making is filling out. He has recognized it. When he started, he didn't want to see an image of the finished piece; he wanted it to come into being on its own. Now he can see what it will be. He puts the image out of his mind, concentrates on details. He knows that finishing this piece will interrupt his progress from apprentice to master in the House of Lippsted. But he does not know where his path will take him after that.

After the dinner, Sven Eriksson comes to the storeroom more frequently. The foreman says little, but he seems troubled. Even though he himself gave permission for it, he has always been disturbed by what the boatmaker is doing in the storeroom. Now that the man from Small Island has been up the stairs to dinner, what is going on in the storeroom seems like an even more troubling disruption of the accepted way of doing things. There is an explosive energy around the boatmaker and what he is building. Perhaps it is because no such work has ever been undertaken inside these walls, with or without permission.

His mind troubled, the foreman mutters that his time has passed. He's lived too long, he tells himself. He's an old man in his dotage, the way his father was for three or four years before he died. Eriksson knows none of this is true. It would be easier if it were. He walks the wall four times, five times.

All around him the smells of the city rise in full power—from layers of manure, fruit in vendors' carts, raw meat behind windows inscribed with letters of gold. The foreman flaps and puffs like a waterbird, trying to put out of his mind the volatile energy he feels around the wordless Small Islander. He badly wants to know what things were like upstairs in the apartment of Herr Jacob Lippsted and his sister Rachel, but he will never ask.

A few days after the dinner the boatmaker tries to return the dinner suit, but the landlady won't accept it. "You might be asked to dinner again," she says. "Then you'd just have to come down and get it. Keep it in your room. I'll come up and brush it."

He hangs it in the wardrobe in his room, which until now has been empty. The landlady is sad to part with the suit, but pleased that it may be worn again at an elegant dinner table. It was not so old when her husband died, the last in a line of dinner suits he ordered from a tailor patronized by many of the elegantly dressed men of the capital. She is moved to think that it might have a new life in the present, reduced as that present might be for her, with its odd boarders, Kierkegaard and alcohol and cigarettes.

While for some reason the landlady is sure the boatmaker will be invited back, he is equally sure he will not. The invitation was a mistake, he thinks, or an elaborate prank. And if he is, by some remote chance, invited back, he will decline immediately. He has no need to be harangued about being a Secret Jew. He is no Jew, has never been one.

But he humors his landlady, appreciating her kindness. He hangs the suit in the wardrobe and returns to his round of working, walking, smoking and attempting to puzzle out Crow's notebook. One night while he is looking through Crow's black scratches for the twentieth time without approaching any closer to the mystery of R and the third stream of Crow's income, there is a knock on his door, something that is unusual at any hour, unheard of this late.

He gets up and opens the door to find the landlady, Kierkegaard and cigarette in hand, sans cats. "You have a visitor," she says. Her voice is even, not too different from usual, but the boatmaker can feel her excitement. He thinks Father Robert has finally found him. In a corner of his mind he has been expecting the priest, Neck and a few other brothers to enter, wrestle him to the floor and take him to the New Land, bound and gagged. He should have run long before. He was an idiot to return to this house.

"A visitor?"

"I think you should go down." She turns and disappears down the stairs. The boatmaker pulls the straps of his overalls over his longjohns, picks up his candle and follows her down between the ancestors until he reaches the bottom and the family's founding knight, dating from only a few centuries after the time of Vashad.

The front door is standing open. In the doorway is a man dressed in the uniform of the House of Lippsted. Behind him at the curb the boatmaker sees a familiar two-wheeled carriage with matched black horses shaking their heads and snorting under stiff plumes. The shades are drawn over the windows.

"Miss Rachel Lippsted to see you, sir," says the servant, his throat clenching around the hateful words.

"Rachel Lippsted?"

"Yes, sir."

"Well . . . send her in," the boatmaker says, trying to recover and speak words appropriate for a gentleman receiving a lady, absurd as such words might seem, spoken by an unshaven man in overalls and stocking feet at the door of a house that has come down many rungs in the world.

The servant retreats to the curb, opens the door of the carriage and extends a gloved hand. Rachel Lippsted steps out, wearing a dress of emerald green with a short cape. She is unveiled, but there is no one on the street to witness her sail across the curb and up the stone steps to the landing, where the boatmaker is standing still as the house, candle flame flapping.

"I apologize for coming unannounced. I know it's not civilized. I hope I'm not intruding."

"No."

"Good. You may go, Karl. Return for me in two hours."

"Very good, miss," the servant says, choking on his outrage. He returns to the carriage, takes his whip and abuses the horses through the deserted streets, their hooves loud on the cobblestones, black plumes bobbing.

The boatmaker leads the way up between the landlady's ancestors to his room, holding his candle high. Castor and Pollux escape from the landlady's open door. She rushes out to shoo them back before they can follow the boatmaker and his guest.

Rachel sees the portraits and is struck by the contrast between the shabbiness of the boardinghouse and the nobility of the lineage. Unlike the boatmaker, she knows exactly who the landlady's family is. As she climbs the stairs, feeling each step give and then spring back, Rachel has a moment of fear, wanting to turn back. But it is too late. It was too late the moment she stepped from her carriage to the curb. Perhaps the moment she gave the address to her driver and saw him attempt to conceal his surprise at her poor judgment. Possibly even before that.

She follows the boatmaker to the top of the stairs, turns left down the hall and into the small room with its window overlooking the alley. He offers her his only seat: a simple oak chair from a country kitchen. She removes her dove-gray gloves and drops them into her emerald-green lap. The boatmaker pulls the bedsheets into a semblance of civilized respect, pushes Crow's account book under the pillow and sits on his bed.

"I hope you can forgive the rabbi for his talk about the Secret Jews."

"Where I come from, there aren't any Jews."

"Small Island."

"Yes."

"And how did you get to the capital?"

"I built a boat and sailed to Big Island. I was there for a while. Then I sailed to the Mainland. I landed on the other coast and walked here. I hitched some rides on wagons. But mostly walked."

Rachel Lippsted, astonished with herself but not turning back, knows she has seen this man. Not in her drawing room and not in the compound. Before that. And the memory is connected to big things, important things. But she still can't bring back the scene. The irritation caused by this unsatisfied curiosity is part of the reason she is here—but only a small part.

The boatmaker, on his side, remembers each time he has seen the woman sitting in his worn country-kitchen chair, everything she said and did. He wants to talk to her about all of that. But he is silent.

"Do you mind if I smoke?"

"No." He offers her one of his cigarettes and takes one for himself, lighting both from the candle. For a while they sit smoking. From the Mint he remembers the stains on her fingers.

"I hope you can forgive the rabbi. He is really all the family we have. Our parents died when we were young. Jacob is two years younger than I am, although he thinks he's my father." She laughs, holding the cigarette up, the ash long, looking for a place to put it.

The boatmaker stands and offers the candlestick, which he has been using as his ashtray. She tips ash into the upturned brass base and looks up at him. He rubs his cigarette out in the candleholder, takes hers and puts it out, sets the candleholder on the washstand and pulls her into his arms.

She resists at first, holding herself back, turning her mouth to avoid his rough face. Her turning away makes him more forceful and demanding. She begins to give in.

She knows this is what she has come for. *Asking for forgiveness for the rabbi.* It embarrasses her. The rabbi doesn't need this man's forgiveness—or anyone's. The boatmaker's kisses heat her. Shame heats her. She gives in.

The boatmaker undoes her elegant clothes a layer at a time until he has freed her body into his hands. She is small, but fuller than he imagined, smooth and resilient, folded and secret. He puts the candle out and, though no one can see into the room, draws the curtain.

He stands over her while he removes his clothes. The last thing he does before entering her is to feel under the pillow for Crow's notebook. He takes it out and lets it fall. She hears the notebook hit the floor, but she is already lost, and the sound could be anything: a pushcart in the alley, the cry of a peddler, a bird on the windowsill, confused about the direction from which the sun will rise.

Afterward, they lie smoking, looking at the ceiling, each engaged in very separate thoughts. Rachel Lippsted cannot decide whether what she has done is in obedience to her brother's wishes or a terrible defiance of them. Surely, she thinks, a single act cannot be both compliant and defiant.

Rachel has great respect for her brother's knowledge of the world. He has tried to guide her into marriage, arranging proposals from the sons of wealthy Jewish banking houses in Berlin, Paris and Vienna. She has rejected all of them, some quite abruptly. Her brother has never chastised her for refusing, but she can feel his concern that she will never marry and leave the deeply familiar routine of the townhouse where the two of them live together like jewels in a black velvet case.

In all those situations, she understood her brother's intentions clearly. But now she is confused. Didn't Jacob invite this strange man to dinner? And wasn't that an act almost as unexpected and mad as what she has done tonight? Isn't her act, impulsive as it was, an extension of his? She thinks and thinks, but cannot decide. Still, she is sure that her opposing currents of feeling toward her brother are part of what is drawing her to this strange man.

She turns on her side and reaches over to stroke the boatmaker's face, feeling the roughness of his beard, the prickle of mustache. She raises herself over him where he is lying on his back and slaps his face lightly, teasingly. She feels so much more worldly than he is. It is as if they are from different realms: she the sky, he the earth. She saw from the way he behaved in their drawing room that she knows a thousand things he does not know, may never know. She knows she could tease and mock him—and she will. At the same time she cannot deny that, regardless of the enormous differences between them, regardless of her tangled motives, she has given herself to this strange man from Small Island. The gift is irrevocable.

She remembers how she felt with her father when she was eight years old: cherished, in her place, his love restoring order to a universe that had become chaotic following her mother's death. Her brother and the rabbi, each in his own way, give her some of that feeling. But for reasons unfathomed and unfathomable, the boatmaker, with his Small Island smell of earth, stone and sea, gives her much more. She has surrendered. She is not afraid. Surprised—very—but no longer afraid. They crush out their cigarettes, close the distance between them.

When she leaves, he pulls his longjohns on and stands in the center of the cold room watching what has just happened play through his mind over and over again. He sees the chair where she was sitting when he pulled her up to him. The narrow bed where he stood looking down at her waiting for him, watching him, her body white and smooth, dark at the center. He walks to the window and pulls the curtain back, looking down into the alley, where he saw Crow and White alive for the last time. Crow's notebook sits on the floor under the bed where he dropped it.

He picks the notebook up and skims through it in the moonlight. Finding nothing new, he closes the notebook and lifts the lid of his cache. Even with what he keeps in the sealskin bag, there is quite a bit of money under the floor. In this moment, his questions about money seem as childish as the red and blue sails on the boats the boys push out into the center of the pool in the Royal Gardens. Perhaps the secret of money, the secret he has been searching for all these months, is simply that to be happy you need to have enough money that you don't have to think about it. He laughs at himself. Rachel Lippsted makes him want to laugh at himself. She makes him feel foolish, a little crude, possibly even childish. He feels a little of the anger he felt toward the woman of the town. But he softens quickly, because he knows that, deep down, this woman, in spite of her teasing superiority, her wealth and breeding, belongs to him. The boatmaker has accepted Rachel Lippsted's startling surrender. There will be none of the rage he felt on Big Island.

He puts the notebook back in the cache and sets the green floorboard in place. He lies down and twists the rumpled sheets around him. Through the window, he can see that the sky has begun to change. Everything is smiling. Outside, a miracle is about to take place: the dawn of a perfectly ordinary spring day. In an hour the boatmaker will dress and then drink his coffee from the bowl offered by the landlady. The landlady will say nothing about the events of the previous evening. He will treasure her silence. He will pull on his canvas jacket, finish his coffee and go out into the Old Quarter, its streets alive with the smell of food and the sound of business waiting to be conducted.

CHAPTER 22

Rachel's third visit to the boardinghouse comes on a beautiful spring night with a sliver of moon in a blue-black sky. The boatmaker is standing with his back to the room, looking out the window. The moon and sky make him think of his journey to Big Island: how huge the sky was, how well his boat sailed. He thinks of where the boat is now, wonders whether he will ever see it again. Asks himself whether Small Island is still his home. And if it isn't, what is?

At that thought he feels her touch on his back and smells her scent, which reminds him of spring flowers under rain, beneath it the smell of her. She leans into him, her head resting on his back, reaches around and joins her hands on his chest. They stand that way for a while in the moonlight. Then they enter the world that they create together between the Old Quarter and the moon.

After, he rises from the twisted sheets to bring them cigarettes. She is pleased by the leanness of him. At the center of his body his skin is white, but there is color in his neck, face and forearms, even after the long Mainland winter.

They lie back, smoking, safe in their world, which for the moment exists only on his narrow bed. When they are in this world, neither of them wants to leave it to enter everyday reality. For that reason they have shared little about themselves. Even the few stories they have told each other have been told the way you would tell an acquaintance, not an intimate. But as he lies smoking, feeling her beside him, the boatmaker knows he is about to bring them out of their little sphere into the outside world—or bring the outside world onto this bed with them.

Raising himself on an elbow and looking down at her, he says: "I saw you once before."

He is giving her room, not touching her. She is not interested in talking, wishes he would be quiet, press closer. She resents the space between them, which is oddly shaped, filled with cigarette smoke and moonlight.

"In the compound? Yes, I saw you. I still see you sometimes, standing there in your canvas jacket. But I am *proper*, you know, well brought up. I was raised in the capital and educated in Paris. And so I say nothing.

What would people think if I stood in the courtyard and shouted to anyone who could hear me: *Look! Look! This is the man I love. Look at him there in his jacket, his arms full of wood!* Imagine how their faces would change! But I don't do that. I am nothing if not well behaved. At least I was before I met you," she says, exhaling gray smoke through a smile that is about to turn into the laughter the boatmaker now cannot imagine his life without.

She is surprised he seems so serious. She knows he is a serious man, but until now, she has always been able to make him smile, even laugh at himself—and has taken great pleasure in those acts.

"Not in the compound. Before I came there."

"When?" She lets ash fall on them and on the sheet. He takes her cigarette, gets out of bed, crushes both cigarettes in the base of the candlestick and comes back to sit on the edge of the bed.

"At the Mint. On the king's birthday. Not last year. The year before."

She sits up and looks at him. "So *that's* where I saw you! I couldn't remember. I knew I had seen you before. You seemed so familiar. But I couldn't remember where or when. It was like an itch in my brain; I couldn't scratch it. So that's where it was!" Her face shines. The mystery is solved. There is no reason for him to keep on being so serious.

She reaches for him. He knows she wants him to close the distance between them, take her again. But he stops her. Not roughly, but firm.

"You were giving your lecture. There was a man yelling about the Jews. You did something with the desk. The police came and took him away. But not roughly. I know how the coppers can be when they want to. They were gentle with him. It was a game."

"*Rademacher*," she says, her face clouding. "*A very dangerous man.*"

"Who is Rademacher?"

"An agent of The Brotherhood. And the police also, no doubt. There is often so little difference between them."

"*The Brotherhood* newspaper?"

"They publish that hateful paper, yes. And do other things. They are a secret society that is in fact not so secret. At the heart of it is a small group of powerful men: retired army officers, businessmen, politicians, high men of the Church. My brother knows all of them. We have been to their houses and they to ours. In public they are polite enough to us. But deep down they are frightened—of losing their country, of us, of things changing. And as a result they are filled with hatred. So far the king has kept them in check. But there are limits to any man's power—even the king's."

He can tell she wants to smoke. He gets them another pair of cigarettes and stands before her. "Why would he show up at your lecture, this Rademacher?"

"Who knows? Perhaps he was drunk. Drunk and full of whiskey courage. Then again, he might not have been afraid even if he was sober. Perhaps it was just an amusement. A pleasant way to pass the holiday when he was liberated from his other duties." Rachel Lippsted laughs without happiness.

The boatmaker doesn't like to see her in this mood. But he does not want her to stop talking. Someone is finally telling him at least a few of the things he has wanted to know for a long time. He lights the cigarettes and hands her one. They sit side by side on the edge of the bed, smoking.

"Rademacher is a powerful agent of The Brotherhood," she says. "A man to be feared. But also a man with a wild streak. Perhaps that is why he is still out there in the field running his stable of corrupt little agents. I must admit that in a strange way—very strange, coming from me—I admire Rademacher. With his connections and experience, he could be sitting in a wood-panelled office somewhere, shifting papers from box to box. But he remains on the outside, in the middle of the action. I admire that in a man—even an evil man."

She pauses and exhales, long and slow, gazing at the green floorboards. Then she turns to look straight into the boatmaker's eyes.

"And here's something that may surprise you. You know Sven Eriksson, the foreman you admire so much? He and Rademacher were childhood friends. They grew up together in the same village. Now they hate each other. What kind of world do we live in, where boyhood friends from the same village grow up to be sworn enemies who would kill each other if they got the chance?"

The boatmaker hears her question, but his mind is still engaged with the riddles he has been pondering so long.

"You handled it well—when he got angry."

"I was upset. You can imagine. But I wasn't afraid for my life. I have no doubt that Rademacher is capable of great violence. But he wasn't going to spill my blood in the Royal Mint on the king's birthday. He knew that. I knew that. Still . . ."

She reaches for him, and this time he doesn't stop her. Their coming together is as powerful as before, but also different: The outside world has entered the space between them.

Two days later the boatmaker is deep in the storeroom when the foreman comes to stand over him and his work. It is late in the day. Sven Eriksson looks from man to wood and back. "You are again invited to dine—upstairs." He turns and leaves.

In the boatmaker's room the dinner suit hangs in the wardrobe. The landlady has been brushing it every few days, hoping it will be worn again. He takes it out and dresses slowly. His fingers, so skilled with tools, are less deft when it comes to putting on an old-fashioned dinner suit. The landlady will help him with tie, cufflinks, studs for the boiled shirt. The boatmaker, who has never before wished he had a mirror to see himself in, now wishes he had one.

He tucks himself into the trousers, pulls the halves of the shirt together, pulls up the braces. Fingers his nose, wondering how much the scar has faded, how obvious it still is. He has told no one how he got it. Rachel has asked, of course. He gave her the usual story—an accident on a building site—a story that is little more than a painted wooden toy given to a child to stop its crying. Rachel knows that, but she already understands the boatmaker well enough not to press further. He sits on his bed, waiting for the landlady to come and help him finish dressing. It is late in spring, still light past seven.

Outwardly the second dinner is not very different from the first. The same group convenes in the drawing room among paintings that resemble colored snowstorms. There is the whiskey, with its luxurious and elegant burn, the table heavy with silver and crystal in the wood-panelled dining room.

But under the surface different currents are flowing. Rachel Lippsted and the boatmaker glow like fireflies, pretending not to know each other. The rabbi stays away from the subject of the Secret Jews, instead making surprisingly worldly and sophisticated small talk including witty remarks in several languages. Jacob Lippsted, having been a selfless and gracious host at the first dinner, is flushed and full of himself, enjoying much of his own glorious deep red wine as he talks about what is on his mind rather than bringing the others into the conversation one at a time in their turn.

"We are racing the king. In June at the Royal Racecourse. A challenge match: his horse against ours. Medieval, don't you think? Two champions enter the lists on behalf of two great houses, sporting colored silks. But this race is the opposite of medieval. The king is a great modernizer. He is opening our small, backward country to the world. The race is a part of that opening. There is no money riding on it, nothing but a handshake. But for the king to shake *my* hand and take this wager means a deep change in the kingdom. He is the king, but he is meeting me, meeting this house, as he would any of his citizens. That is progress."

He lifts his glass, half full of wine the color of a ripe plum: "To our king. To a wider world where we all stand equal." They drink, his listeners careful with their own thoughts.

"And may this race, though just a symbol, bring many opportunities to us. May the House of Lippsted grow and prosper. May our partnership with the king lift us beyond even the greatest successes of our past." All four drink again, tasting the wine and the words.

Turning to the boatmaker, Jacob says: "Our horse is every bit a match for the king's. You must come with me to see him." He gives his sister a look that is meaningful, his dark eyes on hers, speaking the language of a kingdom of two. He is startled to find that her eyes are opaque to him. She is flushed. She has drunk more than usual, he thinks, explaining her opacity that way.

The rabbi looks at the three young people with pride and affection. How beautiful they are, he thinks. Even the man from Small Island has crept into the rabbi's open heart. But at the same time he feels a fear that rises from the memory of his people, from all the things Jews have suffered at the hands of Christians. Jacob Lippsted's pride, his display of power, make the rabbi uneasy. The rabbi knows better than the young people that in the history of his tribe calling proud attention to oneself and one's power has brought down disasters and punishments. First from Ha-Shem, later from the Gentiles, who might even (who can say?) be themselves an instrument of Ha-Shem. The rabbi knows that if he tries to explain his concerns, Jacob Lippsted will laugh, tell him to abandon tribal superstitions and join a world that is rapidly changing.

The boatmaker doesn't know whether he should take seriously Jacob's suggestion to come and see the great horse that will run for the House of Lippsted. But not long after this dinner, on a fine day when spring is flowing into summer, he finds himself in the black carriage that brings Rachel to his boardinghouse. He thinks he can smell her scent rise from the black leather. By now he is aware that this scent, of spring flowers under rain, has a name: Lily of the Valley.

As the carriage rolls toward the countryside, the boatmaker is embarrassed by his jacket, the costume of an apprentice. He is not ashamed of his work. Not at all. He is proud to serve under Sven Eriksson, to work among his men, every one a serious and capable worker, some revered masters of their craft. But next to Jacob Lippsted, who leans back on black cushions smoking a cigar and letting his smoke drift out the window, wearing a brown tweed suit cut and sewn by hands as skilled as the ones that make Lippsted furniture, the boatmaker feels poorly groomed.

Jacob Lippsted's suit fits him as if it knew him as well as his mother did, giving him room where he needs it, holding him snug where it should do that. It is a suit for the country, matching brown boots and the brown gloves held in his left hand while he smokes with his right. It is not only the suit that makes the man seem so well groomed. Jacob Lippsted seems more at ease with himself than anyone the boatmaker has ever known. It does not surprise him that the man with the dark eyes and neatly clipped beard can speak as a peer to the king.

"I'm glad you're coming with me. I am. I want you to see this horse. And meet his trainer. An odd little man, Donelan—but a genius with animals. He knows this horse. No one could have told us when we bought him at auction as a colt that he would come this far. He had courage—no question of that—and raw power. But he was ornery. When he raced, you never knew whether he was going to run like the wind or bolt to the stables when the gun was fired. He was a handful—more than a handful! I was ready to give up on him and put him out to stud. And he will be a great stud horse one day. He has wonderful bloodlines, going all the way back to the

Byerly Turk. You can't have nobler blood than that, even if you are the king himself. Who's a very good chap, by the way, with a wonderful sense of humor, even about himself."

"Donelan?"

"Yes, Donelan. Oh, you mean the name. He's an Irishman. I see why you're puzzled. Not many of those on the Mainland, are there? He came with the colt when we bought him. Refused to be parted. He was as ornery as the colt. But he must have known what the horse could be. There are many kinds of knowledge in this world. The rabbi has one kind. I know you think he's a cracked old egg, with his babble about Secret Jews, but you will see in time. He's a man of rare depth, Nachum Goldman. You have another kind of knowledge. My sister has another."

Jacob Lippsted leans out the window, exhaling a long stream of smoke, eyes turned from the boatmaker to the rich farmland left by the glaciers when they retreated thousands of years before.

"When we bought the colt, Donelan knew something about him that no one else could see yet. He was willing to make powerful people angry in his stubbornness and his refusal to be parted from the colt. But he's been proved right, many times over. He's made something great of this horse. I wouldn't say tamed, because he isn't tamed. You'll see. You wouldn't want him to be tamed. The same way you wouldn't want your best general to be tamed. The way Napoleon was never tamed. They could chain him to a lump of rock no bigger than Small Island—but never tame him. Well, here we are. Soon enough, you'll see for yourself," Jacob Lippsted says, tossing half of a very expensive cigar out the window.

The carriage turns through a gate in a wooden fence. At the end of a gravel drive stands a group of large, well-kept stone buildings. On the front of the largest, in the center, is a metal *L*. The carriage stops in front of it, and the men climb out, stretching their legs. The black horses snort and shake their heads. The driver leads them around the corner and out of sight.

Inside the barn is the rich smell of a place where horses live: sweat, hay, grain, manure, saddle soap, leather. Everything is quiet. No one seems to be waiting for the two men to arrive, even though one of them owns everything in sight, right down to the last water bucket and the dipper in it. Each stall they pass has a brass plate bearing a name. They walk through the straw until they come to a stall twice the size of the others, with *Bold Prince* inscribed on its brass plaque.

In the stall are a pony and a man wearing a worn tweed suit with a vest and flat cap. Towering over them is a brown horse with a black mane and tail. The horse is tall, but his leanness makes him seem even taller than he is. He tenses at their appearance. The boatmaker remembers the newspaper in the barbershop. One of the silhouettes facing each other on the front page has sprung to life.

"Hello, Donelan," says Jacob Lippsted, at his ease but not barging into the stall. "How is the mood today?"

"Changeable as always, sir. Thunderclouds early, then patches of sun. But we're always on the lookout for sudden storms. It's spring, after all."

Donelan speaks the language of the Mainland well enough to banter with Jacob Lippsted about the horse in their own code. But he speaks with an accent. It is unlike any accent the boatmaker knows, like an English accent but not quite the same. The big horse relaxes at the sound of the little man's voice.

"Donelan, this is a friend who has come to us all the way from Small Island. I would appreciate it if you would all make him welcome. Do you think the weather will hold long enough for us to come in?"

"I think it might," Donelan says, coming to the gate. At he reaches to open it, the boatmaker sees that the Irishman's hands are twisted. He uses them like blunt tools.

Donelan gets the gate open, and they step in. The big horse backs into a corner of the stall, his eyes expanding until white shows all the way around the irises.

"Come on," the Irishman says, closing the gate, "it will be alright. We'll be friends soon enough. Give this to the pony," he says, pressing a lump of sugar into the boatmaker's palm. "Here you go, Fannie. Let's see what this fellow has brought you from town."

The boatmaker shows the sugar and the pony comes toward him, looks him up and down, accepts the sugar and lets him stroke her muzzle. Some of the tension leaves the stall. The brown horse takes a step toward the rest, less white showing in his eyes.

"Ah, yes, your majesty," the Irishman says, "it's alright. We're all going to be friends, whether our bloodlines go all the way back to the days of the prophet Mohamet or only to Small Island."

He moves quietly to the big horse and leans into his shoulder, as if he were leaning against a brown-and-black wall. The horse turns his head, reaches down, takes the flat cap in his mouth, holding it up and out of reach.

"Well, well, well. We are playful, are we not, my prince? The air of Small Island must agree with you."

He turns and swats the horse on its shoulder, at which the pony comes to intervene, putting her head under the Irishman's armpit and demanding her rightful place in this small kingdom.

After his visit to the barn, the boatmaker's life settles into a new rhythm. When he is in the compound, he spends more and more time in the storeroom. And he spends his time mostly as he wishes. Eriksson does not come after him to pull him back into his apprentice duties. What he is working on in the storeroom grows toward completion. When he leaves after wrapping the canvas around it, it is taller than the boatmaker himself.

In the courtyard he sometimes passes Rachel Lippsted stepping down from her carriage. As they pass, neither betrays the other. When she goes into the house, he couldn't say what she is wearing. She, on the other hand, notices everything about him. The scar on his nose, which is now just two light lines. His brown hair, which is continuing to thin. In the end he will be bald, she sees, unlike her brother, who retains all of his thick black hair. The boatmaker's baldness won't matter. In fact, the differences between the two men please her.

When he is not working, the boatmaker often goes out to the stables. The barns are on the other side of the city from the New Land, in a different landscape. Here it is green and rolling, with big estates among the farms and houses, glossy horses in rich pastures. He rides the tram to the end of the line, looking out the window and thinking about Father Robert and Neck. At the end of the line he gets off and walks the rest of the way or gets a ride in a wagon filled with vegetables.

He is drawn to the barns by the warmth he feels in the stall with the Irishman, the horse and the pony. Their kingdom is comfortable, though not always peaceful. The Irishman sometimes goes silent, radiating cold melancholy. The big horse rears over his small subjects, showing his teeth. The pony snaps with hers. But these moods pass quickly, and no grudges are held. Although the man from Small Island is only a visitor in this tiny kingdom, they have come to accept his presence.

Like his time with Rachel, the boatmaker's visits to the barn are a nourishing secret. He witnesses the care the Irishman takes with the horse: his feed, the well-planned workouts, the rubdowns afterward. Leaning on the fence around the track behind the barns, the boatmaker watches as Bold Prince is put through his paces by his jockey, Staedter. The big brown horse goes slowly to warm up, then circles the track at full power. The horse loves to run; Staedter rarely needs his whip. The ground shakes as they roll past, the jockey in his red-and-white Lippsted silks. Clouds of dirt burst upward. Breath thunders in and out of the horse's flaring nostrils. Standing at the rail, the boatmaker wonders how there could be another horse in the kingdom capable of giving this one an honest challenge.

CHAPTER 23

The race between Bold Prince and The Royal Champion is scheduled for a Saturday just before Midsummer's Eve. On the first day of June, the handbills begin appearing in the Old Quarter. At first there are just a few, put up during the night. As he walks to work, the boatmaker sees the rectangular sheets on walls, lampposts, doors. At the top, *The Brotherhood* is printed in the spiky type of the newspaper's logo. Below, a headline in rounded modern type screams: *Stop the Abomination!* Below that is a single column of smaller type:

> Brothers! The horse race between the Crown and the House of Lippsted is an abomination. The Jews are foreign parasites, an infection in the blood of our Mainland. It is outrageous that they have the audacity to challenge the king whose ancestor was converted to the love of Christ by Vashad of sainted memory.

Brothers! We must unite to purge these parasites from our blood! But they are not the only ones who undermine us. The king himself is far from blameless. Even though the spirit of our warrior forefathers runs in his veins, he pollutes himself by stooping to a public display of equality with these worms that invade our flesh and our soil.

Brothers! We must cleanse our cities and towns, our nation! The Mainland must be made pure again through sacrifice. We must rise and rid ourselves of these rootless foreign oppressors—and all who give them comfort. Help us stop the abomination! Join us! Follow The Brotherhood into the New Land!

On his way to the compound the boatmaker uses a fingernail to lift one of these handbills from a brick wall. He reads it, folds it and puts it in the pocket of his canvas jacket before walking on.

As each June day dawns hotter and brighter than the one before, more of The Brotherhood's handbills appear in the Old Quarter, posted invisibly during the night. Soon they cover the walls, hiding the older layers underneath them: images of the king, posters from the previous summer advertising a circus whose star attraction was a pair of Siamese twins, advertisements for diviners offering miraculous solutions to all manner of problems—drink, rheumatism, failing potency, missing wives.

In the morning the news is there for everyone to see. Gentiles cluster around the bills and talk, some clucking and shaking their heads, some murmuring their approval. Jews stop and read, then move on without speaking.

As the handbills appear, the boatmaker sees things he has not seen before on the Mainland. Drunken workingmen bump Jews off the sidewalk into the street. There are broken windows in Jewish shops. The shopkeepers stand on the sidewalk examining the damage, looking puzzled and frightened.

The weather stays beautiful and warm. Fresh green leaves unfold on the trees that line the long allée in the Royal Gardens around the Winter Palace. The pond near the palace is full. Boys use sticks to push their boats out into the center, where they catch the breeze that comes flowing down between the plane trees.

At night Rachel comes to him. As they lie together, she reaches out to touch the scar on his nose. Since he refuses to tell her how he really got it, she has been forced to make up her own explanation. In Rachel's story, the boatmaker's scar is the remnant of a mysterious Small Island initiation rite. Although her education is not as

extensive as her brother's or the king's, she is as well educated as any woman on the Mainland. At university she
read accounts of rituals practiced by tribes in Africa and
on the Pacific Islands. She knows that cutting, bloodletting and scarring are often required for a boy to become a
man. She imagines similar things happening in the darkness of Small Island. To her, the boatmaker's silence, his
refusal to discuss the scar seriously, are part of the ritual.
The men of the tribe have been sworn never to talk about
it with anyone—especially not a woman. Her story began as whimsy. But it soon lost its fictional quality and
became a part of her experience of the boatmaker, as real
as any other part of him.

"I don't believe you got this at work."

"No?"

"No, I don't believe it. You are too careful. Too careful
with tools, at least." She laughs. "I think this is something
you got in a rite of initiation. I think you are a tribesman.
Not really civilized at all."

The boatmaker is getting used to this woman's teasing humor; he is smiling at her in the dark.

She covers his eyes with one hand. With the other
she reaches for him and finds him surging toward her.
He pulls her close, rolls onto her and holds her down, his
eyes covered by her hand.

He lashes himself to her the way two fishing boats are lashed together to ride out a squall—out of sight of land, yawing and bucking while the thunder shakes them and the lightning passes over in the dark. The two boats remain that way, gunwale to gunwale, until the storm has passed, the wind eases, the rain softens and the sky begins to lighten. Then the sailors check the rigging and the soundness of the hulls to see how they have weathered the storm.

Afterward, as they lie smoking, Rachel Lippsted's mind is running over her own motivations. Despite having been in this bed many times, she still cannot decide whether in being here she is following her brother's will or rebelling: extending their family or leaving it behind her.

The boatmaker is not thinking about Rachel. He is thinking of the handbills that appear each night in the Old Quarter, their words so much like those of Father Robert's sermons. He knows how dangerous the priest can be. But he does not share his fears with Rachel. He does not want word to reach Jacob Lippsted, with only days remaining before the race. He knows how important this race is to Rachel's brother.

The morning of the race is bright and clear, the sky a blue army on a long retreat from the earth. The boatmaker rises, relieves himself, washes at his basin, wonders how things are going in the barn. The Irishman knows it is the big day. Does Bold Prince? Does the pony? Perhaps they have already been brought to the stables at the Royal Racecourse. He's stayed away from the barn for the last two weeks, to allow them to prepare. Nor has he seen Jacob Lippsted, who will watch the race with the king. He isn't sure where Rachel and the rabbi will be sitting. Probably they will not be in the royal box, which will be filled with princes, dukes, soldiers and businessmen, some no doubt members of The Brotherhood.

The nightly fall of handbills has become a blizzard blanketing every wall of the Old Quarter. Their message inflames the Christians and frightens the Jews, who have begun to stay indoors unless they have an errand to run, and then they do it without lingering. The boatmaker hears of meetings, some of them at the Grey Goose, where direct, violent action is discussed.

He pulls on his overalls and canvas jacket, laces up his boots. Puts cigarettes in the pocket of his jacket, feels the handbill he removed from the wall when they were first appearing, like the first flakes of a blizzard. He drinks coffee with his landlady. He can tell she wants to talk, but he has no time to listen to her concerns about the changes taking place in the Old Quarter.

Outside, the streets are empty, which is highly unusual for a Saturday. It is the Jewish Sabbath, so he is not surprised no Jews are abroad. But there are almost no Gentiles either. Usually the streets and Christian shops are bustling on Saturday, which is the time for a half-day of work and a long night for celebrating with music, drink and women of the town. Now the sidewalks are empty. Shopkeepers stand in front of their shops, looking left and right down empty pavements. The barber stands at his door in apron and striped sleeves. He nods to the boatmaker. The newspaper dangling from his right hand is *The Brotherhood*. Inside, the bench where the native sat snoring is empty.

The race is at noon. The boatmaker wants to be there early, to find his way through the crowds, say hello to Donelan and pat the big horse before everything happens. First, though, he must pay a visit to the compound.

As he enters the gate, he sees Sven Eriksson crossing to the townhouse. The door opens. The long canvas coat disappears. The door closes.

In the workshops and storerooms only half the usual number of men are present. The workers in the compound never speak much to the boatmaker. Today it seems they are not speaking much to each other, either. The only sounds are boots on flooring, wood being set down, tools being taken out and used, brushes swishing as they spread oil and varnish on clean wood.

In the storeroom the piece he has been working on sits under worn canvas loosely tied with old rope. He unties the rope, lets the canvas fall. What he has been working on stands complete: the boatmaker's version of the secretary from Father Robert's office. It is made of walnut, dark and austere, built as two separate pieces that can be taken apart for moving. The top half has bookshelves, gothic arches holding the glass. The lower half is a writing desk that folds down, revealing drawers and cubbyholes. Below the desk are three large drawers. All of it is made to last for generations.

Now that it is finished, the boatmaker can see the whole piece clearly. But he does not know how well he has done. All he can do is leave it for Eriksson, who will tell him whether or not he has made a piece of Lippsted furniture. Regardless of the answer, he knows he will not be returning to the compound as an apprentice. He takes off his canvas jacket and hangs it on a nail next to the secretary, handbill still in the pocket. Canvas and rope lie in a heap, their work done. The boatmaker turns and heads out of the storeroom into June sunshine.

As he approaches the racecourse, the crowds thicken and he moves with them as they home in on their destination. All around him are men in work clothes: denim, corduroy and canvas, with heavy boots, rough hands and flat caps. The gentry are in their carriages, being carried toward their own entrances. Among the workers, the feeling is not of holiday, as it was on the king's birthday. Instead, it is sour, with muttering and angry talk, bottles and flasks passed from hand to hand, along with the handbills of The Brotherhood. Those who can read are reading the words of the bills to those who cannot.

The crowd ahead of the boatmaker parts. The race-course comes into view: a long oval of brown earth, firm and dry, enclosed by a tall wrought-iron fence like the one around the Winter Palace. At the far end stands the main building, built of brick, with a slate roof overhanging boxes for the gentlefolk. The royal box is at the very front, down at the level of the track. Uncovered grandstands for ordinary citizens extend from the main building like long arms embracing the track. These stands are filling with workingmen, a hum of talk and drink running through them. Above the roof of the main building two flags are flying. One is the flag of the kingdom, with its blue and yellow quarters. The other is the king's battle streamer, a long, narrow white pennant with a red cross. Under the slate roof, the royal box and the boxes nearby are empty.

The boatmaker makes his way through the crowd, an unremarkable worker wearing overalls and boots, with a drooping mustache and a scar on his nose. He doesn't enjoy crowds, doesn't like being pushed, shoved, even brushed by people passing by. He picks his way among brown cloth, blue cloth and canvas, finding openings, turning sideways to let beefier men pass without touching.

In back of the main building he finds a door that seems to lead to the stables. He passes through and finds himself in a small area between buildings, enclosed by an iron fence. At the far end, in front of the door leading to the stables, stands a beefy policeman rocking gently back and forth, holding his truncheon against two rows of silver buttons that rise over his blue belly like a road climbing through a mountain pass.

"No entrance. Horses, horsemen and owners only past this point."

"Donelan asked me to come back and say hello. The trainer for the House of Lippsted."

"Yes, I know Donelan. He asked you to come back, did he? You don't look like much of a horseman to me."

"No. But Donelan asked to see me." It isn't true. But the boatmaker doesn't think the Irishman will mind. And he wants very much to see the three of them before the starting pistol is fired.

"Alright. Go ahead. You look harmless. But if I find that Donelan hasn't asked for you . . . If I find out, for example, that you're one of those newspaper johnnies in some sort of disguise, I'll find you. Even in this unholy mess of a crowd, I'll find you—and make you regret your bitch of a mother ever whelped you. Do I make myself clear?" he asks, tapping the truncheon into a meaty palm.

The boatmaker nods. The policeman moves aside to let him into the barns. He turns right between rows of empty stalls. Then he turns left and sees Bold Prince through an arched doorway that leads to a stall larger than the rest, straw piled on the floor. The big brown horse is bucking and rearing, his eyes wide and white.

The boatmaker runs toward the arch. As he reaches it, a man comes rushing out past him. He is sure it is the man he saw at the Mint. *Rademacher. A very dangerous man*, Rachel had said.

Inside the stall, the tall brown horse and the pony are backing into a corner, the pony in front, protective. The Irishman is lying crumpled in the straw. The boatmaker kneels beside him. A bruise is spreading across Donelan's cheek. His flat cap is lying in the straw. A large syringe, half-full of milky liquid, stands up out of his chest. There isn't much blood.

He takes Donelan in his arms, smells tobacco, horse, cologne and a sweetish smell he can't identify. The color has drained from the trainer's features. He does not seem to be in pain, but he is weakening moment by moment.

"The horse?" he asks in a wisp of a voice.

"Fine."

"Get him to the track. He must race."

The boatmaker doesn't know whether to remove the syringe, which is deep in Donelan's chest. Then the Irishman's body goes limp, and the boatmaker knows he's gone.

Staedter, the jockey, appears in the arched doorway holding the racing saddle with the bridle draped over it.

"Donelan's dead."

"*Christ!* Who did it?"

"Rademacher."

"Who's that?"

"It doesn't matter. I think they were trying to get to the horse and fix him so he couldn't run."

"*Jesus Christ!*" The jockey looks at the animals in the corner, cowering and showing their teeth. He kneels on one knee to look at Donelan, careful not to get spots on his gleaming white jodhpurs or the silk blouse in Lippsted red-and-white.

"You've got to get him out of here. The horse will never calm down with the body in the stall." He rises, takes two small steps toward Bold Prince, stopping out of range of hooves and teeth, turns and barks at the boat-maker: *"Get him out of here, I said!"*

Suddenly the archway is filled by Eriksson in his long canvas coat, followed by two journeymen the boatmaker recognizes from the compound.

"We need to move him," he says, looking up at the foreman, who kneels down and presses two fingers against Donelan's neck, then nods to the men behind him. The two of them pick Donelan up under his arms and legs and carry him out.

"What happened?" the foreman asks.

"Rademacher," the boatmaker says. The foreman looks startled, then thoughtful.

"We must tell Herr Lippsted."

"No," says the boatmaker. He has never given Eriks-son an order, never even thought of doing such a thing. He isn't sure how he has the courage to do it now, but he is certain Jacob Lippsted must not know about Donelan until after the race. The horse is not harmed. The race must go on. With his last breath, Donelan had said so. The two men stand up out of the straw, one more than a head taller than the other. They look at each other, dark eyes into light, for what seems like minutes.

"Alright," says the foreman. "I'll have Donelan taken away. Some of the men will stay here to guard the stall.

They're not armed, and we don't have time to go back and get weapons. But I think we'll be safe. I doubt that he'll come back now. He was after the horse?"

"Yes." The boatmaker bends down, picks up Donelan's cap and hands it to the foreman.

"And the little Irishman fought like a demon to keep them from hurting him."

"Yes."

"*A bloody mess.*" The boatmaker knows Eriksson means not just what has happened in this stall but everything outside as well: the boiling city, the crowd drinking itself into a rage as it fills the stadium, the hateful newspaper, the poisonous handbills.

Turning to the jockey, the foreman asks, "Staedter, can you manage here by yourself? We have men outside."

"*I can if you will by God get out of here.* The horse won't calm down until you leave. And the race goes off in *fifteen bloody minutes.*"

The boatmaker and the foreman exchange glances. Neither likes Staedter, but the jockey has a job to do that no one else can do—and he knows his work.

The boatmaker leaves the stables to find a place where he can watch the race. He wants a place outside the iron fence, with open streets at his back. It is a day to have room to run.

At the end of the track farthest from the royal box, he finds a good spot. He will have to watch the race standing, but there is plenty of room to turn and run, and he has a clear view down the track to the main building. He cannot make out every detail under the slate roof flying its two flags. But he can see the scarlet tunics of the King's Own Guard on the track in front of the stands, white gloves on their rifles. He knows the king will enter last, to the sound of a brass band, joining Jacob Lippsted and a few others in the royal box.

All around the royal box, the boxes for the nobility are filling with refined chitchat. Along the straightaways, the stands for commoners are full of excited babble. Outside the fence, near the boatmaker, stand the workers who could not afford a ticket or chose not to buy one. They seem even poorer, drunker and angrier than the men in the stands. All around him, the boatmaker hears words that have leaped off the handbills into the mouths of the people. *Disease. Parasites. Purify.*

Down at the other end of the track there is a commotion as the king enters and takes his seat. When everyone is settled, the royal chamberlain, in dark coat and long tails, walks out from under the stands. Standing in front of the royal box, on the white line marking start and finish, he takes papers from an inside pocket and reads. His remarks are carefully written and appropriate for the day, praising the king for his liberality, his modernity, his far-sightedness, his boldness in welcoming the future to the Mainland.

The chamberlain is too far away for the crowd around the boatmaker to make out his words clearly. The speech goes on and on, tension rising in the crowd. When the chamberlain finishes, there is no cheering, only polite applause from the high-born.

The chamberlain bows and recedes. A brass band in dress blue marches out onto the track, instruments gleaming, and begins to play. The sound is thin and distant, but the boatmaker can hear the national anthem, its tune going all the way back to the time of the sea-warriors. After the anthem, the band plays the hymn that has for centuries accompanied the Mainland's army and navy into battle. The music that accompanies the words *a mighty fortress* comes down the track, the words humming involuntarily in every brain from hundreds of repetitions over a lifetime.

The wind dies. The flags crumple and spill down their poles. The music stops. The band carries their golden instruments back under the stands. The wind picks up again. The flags belly out: the blue-and-yellow rectangle and the white streamer sliced by the cross.

Down on the right, from the opening the band marched out of, comes The Royal Champion, ridden by a tiny jockey wearing blue-and-yellow silks. At the sight of the never-defeated black thoroughbred, the crowd opens its throat and sends out a roar of love and willingness to die—and kill—for the homeland. A groom leads the Champion, who is dancing, lighter than air.

The black horse passes the royal box before being turned and brought back to the starting line. The horses will start in front of the stands, make the first turn immediately, go into a long straightaway, sweep around the turn in front of where the boatmaker is standing and head down the other straightaway into the final turn. They will finish where they started: in front of the royal box, before the eyes of the king and Jacob Lippsted.

A moment later, Bold Prince is led out to a low grumble from the crowd. He is taller than the royal horse and thinner, obviously powerful but not nearly as elegant as the black horse. He is not floating. A groom in red-and-white leads the horse and Staedter. The boatmaker sees the jockey talking to the big brown horse, stroking his neck. Bold Prince walks slowly, head down, as if he is in pain. The boatmaker wonders whether some of what was in the syringe did reach its mark before ending up in the chest of the Irishman.

The groom gets Bold Prince turned in front of the royal box and brings him up level with The Royal Champion. The noise in the stands quiets. A man in a dark suit steps onto the track, a silver pistol at his side. The grooms release their horses. The starter raises his silver pistol. When the report reaches the boatmaker at the far end of the track, the horses are already running.

The black jumps off the line into the first turn, taking the inside. The Royal Champion runs with speed and grace, his jockey holding him back, horse and rider appearing to be as untroubled as if they were out for a training gallop. The brown is running, but the boatmaker can see that he is not himself.

On the far straightaway, both horses take the inside, Bold Prince breathing the Champion's dust. The boatmaker sees Staedter urging the brown horse on. He is not using his whip. As they reach the end of the first straightaway the gap widens to three lengths, then to four.

If the race continues like this, the king's horse will win by many lengths. From the crowd in the stands and along the fence comes a deep rumble of satisfaction. All is right with the world. The cosmic order has held. Tonight, glasses will be raised to the king who put the Jews back in their place. The Jews of the Old Quarter will be relieved that things have begun to return to normal. The handbills from The Brotherhood will be replaced by the usual advertisements for circuses and miracles.

Unlike the men around him, the boatmaker is not yelling; he is simply watching. He can feel his own disappointment. But perhaps it is for the best, he thinks. However it has come about—whether Rademacher actually reached Bold Prince with his syringe or not—it may be the better outcome. The crowd will be calmed. There may be sporadic violence but no mob out of control in its rage and bloodlust.

The horses come into the turn in front of the boatmaker and swing around, both on the inside. He sees desperation on Staedter's face. As they come out of the turn into the second straightaway, the jockey begins using his whip. Staedter strikes Bold Prince's neck and shoulders. As he brings the whip down, the jockey loses control. He is no longer a calm strategist, a skilled technician, winner of many races. He is a man in a rage.

Whether it is because of the pain, or the outrage at being treated with such disrespect, Bold Prince wakes up and starts to run as the boatmaker has seen him run many times. On the second straightaway it looks as though The Royal Champion has slowed to a walk, though the boatmaker knows he is moving just as fast as he was before. The tiny royal jockey, shocked at the pounding coming up behind, begins whipping his horse. The black responds, but the gap continues to close: three lengths, two, then one.

Looking down the straightway, seeing the horses from behind, the boatmaker cannot tell who is in front. As they thunder into the far turn, Staedter swings Bold Prince to the outside, around the black. They pound past the finish line, necks stretched, nostrils wide. As they reach the royal box, the boatmaker can make out the brown head on the outside, just in front of the black.

CHAPTER 24

An angry howl goes up from the crowd. The horses whip around the first turn again, slowing with each stride, jockeys standing in the stirrups. They come to a walk in the middle of the straightaway before the jockeys turn them back toward the main building. Grooms run out to lead the horses to the safety of the barns.

As horses and riders vanish, the entire racecourse bursts open like the mouth of a volcano. Out of the opening comes a molten wave of sound, different, louder than the first angry cry. The royal guard, their bayonets fixed, surround the king and his guests and lead them from the royal box to the carriages.

At the other end of the track and outside the iron fence, the boatmaker cannot make out individuals, but he knows Jacob Lippsted is within the wall of scarlet. Rachel must be nearby, among the gentry scrambling for their horses and carriages.

The whirlwind of sound fills and overflows the race-course, like lava rolling down the slopes of a volcano. It begins to harden, take shape. Words rise out of the chaos. "Death," the chant goes up. "Death to the Jews!" Then it finds its rhythm and begins repeating: *"Death, death to the Jews! Death, death to the Jews!"*

The crowd of workingmen pours out of the entrances and away from the track. The boatmaker threads his way among them. Here and there men are clustered around someone speaking the words of The Brotherhood's handbills. The boatmaker stops at each speaker, expecting to see Rademacher, but the very dangerous man is nowhere to be seen.

The boatmaker hurries through the streets, sometimes stepping out of the way to allow shouting men to run by. He smells smoke.

He leaves the crowd on the boulevards and takes a route that leads him down narrow streets and alleys, pausing at the intersections with the major streets to let a flood of angry workingmen stream by, whipped into a rage by the speakers. As it moves, the angry crowd has settled on its destination: the Old Quarter.

As he enters the streets of the Old Quarter, the boatmaker sees the mob has been there before him. Pushcarts are overturned. Fruits and vegetables spill out onto the pavement, crushed to pulp. From under one or two carts he sees legs outstretched.

All around him, armed with sticks and cobbles, the men of the Mainland are breaking the fronts of stores owned by Jews. All the stores are closed, and most have their shutters down. But the mob knows which stores have Jewish owners. Glass breaks, wood splinters, locks and hinges groan before giving way. Once the façade is broken, men rush in to grab and carry out whatever they can lay their hands on: barrels of pickles, cheeses, pots and pans. The boatmaker sees two men running, holding up a side of beef, one at the front, the other at the rear. They are giddy, laughing and running away before stronger predators arrive to snatch their prey.

As he makes his way through the mob to the boardinghouse, the smell of smoke thickens. Yellow flames curl up inside smashed storefronts, tearing at walls and floors. The boatmaker feels the heat on his hands and face.

Freed of the crowd, he is moving swiftly over the last few blocks to the boardinghouse when he stops and presses himself against the side of a building. Two familiar figures are coming down the steps of the once-elegant townhouse. He has imagined them at his door so many times that they do not seem real now that they are actually there. The blond priest built like a wrestler and the misshapen man in the woolen robe hurry down the steps and disappear into the crowd. They give no sign that they have seen the man pressing himself into the brick of the wall, his heart pounding so hard it might explode.

In his room the boatmaker stands looking out the window over the Old Quarter watching orange columns shoot up over the crooked line of roofs and dormers. Through the open window he hears shouting in narrow streets and running on cobbles. After watching for a long time he lies down and waits while the sky coagulates and the fires burn themselves out. The sounds of running and glass breaking finally exhaust themselves. What is left is a smoky night different from all other nights.

He wakes in his clothes to a knock at his door. He gets up without lighting his candle and and opens the door.

The landlady stands in the doorway, an ancient paisley shawl wrapped around her shoulders. For once she has no cigarette, no book, no cats. But the smell of whiskey accompanies her. She sways like a pine tree in a strong breeze, tilting away from the wind, then back to center.

"Let me in," she says. "And close the door."

The boatmaker stands back. The landlady enters the room, bracing herself against the washstand. Reaching under her shawl, she pulls out two envelopes and hands them to him. One is long, rectangular and official-looking. The other is smaller, squarer, more personal. Each bears his name in a different well-educated hand. He takes the envelopes, looks at them and tosses them on the bed, where they land side by side, face up.

The landlady makes no move to leave. He wonders whether she is waiting for him to open the envelopes and read the letters in her presence. Or perhaps, after climbing the stairs in her drunken state, she has reached the point where she is afraid that if she moves, she will fall. Or perhaps, on this night of nights, she is afraid to be alone in her room with only black-and-white cats for company.

He points her to the worn country chair where Rachel Lippsted has sat many times.

"I thought our kingdom was past this," the landlady says, sitting and reaching under her paisley shawl for a flask. She offers it to the boatmaker. When he refuses, she takes a long pull before replacing it.

"Has it happened before?"

"*Has it happened before?* Where were you born? Oh, I forget. Small Island. No doubt such things don't happen there. They do here. The last time was more than fifty years ago, under the old king."

She takes out the flask and drinks, this time not bothering to offer any to the boatmaker.

"*The smell*," she says. "The smell is always the same. You smell it as a girl. You think you will never have to smell it again—and that you will forget. But certain things you can't forget. The noise perhaps, even the blood on the pavement the next morning. But you do not forget the smell."

Her head falls forward. She is silent. The boatmaker looks at the top of her gray head, assuming she has passed out. He wonders how he will get her down the stairs to her room. But then her head comes up.

"No matter what those letters say, *do not go out tonight*. Wait 'til tomorrow. By then it will be over. The anger will be gone, for a while. They will no longer know who they hate more—the Jews or themselves. Then you can go out. Tomorrow. Even early. *But not tonight*. Understand?"

Much as he wants to go and find out whether certain people are safe, the boatmaker cannot argue with her; she has seen all this before.

The landlady raises herself slowly, drawing her shawl close and listing like a schooner under full sail, leaving a cloud of whiskey in her wake.

As she opens the door, the cats leap up the stairs and rub against her legs, purring loudly. Without acknowledging them, she pulls the door closed and makes her dignified way down the stairs.

The boatmaker stands in the middle of the room looking at the envelopes on his bed. He opens the larger one. Inside is a letter in a firm black hand. The controlled handwriting covers two large cream-colored sheets of heavy paper.

My brother in Christ,

I believe I can still call you that, even though you have deserted us and the New Land for reasons I can only surmise; only Our Father can fully penetrate the mystery of another man's heart. But that does not prevent us here below from trying to understand. We must try, brother. We have no choice but to act, even though we know His Truth only in brief flashes of illumination.

Since your departure, I have prayed many nights on my knees for acceptance of His will and for clarity regarding your behavior. I know that Jesus, the first Christ, was afraid of His destiny. Even near the end He prayed that the cup might pass from Him. I am sure that you—only human after all—have made the same request many times. What is more, since leaving us I know that you have become entangled with the Jews in ways I can only speculate upon. I have spent many nights on my knees asking for guidance in understanding these matters with, I admit, limited success.

I remain convinced, however, that you are the one I believed you to be: an essential part of the New Son of Man. The one who was the fourth, sent to complete the circle. And that by balking your fate, as our brother Jesus contemplated but refrained from doing out of His deep love for the world, and His compassion for our suffering, you have interfered with the will of Our Father and jeopardized His plan for the rebirth of the Mainland—indeed, of the entire world.

In sum, my brother, I cannot help but hold you personally responsible for much of the evil that has come to pass in these painful days. A deep change was intended for our Mainland: a cleansing and renewal, a purification and return to our roots. But it was meant to be peaceful, without unnecessary shedding of blood. If you had followed through in the part that has been ordained, I believe that our king, and many others, would have had their eyes opened in a gentle manner, without the violence of *these last days. Many now lying dead in the streets of the capital would be alive, the possibility of Salvation before them.*

I have great sadness from all this, brother; my heart is sore, torn in half. And I believe that because you have flinched and let the cup pass from you, you bear much responsibility. Yet such is His mercy that, if you are willing to return to the New Land and join, as you were meant to join, with your three brothers, a great deal of bloodshed may still be avoided, and the great renewal returned to its original, peaceful course.

At the New Land we are on our knees, brother, awaiting your return, arms and hearts open, our love for you unchanged despite your abandonment of us and our sacred cause.

Father Robert's signature is large and strong, underscored with a flourish. The priest's last name, which the boatmaker had not known, is the name of a family as old and noble as the landlady's. Below the signature, the priest has added:

For as the body is one, and hath many members, and all members of that one body, being many, are one body, so also is the Christ. For by one spirit are we

all baptized into one body, whether we be Jews or
Gentiles, whether we be bond or free, and have been
all made to drink into one spirit.

The boatmaker drops the priest's letter on the bed and opens the smaller envelope. As he lifts the flap the scent of Lily of the Valley rises from light blue sheets with a message in dark blue.

My sweet Small Island man,

What the rabbi feared has come to pass. We are leaving for such safety as we can find. I scrawl to you in haste. By the time this reaches you, we shall be gone. Should you wish to join me, I have enclosed a map. If you choose to come, commit the map to memory. Whether you intend to join us or not, destroy the map after you have looked at it. Do not leave it behind. *I know you too well and I love you too much to ask you for anything, but under these circumstances there are two things I would make known more directly than I would at another time. The first is that if you want me, I would be your wife. I belong to you. I have known this for some time. I believe you know it too. The second thing I must tell you is that there will be a child. Even in the face of these facts, I demand nothing. I write only to share what I know with you and allow you to make your decision. Should you wish to join me and the child that is to be, this map will show you the way. Joining this family is no simple matter. But I have no doubt you are capable of it—and of much more. If you choose to join me, I wait for you with more than love. If you do not, or cannot, for whatever reason, I will still wish you well: on the Mainland, on Small Island or on the sea. I shall bear you no ill will. On the contrary, regardless of your choice, part of me will always be in your little room up the stairs, with just enough space between us for the moon.*

Your Rachel

Beyond the boatmaker's window the fires have died down. The streets are quiet. The landlady was right: Tomorrow he will be safe. After the bloodletting, the men of the Mainland will wake in a stupor of self-hatred. He stands at his window, knowing it is the last time he will see this view.

When the sky begins to lighten, he goes to his cache, removes his money, the sealskin bag and Crow's notebook. He sits on his bed with the letters beside him and thumbs through the notebook one last time. Now he realizes that *R*, the letter that has puzzled him for many months, must stand for Rademacher. Rademacher and The Brotherhood were one of Crow's sources of income, along with White's pay and, if he wasn't losing, his gambling. Rademacher's *corrupt little agents*, Rachel had said. Crow and White must have been two of those corrupt little agents. Certainly they were corrupt. Crow at least; White simply loved Crow.

Crow must have told Rademacher about the boatmaker, his name being part of the fascination. Rademacher ordered the beating. Afterward, Rademacher had him delivered to the hospital, into the hands of Father Robert, who would also have been fascinated by his name. Despite its appearance, the beating was not a robbery: It was a way for Rademacher to get him to the New Land. The shouts of "Where is the money?" must have been an attempt to confuse him—or perhaps just a private joke of Crow's, a reference to the boatmaker's obsession. After the boatmaker was safely on the New Land, Rademacher must have delivered Crow and White to Father Robert, to shut them up—and impress the boatmaker with how far the New Land was willing to go on his behalf.

As these puzzle pieces fall into place, another memory rises to the surface of the boatmaker's mind. He remembers Father Robert telling him about how the

Crown's debt to the House of Lippsted had been split up into many slivers to conceal it from the people. He recalls how excited and angry the priest was as he talked about the connivance between the king and Jacob Lippsted. Now he realizes the priest was sharing secrets that must have come from the network of spies and informers run by Rademacher. And he sees that the New Land and The Brotherhood are closely joined in a dangerous conspiracy that reaches all the way to the palace itself.

Now that his eyes have been opened, the boatmaker would like to stay and think over everything he's learned. But he can't. He must move. Though the city is quiet in its hangover of self-loathing, this calm won't last.

He undresses and straps the sealskin bag to his body before putting his clothes back on. He goes to the wardrobe, opens it and takes out the black suit, shirt, tie and the strangely feminine shoes and socks. He wraps the suit in one of his sheets and knots the sheet in a bundle.

The map on the back of the second page of Rachel's letter is drawn with Eriksson's mathematical precision. They are in a forest located to the south and east, toward the European border, in a region where the boatmaker has never been. He memorizes the map before gathering up the envelopes and the closely written pages that were delivered in them.

He kneels on the floor, puts the letters down and lights them. They blaze in a tiny holocaust, words vanishing into transparent blue, yellow and white flame. He makes sure nothing in the room catches fire, then crushes the ash.

He picks up Crow's notebook, which is too big to burn. He will find a place to drop it in the river and let the brown tide of Vashad carry Crow's scratches—his calculations of loyalty and its opposite—to the sea.

He goes down the stairs between the ancestors of this house and out into a city sleeping off its blood sacrifice and burnt offerings.

On the wall around the Lippsted compound someone has written in red paint *Our sacred land*. Scattered around the large red letters are offensive names for Jews. Down in one corner of the wall the boatmaker sees *The Sons of Vashad*, written in yellow paint. It must be another organization, one whose name he hasn't heard before.

In the compound the ashes are smoking. The warren of workshops clustered around the townhouse is gone. The workshops were wood. They burned easily, leaving nothing but foundations, in some places not even those. The boatmaker can see clear across to the rear wall, ordinarily a ten-minute walk through a tangle of outbuildings.

On the ground, from one wall to the other, a layer of fine gray ash covers remnants of what would not burn: tools, glass, metal. The façade of the townhouse is still standing. Through openings where the windows were, the boatmaker can see the endless summer sky.

Careful to avoid the smoldering rubble, he picks his way through to where his storeroom was, feeling the heat through the soles of his boots. The storeroom is gone, only an outline of the foundation remaining. Where he left the secretary, he sees bits of burned canvas and a few gray outlines of the desk. He touches the gray with the toe of his boot and it dissolves into ash, lifted across the compound by the breeze.

The boatmaker wonders whether Eriksson saw his work before it burned. Probably not. There was the commotion around the race, and afterward the mob. The foreman could hardly have had time to go into the storeroom and examine the boatmaker's personal project. The boatmaker feels a deep disappointment, thinking of all the work that went into the secretary and the fact that Sven Eriksson will never see it to give it his blessing.

Then his disappointment lifts. What he made was good. He doesn't need anyone's approval to know that.

From outside the wall come voices, low and rough, of men recovering from the convulsion of the night before. He walks through the gap in the wall where the gate stood. He looks both ways and sets out, boots on a street of the capital, where a thousand cords of wealth and power are braided into one.

CHAPTER 25

The city the boatmaker passes through as he leaves is mostly empty. But here and there groups of men roam the streets, some looking for stores to loot, others wandering, looking for leaders to tell them what to do next on this unsettled morning. Some of the men wear black armbands with a symbol the boatmaker hasn't seen before. Inside a white disc sits a crimson triangle. At each of its three corners is one of Vashad's blackbirds, dark and crude.

As the boatmaker leaves the Old Quarter he sees handbills marked with the triangle and blackbirds. These new handbills, in the old spiky type, are more overtly violent than the leaflets from The Brotherhood. They focus less on the king and more sharply on the Jews, calling for a final purification. They are signed *The Sons of Vashad*.

He gives the men on the street a wide berth and moves on. There are no police to be seen, and no soldiers, except those guarding the largest royal buildings. Outside the Mint stands a ring of royal guardsmen. They are wearing combat blue rather than dress scarlet, are heavily armed and look deeply uninterested in idle conversation. Leaving the city, he sees more groups of the Sons of Vashad in their red-triangle armbands. Some carry long, heavy sticks; he thinks he sees one with a pistol.

The boatmaker's journey to the place marked on Eriksson's map takes two days. The camp is deep in the woods. On reaching it, the first thing he sees is a man lounging at the base of a tree on the far side of a stream, shotgun cradled in his elbow, smoking.

As the stranger approaches, the sentry drops his cigarette in the stream and steadies his gun, its muzzle pointed at the boatmaker's knees. When he gives his name, the sentry tells him to wait. He disappears, returning a few minutes later trailing a taller figure, who also carries a shotgun. Eriksson has shed his canvas coat for a leather jacket and flat cap; he seems quite comfortable with the gun.

The foreman gestures the boatmaker across the stream. He picks his way across flat stones, the dinner suit wrapped in its torn sheet held over his head.

When the boatmaker has crossed the stream, the foreman leads him along a narrow path in the dark. To one side he sees men, barely visible in dark clothes, and tents pitched between the huge trunks of ancient trees. This forest, far from the city and part of a royal preserve, has never been logged. It smells prehistoric, ripe with birth and death. Up ahead, torches throw light on a clearing. At the center of the clearing is a platform made of unfinished pine boards, flanked by four large white tents, each with its flap down.

The foreman sends the sentry back to the stream. Torchlight illuminates many sets of muddy footprints on the boards, some made by a woman's boots.

"Did you have trouble on the way?"

"No, they left me alone."

"That's good."

"I stopped in the compound."

"Gone?"

"Yes."

"We got out just in time. A few more minutes and we would have been in the ashes ourselves, with no stories to tell our grandchildren."

"The façade was the only thing standing."

"The house can be rebuilt. The compound has been rebuilt before."

"Everything else is gone."

"Yes, the wood, the pieces in the workshops. We will make new ones. There is more wood in the world."

"I suppose."

"Believe me, there is. The House of Lippsted has been through this before. Fifty years ago was the last time. Even though I've never been through it myself, I have a sense of how things will go from here. Some from the compound have left. But those who have remained until now will stay with us. They are solid, like well-built furniture." The taller man laughs, deep shadows painted on his face in the torchlight.

"By the way," the foreman says, reaching in the pocket of his leather jacket and taking out his pipe. He lights the pipe gracefully around the shotgun. "I saw your piece in the storeroom before I went to the track. A Lippsted secretary. Very nice. Two generations ago that was one of the best-known pieces in the line. Not that we made many of them. They were famous because it's damned hard to make one without metal fastenings. You did a nice job."

"Thank you."

"Not easy to find, these days. They are considered old-fashioned. Where did you find one to learn from?"

"In the place I was before."

The foreman smiles at the boatmaker's terseness. He inhales and lets his smoke rise toward the torches.

"Well, if you are not a master of the craft, you are not so far away from being one either. I am not sure whether what you made in the storeroom was really a Lippsted masterpiece. Perhaps a few too many touches of your own. I was skeptical, you know: an untrained man in the back of a storeroom. But what you made was good. Maybe a masterpiece, maybe not. But in its own fashion—very good."

The boatmaker, pleased and embarrassed, looks at the splatter of bootprints. In the torchlight they are black against the pine boards.

"Who is so loud at this hour?" Rachel Lippsted's head emerges from one of the tents, curls framing her face, her eyes heavy with sleep. The foreman touches his cap and retreats into the darkness beyond the ancient treetrunks.

In the tent nothing needs to be said. When she saw him talking to Sven Eriksson, the questions in her letter were answered. He has things he wants to talk about, but they are difficult, requiring what for the boatmaker amount to extended conversations. He doesn't have the strength for that; he has eaten little on his journey.

He lays his bundle on the floor of her tent and joins her, head against her chest. The boatmaker knows little about how a child grows inside its mother. As he leans against Rachel, he wonders whether he will hear two hearts instead of the one he knows. But it is just the single, familiar beat.

She gathers his head to her, feeling his body uncoil. Lying on the camp bed, the boatmaker feels as if he is still on the road, his legs never stopping, consulting the map engraved in his mind. The thoughts he could not afford while he was on the road flood in. He wonders whether the families in the lighted farmhouses he passed were gathered around their kitchen tables reading *The Brotherhood*, whether the Sons of Vashad have spread from the city to the countryside. He wonders what happened to Donelan's body. The foreman would never have left it in the stables at the track if he could help it, but his main thought must have been to get Jacob Lippsted and his sister out of the city before the mob reached the townhouse. And what of the horse who woke from his trance and ran like a brown demon? What of the pony who became a friend for a lump of sugar?

Rachel leans over him, watching the muscles of his face work as he lies exhausted between waking and sleeping. She sees his mouth move, thinks she can make out words, but when she leans in, her ear brushing his lips, the only word she can make out is *Vashad*.

She leaves her ear on his mouth for a moment, not listening, just feeling the warmth of his lips. He turns over and his body softens.

She eases off the narrow bed, finds a blanket and covers him without removing anything except his boots, blunt and muddy, which she puts under the bed.

She pulls up a camp chair and sits, watching him as he tosses and speaks snatches of conversation she does not understand, talking to people she does not know: a woman named Karin, his mother, someone with the comical name of Crow, a priest. He tosses under the blanket, mumbling, finally lying still as light begins to change the color of the canvas.

Early the next morning, her brother's dark head appears inside the flap, inquiring wordlessly whether she is decent. She looks at the bed, at her brother and raises a finger to her lips. The dark head disappears. Outside, low voices signal the beginning of the daily routine in this camp pitched in a royal forest near the border with Europe.

A little while later the boatmaker opens his eyes and sees the shadows of leaves on canvas. For a moment he thinks he is on Small Island, building his boat in the shed. Then everything that has happened returns and fills him with his own story.

He throws off the blanket, washes his face in a basin, sits in the camp chair to pull his boots on. All around him are her possessions: a steamer trunk set on end serving as an armoire, books in French and English, a silver mirror, comb and brush. He has never been in her bedroom before. Her possessions are things he cannot imagine anyone owning; her ways of being cared for are beyond his ken.

Outside on the platform four men of different heights stand in June sunshine. The foreman in his leather jacket, shotgun in the crook of his arm, towers over the others. Jacob Lippsted, in shirtsleeves, a vest, dark trousers and tall riding boots, is in the middle. Shorter are the rabbi and an even smaller man who looks much like him.

All four heads turn to the boatmaker. Conversation stops. Jacob Lippsted steps up to him, grasps him by the shoulder and shakes his hand. "So Eriksson's map served you right?"

"It was clear."

"I'm glad you made it. My sister will be pleased. *Is pleased*, I should say. This is the rabbi's brother, by the way, Meyer Goldman. You'll be visiting him in due course."

Jacob Lippsted seems in good spirits, in command here in the woods as he was in the compound, apparently untroubled by the destruction of his home.

"What can we get you? Breakfast? You must be hungry. No trouble on the way?"

"Not really. Mostly it was quiet—after." He wants to talk about the Sons of Vashad but knows he must wait. "Breakfast would be good."

"Eriksson, would you help our friend find a meal? And after that, a visit to Meyer's quarters. You'll find we're well equipped."

Jacob Lippsted rubs his hands together, a man with a full program, eager to begin the day. Meyer Goldman gives the boatmaker a nod that is not entirely friendly.

Eriksson leads him into the woods, passing smaller tents hidden among the trees. Beyond the tents, the boatmaker sees a picket of armed men in leather coats.

They reach an open area with a cooking fire and men eating, weapons within easy reach. The boatmaker recognizes the men from the compound. They nod, finish their food, pick up their guns and head to the woods. The cook hands the boatmaker a metal plate, and he realizes how hungry he is. When he's cleared three plates and emptied two metal mugs of coffee, Sven Eriksson returns to lead him deeper into the woods. On their way they pass a new clearing in which men are cutting saplings and erecting a canopy of green branches under the larger canopy formed by a grove of old oaks.

"The horse?" he asks Eriksson.

"Safe in the country. Fannie, too."

"Staedter?"

"Now, that man is a survivor if ever there was one. He slipped away after the race. Believe me, he'll be fine. Who knows? He may even be one of *them*. Never did like the man much, to tell you the truth. Got the job done, though, didn't he?"

"The horse seemed like he was in a trance. I thought maybe they'd gotten to him after all with the syringe."

"I don't think so. I think he was grieving for Donelan. And he snapped out of it just in time." The foreman paces silently on his long legs. Then he says softly, "The scum. Killing an old man with arthritis who was trying to protect a horse." He spits to the side of the trail. Silence resumes.

The foreman leads him to a small tent standing by itself in the woods. "There you go," he says, turning to leave, shotgun over his shoulder.

Inside the tent Meyer Goldman sits on the floor cross-legged, an unfinished jacket in his lap. He untangles himself and rises. "So, the famous man of Small Island comes to visit the humble tailor."

When the boatmaker is silent, Goldman continues. "Come for the wedding suit, have you? I'm told you wear a dinner suit well, though no one could tell that by looking at you." He has the same accent as his brother, the same love of words. But some of the twinkle is missing.

"Well, don't just stand there. Take off those boots and overalls. How do you think suits get made? By themselves? That's not the way it happens. Not even here in the forest. No. We take the measurements, then cut and sew and back and forth until the garment is finished. And if we find ourselves in the woods, sitting in the dirt like barbarians rather than in the capital like civilized men, then that is where we do our work. Step lively, Small Island man. If you are going to marry Miss Rachel Lippsted tomorrow in that huppah they're building next door, you'll need to do as you're told."

The boatmaker wonders if the rabbi's brother is a drinker. He doesn't smell alcohol, but the stream of words reminds him of a certain kind of drunk.

He takes off his clothes and stands naked. He is short enough that he does not have to stoop under the roof of the tent as the tailor takes measurements for the first suit of clothes that has ever been made for him. From the moment he arrived at the camp he has felt the power of the House of Lippsted around him, arranging everything. He feels that it would be easy to let himself go and allow these arrangements, made effortlessly smooth by the lubricating power of money, to carry him along. But that is not the way the boatmaker has set his course.

"I have a dinner suit. I don't need a new one."

"What?" the tailor says, tape measure around his neck. "Don't play the fool with me, man of Small Island."

"I'm not. The one I have is the one I'll wear."

"Then what are we bothering with all this for?" The tailor flings his arms wide. On his face is an expression like curdled milk.

"I'd like a suit like the ones Herr Lippsted wears. In brown tweed. With a vest."

"And you think we're running a dry-goods store out here in this goyishe wilderness?" But there is a hint of amusement in his outrage, and the boatmaker sees a little more of the rabbi in him.

"We'll see what we can do. But I can't promise it for tomorrow. Now put your Small Island potato sacks back on and be gone from my respectable place of business." He is mumbling to himself as the boatmaker leaves the tent, glad to stand outside in the sunshine, fully clothed.

He walks back alone through the woods, the warmth of a summer's day spreading under the leaves. The square between the tents is empty. He lifts the flap of Jacob Lippsted's tent, asks permission to enter.

The scion of the House of Lippsted sits behind a folding desk, papers and account books stacked neatly in front of him. His jacket hangs on the back of his chair. He looks clean and collected as he motions the boatmaker to a camp chair.

The two men talk over the events of the past few days and discuss the future. Jacob is certain he will be able to return to the capital and rebuild. He has confidence in his relationship with the king, though he says nothing about whether they are in communication. He is interested in the boatmaker's plans for returning to Small Island and building something of his own there. He is sober when he hears about the Sons of Vashad. He seems distressed only when the boatmaker describes the bodies under the broken pushcarts. Then he puts his head in his hands. But his composure returns quickly.

The boatmaker leaves the tent and stands on the platform. The sun, moving toward the peak, warms his back and arms. He turns his face up, feeling for the first time in many weeks the release of the tension that was bound up in the race. Even though his secretary is nothing but pools of gray ash, Sven Eriksson has seen it and blessed it. The boatmaker is no longer an apprentice. And he knows where he is going from here.

As he stands, face offered to the sun, he feels her leave her tent, step on the boards and press herself against his back. Holding him, she pulls him back, a step at a time, until they are moving backward in a gliding dance:

a fantastic animal with four legs, their heads facing the same direction. She lifts the flap of her tent with a free hand, and they pass into her world.

She releases him and turns him around. He sees that an oval metal tub has been brought into the tent. She removes his overalls slowly, looking him in the eye as she undoes the buttons at the shoulders, pulling the fabric down. She removes his longjohns a little at a time, reaching her hands inside. She pulls them down and descends with them until she is kneeling before him. He lifts one foot, then the other out of the garment, which she lays on the floor. She embraces his knees, kissing the flat knob of each in turn, allowing the rich, loamy, acrid smell of him and his time on the road to fill her.

She moves behind him and guides him into the tub. The water is hot but not scalding. He lowers himself, soaking while she sponges him. She washes him now as the man who is about to be her husband, not as the odd stranger she meets in a shabby rooming house in the Old Quarter. Each part she touches is part of her husband, the father of her child, who will soon be a member of the House of Lippsted, playing a role that is yet to be written but for which she is sure he was born. He closes his eyes, enjoying the sensation of being touched by her.

Kneeling beside the tub, she says: "You know, in being with you, I didn't know whether I was doing what my brother wanted or something that he would be shocked by—or even hate. He does not explain everything. That is not his way. He puts things in front of people and sees what they do. Do they come forward and take what is offered? Do they run? Do they freeze? I've seen men—and women—do all of those things while he watched without giving a sign. I can tell you it made some of them crazy. He hasn't yet given me any signs. And I'm still not sure I know the answer. But it doesn't matter. He seems happy. And I know I am. I'm sure he will put things in front of you and see how you react. You are free to choose what you wish. I will be with you regardless of what you choose and what you leave from among what he offers."

Her voice pours over him like the warm water she uses to rinse his body. He hears what she says about her brother. But he knows he will make his own way, not simply choosing from among what his wealthy, powerful brother-in-law sets in front of him. He has already shared his plans for Small Island with Jacob Lippsted. He feels no need to explain them to Rachel yet. She will find out soon enough. He closes his eyes, and she begins sponging him off.

He stands. She wraps him in a towel and leads him to her camp bed. Her world remains strange to him, but he does not question his decision to come here, to enter that world. He has not questioned it since he burned the letters in his room, took his bundle and set out on the road leading to this forest. Lying with her, seeing himself reflected in her eyes, he is thinking of the words in her letter: *There will be a child.*

The child is already with them on this camp bed, he thinks. It is simply waiting for the right time to join them, to enter the space where the moonlight was when they lay in his little room over the alley.

He thinks of the girl on Small Island. She was sometimes clinging, sometimes grave. Sometimes she seemed afraid of him, perhaps because he was so different from her father. His child will not be afraid of him. He knows it will be a boy. He will teach his son everything he has learned on Small Island, on Big Island and the Mainland. The child will know so much more than the boatmaker does.

"Must I be gentle with you now?" he asks, reaching out to touch her belly.

"Be gentle with me? Always," she says, looking at him with a smile. She pulls his face to hers, covering his eyes so that he is blind, bound to her, and speaks directly into his ear. "*Always. You must always be gentle with me.*" She pauses a moment and then resumes, her lips on his flesh: "*Always. Never. Always. Never. Always.*"

CHAPTER 26

The boatmaker wakes early and disentangles himself from his bride. He pulls his clothes and boots on and steps out into a bright day. The foreman is standing on the platform, drinking coffee from a tin mug. He finishes the coffee and ducks into Jacob Lippsted's tent, where he stays a few minutes, emerging without his mug. He touches his cap to the boatmaker and goes down a path into the woods.

As the boatmaker stands on the platform in the sunshine, the things that happened in the capital are difficult to believe. He wonders what the Old Quarter looks like, how much of the city is controlled by men wearing the triangle armbands of the Sons of Vashad. He steps off the platform and takes the path to Meyer Goldman's tent.

He has no idea how the tailor managed to find the fabric, but his suit is nearly finished. He expects a harangue along with the suit, but the smaller Goldman has nothing to say beyond what is necessary for the practice of his craft: *Enough room? Does this pinch? Raise your arms.*

The tailor's eye is superb: The suit fits beautifully, needs only a last few adjustments. There is no mirror, but the boatmaker needs no mirror to see where he will go in this suit. His plans for Small Island are taking clearer shape every day. As he did in the compound, on Small Island he will do something that has never been done there.

"Thank you," the boatmaker says. The tailor says nothing.

"I also need shoes to go with the suit, along with shirts and ties. All of it must be shipped to Small Island, to the general store in Harbortown on the steamer. It must arrive within the month."

Giving orders has already begun to feel less strange. But the tailor doesn't make it easy for him; his face shows no expression. He can't decide whether Meyer Goldman is happy to be of service, outraged or something else that can't be read in his features. As he leaves the tent, the tailor is sitting cross-legged on the floor, bent over his work, humming tunelessly to himself.

In their tent the bed is empty. The boatmaker sits in the chair listening to the birds crying the headlines from tree to tree: *Very curious events! More tents than usual in the woods! A virtual city! Erected by humans who have guns but are not hunters! Fine weather continues through the week.* Rachel enters bearing plates. They eat without talking, conscious that it is the first meal in their home.

When they are finished, she takes him by the hand and leads him into the tent to the left, where the rabbi is sitting at a camp table. The table is identical to the one in Jacob Lippsted's tent. But instead of neat stacks of documents requiring action there are mountains of books in Hebrew, German and the language of the Mainland. The tent cannot have been pitched more than a week, yet it has the feel of a scholar's study, uncleaned for decades. On the camp table are layers of paper, a tin of watercolors and brushes in a glass. A broad white sheet sits in the middle, covering something brightly colored that peeps out from underneath. Behind the desk sits Rabbi Nachum Goldman in shirtsleeves and skullcap, perspiring.

"*So.* The man from Small Island," he says without getting up.

"Yes."

"And under such different circumstances. About to become a member of the family. Although my theory is that you were one of us already—whether you knew it or not." The rabbi smiles a childlike smile that says: *You see, I can't help myself. Don't be angry!*

"Rabbi, you promised you wouldn't bring that up again," says Rachel, pressing herself into the boatmaker.

Her warmth pleases his body. Nothing anyone could say at this moment would hurt very much. It feels as if there is a layer of something soft between any possible pain and his brain. He has felt this before only when he was drunk. Yet he has drunk nothing in many months, except a little at the townhouse, out of a desire to be polite. *There will be a child*, he thinks. He wonders if the rabbi knows, whether Jacob does. He assumes they do. Even that knowledge, which would ordinarily make him feel as if layers of his skin had been peeled off, leaving his entire body raw, red and exposed, causes no pain. The boatmaker is foolish in his happiness.

Rachel moves to the camp table and lifts the large white sheet that sits in front of Rabbi Nachum Goldman. Lying under it on a sheet the same size is a large circle in black ink. Inside the circle are fields of bright color. Over the fields of color are lines of Hebrew, places for signatures at the bottom.

"The *ketubah*," she says, "our marriage contract. Here in the woods the rabbi has been practicing his magic."

"Not magic, child. Tradition. The customs of our people. *Baruch Ha-Shem*."

"Isn't it the same thing, Rabbi?" To the boatmaker she says: "The rabbi didn't think I would ever get married." She reaches out and touches the old man's cheek. The boat-maker is surprised by the familiarity. Like Jacob Lippsted, the rabbi has an aura of not being easily touched. But the older man smiles and holds her hand against his cheek.

"I turned down so many *more appropriate* suitors. Isn't that right, Rabbi? Men from great Jewish families, with fortunes as large as our own. And in the end I marry this man from Small Island. Nobody knows who his people are. I don't care. All I know is: He's the one I've been waiting for. And whatever they say or don't say, I know they're happy for me."

She buries herself in the arms of the boatmaker, who looks over her at the rabbi. The men exchange expressions of masculine understanding, intended to show how patient they are with women, with this woman in particular.

"They had it wrong," Rachel says, stepping back, "all of them. My brother is the one who will never marry. Which is why this child is so precious."

There is a moment of quiet in which each of the three people in the tent is harboring a deep, individual response. The rabbi breaks the silence to explain the meaning of each line in the colored marriage contract, then describes what will happen in the service that evening under the smaller green canopy.

Toward evening the boatmaker kisses Rachel Lipp-sted and steps out of the tent carrying his antique suit, shoes, socks, undergarments, shirt and tie to a place where he can dress, allowing her the tent.

He looks for a secluded spot, thinking about the wedding customs the rabbi has described. He is to crush a glass wrapped in a napkin—for reasons no one can fully explain. A small piece of bad luck to ward off larger danger? A recognition of the imperfection of all human life, no matter how blessed it may seem? A primitive sacrifice of something valuable? He wonders whether the glass will be one of the crystal goblets from the townhouse. How much planning was made for this wedding as Jacob and his sister fled between rows of burning houses? How sure was she that he would say yes? No one seemed very surprised by his appearance in the forest. Again he feels exposed—but without the usual pain.

He finds a large tree suitable for his purpose and stands on a gnarled root. He takes off his longjohns and pulls on the dinner suit. He is glad to have brought it with him. Amid the Lippsted wealth it is something that belongs unquestionably to him. This is the last time it will be worn. Later, when things are calmer, he will have Meyer Goldman make one to his measurements in the current style.

Balancing on the roots, he pulls on shoes and socks. He finishes, even tying the tie. It is crudely tied, but it will do. The landlady showed him how to do it on his own. Rachel will straighten it.

When he is fully dressed, he leans back against the tree, feeling its rough bark through the fabric of his jacket. He lights a cigarette and stands smoking in the everlasting June twilight.

In the center of the tent Rachel is in white silk from head to toe. Her dress is in a style from two generations before—even older than his suit. She holds a necklace of pearls for him to fasten. He joins the clasp and leans in to inhale the scent of spring flowers. He lays his hands on her shoulders and leaves them there. He will say all the words that need to be said in the service under the canopy of maple branches. But his own promise to her is made in this lingering touch.

He moves in front of her so she can straighten his tie. She brushes the shoulders of his suit, touches her lips to his. Then they walk out onto the platform and down the path to where the others are waiting.

The rabbi and Jacob Lippsted stand under the canopy in the clearing, wearing dark suits. Sven Eriksson and a few of his trusted men are near the opening. The rest of the men are in the trees, taking part while they keep watch. Meyer

Goldman is nowhere to be seen. The boatmaker wonders whether his suit will make it to Small Island in time.

The ceremony is exactly as the rabbi described. The boatmaker makes his way slowly, but without stumbling, responding in Hebrew as he is asked to.

At the right moment, Jacob Lippsted produces a plain gold band. The boatmaker slides it on, feeling himself aroused. When they are finished, he steps out of the canopy and crushes the glass, which gives with a satisfying crack. After that, there is a silence broken by cheers from the men in the clearing and an echoing cheer from the woods beyond.

The guard the boatmaker saw leaning against a tree when he arrived at the camp goes into the shadows behind the canopy and emerges with a fiddle. He begins to play folk songs of the Mainland.

The boatmaker steps up to the foreman and whispers a request. The foreman nods and speaks to the fiddler, who retunes. Then he plays the song of the duck: so clumsy on land, awkward in the water, but with such grace in the sky, because it was born for the sky.

The boatmaker's voice is uneven. He is unused to singing, even when he is alone, much less for anyone other than Crow and White at the Grey Goose when they were all far gone in drink. But he knows this song in his bones, intestines and muscles, not just in his mind. He feels the song, allows everyone to see him feeling it. Rachel wipes tears away with an embroidered handkerchief, then doesn't bother to hide them.

Everyone in the clearing knows this song comes from a region not far from where they are standing, where there had once been a thriving Jewish community. After pogroms in the last century, boiling up from the south and east, the Jews in that region were killed, forced to convert or driven away. Each listener has a distinct and different reaction to the boatmaker's song.

By morning he is gone.

The country the boatmaker passes through on his return seems very different from the one he saw on his journey in from the coast. He takes a different route, starting far to the southeast and winding his way back toward the place where he arrived. When he first landed, hungry and tired, but full of curiosity, the Mainland seemed unimaginably large and strange: a place of myths and legends, warrior kings who went to sea in ships with round shields on their gunwales, sacrificing to pagan gods. On his way back, the country is no more than rivers, trees, hills and fields filled with pigs, cows and bullocks driven by peasants with dung matted in their hair. He bypasses the towns to avoid the Sons of Vashad.

His route to the coast takes him through rolling hills that turn dry as he nears the sea. Trees give way to sandy hills covered with tough grass. The last few hills are bare dunes dropping down to the ocean, which is blue, green and placid in the July heat. On a bluff overlooking the beach he comes to a snug cabin made of wood, set into the hill for protection against the sea winds. Now there is just a touch of sea breeze. Smoke from the cabin's chimney rises and hangs for a moment before the wind spins it out to sea. Even before he reaches the house, the boatmaker smells what he knew he would smell there: meat roasting in its own rich juices.

The door is open. At a wooden table sits a man in undershirt and workpants, suspenders down, face flushed. His round face and white beard make him look like the images of Saint Nicholas on the Advent cards children carry. But his mustache and beard are stained yellow from smoking, he steams with sweat, and there is something in his eyes that is not like Saint Nick.

The man roasting meat seems unsurprised by the appearance of the boatmaker. In fact, he looks as if he has been expecting his visitor any day. This cannot be true. The boatmaker has not set foot in this house for three years, and when he left, he gave no sign he would ever return.

"Come fer yer boat, have ye? I thought ye might. Mainland too much fer ye? Can't say ye look too bad. Not starving, any rate."

"I came for my boat."

"Aye, it's still here."

"In the cave."

"The boys are there. They'll be happy to sell it ye—*at a fair price.*"

The red-faced man with the yellowing beard smiles. The boatmaker suppresses a return smile. He knows what *a fair price* means: *an outrageous price.* Two or three times what they paid him. Maybe more. And they won't have taken good care of it, either. The boat will need work before it can be put in the water. But as long as all the pieces are there, he will be able to make it seaworthy.

On one side of the house, a window overlooks wooden steps leading down to two smaller houses and then to the beach. On the landing at the top of the stairs stands a powerful brass telescope. With the telescope the man at the table can see many leagues out to sea when the weather is fair and the running lights of ships even when it's foul.

This is where the boatmaker landed after sailing from Big Island. He found the old man and his sons friendly. They explained that their meager livelihood lay in scavenging things washed up from wrecks on the shore below. The water shoals there, they explained, in such a way that the shoaling can't be seen until a ship is already over it. Only those who know the coast can land safely. The boatmaker was lucky to land without snagging, or smashing his boat.

After he landed he stayed on the coast for a few weeks, sleeping on the floor of this house, sharing the meat the father roasts continually for his two silent sons. One night in a storm they called him to the beach to help salvage a brig that was foundering offshore. He went into the water again and again, bringing back goods and animals and hoping he could rescue the crew. Strangely, he didn't find any of the crew on board; only goods were saved.

He helped the brothers store their salvage in a large cave with many chambers in the bluff at the landward edge of the beach. The brothers allowed him to see only the largest of the cave's chambers, moving goods into the smaller side chambers themselves. Afterward, they all got drunk on whiskey from the brig. The father and brothers praised the boatmaker's skill in the water, his fearlessness. They offered to take him into the family business. He wondered what kind of living they could make by salvaging cargo from the occasional wreck on this lonely stretch of coast. The shoal must be marked on the charts, he thought. And there was a lighthouse no more than half a mile down the coast.

It was only a week later, when he saw the brothers stacking wood on the beach in a huge firepit that had clearly been used many times before, that he understood the family business. The bonfire fooled a ship's crew into thinking the lighthouse was there, drawing them onto the shoal. By the time the brothers called him for the first wreck, they had already doused the bonfire, killed the brig's crew and thrown the bodies overboard. When he understood the scheme, the boatmaker offered apologies and sold them his boat, accepting little for it. Then he set out for the capital.

Now he is back at this table eating roast meat. The man across from him seems jolly and welcoming. The boat-maker has never said a word to anyone about the business father and sons do here. He hopes they will sell him back his boat and let him go without harming him. If they want to hurt him, there will be no one to come to his aid: This stretch of coast is all but deserted. He eats the meat the old man offers, steaming and bloody. The window of the snug house looks out over the bluff and the wooden stairs to the ocean, shoaling blue, then green, finally a deeper blue, all the way to Small Island.

CHAPTER 27

Inside the cave it is cool and dry. The sons look like twins, wearing the same dark sailor clothes, knitted watchcaps, sporting the same luxuriant dark mustaches. One is slightly taller and heavier than the other. Both are cold to the boatmaker. Before he came, they had never asked anyone to join their business. They were insulted when he turned them down. Because he came from Small Island, which they think of as a wild place, without benefit of law, they assumed he would jump at the opportunity. When he refused, they were angry, wanted to kill him. The father stopped them. They watched with contempt as he left their coast, as if the boatmaker were the runt of the litter. They are surprised to find he is alive and not much worse for wear, aside from being thinner and having an odd scar on the bridge of his nose.

"What do you want with us?" they ask in unison.

"My boat."

"What did the old man say?"

"That you would sell it back to me."

"For how much?"

"A fair price."

Standing on the sandy floor of the cave, the brothers look at each other, suppressing grins. Those words from their father are a signal for them to extort an absurd price from the boatmaker. And they do: three times as much as they paid him for it.

"We've taken good care of it," they say together, one voice a little higher, one a little lower. "We've *improved* it. That's why the price is higher now."

The boatmaker knows that if he is silent and walks away, the price will come down quickly. He is certain no one has shown the slightest interest in his boat in the three years since he has been here. But he didn't come back to haggle with these twin devils. Money has come to mean something different to the boatmaker than it did when he landed on this coast. When he left Big Island, he thought money had a power of its own, a kind of magic. After all his experiences on the Mainland, he no longer believes money is magical. It is a tool like any other. A tool that is very sharp, capable of cutting if not used correctly, but also capable of producing beautiful things. The magic—if there is any—lies in what is done with money, not in the money itself. When he returns to Small Island, he will be a different kind of workman, and money will be one of his tools.

"Fine," he says. "That's a fair price."

The brothers exchange looks of puzzled disappointment. They would have come down to a slightly more realistic price—still theft, but a little more reasonable—even if the boatmaker had not threatened to walk away. They wanted him to be shocked by the price but afraid to negotiate aggressively. They wanted to play with him the way a kitten plays with a baby bird in the angle of a stone wall. When he is not afraid and shows little interest in the price, they feel cheated.

The brothers lead the boatmaker out of the cave's main chamber and into a smaller side chamber. Wooden cases are stacked along the walls, stamped with the names of companies from all over the Mainland and Europe. In front of one of the stacks is his boat, lying on the sand, mast and sail beside it. The hull, fittings and trim, along with everything in the cockpit, have been covered with several coats of white housepaint. The compass is not with the boat. The boatmaker turns his back to the brothers, reaches into his sealskin pouch and takes out the amount the brothers have named. He hands it to the taller one.

"Why did you paint it white?"

"We were *taking care of it*. We thought you might come back. We wanted it to be in good shape."

"Where's the compass?"

"Oh, we have that, too." The slightly shorter brother goes through an opening at the rear of the chamber and returns with the compass. They have torn it out even more roughly than the boatmaker did before he pawned it. But it is intact.

"Help me get the boat down to the beach," the boatmaker says, unable to bear being in this cave with these men for another minute.

On the beach he strips to his longjohns, keeping his gear in view. The brothers stand on the beach talking quietly in the accent of this part of the coast, where earlier ways of speaking have survived for many decades, even centuries, after they disappeared from the rest of the Mainland.

When he landed here, the boatmaker thought that perhaps all of the Mainland was pickled in the salt brine of its past this way. It was completely unexpected, since he had come from one of the most backward parts of the entire kingdom. Yet he landed among men who spoke a language that seemed old-fashioned even to a Small Islander. It took him only a day or two after leaving the father and sons to realize that this stretch of the coast is a world unto itself, where old ways—both good and bad—have been preserved by isolation.

Out of the corner of his eye, he sees the brothers talking in low voices. He knows they still bear a grudge, would like to hurt him. He trusts their father will keep them from harming him while he stays. But he has no interest in spending any more time in this place than is absolutely necessary.

He looks over boat, compass, mast and sail, rudder and centerboard. Everything is there, though covered in layer after layer of creamy housepaint. The touch of these men on his boat disgusts him as much as if they had touched his own body. He asks them for tools, knowing there are many scattered through the chambers of the cave. They bring out a selection of tools, asking for more money, which he gives without arguing.

Among the things he chooses, he makes sure to take a whetstone and a large knife with a fine curved blade of German steel. He will sleep holding this knife and the sealskin bag containing what is left of his money and a note with a few words written by Rachel on their wedding night, when, for a few hours, two people who had rarely been happy were happy together, and each thing was in the place intended for it. Though the handkerchief from his mother is long gone from his pouch, he remembers every detail she stitched there: the houses on the bluff above the harbor, the curve of the shoreline, the three harbor seals in green, one large and close by, the other two small and farther off, near the shore.

The brothers retreat into the cool of the cave, where they can watch the boatmaker on the beach, working in his long underwear. He begins by taking things apart. The thwarts come out. The decking comes off. The centerboard and rudder lie on the sand, along with the unstepped mast and his compass, which he has covered with his clothes.

Soon he is drenched in sweat. He strips off his long-johns, tears a rag into strips and fashions a loincloth and turban. He puts them on and works in the unblinking sun like a visitor from another continent.

He needs buckets and turpentine. He gets them from the brothers, who stand smoking in the back of the cave. He wonders how long it has been since they used their bonfire to decoy a ship onto the shoal. He wonders whether, if the time between wrecks is too long, they begin to fight each other out of boredom.

The brothers don't bother to hide their smiles when they see the boatmaker come up the beach into the cave dressed in loincloth and turban. But they give him what he needs without demanding more money. They sense that his hand has closed. They saw the knife he chose from their goods.

The boatmaker dumps the brass fittings into buckets of turpentine and waits for the clear piney-smelling liquid to work. He begins removing white paint, layer by layer, from the hull. Under his hands, the wood of Small Island—maple, oak, spruce and pine—begins to show. He uses his curved knife, two chisels, a file and a plane to remove the paint. The boat is all curves, with few of the regular surfaces of a table or a chair. Each piece must be worked separately.

As he works, he thinks of Lippsted furniture and the craft of building without metal fastenings. He wonders whether a boat could be built entirely without metal. Then he wonders how things are for Rachel and the camp. By now Sven Eriksson has undoubtedly moved them to another part of the royal preserve, to prevent them from being discovered by less charitable observers than the birds of the forest.

The boatmaker has the feeling Jacob Lippsted knows what he is doing and that, even if he overreached in challenging The Royal Champion, he will be able to guide his people back to the capital and restore his relationship with the king. He knows that the hatred of Jews on the

Mainland will not disappear. But it may recede, as the spring floods of the mighty Vashad do, leaving behind splintered houses and wagons, bloated corpses of cows and horses, the earth rich and ready for seeding.

In the endless July days, as he brings the hull of his boat back out from under its coat of paint, the boatmaker's skin turns red, then brown. He makes himself a larger, more elaborate turban and soaks it in water several times a day while the brothers laugh at him from the mouth of the cave. From time to time he changes into his clothes and goes up to the little house on the bluff to sit and eat roast meat. The old man offers to let him sleep on the floor of the cottage, where he slept the first time he was here. The boatmaker declines and offers to pay for his food, an offer that is also declined. He descends rickety stairs to the beach and sleeps next to his boat, pulling his clothes around him for warmth. On this part of the coast, the nights are cool, even in July.

Each morning he wakes, takes off his clothes, dons loincloth and turban and goes to work. When the brass fittings come out of the turpentine, they are mostly clear of white paint. But each piece must still be worked with a knife and a rat-tail file to remove as many as possible of the last small white flecks. Then the fittings go back in the turpentine.

When he has finished with the fittings, he returns to the hull, decking and thwarts. The patches of wood grow until they are almost as large as the areas of paint. Then the balance shifts: The painted areas become islands in a sea of wood. Then those islands shrink to flakes. The work can't be hurried, and the boatmaker doesn't try, although he knows the end-of-summer storms are coming, and he should be on his way.

After many hot days on the beach, all the paint is gone. It has been demanding, intricate work to remove every last white dot, but he has done it. When the wood is clear, he examines his rigging and compass. The mast, gaff and sail are sturdy and unbroken. The compass is working, pointing north to the magnetic pole that lies beyond the most remote of the kingdom's northern islands. He begins varnishing the wood, giving it two and then three coats. He lets the varnish dry before putting the pieces of the boat back together, wood first, followed by the brass fittings. He mounts his compass on the foredeck, repairing the damage done by the brothers.

Then he begins caulking. Between every curved strip of hull, steamed to fit in the shed on Small Island, is a gap that must be made watertight. While the boat sat in the cave, the seams dried out and spread. Now they will be tight again, and the collection of lifeless pieces will become a boat. When he finishes caulking, he hauls his boat down to the water, eases it in and stands in the sea, cold even in summer, a small brown man in turban and loincloth watching the hull swell and the seams tighten.

When the boat is seaworthy, he steps the mast and checks the rigging. Everything has survived. He looks the boat over one last time before provisioning it for the return journey. He will not put in at Big Island, so he must be prepared for the full sail of almost two weeks. He is late, he knows, too close to the late-summer storms between Big Island and Small Island. But the work could not have been done faster.

As he looks over his work, the image comes to him of the native islander on the bench in the barbershop, under the engraving of The Royal Champion. He goes to the brothers, who have in their cave almost everything that has ever been bought or sold on the Mainland.

In a small chamber he finds the sealskins he is looking for. He goes back to the boat and extends the decking over most of the cockpit, leaving a small square opening at the stern. Out of sealskins from the cave, he cuts and sews a parka like the one the native wore, with a hood fitted to his head and shoulders. He fastens the edges of the sealskin to the gunwales and makes the seams as watertight as he can. Nothing will prevent the fiercest storms from drowning him, but the hood might help keep his boat from swamping in a storm that isn't too violent.

The brothers watch, nudging each other in amusement. Far from wanting to hurt him, they are now sad to see the boatmaker leave. He has proved more entertaining than they could have imagined before he arrived. When he leaves, he doesn't bother to say goodbye to them. He does mount the stairs to bid farewell to their father, who is surprisingly emotional.

His boat provisioned with bread and water, his head covered by his new sealskin hood, the boatmaker sets a course for Small Island, which is a gray dot over the horizon. His course takes him north of Big Island. He passes it after six days. A place that was once his goal, mysterious, alluring as a dream, is now just a small green smudge off to port.

The winds are from the south, strong and steady. He makes good time, bailing as the seams expand and the hull comes together and rides lightly on the swell. He stays awake, keeping an eye out for the storms he knows are coming.

Twelve days out, past Big Island, on the final leg, unable to keep his eyes open, the boatmaker falls into a deep, exhausted sleep. He dreams he is sailing his boat, which is much the same as in daylight. The voyage is the one he is on. But in place of the familiar night sky an enormous wooden dome curves above him. The dome has been carved out of beams pressed together so that their square ends look down on the boatmaker. The entire bowl of the sky has been carved out of the endgrain, the hardest part of any wood to work, impossible to plane, saw or even chisel. Speckled through the endgrain like thousands of stars are dark dots marking the channels that nourished the living wood.

The boatmaker looks up, amazed. How could anyone have carved a dome stretching from horizon to horizon out of the endgrain, tough as iron?

Then, high above him he sees a single white gull soaring, its wings spread as it turns in a huge, lazy circle. One wing must have a blade on its leading edge, because the gull trails a shaving, smooth and brown. As the gull circles, the shaving lengthens and dangles over the sea. The boatmaker stares up, stunned. It would be impossible for the world's mightiest craftsman to produce a smooth, unbroken shaving from this much endgrain. Yet the gull does it without any apparent effort, as if it were simply gliding on the wind.

He wakes upside down, cold water in his lungs, not knowing where he is. Holding the little breath he has, he reaches into the boat, floating above him, for something to cut the sealskin that binds him to the hull. Just as he is sure he will pass out and drown, his hand closes on the knife he bought from the brothers. In one final effort, he cuts the sealskin and swims out from under his boat.

The sky is dark. It is raining, but the storm that capsized him while he dreamed of the wooden dome of the sky has moved off. Rain is falling gently on the upturned hull. He gasps, filling his lungs with air, retching salt water, kicking slowly to hold himself up in his sodden clothes, then draping himself over the hull and holding on to the wood. He is sure he has been dismasted, but he can step the mast with the tools he has. Hanging on to the hull, chin on the wood, still coming out of the dream of the gull, he sees a dot up ahead. Dawn has revealed a tiny flaw in the horizon: Small Island.

It takes him twelve hours in and out of the water to right his boat, step his broken mast and bail enough water to begin making way. When he is done, he is half dead, chilled to the bone. His teeth will not stop chattering. He holds his jaw closed with one hand, tiller and sheet in the other. The sun warms him a little as he sails. Then the sun goes down, and his teeth begin chattering again.

The next morning at dawn he enters the main harbor below Harbortown. His boat comes into the wind shadow of the island. The sail empties and flaps at the luff. He releases his jaw, reaches for the halyard and drops his sail, the gaff falling with a crack on the boom. He will paddle the few hundred yards to the gravel beach.

He reaches for his paddle, then stops at what he sees in the calm waters of the harbor. A seal has surfaced off his starboard bow, quite close, face sleek, nose and whiskers pointing to port. Off to port and close to shore, two seals emerge at the same moment and face each other. For a moment, it is exactly as it was on his mother's handkerchief: the buildings on the bluff, the curve of rocky shoreline, the three seals. Then all three seals vanish into their own ripples. The boatmaker paddles for the beach. On the bluff, no footsteps echo from the wooden sidewalk. He has lost track of the days of the week. It must be Sunday.

CHAPTER 28

On an ordinary Monday toward the end of summer, the small bell over the front door of the general store in Harbortown rings as the door opens. The woman of Small Island stops, her feet held to the floor.

His features are the same, but his face is different. He is dark from the sun, past burned, darker than she has ever seen him. Standing out, white against the skin of his nose, is a scar like an X. The drooping mustache is the same, but the baldness has expanded across his scalp.

She has never imagined she would see him again. At the beginning, she told herself he would return, but she didn't believe it; she has acted on what she believed. The opening of the door and the entrance of the boatmaker, looking like a stick hardened in fire, erases a large piece of what she thought she knew.

It is mid-day, and there are no customers in the store. The boatmaker sees the woman start. The high, bright sound of the bell fades away as he stands at the door waiting for her to regain her composure. She looks as if she's had a visitor from the spirit world. But the boatmaker is no ghost. Everything about him is solid: his boots, his hands, his sunburned face, his boat hidden in the woods that drop down below Harbortown.

The general store is not large, but it takes a long time for him to cross it: three years. Then he is beside her, taller than she is, though not by much. He takes her shoulders and pulls her to him, kisses her on her cheeks—first one, then the other. It is a gesture never seen before on Small Island.

"Do you have a package for me?" asks the stranger. "From the Mainland."

There is a package for him. It is bulky, wrapped in tough paper, mailed from a place she's never heard of. The package arrived a few days ago. It's sitting in the back room, where they keep the things that come in on the steamer. When it was delivered, she ran her hands over the brown paper, examining the unfamiliar writing. Wondered what was inside. Imagined it must be a mistake. From time to time, parcels arrive for people who don't live on Small Island, or people who have died.

She considered opening this package from the Mainland. After all, how likely was it he was still among the living—a man who drinks too much, who sailed away in a boat he built himself? She thought about opening it, but she didn't allow herself. She wasn't certain he was dead. Still, she never imagined he would simply open the door and walk into the general store as if he hadn't been gone for three years without sending a single word.

"I'll go and look," she says, already lying to him. She is giving herself time.

Moving her feet is like uprooting saplings. She parts the purple curtains that screen off the back room. Behind the curtains is a tall white set of shelves, with cubbyholes above for mail and larger shelves for parcels below. His package is on the shelf closest to the floor. The shelf for sorting mail extends out at waist level. She puts her hands on it and supports herself, chest trembling. She is afraid she will vomit on the mail. Then she begins to cry, silently. She doesn't know how to tell him. She had no idea he would return. She must tell him, immediately, what has happened since he left. She didn't think she had these feelings anymore. She wipes her face on her sleeve. Her breathing returns more or less to normal. She turns and goes out through the purple curtain.

"Yes, there's something here for you."

He leaves the store with the package balanced on his shoulder, whistling. Harbortown is the same; he is different.

The bell rings again as he leaves. It may have been five minutes between the two times it rang. An hour later she feels as if she has not moved from the spot where she was standing when he entered the store. People have come into the store, she has served them, they have left. She has no idea what she said, though no one seemed shocked.

The bell rings, and the boatmaker enters again, this time wearing a suit. *A suit!* It is beyond imagining. Valter has suits, yes. The doctor. A few others on the island. But none of them has a suit like this one: in a beautiful brown tweed with a matching vest, cut by someone who knows his body as well as she does. Above the vest is a white shirt with a stiff collar and dark tie. He is shaved and wearing elegant brown boots. Even more than the one who entered earlier, this is a man the woman of Small Island does not know. Perhaps that will lessen her guilt. Still, what she has to say won't come easily.

"Let's take a walk," says the stranger. "I want to show you something."

"I can't leave. Gunnarson will be upset."

"He works for Valter, doesn't he?"

"Yes."

"Then it will be alright."

He takes her by the arm, guides her out of the store and stops to wait for her to pull the shade and lock the door. As they walk, he looks sideways to see how she has changed and how she has not. Mostly she is the same.

Out where the sidewalk ends, not far from the top of the bluff, he takes her arm and they climb down over rocks and roots to the gravel beach where the longboat from the steamer puts in. The tide is far out among gray rocks, seawater swirling in the tidepools. He looks along the sweep of the harbor, sizing things up. He has had his plan in mind for a while; now he is sure of it.

"How is the girl?"

"She's fine. A bigger girl. You wouldn't recognize her."

"I would."

She knows she must tell him now. "We . . ." She starts to speak, then stops. "We . . ." The tears come again. He takes her by the shoulders.

"What is it, Karin? What's wrong?"

She buries herself in his shoulder and speaks, her voice muffled by brown tweed. Between each phrase is a sob.

"We've gone back to Valter. The girl and I. I'm so sorry. I didn't know if you were coming back. I didn't even know if you were alive. I never heard from you. It's been three years." She's quiet. Then she looks up into his face and says: "Forgive me."

He pulls her closer. "Of course I forgive you. You never heard from me. You had to take care of yourself—and the girl. You've done nothing wrong."

So that's why she looked stricken. He is relieved. All this can be easily addressed. There is no reason for her to feel guilty. He never intended to return to his life on Small Island as it was before. He decides not to tell her yet that he is married, his wife pregnant with their child. There will be time for that later.

Now he wants her to move beyond her sorrow and guilt. He needs her attention for something more important.

"Listen, Karin. I'm going to build something. Right here."

"What?" This is so far out of the train of her own thoughts that she isn't sure she has heard him correctly.

"I'm going to build something here."

"What are you going to build?"

"A boatyard."

"A boatyard. What is that?"

"A place where boats are built and repaired."

She steps back to take him in, this stranger with the sunburned face, the scar, the elegant suit, the Mainland manners. She hears him describe his plans for the thing he calls a boatyard and the business empire it will be a part of, which he is involved with in some way. But she isn't paying much attention to his words. She is confused, her feelings shifting. All she hears is the steady, determined tone. As if he hadn't heard anything she just told him—or it didn't matter. She feels a first twinge of anger.

"I'm going to build it right here. I'll buy the land a parcel at a time. I'll find men to work for me. If I can't find them here, I'll go to Big Island—all the way to the Mainland if I have to. I don't care. I'll find men who want to work and know how to work."

She says nothing, hugs her arms to her, feeling suddenly cold.

"And I'm going to change my name."

"Change your name?"

"Yes. I'm going to be called Boatmaker."

"*Boatmaker*. What kind of name is that?" She laughs.

"It's the name I will have."

"But you already have a name," she says. "A perfectly good name. Vilem Lippsted. The same as your father. Everyone here knows what your name is."

"*Was*. They know what my name *was*. Now it's Boatmaker. Vilem, they can take or leave. Boatmaker is my name now. And there will be a boatyard on this beach. Called The Three Seals."

What nonsense this man talks. If he stays on Small Island, she may run into him on the sidewalk in Harbortown. But it will be easy enough to ignore him, with his talk of boatyards and a new name. No one on Small Island will understand him. They will laugh at him. Call him crazy. The boatbuilder families will fight him with all their strength. No one will work for him. It is all a fantasy, some dream he dreamed on the Mainland. He is bound to fail. Small Island does not take kindly to change.

She will leave the stranger right here, have no more to do with him. But before she walks away, she has one more task.

"There's another thing I need to tell you."

He says nothing, lost in his plans for The Three Seals Boatyard.

"Your mother."

"How is she?"

"She's gone. A year ago, at the end of the winter. That winter was long and hard. They found her at her house. Pneumonia. She'd been dead a week. She's next to your brother."

They turn and go back over rocks, under branches, over the roots of gnarled trees to the top of the bluff. He leaves her at the general store and turns off into the woods.

He isn't interested in meeting anyone he knows or answering any questions. In time he will reintroduce himself, buy the parcels of land he needs, explain the idea of a boatyard and begin hiring. He knows he will meet resistance. As he walks along in his suit and boots, he thinks of Sven Eriksson, who seems equal to anything. He will try to be like that. He is no longer a drunken young man with a feeling for wood. He is a force—a force backed by money.

He finds the path as if he had walked it the day before. It's sunny, the wind rising and dying in a nervous rhythm. The smell of pine is strong. The woods open, and he is in the clearing leading to the oak where his brother is buried. High above him, oak leaves rustle.

His brother's stone is in its familiar place. Someone has trimmed the grass around it. A few feet away, close to the roots of the oak, is another stone, with his mother's name and dates. He kneels, runs his hand over his mother's name incised in stone: a city man wearing a suit cut by a tailor who sews even better than his mother did. A man who has seen things no one on Small Island would understand or even believe. And is now back at the base of the tree whose roots go all the way down to where Small Island itself is anchored.

As he runs his hand over the stone, the tears begin without will or permission. He feels that everything he has done has been for nothing. He has returned too late. His mother will never see him in his suit and boots, never know the man he has become. He will never be able to show her that he is as good a man as his brother would have been. His body shakes with loss, tears staining his face and new shirt. She is gone. He will never have the love he sailed so far for.

He finds himself lying in the grass, sobbing. Cheek against his mother's stone, he sees tiny flowers peering at him between the green stalks of grass. The flowers have six petals, each the blue of the blue wolf. He doesn't recognize them. Rachel will know their name, in Latin and in the language of the Mainland. He pulls two flowers, rubs them against his face, finds they have no smell. His tears begin to dry. Looking into the tiny flowers, he feels his mother present, but in a different way, not smelling of drink, tearing with fists and words. Instead she is smiling at him, shining silently through the blue petals. It is not too late, after all. What he has received is not as he imagined it would be, but it is much more than nothing. Even in this first moment of understanding, he knows it will take years to know just what it is that he has been given.

The boatmaker rolls over. Above him oak leaves move back and forth, allowing the fleeting Small Island sunshine to pass through. He shields his eyes, holding a miniature bunch of blue flowers over his head, looking through them to the sky. He thinks about his other home, in the capital. Jacob Lippsted will rebuild. The men who were with them in the forest will again make the famous Lippsted furniture, using designs handed down from generation to generation. He will bring Rachel and his children—he knows there will be others after this first son—to Small Island. Rachel will spend time here, to be with him and see where he comes from. They will build a house in Harbortown, facing the wooden sidewalk, with a view of the curving harbor and the sea. But he knows she will never permanently leave the rebuilt townhouse with its beautiful tapering façade. The boatmaker will begin a new life, lived between these two worlds, old and new. He will travel farther, even past the Mainland, to Europe and beyond. But he will always return to Small Island, where he began: a rock in the gray sea, the visible tip of an axis that reaches all the way to the center of the earth.

GRATITUDE

Getting *The Boatmaker* launched was not an individual task. My gratitude to those who contributed comes in layers and in depths. ✦ The guardian angel of this entire project has been Jeanne McCulloch. Jay was the first publishing professional who thought this book deserved to be published. And she backed up her opinions with action. She has become not only a mentor but also a wonderful friend. ✦ Jay introduced me to the remarkable folks at Tin House Books, beginning with Meg Storey, a deft and insightful editor. The boatmaker's vessel is much sleeker and sturdier than it would have been without Meg's touch. Nanci McCloskey's enthusiasm and savvy about marketing have been instrumental in getting *The Boatmaker* down the ways. Jakob Vala's fine eye has given the words a cover and interior design that bring out the best in them. ✦ Lauren Cerand has been much more than a very effective publicist. She has been the trusted guide every first-time author needs to the rich and rapidly changing world of book publishing. ✦ Every writer needs an inner circle of Old Believers who read his work before it is ready for the eyes of the world. I have been fortunate to have three: Alan Benditt, Nina Sernaker and Elisabeth King. With infinite care and love, they read an early draft of *The Boatmaker*. Their response made me feel there was something in this tale worth pursuing. Elisabeth deserves special mention for her selfless love and support. ✦ Deeper down is the family, which is the matrix from which everything comes. I am grateful to my other brothers, Joshua and Charles Benditt, for their enthusiasm on reading the manuscript in draft. Long ago my mother, Marcella Benditt, kindled my love of reading and writing. She taught us what a well-made thing looks like. ✦ Finally, all the way down, near the keel of the dream, where there are no images, this book is dedicated to the memory of my father, Earl Benditt, who was an original and a boatmaker. *Godspeed, Skipper.*

✦ COLOPHON ✦

The text of this book is set in Adobe Jenson Pro, an old-style typeface designed by Robert Slimbach. It is based on the work of Nicolas Jenson, a fifteenth-century engraver and coin forger. The italics were inspired by those of Ludovico Vicentino degli Arrighi, a papal scribe in Renaissance Italy. Chapter headings and folio elements are set in SeriWood, as digitized by Terry Koppel from a collection of wood type.